# PALACE OF THE ALMIGHTY

Christopher Mitchell is the author of the epic fantasy series The Magelands. He studied in Edinburgh before living for several years in the Middle East and Greece, where he taught English. He returned to study classics and Greek tragedy and lives in Fife, Scotland with his wife and their four children.

By Christopher Mitchell

The Magelands Origins

*Retreat of the Kell*
*The Trials of Daphne Holdfast*
*From the Ashes*

The Magelands Epic

*The Queen's Executioner*
*The Severed City*
*Needs of the Empire*
*Sacrifice*
*Fragile Empire*
*Storm Mage*
*Soulwitch Rises*
*Renegade Gods*

The Magelands Eternal Siege

*The Mortal Blade*
*The Dragon's Blade*
*The Prince's Blade*
*Falls of Iron*
*Paths of Fire*
*Gates of Ruin*
*City of Salve*
*Red City*

*City Ascendant*
*Dragon Eyre Badblood*
*Dragon Eyre Ashfall*
*Dragon Eyre Blackrose*
*Dreams of Kell*
*God Restrainer*
*Holdfast Imperium*
*World's End*

## The Magelands Dominion

*Serpent Dominion*
*Demon Witch*
*Death Seer*
*Blood Burden*
*Kin Strife*
*Tempest's Edge*
*Creator of Worlds*
*Palace of the Almighty*
*Sapphire Throne*

## Masters and Makers

*Fall Seldom Kings*
*The Making of Abigone*
*Whalebone King*

Cover Design by Sasha Almazan and Gene Mollica, G&S Cover Design Studio. LLC.
Maps by Irina French


Brigdomin Books Ltd
First Edition, November 2024
Ebook Edition © November 2024
ISBN 978-1-915978-47-9

# ACKNOWLEDGEMENTS

I would like to thank the following for all their support during the writing of the Magelands Empire - my wife, Lisa Mitchell, who read every chapter as soon as it was drafted and kept me going in the right direction; my parents for their unstinting support; Marilyn Hopwood for reading the books in their early stages; James Aitken for his encouragement; and Grant and Gordon of the Film Club for their support.

Thanks also to my Advance Reader team, for all your help during the last few weeks before publication.

## DRAMATIS PERSONAE

**Pebble Strand Marine Base**

**Cael Holdfast**, Ensign, Imperial Marines

**Dodd**, Ensign, Imperial Marines

**Audrey Longhold**, Ensign, Imperial Marines

**Plateau City – Imperial Court**

**Thorn Holdfast**, Empress

**Naxor**, Imperial Chamberlain

**Brogan ae Bridget**, Herald of the Empire

**Slaeon**, Imperial Treasurer

**Bedig ae Brannig**, Lord Marshal

**Martius Claudian**, Imperial Adjutant

**Caelius Logos**, Imperial Quartermaster

**Jannis Holdsmith**, Chief Jurist

**Van Logos**, Ambassador from the City of Salve

**Plateau City – University**

**Cole Holdfast**, University Student (19)

**Arrosa**, University Student (17)

**Kyra Holdfast**, Karalyn's Daughter (18)

**Dazi**, University Student

**Larron**, Student Council Vice-President

**Larig**, Larron's Twin Brother

**Lorrie**, Larron's Father

**Lena**, Larron's Mother

**Avril**, Student Council President

**Elbannon**, University Professor

**Gallea**, University Professor

**Nadia**, University Professor

**Ravi**, University Professor

**Achan**, Visiting Professor

**Rosie Jackdaw**, Visiting Professor

**Hold Fast Estate, Holdings**

**Celine Holdfast**, Estate Manager

**Colsbury**

**Karalyn Holdfast**, Immortal Dream Mage

**Carden Holdfast**, Karalyn's Son (3)

**Caitlyn Holdfast**, Karalyn's Daughter (1)

**Kelsey Holdfast**, Unemployed Writer

**Calpurnia Holdfast**, Kelsey and Van's daughter (8)

**Caelius Holdfast**, Kelsey and Van's son (5)

**Shella**, Imperial Chancellor

**Lucius Cardova**, Imperial Constable

**Olo'osso**, Retired Pirate

**Frostback**, Silver Dragon

**Halfclaw**, Blue/Green Dragon

**Lord Sigum's Dragon Team**

**Lahnos Laimos**, Commander, Imperial Army

**Sigum Mon Sigel**, Dragon, and Friend of Lahnos

**Efizel**, Bullan Sergeant Major

**Gaddiz**, Bullan Corporal

**Quicklime**, Eastern Rim Dragon

**Ora'lya**, Quicklime's Rider

**Gallantmorn**, Eastern Rim Dragon

**Annu'tila**, Gallantmorn's Rider

**Duskshade**, Eastern Rim Dragon

**Idali'rona**, Duskshade's Rider

**Ochretail**, Eastern Rim Dragon

**Cloudeye**, Eastern Rim Dragon

**Mayscale**, Eastern Rim Dragon

**Athumia**

**Bailey**, Theodora's Brother

**Bauchlie**, President of Zamata

**Famula Min Gahad**, Queen of the Dominion

**Abda Min Gahad**, Famula's Sister

**Konran Mon Gahad**, Famula's Brother

**Tirna Min Gahad**, Famula's Sister

**Ulna, Dragon Eyre**

**Blackrose**, Queen of the Eastern Rim

**Maddie Jackdaw**, Blackrose's Rider

**Sable Holdfast**, Retired Agent

**Alara'osso (Lara)**, Sable's Partner

**Anaj'osso (Joss)**, Sable and Lara's Son (5)

**Alindi'osso (Lindi)**, Sable and Lara's Daughter (1)

**Millen**, Friend of Blackrose and Sable

**Clackenbaird, Kell**

**Corthie Holdfast**, Farmer

**Aila Holdfast**, Purveyor of Whisky

**Killop Holdfast**, Corthie and Aila's Eldest Son (12)

**Konna Holdfast**, Corthie and Aila's Eldest Daughter (10)

**Cairney Holdfast**, Corthie and Aila's Son (8)

**Carter Holdfast**, Corthie and Aila's Son (6)

**Clova Holdfast**, Corthie and Aila's Daughter (4)

**Carron Holdfast**, Corthie and Aila's Youngest Son (2)

**Ceres Holdfast**, Corthie and Aila's Youngest Daughter (6 Thirds)

**Kilholm**, Corthie and Aila's Cook and Housekeeper

**The Immortal Prisoners**

**Edgar**, Brother of Edmond

**Allura**, Daughter of Edmond

**Ward**, Son of Edmond

**Ballatar**, Grandson of Edmond

**Crennic**, Grandson of Edmond

**Others**

**Doune**, Marine Captain, Seaborne Company

**Elmhirst**, Ancient, and Ruler of the Doomed Worlds

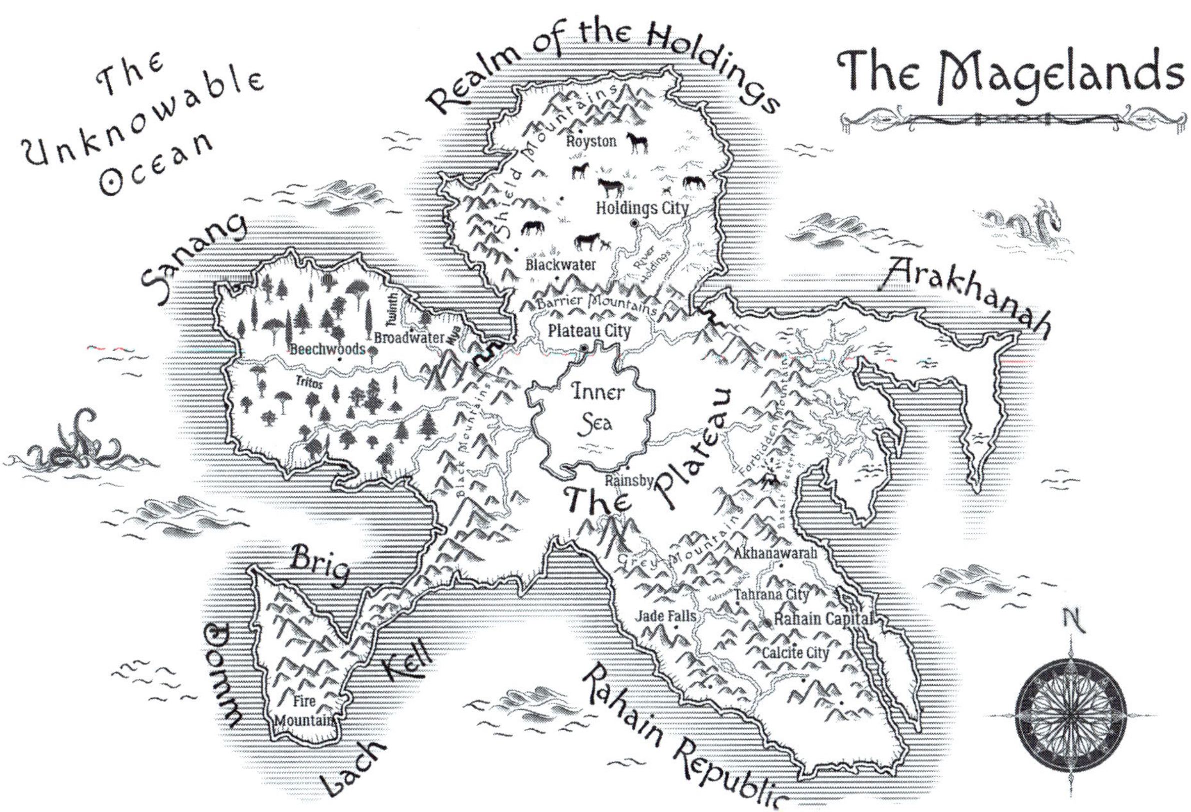
The Magelands
The Unknowable Ocean
Realm of the Holdings
Shield Mountains
Royston
Holdings City
Blackwater
River Holdings
Barrier Mountains
Plateau City
Sanang
Twinth
Broadwater
Beechwoods
Tritos
Inner Sea
Black Mountains
Rainsby
The Plateau
Forbidden Mountains
Basalt Desert
Arakhanah
Grey Mountains
Akhanawarah
Tahrana City
Rahain Capital
Jade Falls
Calcite City
Rahain Republic
Brig
Kell
Lach
Domm
Fire Mountain
N

# CHAPTER 1
# ENSIGN HOLDFAST

**Pebble Strand, The Plateau – 2nd Day, Last Third Winter 544**

The hull of the small vessel ground its way up the beach through the pelting rain, and the eight officer cadets on board jumped over the side. Cael landed in the thigh-deep water, gripped the rope strung along the port side of the boat, and the cadets pulled together, dragging the craft further up the beach. One of them lost his footing and went under for a few moments, before being hauled back up by a watching instructor.

'Secure the vessel!' cried a Holdings sergeant.

The marine cadets pulled on the ropes, and the craft lurched forward again, its stern rising out of the water. Up on the narrow deck, the craft's only sail was straining in the winter wind, and the hull lunged to the left, scraping its keel on the sand, and almost crushing one of the cadets.

'Who is in charge of this cutter?' shouted the sergeant.

Ensign Dodd stood to attention, as the rain gusted into his face. 'Me, sergeant.'

'Why hasn't that sail been lowered, cadet?'

'I forgot to issue the order, sergeant,' said the drenched Kellach man.

'Then do it now, you unfathomably stupid imbecile.'

'Yes, sergeant.' Ensign Dodd turned to the rest of his crew. 'Get that sail down!'

Cael and a couple of others clambered up onto the unsteady deck. The wind had increased, and the craft lurched again, as the sail flapped and billowed. One of the cadets was loosening a rope when a winch broke free. It flew across the deck and hit the cadet's right hand, crushing several of her fingers. The cadet cried out in pain, and the sergeant climbed up onto the deck. He strode over to the injured cadet, as Cael and the others lowered the sail.

The sergeant examined the wounded hand, then he glared down at the beach.

'Ensign Dodd,' he said, 'I think it's safe to say that you will not be put in charge of any more of Her Majesty's marine cutters any time soon.' He turned to Cael. 'Ensign Holdfast, take Ensign Longhold to the infirmary.'

Cael hurried over to where the sergeant was crouching by the injured cadet.

'I'm fine, sergeant,' said Ensign Longhold, as the rain soaked the deck. 'I don't need to see a doctor.'

The sergeant prodded a finger into the back of Ensign Longhold's right hand, and she grimaced in pain.

'You don't look fine to me, cadet,' he said.

She got to her feet, holding her injured hand, and Cael helped her climb down to the sand. As the rest of the crew packed up the vessel's equipment, Cael and Ensign Longhold hurried up the beach towards the buildings that marked the edge of Pebble Strand Marine Base. The paved streets that ran through the large compound were streaming with water; then, as quickly as it had started, the rain stopped, and the sun broke through the clouds.

'How's the hand, Audrey?' said Cael.

Ensign Longhold narrowed her eyes at him. 'I've had worse. The battle-vision is taking the edge off. And I know the way to the damn infirmary. I don't need anyone to walk me there.'

Cael shrugged. 'It got me out of stowing away the cutter. It'll be light duties for you for a while. I'm a wee bit jealous.'

'I'll ask the doctor if there's any salve. Light duties mean I won't be able to sit my sailing assessment. I'll have to re-do the entire fucking course if it doesn't get better in time.' She eyed him. 'When does your leave start?'

'Soon,' he said. 'If I could see the sun, I might have a better idea of exactly when.'

'Are you going to do it? Are you going to ask her?'

Cael glanced down, then he nodded. 'Aye.'

She laughed. 'Good luck.'

'Thanks.'

Cael stepped over a large puddle and walked into the infirmary building, with Audrey Longhold beside him. They strode over to the duty nurse, who was attending a marine with his arm in a sling.

'I'll leave you here,' said Cael. 'I hope your hand isn't too bad.'

'Thanks, Cael,' said Audrey. 'I'll see you in a couple of days when you get back.'

Cael walked outside and felt the cold wind as it blew away the clouds. He glanced over in the direction of the beach and boatyards, and took a cigarette out of a packet. He lit it with a match, and gazed around at the sprawling marine base. It lay next to five miles of golden beaches, and had its own harbour, from where the trainee marines could hone their maritime skills. Forested hills ran to the north of the vast camp, and it seemed that when they weren't in the water, the young cadets were in the woods. The sun came out, and Cael glanced at its position. Not long to go. He took a deep breath, and tried to prepare himself.

Two sergeants approached from the left, and Cael dropped the cigarette and stubbed it out beneath a boot.

'What are you doing here, Ensign?' said one of the sergeants. 'Are you sick?'

'No, sergeant. I was escorting a colleague to see the doctor.'

'Get back to your post,' said the sergeant. 'Her Majesty doesn't pay you to stand around.'

'Aye, sergeant.'

Cael set off towards the beach, but before he reached it, the afternoon bell sounded. Cael smiled, and turned around.

'Are you lost?' said the sergeant.

'My two-day leave pass has just begun, sergeant,' he said.

The sergeant held out his hand, and Cael passed over the slip of paper.

'Ah,' said the sergeant, as he read. He nudged his colleague. 'Did you realise that we were in the presence of bleeding royalty, eh? This lad's a fucking Holdfast.'

'Is that right?' said the other sergeant. 'We'd better watch what we say to the little bastard.'

The first sergeant passed the slip back to Cael. 'Don't go disgracing the good name of the Imperial Marines while you're out getting drunk, Ensign Holdfast.'

'I wouldn't dream of it, sergeant,' said Cael.

'Carry on.'

Cael strode away, heading towards his company's barracks. The trainee officers were kept away from the mass of raw recruits, and had their own dining, exercise and training facilities. They also had their own cadre of sergeant instructors, who seemed to take particular delight in seeing the future officers of the service suffer. The barracks were deserted when Cael arrived. He grabbed a towel, pulled off his drenched uniform, and stood under a hot shower for a few minutes, letting the water warm him up after the freezing cold of the Inner Sea. He dried himself, then dressed in his Number Three uniform. All cadets were forbidden from wearing civilian clothing until they had been commissioned as second lieutenants, and Cael wondered what his family would think when they saw him. He packed a bag by his bunk, then he tidied up his area. He made his bed, dropped the towels and wet uniform into the communal laundry basket, and swept the floor next to his bunk.

'I never once saw you tidy your room,' said a voice.

Cael turned, and saw his mother standing a few yards away.

'You're not supposed to be in here, Mother,' he said, as he placed the brush into a cupboard.

Karalyn smiled. 'You look like your father.'

'Aye?'

'Aye. And I checked that no one else was in here before I travelled.' She walked up to him and they embraced. 'You've broadened out.'

'That's what five thirds of hiking through the woods will do,' he said.

'You weren't hiking through the woods today; you were out sailing. And before you say anything – of course I've been keeping an eye on you. Not every day; but now and again. If I were you, I wouldn't tell Arrosa how pretty Ensign Audrey Longhold happens to be. My mother probably knew her parents up in Hold Long.'

'How is Arrosa?'

'She's pretending that she isn't excited to see you.'

'I'm not even sure if Arrosa and I are still...'

'You've been writing to each other.'

'Aye, but I haven't seen her in five thirds. She will have made new friends at university. All I am saying is that I'm prepared to be disappointed. I can hardly expect her to wait for me.'

His mother frowned. 'You haven't strayed, have you?'

'No. I told her that I would be loyal, and I have.'

'Then why would you expect her to behave differently?'

'I'm not expecting anything.'

She frowned. 'Are you all right? You seem a little nervous.'

'I'm fine. I need to let the duty officer know that I'm about to leave Pebble Strand.'

'I'll walk with you.'

Cael eyed her.

'Are you ashamed to be seen with your mother?' she said.

'No, but we're Holdfasts, and not only that, my stepfather is Imperial Constable and Commander-in-chief of the armed forces, and my aunty is the Empress. Every instructor in Pebble Strand knows who I am, and I don't want anyone to think that I get any special treatment.'

She rolled her eyes. 'Fine. I shall remain invisible to everyone except you.'

Cael picked up his bag, and they walked out of the barracks. The last of the rainclouds had been blown out to sea, and the sun was shining down upon the marine training facility.

'So this is where Thorn has been spending all of the taxes we pay,' said Karalyn. 'Do the marines really need such an enormous base? How old is Pebble Strand?'

'It opened three years ago,' said Cael.

'And how much did it cost?'

'I have no idea, Mother.'

Squads of drenched cadets approached from the left, and Cael saw the other members of his class.

'Are you off on leave, Cael?' said Dodd.

'Aye. Two days.'

'How's Audrey's hand?'

'I left her with a nurse. When you visit her, tell her I hope nothing's broken.'

'I will. See you later.'

Cael walked to the other side of the road and entered the administrative building for the officer cadets. He gave his pass to the officer on duty, who read it, stamped it, and handed it back to Cael without a word. Cael walked back outside, where his mother was waiting for him.

'Are you ready?' she said.

'Very,' said Cael.

The air shimmered, and they appeared on the street outside the Holdfast townhouse in Plateau City.

'I need to have a quick word with you before we go in,' Karalyn said. 'Kyra is here, and she might make a few comments about the marines. Please don't rise to the bait. This is Carden's birthday party, not a political wrestling match.'

'Why would she say anything about the marines?'

Karalyn narrowed her eyes. 'I forgot that you missed Kyra's act of defiance against Thorn. It happened while you were trapped upon your world with Cole and Arrosa.'

'Arrosa mentioned something about it in a letter,' he said. 'As far as I could tell, my sister is turning into you – a pacifist.'

'She isn't turning into me, Cael. I've always believed in staying out of politics, but Kyra's views have... hardened. She has been helping to organise protests against the conflicts in Rahain and Rakana.'

Cael shrugged. 'It's just a phase.'

'Maybe.' Her features softened, and she reached out to tidy Cael's hair. 'What happened to my little boy?'

Cael smiled. 'What happened to my tall mother? In another year I'll look older than you.'

'I know. Your father would have been very proud of you. He loved the marines.'

'It was the right choice,' said Cael. 'For me, I mean. It's been hard, but I think I know what I want to do with my life.'

'You only have to stay in the marines for three years,' she said. 'That was the deal.'

'I know, but I enjoy it, and I think I can make a difference. Once I've been commissioned, I'll be leading my own squad, and then, within a couple of years, I might make first lieutenant.'

'Am I going to lose you to the military?'

'Why not? Both of your parents were in the armed forces. And Uncle Corthie. There should always be a Holdfast in uniform; I'm just keeping up the tradition.'

'Saying things like that will make Lucius very happy, but not your sister. Or Arrosa, for that matter. Come on; let's go inside.'

Karalyn led him up the stone steps, then she opened the front door of the townhouse. Cael closed it once they had entered, and they walked into the large living room. A long table had been placed by the bay windows, and around it were sitting Cardova, Kyra, Cole, Arrosa and Kelsey, while Carden was running around on the carpet wearing a paper crown. Kelsey's two children, Calpurnia and Caelius, were sitting by the fireplace, while little Caitlyn was in a highchair next to Cardova.

Cardova smiled as he got to his feet. 'Ensign Holdfast.'

Cael saluted. 'Commander.'

Cardova extended his hand, and Cael shook it. Kelsey and Arrosa also stood, and both walked round the table to where Cael was standing.

'Pyre's arse, Cael,' said Kelsey. 'You look like a damn marine.'

'I would hope so, Aunty,' he said. 'How are things? Are you living in Plateau City?'

'No,' she said. 'I'm staying on Colsbury, but Karalyn very kindly offered to bring us all down here for the day. I'm writing a book about the history of the Star Continent.'

'It's very good,' said Cardova.

'I need something to do to pass the time when the children are at school,' said Kelsey. She glanced at Arrosa, who was waiting in silence. 'I think someone else wants to say hello, nephew.'

Cael gazed down at Arrosa. He had been wondering how to approach her, and had gone over several conversations in his head in the days leading up to his two-day pass. She gazed back up at him, and the silence stretched out.

'I…' he said, then he shook his head. 'I can't do this with everyone watching and listening. Will you come with me to the balcony, Arrosa?'

'All right,' she said.

He glanced over at Kyra and Cole. 'I will catch up with you soon,' he said, then he took Arrosa's hand and they left the living room. They went up the stairs to the first floor, and walked out onto the balcony. The sun was close to the horizon, and its rays were lighting up the waters of the Inner Sea. Cael breathed in the sea air, and it reminded him of Pebble Strand.

'Five thirds,' he said. 'It's a long time. I missed you.'

'I worked out that it's the longest time we haven't seen each other since I got here from Athumia eight and a half years ago,' Arrosa said;

'and it came right after we started... whatever we started. Cole said it was ironic. I told him to shut up. Are we still... something?'

'I want it to work,' he said. 'This feels right, but I realise that it isn't fair on you.'

'But don't you get more leave once you've been commissioned?' she said. 'I thought the worst was over – the training. You only have one month to go.'

'But then I might get sent somewhere.'

'Are you trying to tell me that we shouldn't see each other any more?'

'I'm trying to warn you that it won't be easy. I don't have much to offer you, Arrosa, except long periods apart.'

'You're still an idiot,' she said. 'I don't care how difficult it is; I want to see if you and I can build something together.'

He put his arms round her waist and they kissed.

'I missed you, too,' she said. 'I've missed arguing with you. Arguing with your sister is a lot less fun.'

'Do you love me?'

'Yes.'

'Then...'

'Yes?' she said.

'I want to ask you something,' he said, taking her hand. 'I think we should get betrothed. Tomorrow. I don't want anyone else, and I want to prove to you that I'm committed.'

'Are you serious?'

'Arrosa, I want to spend the rest of my life with you.'

'I think I need to sit down,' she said.

They sat by the balcony table, facing each other as the sun set over the Inner Sea.

'I wasn't expecting this,' she said. 'I thought we were going to pick up from where we left off. Are you sure it isn't a reaction to coming home for the first time in months?'

'I've been planning this moment for thirds.'

'You didn't mention anything about it in your letters.'

'I wanted to say it in person. Do you need more time to think it over?'

Arrosa gazed out at the dying rays of the sun upon the surface of the sea, then she smiled.

'All right,' she said. 'I accept.'

Cael smiled back at her and they kissed again.

'People will say we're being stupid,' she said.

'I couldn't give a fuck. I want you to be my wife, Arrosa. We've known each other since we were children, and I don't need more time to think about it.'

'Are you going to make me a Holdfast?'

'Aye. Arrosa Holdfast.'

'Then why don't we get married now?' she said. 'Why bother with a betrothal?'

'Because you're still only seventeen,' he said.

'People can get married at seventeen.'

'Only if they have their parents' permission. My mother is your legal guardian; she might object. I'll have to finish my training first, and I'd rather get married in the spring or summer, after your birthday. Don't you want the chance to plan a big wedding?'

'Where would we have it? Colsbury?'

'Aye.'

'A few ideas are already springing to mind,' she said. 'Leave it with me.'

Karalyn tapped on the glass of the balcony door. 'I hate to interrupt, but we have a birthday cake for Carden.'

Cael glanced up at his mother.

'From your smiles,' she said, 'I'm guessing that the romance continues?'

'We're getting betrothed,' he said.

Karalyn narrowed her eyes. 'I see. Congratulations.'

'We've chosen early summer for the wedding,' Arrosa said. 'It'll be in Colsbury. We'll have to see when Cael has enough leave for it, though, and work out the exact dates later. Will you help me organise it, Karalyn? Could we get married in the gardens? Will you help me find a dress?'

'A betrothal I can accept,' Karalyn said, 'but why the rush to get married? Maybe the following summer would be a better idea.'

'Why?' said Cael.

'You will both be eighteen if you marry this summer,' she said. 'In fact, Arrosa will have just turned eighteen. I think it's a little young.'

'I can see why you'd think that, Mother,' said Cael; 'but we've known each other for a long time.'

'Aye, and if my memory serves me correctly, you did not get along for much of that time. Does this come from being apart for so long, Cael? Are you worried that Arrosa will drift away if you don't get a ring on her finger? And I'm surprised at your response to this, Arrosa. Cael is your first boyfriend. Let's all try to think rationally about this before we make any definite decisions.'

'You wouldn't be able to stop us,' said Arrosa. 'As soon as I'm eighteen, I can choose for myself.'

'You are right,' said Karalyn, 'but wouldn't you rather have my blessing and my support? I love you both dearly, and I am trying to help you. I'm not saying no – I'm saying let's have some time to think it over. And now, I have to ask – are you pregnant?'

Arrosa's face flushed, and she looked away.

'That would be an impossibility, Mother,' said Cael. 'We haven't... reached that stage.'

'Oh. I see,' said Karalyn. 'Well, now I feel a little awkward. Cake?'

'Aye,' said Cael, 'but first, you should know that we're going to register our betrothal at the ministry offices tomorrow. Will you come with us? You will need to sign a declaration stating that you give permission for Arrosa, as she is still your ward until her birthday.'

'I see you have been researching this, son,' said Karalyn. 'Aye. I'll come with you, on the condition that we sit down afterwards and work out a reasonable plan. Don't mention any of this to Lucius; I will tell him when I get a spare moment. And if you say anything to your Aunty Kelsey, expect to hear a whole litany of reasons why it's a stupid idea. Your aunt has soured on the concept of marriage recently.'

Cael and Arrosa got to their feet, and they followed Karalyn from the balcony.

'Did you read my mind before you asked?' Arrosa said, as they walked towards the stairs.

'No,' said Cael. 'Your thoughts are your own; you know that. I haven't read your mind in years.'

'Well, maybe, you know, if you wanted to, you could use your vision to keep in touch when you go back to Pebble Strand. I don't mind if you go into my head for that. It would be better than writing letters.'

'I can show you how to make a projection of yourself,' said Karalyn. 'That way, Arrosa will think you are in the same room.'

'You shouldn't be listening to our conversation, Mother.'

'Then you shouldn't be talking where I can hear you.'

They went down the stairs and entered the living room. Kelsey was standing by a large cake, and Cardova had lifted Carden up onto his shoulders.

'He's too young to even know it's his birthday,' said Kyra.

'That doesn't matter,' said Karalyn. 'This party is for all of us.' She smiled. 'My four... no, five children – all in the same place at the same time. Damn. Now I'm sounding like my mother again.'

That evening, Cael, Arrosa, Cole and Kyra decided to take a few bottles of wine and sit out on the same balcony where Cael had proposed. Cael listened for a while as the three students talked about university. He felt that day's training exercises catch up with him, and he yawned.

'What's wrong?' said Kyra. 'Tired already?'

'I was out on the Inner Sea in a small boat all day,' he said. 'If I were in Pebble Strand, I'd be in bed by now.'

'What's it like?' said Cole. 'You look healthy enough.'

Cael smiled. 'It's been great. Hard work, every day, but it's better than I'd imagined. So far, we've been taught how to sail and repair boats; we've been swimming in the sea, hiking and camping through the forests and hills; we've had endurance marches, hand-to-hand combat, horse riding, cooking, sewing...'

'Sewing?' said Kyra. 'I have a tear in a dress that you could take a look at.'

'And those are just the practical courses,' Cael went on. 'We're also being taught about every battle and conflict that the marines have taken part in, as well as tactical theory and leadership.'

Kyra shook her head. 'They are training you to become an obedient killing machine, brother. Is that what you want?'

'I want to protect the Empire from its enemies.'

'And who chooses which enemies you will fight? You will be fighting to further Thorn's ambitions.'

'She's called the Empress,' said Cael. 'Don't disrespect Her Majesty.'

'What in Pyre's name has happened to you, brother?' said Kyra. 'Five thirds in the marines, and you're spouting imperialist propaganda? I wasn't *disrespecting* your precious Empress; I was exercising my right to free speech.'

'That's one of the freedoms I'm protecting.'

'How was slaughtering eighty thousand Rahain civilians protecting free speech? And don't get me started on the atrocities being carried out in Rakana. We have invaded our two neighbours – how is that protecting anything?'

Arrosa groaned. 'Don't do this, please.'

'Is the truth too much for you, Arrosa?' said Kyra. 'I know you like to close your eyes to what is happening in the Star Continent, but people who stay silent about the atrocities are complicit in the crimes of the Empire.'

'Don't talk shite,' said Cael. 'Complicit, my arse. Do you think we should abolish the armed forces?'

'Aye,' said Kyra. 'I do. The marines aren't the worst, but what about the Sanang divisions? And what about the Banners? I'd rather have no army than an army of war criminals.'

'And then who would protect the Empire?'

'Fuck the Empire.'

Cael sipped from his wine glass, as the others sat in silence.

'Nothing to say, brother?' said Kyra.

'I don't want to fall out with you over this. We should change the subject.'

'Why? The truth can be uncomfortable, but that doesn't mean we should avoid it.'

'This is what she's like at university,' said Arrosa. 'Every day feels like a political struggle.'

'How would you know?' said Kyra. 'I barely see you at university.'

'And why's that?' said Arrosa. 'It's because you have a new group of friends. You avoid Cole and me. We aren't radical enough for you.'

'You are a child,' said Kyra. 'Maybe if you grew up a bit, you might understand more about the world.'

'That's my future wife you're talking to,' said Cael. 'I will take her side over yours, sister.'

Kyra stared at him, then she burst into laughter.

'You and Arrosa?' she cried. 'You're getting married? That's the funniest thing I've ever heard. I can't work out which of the two of you is more deluded than the other.'

'You're getting married?' said Cole.

'We're registering our betrothal tomorrow,' said Cael. 'Will you be my best man?'

'Uh, sure,' he said. 'Thanks, and congratulations. When's the wedding?'

'It's never going to happen,' said Kyra. 'Cael thinks he's the mighty defender of our freedoms, and Arrosa is a needy little girl who hasn't the first clue about relationships. Married? You fucking idiots. Mother will forbid it. It's practically like incest.'

'Fuck you,' said Cael. 'Arrosa and I aren't even remotely related. She's a Gunstian. She's from another world altogether.'

'Mother wanted to adopt her as our sister.'

'Aye, but she didn't. And Mother has already agreed. She's coming with us to the ministry offices tomorrow.'

'What? No. Mother said that? Is she insane?'

'I think you will both be very happy,' said Cole, raising his glass.

'Thank you,' said Cael.

'Yes, thank you, Cole,' said Arrosa. She glanced at Cael. 'I told you that people would think we're being stupid.'

'Aye,' said Cael, 'but I didn't expect my sister to be one of them.'

'You *are* being stupid,' said Kyra. 'You are the first boy Arrosa has ever kissed; and your own record of dumping girlfriends hardly inspires me with confidence. Why don't you just stay boyfriend and girlfriend for a while, before you take such a drastic step?' She frowned. 'Or, wait a minute. Arrosa, are you...?'

'No, I'm not,' said Arrosa. 'Your mother asked me the same question. I am not pregnant.'

'Everyone is going to ask you that.'

'I don't understand where this opposition is coming from,' said Cael. 'Plenty of people get married at our age. It's not as though Arrosa and I have just met. It's not love at first sight. We've known each other for eight years.'

'You fought for most of that time.'

'That was my fault,' said Cael. 'I was too immature to understand my own feelings, and I was angry at everyone and everything. That's over now. I learned a lot about myself when we were trapped on World Three. I learned what was important, and I realised how much I loved her. You are going to come to the wedding, though, aye?'

'If there is one, brother, I'll be there,' Kyra said. She got to her feet. 'I'm going to bed.'

'Then I should probably go, too,' said Cole.

'We'll see you in the morning,' said Kyra, then she and Cole left the balcony.

Cael lit a cigarette.

'Are you regretting asking me?' said Arrosa.

'No,' he said. 'I'm disappointed in Kyra's reaction, but I know what I want.'

'If we're getting married,' she said, 'should we talk about the future? For example, do you want children?'

'Aye. Do you?'

She nodded.

'Not as many as Uncle Corthie and Aunty Aila, though,' said Cael.

'Would we buy a house? Where would we live?'

'I like Colsbury,' he said, 'but it's cut off from everywhere else. What about here, in Plateau City? Or *here*, in the townhouse? No one's living in it at the moment, not after Aunty Kelsey moved out.'

'How long will you be in the marines for?'

'Forever, I hope. But not on active duty. I could get a staff position in a few years, and work in an office.'

She nodded. 'It's going to be hard when you go back to Pebble Strand.'

'Would you rather I resigned from the marines?'

'You promised the Empress you would serve for three years, and I think you should keep your promises. Also, if you love it, then you should stay. Should we call it a night?'

He stubbed out his cigarette, and they got to their feet.

'What room are you in?' he said.

'I'm on the top floor.'

They walked off the balcony and climbed the stairs. They reached the third floor, where Cael had a room, and he paused by the door.

'I know what you want,' she said.

He smiled. 'But?'

'I want to wait until we're married,' she said. 'Are you all right with that?'

'I'm not sure why we have to wait.'

'Because that's what I want, Cael. You were right before – I'm Gunstian, and Gunstians wait until they're married. I have never been with anyone, and, once we are married, I will never be with anyone but you. Why did you think I suggested we hold the wedding right away?'

He kissed her. 'Good night, Arrosa.'

'Good night, my beloved Cael.'

She turned away and climbed up the next flight of stairs towards the top floor of the townhouse. Cael watched her, then he opened the door and went to bed.

# CHAPTER 2
# PROFLIGATE

**Plateau City, The Plateau – 18th Day, Last Third Winter 544**

Kyra and Dazi walked out of the large lecture hall and joined the milling crowds of students in the quad.

'How did you get on?' said Kyra.

Dazi's big eyes gazed up at her. 'It was terrible,' the young Rakanese woman said. 'I wasn't expecting a question on Holdings constitutional reform. It's so unfair – we get one lecture on the subject in the entire term, and they include it in the examination? I couldn't remember anything. What about you?'

Kyra shrugged. 'It was all right.'

'All right? I know what that means, Kyra. It means you'll probably get the highest grade of anyone in the whole year. Again. I like being friends with you, but it sometimes makes me feel as though I'm the stupid one.'

'You're not stupid, Dazi; but maybe constitutional theory isn't your best subject. And I had an unfair advantage – it was my grandmother who enacted the Holdings reforms, during her time as First Holder. If Daphne Holdfast had become Empress, then she might have instituted democracy over the entire Empire, not just in the Holdings, and then we would have a leader chosen by all the people, instead of by a small handful of elitist mages.'

Dazi laughed. 'But *you* are one of those elitist mages, Kyra. You have a vote.' She tapped Kyra on the arm. 'Look – there's your cousin and stepsister, coming out of the canteen.'

Kyra turned. Arrosa and Cole were walking into the quad, their book-filled bags slung over their shoulders.

'She isn't my stepsister,' said Kyra, 'but she wants to be my sister-in-law. She's got her claws into my brother.'

'I heard she got into trouble for accusing one of her teachers of being a liar.'

Kyra watched Cole and Arrosa talking to each other as they crossed the quad.

'It must be nice not to be the only Holdfast here any more,' said Dazi.

'Arrosa isn't a Holdfast.'

'Not yet, but she will be if she marries your brother.'

'My brother is going through a strange phase at the moment,' Kyra said. 'He had a... difficult summer, and got sent to the marines as a punishment. He was telling me all kinds of nonsense when he was last home. He'll grow out of it soon, though; just as he'll grow out of his weird Arrosa infatuation.'

'She is pretty, though; you can't deny that.'

'And? Cael has gone out with several pretty girls, but it always ends the same way – he gets bored and dumps them. He thinks he's in love with Arrosa, but he's not.'

'Do you think he will be sent to Rahain or Rakana?'

'I hope not.'

'I wish I knew what was happening in Rakana,' Dazi went on. 'My folks in Amatskouri have been blinded by old rivalries; they think the invasion was a good idea. We had a big argument about it when I went home for Winter's Day. My father told me that I was upsetting my mother by talking about the massacres that have taken place; he said I ruined the holiday.'

'It takes courage to stand up for your beliefs, Dazi. Look what happened to me when I protested the war in Rahain. The Empress hasn't spoken to me since, and I'm not allowed to go inside the Ministry of the Plateau.'

Arrosa and Cole entered a wing of the university and disappeared from sight.

'We have an hour until our next class,' Dazi said. 'What do you want to do?'

'I need to go up to my room,' said Kyra. 'I left my books there this morning when I went down to the examination. I could meet you in the library in fifteen minutes.'

'Okay,' said Dazi. 'I'll see you there.'

Kyra turned toward the accommodation wing and set off, passing through the crowds of students. She walked into the building, and ascended several flights of stairs to reach the floor where her room lay. She unlocked her door and went inside. The room was a mess. She had been studying late into the night, and had almost overslept, and so had left the room in a dire state. She began rummaging around in a pile of books and folders, looking for the volume she needed for her next class.

'Good morning, daughter.'

Kyra sighed, and turned towards the doorway. Standing there was her mother.

'Can I help you?' said Kyra.

'Maybe,' said Karalyn. 'May I come in?'

'If you want.'

Her mother walked into the small room and closed the door. 'I'm here about Cael.'

Kyra's eyes widened. 'Has he left the marines?'

Karalyn eyed her. 'No. Why would he do that? He's having the time of his life, by all accounts. I wanted to talk to you about his betrothal to Arrosa.'

Kyra sighed again, and continued looking through her things.

'I know that you're still angry with me,' her mother said, 'but what should I have done? If I had refused to go to the ministry offices to give permission for Arrosa to become betrothed, then both she and Cael would have waited until she was eighteen and done it anyway. This way, I can still exert a little influence over their actions.'

'How do we stop them, Mother?'

'Do we want to stop them?'

'Obviously. Why else would you be here? You want my help in preventing this idiotic marriage from going ahead.'

'My interest is not so much in stopping them, as it is in slowing things down. As soon as Arrosa turns eighteen, then, legally, both she and Cael will be adults. They need to be allowed to make their own mistakes.'

'This mistake will wreck Cael's life.'

Karalyn narrowed her eyes. 'Let's sit down for a moment.'

Kyra cleared space on the room's only two chairs, and they sat.

'We might be approaching this from different angles,' her mother said. 'I'm not trying to stop my son from marrying the girl of his dreams. If he loves Arrosa, and if she loves him in return, then why shouldn't they get married? All I am trying to do is delay things. If we can persuade them to postpone the marriage for two years, then that will give them enough time to think it over. Arrosa is so inexperienced in these matters, and, let's face it, Cael has been more than a little mercenary in his past relationships. They are both too young to know what they really want. But, if they delay for two years and then, at the end of that, if they are still together, then there is no reason why they shouldn't get married. Do you agree?'

'I don't know if I trust Arrosa, Mother. She has been clinging onto our family for years. She wanted you to adopt her, but that didn't happen, so now she wants to marry Cael.'

'I didn't adopt her because both she and Cael begged me not to. Besides, I have no desire to prevent Arrosa from becoming a Holdfast. She might not be my natural daughter, but I love her.'

'I have no idea why.'

'You know what happened to me on Athumia,' said Karalyn. 'Arrosa lost everything, and yet she helped me through one of the most difficult times of my life. Do you think I should have then abandoned her, Kyra? Should I have left her on Athumia, at nine years old, to fend for herself? Have some compassion.'

'I understand all that. Did I ever complain about her while she was living with us in Colsbury? No, I didn't. I was welcoming, even though I didn't particularly like her. It was Cael who was always objecting to her presence. But now she's almost eighteen, and I'm tired of pretending to get along with her. She'll be an adult soon, just as you said. It's the perfect time to cast her adrift. You've done your job. You took care of her when no one else would. You fed her, clothed her, and gave her a place to stay, but there's no reason why this generosity should extend into adulthood. I presume you are paying her university fees?'

'Aye.'

'She'll be expecting you to pay for the wedding, too.'

'I'll be happy to do so, if they wait.'

'And if they refuse to wait? What if they insist upon getting married as soon as she turns eighteen?'

'Then I won't be able to stop them, but I won't be paying for any lavish ceremony.'

'But you'll pay for a modest ceremony?'

Karalyn raised her palms. 'Maybe. I'm not sure. I don't want to drive them both away. Will you speak to Arrosa? Try to gently persuade her that a two-year betrothal is in her best interests.'

'I doubt she'll listen to me, but I'll try. Did you really ask her if she was pregnant?'

'Did she tell you that? I had to ask.'

'I asked her the same question, though I knew it was unlikely. Arrosa believes in waiting until she is married. She used to tell me this when she was younger.'

'Does she still believe it?'

'As far as I know. Why don't you just read her mind? It would save a lot of guessing.'

'It's wrong to take advantage of our powers like that. People should be allowed to have their own thoughts. We should only read minds in an emergency.'

'Cael getting married to her would be an emergency. Maybe I should read her mind.'

Karalyn shook her head. 'I know that you've tried, daughter. You don't understand the Gunstian language.'

'Fine. I've tried. Not for a while, though. Do you speak Gunstian?'

'Aye.'

'Then it will have to be you.'

Karalyn got to her feet. 'I'd better go. Talk to Arrosa.'

'All right.'

The air shimmered, and her mother disappeared. Kyra rolled her eyes, then went back to searching for her book.

'But,' said Professor Nadia, 'if the pressure in the boiler gets too high, there is the risk of an explosion. One such explosion occurred in the city of Granite Heights over thirty years ago, killing eighty workers employed to maintain the heating system. This is why it is vital to ensure that the safety procedures are adhered to at all times.'

She turned away from the class, and gestured towards the large blackboard. As she began to write, Kyra nodded to her classmates. A few glanced away, but around half got to their feet as Kyra stood.

Nadia narrowed her eyes. 'Why are you all standing? The class hasn't finished.'

'Will you condemn the slaughter of civilians in Rahain and Rakana?' said Kyra.

'What is this nonsense?' said Nadia.

'Will you condemn the killing of Rahain and Rakanese children by the imperial armed forces?' said Kyra.

'This is a classroom,' said Nadia, 'not a political assembly. Sit down, at once.'

Kyra stared at the professor. 'We refuse to be taught by an imperialist aggressor. Do you condemn...'

'I shall not pander to your juvenile demands,' cried Nadia. 'Either sit down, or get out!'

Kyra picked up her bag and began to walk to the door, followed by the others who had been standing.

'I am warning you, Kyra Holdfast,' said Nadia. 'If you leave, you will fail this course. You will not be welcomed back into this classroom, and I will have your name struck off my register.'

'I will not be blackmailed into supporting war crimes,' said Kyra.

'You are out of your mind, girl. And to those of you who are thinking of trailing along after Miss Holdfast, I say be very careful. You are at university to study, not to ruin your career prospects.'

'We are not intimidated by your threats, Professor,' said Kyra. 'Our principles shall not be compromised.'

She opened the classroom door, and stepped out into the corridor. A dozen other students walked out after her, and Kyra closed the door.

'Did you see the look on her face?' said one. 'I thought her head was going to explode, like a boiler.'

'What should we do now?' said another.

They turned to look at Kyra.

'You can choose if you want to attend Professor Nadia's next lesson,' Kyra said. 'We've made our point.'

'But you won't be allowed back in.'

'I know,' said Kyra. 'I didn't think much of her class, anyway. Dropping this subject will allow me to concentrate on the others.'

'I think I'll go to the canteen and get some coffee,' said one of the students.

The group began to disperse. Kyra walked down a flight of stairs, then she saw Arrosa coming out of a classroom. The Gunstian girl was talking to a few of her classmates, but she hadn't noticed Kyra. Kyra remembered what her mother had said, but decided to carry on towards the rooms of Professor Achan. She could catch up with Arrosa another time.

She walked along a corridor until she reached Achan's office. The door was open, and the professor was seated at his desk. He glanced up, and smiled.

'Come in,' he said. 'Come in and close the door.'

Kyra walked in. She shut the door, and walked over to the desk. Achan gestured to a seat, and Kyra sat down.

'Did you go through with it?' said Achan.

'We did. Half of the class walked out.'

'Well done,' said Achan. 'Will there be any consequences?'

'I have been ejected from her course. She told me that my name would be stricken from her register. I... I wasn't expecting that.'

'But it is not the first time you have left her classroom.'

'I know, but... I didn't think she could do that. I now have two hours every day with no classes, and it's too late to pick another subject. It means... damn it; it means that if I want my diploma, I will have to come back next year to earn enough course credits.'

'So you come back next year. There's no harm in eking out your time at university. In fact, try to see this as an opportunity. You suddenly have extra time on your hands and, next year, you will only have to attend one course, to make up for losing Recovered Rahain Technology. What could you do with that time? What if I were to tell you that I could secure you a place on the Student Council? If you assisted them in a lowly role for the remainder of this year, then next year you could run for president. Being on the Student Council would give you ways to reach every student at the university. You could organise mass meetings, and have access to the printing press. Your voice would be amplified, Kyra.'

'Will you be here next year, sir?'

'My placing was for one year only, so I am due to return to the City at the end of spring. However, my lectures have been over-subscribed, so I could make a case that I deserve another year. And I confess that I enjoy it here. There is certainly nowhere in the City that rivals this university. The exchange of information, the resources in the library, the freedom to experiment and try out new ideas – I love it all. Regardless of what else you may think of Kelsey Holdfast, as patron of the university, she was responsible for attracting the best professors on any of the allied worlds.' He smiled. 'Apologies – that was a very longwinded answer to a simple question.'

'I hope you stay, sir. If I knew that you would still be here, then I wouldn't mind coming back for a fourth year.'

'I am flattered to hear you say that. Would you like me to speak to the selection committee of the Student Council on your behalf?'

'Aye. Thank you.'

'It's the least I can do for a student who shows such promise and courage. Now – on to darker matters. It has disturbed me in recent thirds that the imperial authorities are not allowing reports from occupied Rakana to reach the public here in Plateau City. We know that the Empire invaded under the flimsiest of pretexts at the beginning of autumn; and we know that the imperial armed forces are occupying Arakhanah City, but that is the full extent of our knowledge. What are they hiding from us, Kyra?'

Kyra frowned. 'Was that a rhetorical question, sir? You know that my privileges have been taken away. I am not allowed to attend meetings of the Imperial Court.'

'It was partly rhetorical. Might I ask you a personal question?'

'Aye.'

'It is well known that your mother possesses powers that are wide in scope and potency. She can make herself appear invisible. She can read minds, just as Holdings mages can do. I was wondering – were any of these powers passed on to you?'

Kyra hesitated. 'Why do you ask, sir?'

'Well, it seems to me that there is little difference between illicitly revealing what you heard in a meeting, as you once did for us, and eavesdropping upon those meetings. Do you see any moral difference between the two?'

'Are you asking me to spy on meetings of the Imperial Court?'

'Certainly not. I would never do any such thing. I am merely presenting you with the possibilities, so that you have a choice. Of course, if you are not in possession of any of your mother's powers, then the entire question is moot.'

Kyra said nothing.

'Ask yourself this,' Achan went on; 'if, indeed, you had the ability to discover the truth about what is happening within occupied Rakana, and you knew that this knowledge would inflame the masses, and convince public opinion to turn against the imperialist government, would it not be your moral duty to do so?' He smiled again. 'That is all I am going to say on the matter. For the record, I am not asking you to do anything. I would certainly never ask you to break the law.'

Kyra got to her feet. 'I will consider what you have said, sir. And thank you for offering to speak to the Student Council.'

'My pleasure, Kyra. I will let you know what they say.'

Kyra left the room. With her expulsion from Professor Nadia's class, she had nothing else on for the rest of the day. She thought about using her powers to spy on the Empress. Such a thing would have been inconceivable only a short while before, but hadn't Achan made a good point? She had already revealed the contents of a secret meeting. It seemed hypocritical to think that was fine, while abjuring any use of her powers. Besides, eavesdropping did not mean that she would be obliged to tell everyone everything that she had heard; wasn't she more than capable of using her own discretion and judgement? And wasn't it wrong of the government to be hiding what they were doing in Rakana?

Kyra made her decision, and strode away in the direction of her room.

Half an hour later, Kyra sent her vision powers out of the university and across the New Town towards the Ministry of the Plateau. Despite a gnawing sense of guilt about what she was doing, she pushed her vision in through an open window of the building, and raced it through the marble-lined hallways and corridors. She reached the closed doors of the smaller audience chamber, where she knew the Imperial Court was meeting that day, and pushed her powers in through the keyhole.

Inside, five men and three women were seated around a table. At the far end, the Empress was sitting upon one of her thrones. To her right was Brogan ae Bridget, Kelsey's replacement as Herald; then came Major General Martius Claudian, a veteran from the Banner of the Sapphire Throne. His role of Adjutant had been newly created in the wake of Kelsey's resignation, to take some of the pressure off Herald Brogan. On his right was Caelius Logos, the Imperial Quartermaster, and Marshal Bedig ae Brannig. Sitting opposite the new Herald was Naxor, the Imperial Chamberlain. On his left sat the new Treasurer – a Rahain woman named Slaeon who had been a banker in Plateau City; and on her left was Jannis Holdsmith, who had been appointed to the new position of Chief Jurist at the same time as the role of Adjutant had been created.

Kyra watched at first, her vision not picking up any sound from the conversation in progress. If she stopped at that moment, she told herself, then she wouldn't have broken the law. Watching was not the same as listening. If she went forward with her plan, though, she would have committed treason. Was it permissible to break the law if those who made the laws were corrupt?

She steeled her resolve, and pushed her powers into the mind of Caelius Logos. She burrowed into his thoughts, and looked out from his eyes.

'We don't know the cause,' Naxor was saying. 'All I have is the fevered report from a branch of the local militia based in Hold Stringer.'

'But someone must have killed them,' said Caelius.

'Quite so,' said Naxor. 'The villagers evidently did not tear their own bodies to pieces.'

'Could it be greenhides?' said Marshal Bedig. 'Might some have been hiding in the Barrier Mountains all this time?'

'That hardly seems likely,' said Naxor. 'Frostback and Halfclaw regularly fly over the Barrier Mountains, and I am quite convinced that they would have reported any sightings of rogue greenhides. A more far-fetched theory states that these possible greenhides might have migrated all the way from the Black Mountains of Sanang, but I fail to see how they could have done that without being observed.'

'There would be a trail of carnage leading all the way back to Sanang if that were the case,' said Caelius.

'Is a military response required?' said Adjutant Claudian, 'or can the local militia deal with any greenhides, if it turns out that they are responsible for this massacre?'

'The Holdings militia are not equipped to fight greenhides,' said Bedig.

'Let us pause for reflection before ordering in the army,' said the Empress. 'I tend to agree with the analysis of Lord Naxor – if greenhides were involved, they would have been seen travelling to Hold Stringer. The Ascendants placed no greenhide nests in the vicinity of the Barrier Mountains. For the moment, let us assume that this massacre was carried out by humans, as that is the simplest explanation. Lord Chamberlain, I would like you to assist the Holdings militia with their investigations. If it turns out to be a purely criminal matter, leave it to the Holdings jurisdiction.'

'With all due respect Your Majesty,' said Naxor, 'I am due to return to Rakana in the coming days, to liaise with Commander Lahnos and his team of dragons.'

'Herald Brogan can take over that duty,' said the Empress. 'Please ensure that you show the Herald how to make use of her Quadrant to travel there and back.'

'As you will, Your Majesty,' said Naxor. 'On the subject of Rakana, I would like to propose a further release of funds from the imperial treasury, in order to bolster the new interim Rakanese government that we are setting up. The present level of funding is inadequate. There are hundreds of new Rakanese civil servants who have to be paid, and if we hope to form a battalion of local militia, even more money will have to be found.'

Treasurer Slaeon's tongue flickered. 'I am afraid that is completely out of the question, my Lord Chamberlain.'

Naxor frowned. 'Why?'

'Because the treasury has no money.'

The room stilled.

Caelius laughed nervously. 'Would you mind repeating that?'

'Certainly, Quartermaster,' said Slaeon. 'As of this present moment, the treasury is spending twice what it receives in revenue. Our current out-goings include, but are not restricted to – the occupations of Rahain and Rakana, the subsidies given to the Province of the City, the military handover of the Great Wall, massive infrastructure works in Tahrana City, the Rahain Capital, and Jade Falls, the military build-up in Yearning, the occupation of the Tempest mine in Inopei, the military subsidies handed over to the island of Zamata, and our pension liabilities for all Banner retirees. What remains in treasury reserves has been set aside by imperial edict for the new operations planned for the Western Rim. Without loans, new sources of revenue, or considerable reductions in spending, I fear that the treasury will be bankrupt within six thirds.'

'You... you have got to be joking,' said Naxor, his face paling.

'I do not joke, Lord Chamberlain,' said Slaeon. 'I was appointed as Imperial Treasurer to sort out the financial mess created by years of unbounded profligacy. The truth may be unpalatable, but it nevertheless remains the truth.'

'Did you know about this, Your Majesty?' said Naxor.

'I was aware of the substance of our Treasurer's findings,' said the Empress.

'I take offence at the allegation of profligacy,' said Brogan. 'I was Imperial Treasurer for three years before becoming Herald, and we always had sufficient reserves to pay for all expenditure.'

'Indeed you did, Madam Herald,' said Slaeon. 'However, is it not also true that the reserves became more depleted with every passing year? The Empire has been spending its way through a colossal sum of savings, and that sum has now been exhausted. If one ran a commercial business in this manner, one would not be in business for long.'

'The Empire is not a business,' said Caelius.

Slaeon smiled. 'Your idealism wilts before the naked glare of harsh reality, Quartermaster. Would you now care to hear my proposed solutions?'

'We do,' said the Empress.

'Taxes must be raised,' said Slaeon. 'All taxes, in every sphere of imperial life. Cuts must be made to the reconstruction budget granted to the three occupied cities in Rahain. Cuts must be made to the cost of occupying Rakana. The plans for the Western Rim must be abandoned or scaled back considerably; and subsidies for the City and Zamata must be pared back to the bare bones.'

'That is unacceptable,' said the Empress. 'We concede that some taxes may have to rise temporarily, but we will not countenance any reduction in military expenditure.'

'Then there is but one other recourse, Your Majesty,' said Slaeon. 'Loans. With your permission, I can arrange a meeting with the owners of the Plateau's leading bankers, and we can negotiate terms. It will not come cheap, however. The banks will take their share.'

'Alas that Rahain and Rakana are so poor,' said Naxor; 'otherwise, we could strip their assets.'

'We should table a meeting to go over all taxes and expenditure, Lord Chamberlain,' said Slaeon. 'If you have the stomach for detail, we might be able to find ways to increase revenue without cancelling any future plans. That, allied to a series of negotiated loans, should see us through the coming year. The underlying problem, however, will not go away. At heart, if I may speak frankly, there is a gross imbalance between ambition and available resources. One cannot succeed without the other.'

'Do not turn to the bankers,' said the Empress. 'If the treasury requires a loan, then I will provide the money from the Holdfasts' personal reserves.'

'Forgive me, Your Majesty,' said Jannis Holdsmith, 'but that would be illegal. Only one person has the authority to release Holdfast funds to the government, and that person is Holder Fast.'

Naxor shook his head and laughed. 'So, we shall have to go on our knees, begging Kelsey Holdfast for money?'

The Empress lowered her gaze. 'I shall not beg. Treasurer Slaeon, schedule a full meeting of the Imperial Court, and we shall sift through every line of the budget. Only then, if we cannot find a solution, shall we approach any bankers.'

'As you will, Your Majesty,' said Slaeon.

Kyra cut the connection to Caelius's mind, and found herself back in her room in the university. She felt stunned by what she had heard. How could the Empire possibly be running out of money? Had Thorn so over-stretched herself that the treasury was liable to go bankrupt?

Achan would be overjoyed by the news – if she told him. She imagined the pamphlets that Achan would paste up all over the city, trumpeting the revelation that the Empire was teetering on the brink. Kyra thought about the tired expression on the face of the Empress, and the look of disbelief on Naxor's. As for Brogan, well, it was clear that she was no Kelsey. Despite Kyra's antipathy towards her aunt, there was no denying that Kelsey would have dominated the conversation had she been there.

All at once, the illusion of the Empire's invincibility had been shattered, and its weaknesses laid bare.

Kyra got to her feet, then she sat down again, unable to explain why she was so reticent to let Achan know the truth about the imperial finances. Wasn't this the chance they had been waiting for? With one good kick, the Empire might come tumbling down – wasn't that what Kyra wanted?

'Fuck the Empire,' she muttered to herself.

She got to her feet, left her room, and strode in the direction of Achan's office.

## CHAPTER 3
# THE PROTECTORATE

**Arakhanah City, Occupied Rakana – 22nd Day, Last Third Winter 544**

Lord Sigum soared over the houses and canals of Arakhanah City. Soldiers from the Imperial Army were stationed by most junctions and bridges, keeping a watchful eye on the masses of civilians queuing for food. Huge quantities of provisions had been arriving every day from the Plateau, enough to have staved off the threat of starvation among the Rakanese population

Lahnos glanced down from the back of the silvery-green dragon, his eyes scanning the streets that ran alongside the canals. Much of the city was derelict, and the imperial forces had moved everyone from the outlying areas into the central district, where they were easier to feed and police. Many of the queuing Rakanese stared up at the sight of Lord Sigum flying overhead but, after four thirds, most were used to seeing dragons patrolling the skies above their city.

Sigum banked to the left, and they passed over the wide river that ran through the heart of Arakhanah City. Above the far bank, a smaller green dragon was also on patrol, and Sigum soared over to meet her. Lahnos glanced at the rider secured to the other dragon's harness –

Ora'lya of Dragon Eyre. She waved at Lahnos, and he raised a hand in greeting as the two dragons circled each other.

'Noble Sigum,' said the green dragon, 'how goes your patrol this day?'

'There is little to report, gracious Quicklime,' said Sigum. 'Our mere presence here deters trouble.'

'I believe you are right, my lord,' said Quicklime. 'Shall we descend?'

'We shall.'

The two dragons banked again, then they flew west over the densely-packed streets. Although the city was entirely above ground, it reminded Lahnos of Tahrana City, as so much of it was either ruined or abandoned. What had once clearly been a large population of many millions had been reduced to a fraction of that by decades of emigration, famine and conflict. The first act of the new occupation administration had been to stem the flow of those trying to flee to the Plateau, not by force, but by bringing in enough food and supplies to persuade the Rakanese population to stay in their city. Rebuilding efforts had begun, but they were small in scale compared to what had already been spent in Rahain. Canals were being cleaned up by the local workforce, and bridges repaired, but there was a sense that it was merely scratching the surface of a deep-rooted decay.

Sigum and Quicklime reached a large, enclosed paddock, where the other dragons from the Eastern Rim were standing. Rows of tents ran down one side, and vast canopies of canvas had been erected, to provide shelter to the dragons whenever it rained. Sigum descended first. He landed in the middle of the paddock, and then, moments later, Quicklime landed beside him.

Gallantmorn poked his huge orange head out from under one of the canopies.

'Was there any trouble, Commander?' he said.

'There was none,' said Sigum. 'The city lies at peace.'

Lahnos unbuckled the straps holding him to the harness, then he clambered down to the soft turf. Ora'lya climbed down from Quicklime's shoulders, and the two riders walked over the grass towards each other.

Lahnos put his arms round Ora'lya's waist, and they kissed. He noticed a few of the other riders stare at them, but he didn't care.

'Do you want to get something to eat?' he said.

'All right,' said Ora'lya.

She took his hand, and they walked over to the tents, while Sigum remained behind to speak to Quicklime.

'You know,' said Ora'lya; 'wouldn't it be wonderful if our two dragons got together? I think they're well suited to each other.'

'Sigum might be a bit old for Quicklime,' said Lahnos. 'I'm not sure how that works with dragons.'

'I know that she's a little besotted with him,' she said, 'but maybe you're right.'

Two of the Bullan came out of a large tent as Lahnos and Ora'lya approached.

'Good flight, sir?' said one.

'Yes, thank you,' said Lahnos. 'The streets are busy, but there were no disturbances.'

'We have water and food prepared for Lord Sigum, sir,' the Bullan went on. 'Will Miss Ora'lya be joining us for dinner again?'

'She will,' he said.

They walked into the tent's main area, where two of the other Bullan were preparing food. Internal canvas walls divided the tent into several separate spaces, and there was a hole in the roof of the main area, to allow smoke from the fire pit to escape. Lahnos took a seat, and Ora'lya sat down next to him.

'Will you tell me your names today?' Ora'lya said.

The two Bullan smiled.

'Not today, miss,' said one. 'Maybe tomorrow.'

'You say that every day,' she said.

The Bullan handed them both mugs of steaming coffee.

'Thanks,' said Lahnos.

Efizel emerged from another part of the tent.

'Good afternoon, sir,' he said. 'How was the patrol?'

'Uneventful.'

'I was at the intelligence briefing this morning, sir,' Efizel said. 'There was another attack on a soldier, while you were flying.'

'Any deaths?'

'Only that of the culprit, sir,' said the Bullan sergeant major. 'The soldier was stabbed, but he will live. His attacker was killed by other members of the squad on duty.'

'Thanks for letting me know,' said Lahnos.

Efizel tilted his head, then he walked over to the far corner of the tent to carry on with his duties.

Lahnos turned back to Ora'lya. 'There's very little we can do about these incidents from the air,' he said.

'The Rakanese rebels know that,' said Ora'lya. 'That's why there have been no large-scale disturbances for a long time. Dragons can't do anything against these small attacks.'

'I've been wondering for a while,' Lahnos said, 'if the army will send us back to Rahain. We've achieved everything we can achieve in Rakana.'

'Would you rather be in Rahain?' Ora'lya said.

'I'd rather be here with you,' he said; 'but, from a tactical point of view, Sigum, the Bullan and I would probably be more useful somewhere else. Maybe you, Quicklime and the others will get redeployed as well. Does your deal with the Empire keep you based in Rakana?'

'No. Each dragon and rider had to volunteer for a year's service. I don't think it matters where we're sent.'

'And why would anyone from Dragon Eyre volunteer? I know that other dragons from the Eastern Rim have been sent to the City of Salve; what's the attraction?'

'I think it's become a matter of honour,' said Ora'lya. 'Queen Blackrose first took dragons with her to help the Empress fight the Ascendants. That was... em, almost exactly ten years ago. The dragons who went with Her Majesty and survived, well, they haven't stopped talking about it since. Now every dragon wants to please the queen by volunteering for service. As soon as I became Quicklime's rider, she suggested that we add our names to the list. We had to wait five years to get selected.'

'Five years? That means you were sixteen when you became a rider.'

She smiled. 'I fell in love with Quicklime as soon as I saw her. The normal route to becoming a rider had been disrupted by the occupation of Dragon Eyre for twenty years by Implacatus, and then my home island of Enna was invaded by the Wystians. My family was evacuated to Ulna. When it was all over, and we were allowed to go back to Enna, Quicklime was one of the dragons who settled there, after her old rider had been killed in the fighting. The queen asked for people to step forward as riders, and I jumped at the chance.'

'Quicklime has had other riders?'

'I'm her fifth. There were twelve of us to choose from, and she picked me. You told me that you have been Lord Sigum's rider for eight years, so you must have been, what? – fourteen or fifteen? Younger? You've never actually told me your age.'

'I'm a bit older than I look.'

'Saying things like that makes me suspicious,' she said. 'How did you meet Lord Sigum?'

'We became friends when we were on a long sea voyage, on one of those dragon carrier ships I told you about.'

'Where were you both going?'

'Home. Well, I was going home. I wonder if my little island looks like the islands on Dragon Eyre.'

Ora'lya smiled and shook her head as she got to her feet. 'You always change the subject when I ask about your past,' she said. 'I'm going to speak to the other riders for a moment, while dinner is being prepared. When I get back, I want you to tell me something you haven't told anyone else.'

Lahnos watched her walk out of the tent, then Efizel glanced over at him from the corner of the tent.

'This reminds me of a certain situation with a Lieutenant Dolwyn, sir,' he said. 'Are you about to sabotage your chances of happiness again?'

'I don't know what to do,' Lahnos said. 'I enjoy being with Ora'lya, but I keep forgetting what I can and can't say to her. It's no wonder she's getting suspicious.'

'Do you like her, sir?'

'Of course I do. And Dolwyn was nine months ago. You can't keep bringing that up. Ora'lya is nothing like her. I wish...'

'Yes, sir?'

'I wish I wasn't fucking immortal.'

Efizel frowned. 'Perhaps you have been spending too much time with soldiers from Kellach Brigdomin, sir. A commander should not use such vulgar language.'

'But you understood my point?'

'I did, sir. However, there is little use in complaining about something you cannot change.'

'Should I tell her the truth?'

'Only you can make that decision, sir.'

'Life would be a lot easier if I swore to give up women; you know, like the monks on Zamata. I didn't plan on getting into another relationship; yet, here I am again.'

'If you decide to make an announcement to her regarding your immortal status, sir, then I would suggest that you give me a signal, so that I can shepherd the other Klediomira outside to give you some privacy.'

Ora'lya walked back into the tent. 'Gallantmorn and Duskshade will be doing tonight's patrol,' she said as she sat down, 'which means that we'll be on tomorrow night's shift. I told Quicklime and Lord Sigum when I was walking across the paddock on the way back.'

Lahnos nodded.

'Well?' she said. 'Did you think of something to tell me?'

'I'd rather talk about you.'

'That's sweet, but all we do is talk about me. I'm starting to think that you know everything there is to know about me.'

'I didn't know that Quicklime had other riders before you. Why do you think she chose you?'

Ora'lya raised an eyebrow. 'Is that the best you can do? Are you keeping something from me? You don't have a secret wife hidden away somewhere, do you?'

Lahnos laughed. 'There's no wife, secret or otherwise.'

'Girlfriend?'

'I've... had girlfriends. I'm not being unfaithful, Ora.'

'Don't call me that, or I will start to call you *Lah*.'

'Ora'lya is hard to get my mouth round.'

'Tough shit. It's my name. All right; tell me about one of your previous girlfriends.'

'I went with a girl called Reyn once. She had horns, too, and a tail.'

Ora'lya's eyes narrowed. 'She had a *tail*?'

'Like the Bullan do.'

'She was a Bullan?'

'She was part-Bullan, like me.'

'What happened to her?'

'Well, after we split up, she was murdered by soldiers.'

'Oh.'

'They were on a rampage against the part-Bullan. Dozens were killed.'

'Has there been anyone else?'

'After Reyn, I went with someone called Leona. That was probably the only serious relationship I've been in; well, until you.'

She raised an eyebrow. 'Are we in a serious relationship?'

'I think so. Aren't we?'

'And what was Leona like?'

'Clever, kind, but sad. She had taken the blame for things that weren't her fault, and a lot of the people on the island hated her for it. I stood by her, and so they started to hate me, too. She was also murdered. It took me a long time to get over what happened to her. Years.'

'Years? How long ago was this?'

'I... uh...'

'I have a good memory, Lahnos. You've mentioned Leona before. You said that she ruled the island where you lived. I also happen to know that Karalyn Holdfast returned to the Star Continent eight years ago, two years after she had supposedly died. Sable brought her back, along with a dragon and a man with horns. Do you think these things aren't discussed on Dragon Eyre? Everyone talks about Sable. You must have been with Leona before Sable brought you to the Star Continent. That would make you about thirty. Is that it? You're thirty, but you look younger? I don't care if you're thirty, Lahnos.'

'I'm twenty-nine.'

'Honestly, I'm more annoyed that you kept your age a secret than I am by the age difference between us.'

One of the Bullan coughed quietly. 'Dinner is ready.'

Lahnos and Ora'lya got up and walked over to the tent's communal dining table. Only two places had been set, and Lahnos glanced at Efizel.

'Are you not eating with us?'

The Bullan sergeant major tilted his head. 'Not this evening, sir. I thought you two might like to dine alone.'

Lahnos and Ora'lya sat at the table, while the Bullan filed out of the tent.

'They don't like us arguing,' said Ora'lya.

'Were we arguing?' said Lahnos.

'I want to be able to trust you, Lahnos. Why were you dishonest about your real age?'

'Could we not just eat dinner?'

Ora'lya frowned. 'Maybe I should go.'

'I don't understand; I thought everything was fine. We've been seeing each other for three months, and this is the first time I've seen you look angry.'

'I'm angry because you're keeping things from me. And I wouldn't be angry if I didn't... if I didn't like you so much. You said that we were in a serious relationship, and I want that to be true, but how can I believe that if you won't tell me the truth about yourself? Don't you trust me?'

'All this, because I wouldn't tell you how old I am?'

'It's not just that, and you know it. You've been evasive with me for months. Every time I ask you a question, you change the subject, or refuse to answer. If this doesn't change, then... then there's no future for us.'

Lahnos rolled his eyes.

Ora'lya stood. 'I don't think I should waste any more of my time.'

'Sit. Please,' he said. 'I will tell you if you sit down again.'

She eyed him. 'Tell me what?'

He gestured towards the chair, and she sat down.

'You're not going to like this,' he said. 'In fact, you will probably walk out of the tent when you hear what I have to say. But, if you're sure...'

She glared at him.

'This is the point where I usually stab myself in the arm,' Lahnos went on.

'What are you talking about?'

'I'm immortal. I don't age, and I'll never look old.'

'Are you a demigod?'

'Well, not exactly; but yes, I suppose so.'

'Why would you keep that a secret?'

'Didn't you hear me? I cannot age. In fifty years time, I will look the same as I do now.'

'And I won't. That doesn't bother me, unless you're saying that you would lose interest in me if I'm not young any more.'

'I can never get married. I will not watch my wife grow old and die in front of me. For the same reason, I will never have children, because they won't be immortal. I can't do it. I refuse to watch my children die, while I live on forever, trapped in this body.'

'It sounds, Lahnos, as though you haven't come to terms with the fact you are immortal. Didn't you always know?'

'No. You know I have the Gift of Pain, yes? Well, I have two other Gifts. One of them allows me to kill people by touching them. When that happens, I draw out that person's strength, and take it into myself. I killed a god when I was twenty-one. I stole his immortality, and I haven't aged a day since. You're right, though – I haven't come to terms with it. Maybe in a century or two it will finally sink in.'

'Someone might behead you, or a dragon's fire might turn you into a heap of ashes. You aren't really immortal. Sable killed dozens of so-called immortal gods on Dragon Eyre.'

'I suppose that's true.'

Ora'lya picked up a fork and started to eat.

Lahnos frowned. 'You don't seem particularly upset by my revelation.'

She shrugged. 'Of all the things you could have told me, this was not the worst.'

'I can never have children.'

'You say that now, but people change their minds.'

Lahnos shook his head. 'I should have become a monk.'

'What's a monk?'

'A man who swears a vow of chastity.'

'Why would anyone do that?'

'Religion. Dragon spirits and the like.'

'Do you have any more secrets?'

'I don't think so.'

'Good.'

'We have no future, Ora'lya.'

'Then why did you stop me from leaving the tent? You could have let me walk away. You could have said nothing, and our relationship would be over. You wanted me to stay.'

Lahnos narrowed his eyes.

'All right,' she said. 'If you're going to break it off with me, do it now. Or, we can give it a chance. Do you want to end it?'

Lahnos got up and walked to the tent's entrance. Outside, it had started to rain, and the dragons were sheltering under the great canopies. A few soldiers were guarding the perimeter of the large paddock, and beyond them, the brick houses of the city spread out in dense rows. He glanced back at Ora'lya, who was watching him from the table. He felt trapped, not by her, but by his power to self-heal; doomed to forever repeat the same cycle with every woman he grew to like. The right thing to do would be to break it off, to spare himself the pain that would inevitably come later. Another part of him baulked at the thought of ending it. Ora'lya made him happy, and being with her was infinitely better than being alone and miserable.

'I don't want to end it,' he said. 'I want to be with you.'

Ora'lya laughed amid the thick shadows. 'No, Lahnos; the Wystians are dragons. Uncivilised dragons, who hate humans.' She leaned up on one elbow, and pulled the thin blanket over them. 'I can't wait for spring to start. The Star Continent is so cold.'

'If you want heat, you should try the Holdings in summer,' Lahnos said, as he lay on his back next to her. 'Is it true that Dragon Eyre has perfect weather?'

'It's all I've ever known,' she said. 'Do you think the Bullan have come back yet?'

'If they have, they've been very quiet.'

She traced her fingers down the side of his face. 'Apart from me, how many women have you slept with?'

'Do I have to answer that?'

'You said you were going to be honest with me. I just want to know a bit more about you.'

'You're the fourth,' he said.

'That's fewer than I'd imagined.'

'I stayed away from women after Leona died.'

'You must have loved her.'

'I did.'

'You're my second,' she said. 'I was with a boy in Enna a couple of years ago, but he became jealous of my bond with Quicklime. At least you and I are both dragon riders; we understand what it's like.'

'I'm glad that you know about me,' he said. 'It's a relief. I've been dreading that conversation for a while, because I thought it would mean the end for us.'

'What would you do if I got pregnant?'

'I wouldn't leave you. Karalyn's brother is married to a demigod called Aila. Maybe I should ask her about this. Or maybe I should just ask Karalyn. She's immortal, too.'

'Do you really know all of the Holdfasts?'

'Not all of them. I'm not on first-name terms with the Empress, for instance; but I've fought alongside Sable.'

'You lucky bastard. Sable was my hero when I was growing up. I once saw her when I was on Ulna, when I was twelve, and I nearly fainted in the street. What time is it, do you think?'

'I'm not sure. Halfway between sunset and midnight?'

'Should we light a lamp, or go to sleep?'

'I'm hungry.'

'You should have eaten something for dinner.'

'I was too distracted to eat – first by telling you the truth, and then by... what we did after that.' He kissed her. 'I'm going to get up and have a look for food.'

He swung his legs out of bed, then he rummaged around on the floor of the tent for his shorts, and pulled them on.

'I'll probably be sleeping by the time you get back,' she said.

'I'll try not to wake you.'

He got to his feet and edged towards the canvas door. He pushed the canvas aside, ducked his head, and stepped into the main living space. In the dim light of a solitary lamp, a Bullan soldier was clearing away the plates on the dining table.

'Good evening, sir,' he said.

Lahnos walked over to the table. 'Leave that plate,' he said. 'My appetite's back.'

'Certainly, sir. Would you like some ale to go with it?'

'Yes, thanks.'

Lahnos sat down as the soldier took a tankard and went over to a barrel, which was sitting on a low table by the rear of the tent. Lahnos started to eat. He glanced through the open entrance of the tent, and saw the other Bullan sitting close to Sigum under the stars. The soldier returned to the table, and set the full tankard down. He bowed his head towards Lahnos, then he walked outside to join his colleagues.

Lahnos found that he was hungrier than he had imagined, and he worked his way through the entire plate of food, pausing only to drink the bitter ale. He was raking through the other leftovers for more to eat when the air shimmered, and a woman appeared by the entrance to the tent.

The woman placed her Quadrant into a shoulder bag, then she walked over to where Lord Sigum was talking to the Bullan. A few words were exchanged, then Efizel gestured towards the interior of the tent. The woman turned and, accompanied by Efizel, she strode inside.

Lahnos got to his feet. 'Madam Herald,' he said. 'I wasn't expecting you.'

Brogan glanced at his state of undress. 'I can see that, Commander,' she said.

Efizel threw a tunic to Lahnos. He caught it, and pulled it over his shoulders.

'Would you like to sit?' Lahnos said. 'There's food and ale.'

'It's a little late for dinner,' said Brogan, 'and I apologise for appearing so close to midnight. I had a long list of things to do today, and I am running late. I will sit, though.'

She gestured to a chair, and then both she and Lahnos sat down by the table.

'I will make this brief,' said Brogan. 'You are being redeployed, Commander.'

Lahnos said nothing.

'You have done a good job here in Rakana,' Brogan went on, 'but the Imperial Court believes that your talents would be put to better use elsewhere.'

'Then I have to assume that we're going back to Rahain,' he said. 'Is it time to take another city?'

Brogan smiled. 'I wouldn't trust your assumptions if I were you, Commander.'

'Might I ask, ma'am, when you say I am being redeployed, does that include the other dragons and their riders from the Eastern Rim?'

'It does. You are the commander of this detachment, and you and Lord Sigum will be leading the five dragons from the Eastern Rim. Pack up this camp, and be ready to leave by noon tomorrow.'

'Where are we being sent, ma'am?'

'This information is not to be spread around the army, Commander. You may tell the dragons, their riders, and your Bullan support staff, but no one else.'

'Understood, ma'am.'

Brogan looked into his eyes. 'You are going to Dragon Eyre.'

'I see, ma'am. Why?'

'Queen Blackrose of the Eastern Rim has requested assistance from the Empire. Her realm has been repeatedly attacked by both Wystian dragons and agents from the Unk Tannic, and Her Majesty the Empress has decided that the Empire will lend the queen its full support. You will first be posted to the island of Yearning and, from there, you will be a part of the force that will invade the Western Rim. The initial target shall be Na Sun Ka. Are you familiar with the geography of Dragon Eyre?'

'Not particularly, ma'am.'

'Then ask the dragons and riders from the Eastern Rim to tell you all about it. The invasion will be conducted by a large combined force of dragons, marines and the Sanang divisions. The two dragon carriers from your home island of Zamata will also take part.'

'Where will I sit in the army hierarchy, ma'am? Will the Empire or Queen Blackrose be in overall command?'

'Some of the details are yet to be decided,' said Brogan, 'but I have no doubt that you will have a part to play in the discussions regarding the chain of command. Do you have any other questions? I have three more visits to make this evening.'

'No, ma'am. We will be ready to leave Rakana at noon tomorrow.'

Brogan got to her feet, and Lahnos did the same.

'I will see you tomorrow, Commander,' said Brogan. 'Good night.'

The air shimmered, and the Herald of the Empire disappeared.

The canvas door rustled, and Ora'lya walked into the main living area, a blanket wrapped round her.

'Did I hear that right?' she said. 'Are we going to Dragon Eyre?'

'A place called Yearning,' he said. 'Then somewhere called Na Sun Ka.'

A broad smile appeared on Ora'lya's face. 'We are going to liberate the Western Rim? And Na Sun Ka? We will get to visit the great temples of Sun Ta; the ancient monuments to the dragon spirits. Oh Lahnos, once you have seen the sunlight and the islands of my world – you will never want to live anywhere else.'

'We're not going for a holiday; we're going to fight,' he said.

She walked over to him. 'That doesn't matter. Dragon Eyre will bewitch you, Lahnos; and Lord Sigum, too. Once you have flown over the oceans and islands, your dragon will never want to leave.'

Lahnos laughed. 'We'll see about that. I'd better let the others know.'

'Let me get dressed first,' she said. 'I want to see their faces when you give them the news.'

He put his arms round her, and they kissed.

'I'm glad you're happy about this,' he said.

'Just think,' she said; 'if we get some leave, we could go to Enna, and you could meet my sister and my parents.'

'And would they be pleased to see you with a horned demigod?'

She smiled up at him. 'I guess we'll find out.'

# CHAPTER 4
# PULLED BACK

**Marchside, Kell – 27th Day, Last Third Winter 544**

'Keep your shield up, Killop,' said Corthie, 'and keep your eyes on my sword.'

The boy, just a few days shy of his thirteenth birthday, lifted his shield a little higher, as he and his father circled each other on the muddy field.

'That's it,' said Corthie. 'If you look away, your enemies will strike.'

Corthie lunged forward, and his sword hit the boy's shield. Killop staggered back a few steps, his boots squelching in the mud.

'When's it my turn?' said Cairney, who was watching from the side of the field.

'Later, son,' said Corthie.

The rain started, as grey clouds crawled across the winter sky. The first signs of the coming spring were almost upon them, and the deep chill of the previous few thirds was coming to an end.

Corthie lunged forward again, and Killop cried out as his father's wooden sword battered off his shield. Killop slipped, and fell into the mud.

Cairney cackled with laughter. 'It's my turn now,' said the boy.

'Not yet,' said Corthie, as he extended a hand in the direction of his eldest son.

Killop took his father's hand, and got back to his feet.

'Try to keep your balance,' Corthie said.

'I'm trying, Da,' said Killop.

Cairney picked up another of the wooden swords, and walked across the mud.

'It's not your turn, son,' said Corthie.

Cairney pushed Killop, and the older boy pushed him back. Enraged, Cairney swung his wooden sword, catching Killop in the face. Blood gushed from the older boy's nose, then Cairney punched his brother in the stomach. Corthie dropped his sword and pulled the two boys apart.

'Cairney, behave yourself,' Corthie shouted.

'It was my turn!' the boy cried.

Killop clenched his fists, as his broken nose began to heal.

'Get into the house, both of you,' said Corthie, as the rain grew heavier. 'Training is over for the day.'

The boys glared at each other, as the rain struck their faces. Corthie picked up his wooden sword from the mud, and shepherded his two oldest sons towards the huge farmhouse. The second floor had been completed a few years before, and the home had ten large bedrooms. With seven children, a few of the rooms were still unoccupied, but the house always felt busy, and was rarely in silence. They went through a gate in the side of the field, and hurried towards the main entrance as the heavens opened. Corthie led the two boys into the front hall of the house, then they each pulled off their muddy boots and coats.

'Go for a shower, Killop,' said Corthie. 'Do not wander around the house covered in mud.'

'Aye, Da,' said the boy.

'Cairney, you stay here for a moment,' said Corthie, as the older boy walked away.

'What is it?' said Cairney, a defiant gleam in his eyes.

'You need to watch your temper, son,' said his father. 'You can't go around hitting your brothers and sisters.'

'Why not?'

'Well, Killop is four years older than you. What would have happened if he'd punched you back? And you shouldn't hit your younger siblings, either, as it's wrong to hurt people who are weaker than you.'

'It was my turn, Da.'

'It's your turn when I say it is. Go on, off with you. Get something to eat if you're hungry.'

Cairney ran down the hallway, then turned towards the kitchen.

Corthie tidied up the boots and coats that had been abandoned by the two boys, then he left the entrance hall and walked into the house's large sitting room. Konna was there with Carter, while Carron was sitting on the rug in front of the cold fireplace, playing with some wooden toys.

'How was school today, Konna?' Corthie said.

The ten-year-old girl looked up from her book and shrugged. 'All right.'

Corthie walked over to the table where Carter was sitting. 'What are you drawing, son?'

'A greenhide,' said the boy.

Corthie gazed down at the picture. It didn't resemble any greenhide he had ever seen, but he thought it best not to mention that.

'Very good,' he said. 'Konna, are you watching Carron? Make sure he doesn't get too close to the fireplace; I don't want his clothes all covered in ash again.'

'Aye, Da.'

Corthie left the room and walked through the house to the kitchen. Cairney was there, rummaging around in a cupboard, while their live-in cook was at the stove, preparing that evening's dinner.

'Afternoon, sir,' said the cook.

'Afternoon, Kilholm,' said Corthie. Four-year-old Clova was sitting by the table, and Corthie kissed the girl on the forehead. 'Where's Aila?'

'I think she's still at work, sir,' said Kilholm.

'Does she have Ceres with her?'

'Aye, sir.'

Corthie sat down. It had been a long day, which, as was usual for him, had started before dawn. Cairney, thinking that his father wouldn't notice, stuffed some food into a pocket and ran out of the kitchen.

'I am helping Kilholm, Daddy,' said Clova.

'That's great,' said Corthie. 'You'll be starting school in the New Year, and then you'll get to go down to Marchside every day with your older brothers and sister.'

'I don't want to go to school with Cairney. He's mean.'

'He won't be in the same class as you.'

Corthie heard a noise from the hallway, then Aila walked into the kitchen, a six-third-old baby strapped to her chest. Aila planted a sealed jug onto the table, kissed Clova, and sat down.

'Afternoon, ma'am,' said Kilholm.

'What are we having for dinner tonight, Kilholm?' she said.

'Roasted beef with vegetables from the garden, ma'am.'

'I can't wait,' said Aila; 'I'm starving.' She glanced at her husband. 'Good day?'

'Aye. You?'

'Open that jug and tell me what you think.'

Corthie picked up the jug, and pulled out the stopper. He lifted the jug to his nose and sniffed.

'What is it?' he said. 'I know it's whisky, obviously, but from where?'

'I'm saying nothing until you try it,' said Aila. 'Kilholm, could you fetch us a couple of glasses? Make it three; I'd like you to try it, too.'

'Certainly, ma'am.' Kilholm went to a cupboard, and took out three small glasses. 'Will you be needing some water, too, ma'am?'

'Let's try it straight first.'

Kilholm set the glasses down, and Corthie poured a small measure of golden liquid into each.

'I might fall asleep after I've drunk this,' he said. 'I'm knackered.' He took a sip. 'That's pretty damn good, Aila.'

Kilholm nodded. 'It is very fine indeed, ma'am.'

'It reminds me a wee bit of Severton whisky, though,' said Corthie.

Aila smiled. 'Excellent. It should remind you of Severton, because it has some in it. It's three parts Lachellan, two parts Strathlanach, two parts Pitburn, and three parts Severton Eight-Year-Old. The first barrels of it will be on their way to the Plateau by the end of the First Third of Spring.'

'Has Severton agreed to this?' said Corthie.

'Yeah. Do you remember when they asked if they could store some of their Eight-Year-Old in our warehouses? I inserted a clause into the contract that gave us permission to add some to a new blend. We're paying them for it, of course; well, the cost is being deducted from the rent they pay us. The new blend is going to be the most expensive whisky we sell. I'm thinking of calling it Marchbrae Domlach; you know, because it contains three Lach whiskies and one from Domm. What do you think?'

'Marchbrae is your company, Aila; it's up to you.'

'Then Domlach it is. It's going to make us a fortune, Corthie, even with the new taxes on Lach whisky. Forty sovereigns a bottle will be the asking price.'

Corthie laughed. 'Who's going to pay forty sovereigns for a bottle of whisky?'

'Never underestimate the vanity of the truly wealthy,' said Aila. 'They will pay that amount *because* it costs so much.'

Kilholm smiled. 'Then this is the most expensive drink I've ever tasted, ma'am.'

'The jug is for the house,' said Aila. 'Help yourself, Kilholm.'

'Thank you, ma'am.'

The cook set his glass down by the stove, and got back to work.

'Cairney smacked Killop over the head with a practice sword,' said Corthie.

Aila frowned. 'Did you make him apologise?'

'I gave him a telling off, but no; not yet.'

'Is Cairney in trouble again, Mummy?' said Clova.

'Yes,' said Aila. 'We can't allow him to hit his brothers and sisters.'

'He has a temper,' said Corthie.

'I know,' said Aila. 'Sometimes, I worry that he has inherited too much from my father's side of the family.'

The baby strapped to her chest began to stir.

'It's almost time to feed Ceres,' Aila said. 'Where's Carron?'

'Konna is keeping an eye on him in the sitting room,' said Corthie. 'Carter is there, too.'

'I should say hello to them all,' she said; 'as soon as I finish this glass.'

The air shimmered, and Naxor appeared in the kitchen.

'Am I in time for dinner?' he said.

Aila smiled and got to her feet. She embraced Naxor, and the demigod peered down at baby Ceres.

'Your latest one looks like you, cousin,' said Naxor. 'How many is that now?'

'Seven,' said Aila. 'Five to go.'

'Well, I am not even going to pretend to remember all of their names,' said Naxor. 'Say, is that whisky?'

'What else would it be?' said Corthie. 'This is Clackenbaird, home of the famous Marchbrae Blenders, Copperworks and Cooperage.'

'You missed out Marchbrae Maturations and Maltings,' said Aila. 'We have close to thirty per cent of the entire whisky market on the Star Continent, cousin; and our share is increasing every year.'

'I always knew you would end up fabulously wealthy, my dear Aila,' said Naxor, as he sat down.

Aila refilled her own glass from the jug and passed it to her cousin.

'Is this a social visit?' she said.

'I am afraid not,' said Naxor. 'I bear a summons.'

'If this is about the new taxes,' said Aila, 'tell the Empress that I am happy to pay. In fact, her abolition of Severton's monopoly is the best thing that could have happened to Marchbrae. We can now legally enter every market on the Star Continent. We can even export to the City. I was thinking of flooding Auldan with single malt from Lachellan.

I have a feeling the Gloamers will take to it. And we have a cheaper blend that the Reapers might like.'

'The summons was not for you, dear Aila.'

'Oh.'

Aila and Naxor turned to Corthie.

'What?' he said. 'I had begun to drift off.'

'The imperial summons is for you,' said Naxor. 'I am here to ensure that it is carried out.'

'That can't be right,' said Corthie. 'Why in Pyre's name would the Empress summon me?'

'I am not at liberty to disclose that, not yet,' said Naxor. 'I shall give you one hour to get ready, and then we shall travel to Plateau City.'

'You have got to be fucking kidding me,' said Corthie. 'Oops. Sorry, Clova; daddy said a rude word.'

'Naxor,' said Aila, 'you must tell us what this is about.'

The demigod raised his palms. 'I simply cannot, dearest cousin. I am under strict orders. The matter is of the utmost secrecy, but, I can say this – we are facing a serious and unexpected situation, and the Empress needs your husband.'

'Has anyone else been summoned?' said Aila. 'Sable? Karalyn?'

'Not to my knowledge.'

'How long will Corthie be gone for?'

'Again, I cannot say. A month, perhaps? I do not know.' He glanced at Corthie. 'However, I do know that you will need to bring your stone armour, and your Clawhammer.'

Corthie's shoulders sagged. 'What if I refuse?'

'Then, most unwillingly and with the greatest reluctance, I will be forced to place you under arrest. No subject of the Empire is permitted to refuse an imperial summons from the Empress.'

'What about the farm?' said Corthie. 'I have work to do.'

'The farm is less important than the situation I mentioned.'

'I thought the Empress and I had an understanding,' Corthie went on. 'I was under the impression that I would only have to fight again if the Star Continent was invaded by gods.' He frowned. 'Has the Star Continent been invaded by gods?'

'I can say nothing,' said Naxor.

'Do you have the summons in writing?' said Corthie. 'How do I know this isn't some bullshit story that you've made up?'

Naxor sighed. 'Such unearned distrust.'

'Unearned? Aye, right, Naxor. The problem is that I know you too well.'

Naxor slipped a hand into his robes, and removed a sealed envelope. 'Mark this,' he said, pointing to the imperial seal; 'the Empress herself affixed the wax. And see here,' he went on, turning the envelope over; 'is that, or is it not, your name, Corthie Holdfast?'

Corthie took the envelope and broke the seal with his thumb. He withdrew the letter and unfolded it.

'Shit,' he muttered. He passed it to Aila.

'Do you believe me now?' said Naxor.

'I'm thirty-three, Naxor,' said Corthie. 'I'm too old for this.'

Naxor laughed. 'It amuses me when mortals say such ridiculous things. Thirty-three – old? You are in your prime!'

'I haven't fought in ten years.'

'I am sure it will all come back to you.'

'I don't know where the Clawhammer is.'

'You have one hour to find it.'

Corthie lowered his head until it rested on the surface of the table.

'Are you sleeping, Daddy?' said Clova.

'I hope so,' he said. 'Perhaps this is just a bad dream.'

'Could you leave us alone for a moment, cousin?' said Aila.

'Certainly,' said Naxor, as he got to his feet. He picked up the glass of whisky. 'I shall quaff this while you talk.'

He walked out of the kitchen, and Corthie raised his head.

'Should I also step outside, ma'am?' said Kilholm.

'If you wouldn't mind,' said Aila.

The cook dried his hands and left the kitchen.

'I have no choice, do I?' said Corthie.

'It must be serious,' said Aila. 'I can't imagine that the Empress would disrupt our lives for nothing.'

'If it's to do with Rahain or Rakana, I will refuse to fight,' he said. 'I will not be part of Thorn's ambitions to conquer everywhere in existence.'

'I'm sure she doesn't want to conquer everywhere.'

'What about the children? How are you supposed to run Marchbrae, and the farm, while looking after seven children?'

'I will hire some extra help. Let's face it, Corthie, you could retire if you wanted to. I can appoint a farm manager, and bring in a nanny to care for the little ones while the others are at school.'

'You think I should go?'

'I don't think you have a choice. I would rather you served the Empire than ended up in prison.'

Corthie shook his head. 'I don't... I don't want to fight again. I thought I had left all that behind me.'

'Who are you going to fight, Da?'

Corthie turned, and saw Killop standing by the kitchen door.

'The Empress has asked for me, son.'

'You are the greatest fighter in the world, Da. The Empress must know that.'

Corthie drained his glass of the last of the whisky and pulled himself to his feet. He glanced at his wife.

'It's in the attic,' said Aila. 'Your armour, too.'

'Will you give me a hand to carry it downstairs, son?' he said.

'Aye, Da.'

Nearly two hours later, Naxor was pacing up and down, his impatience clear, as Corthie packed some clothes into a bag. All seven children had been assembled in the sitting room, and Cairney was prodding the Clawhammer.

'How many people have you killed with this, Da?' the boy said.

'Too many,' said Corthie.

'Why do you have to go?' said Konna.

'The Empress has asked me to go, sweetheart,' he said. He picked up Carron, and kissed him, then he kissed baby Ceres, who had been re-strapped to Aila's chest after being fed.

'Are we quite ready?' said Naxor.

'In a moment,' said Corthie. He slung his pack over one shoulder, and the Clawhammer over the other. By his feet was a large crate, containing the blue armour he had taken from the body of Tamid, the Eighth Ascendant, when he had killed him in Pella. He gazed at his children. 'I am going now,' he said, 'and I don't know when I will be coming home again. It might just be a few days, or it might be longer. But, I will be coming back, you can count on that. Be good for your mother, and, you four – work hard at your lessons. Look after Clova when she starts school, and make sure none of the other children bully her. I love you all, and I'm going to miss you.' He turned, and embraced Aila.

'Take care,' she said. 'Don't take any stupid risks. The children need their father.'

He nodded. They kissed, then he glanced at Naxor.

'I will come to see you soon, cousin,' Naxor said, then he swiped his fingers over his Quadrant.

The air shimmered, and Corthie found himself standing in a large central courtyard, surrounded on all four sides by a tall building. He glanced up, and saw the seven stars shining down from the night sky.

'Where are we?' he said.

'This is the Ministry of the Plateau,' said Naxor; 'the Empress's temporary place of residence until the new palace is complete. Can you manage that armour on your own?'

Naxor set off towards a door before Corthie could respond. Corthie narrowed his eyes, then he picked up the large crate, and followed the demigod into the building. They passed several groups of courtiers, officials and soldiers. Most of them didn't stop to look at Corthie, but a few caught a glimpse of the Clawhammer slung over his shoulder and stared. They ascended a flight of stairs, and Naxor led Corthie into a small meeting chamber, where seven others were sitting. Corthie placed the crate onto the floor, along with his bag and the Clawhammer, then he bowed his head before the Empress.

A large smile appeared on Thorn's face, and she got down from her throne, stepped forward, and embraced Corthie.

'Welcome,' she said. 'It is wonderful to see you again, Corthie.'

Corthie suppressed a sarcastic response. 'And you, Your Majesty,' he said.

He glanced at the others in the room. He recognised Caelius Logos, Brogan and Bedig, but there were three he didn't know.

'This is the Imperial Court, Corthie,' the Empress said. 'Take a seat, and we will tell you why we have asked you to come here.'

Thorn returned to her throne, and Corthie sat down at the other end of the table. Naxor also sat, and the room stilled.

'I wish we could have been reunited under more pleasant circumstances,' said the Empress, 'but the truth is that the Empire needs your strength, Corthie.'

'Have we been invaded, Your Majesty?' he said.

'In a manner of speaking,' she said. 'However, in this case, the invaders arrived here some time ago, but we were unaware of their presence. Chamberlain, please explain the situation to Corthie.'

'Yes, Your Majesty,' said Naxor. He turned to Corthie. 'Some ten days ago, we in the Imperial Court received a report from a branch of the Holdings militia. The report stated that twenty-seven men, women and children had been brutally murdered in a small village in Hold Stringer. Their bodies had been torn to pieces. At the request of Her Majesty the Empress, I journeyed to Hold Stringer for myself, in order to liaise with the local authorities there. I saw the bodies, and I can confirm that there was evidence that some had been eaten. At first, it was assumed that a murderous band of Holdings criminals had carried out the attack, and that perhaps wolves had descended from the Barrier Mountains to feast upon the remains of the villagers.'

Naxor glanced at Corthie, who did not respond.

'A further three attacks have been subsequently reported,' Naxor went on. 'All bear the same features – bodies ripped apart and half-eaten; and all within a ten-mile radius of the first village. Local militia have been evacuating other villages in the vicinity but then, last night, a dozen members of the militia came to a similar end. Over one hundred and fifty dead in ten days, Corthie.'

'Who is doing this?' said Corthie.

'We do not know for certain,' said Naxor. 'A few witnesses have submitted testimony, but their accounts could scarcely be believed. One old man insisted that he had seen what could only be described as... well, as a flying greenhide. Others reported seeing creatures that also appear to have been greenhides, but they were claiming that the beasts were far, far larger than any normal greenhide.'

'A queen?' said Corthie.

'Possibly. I was rather reluctant to give any credit to these wild tales. The fact of the matter is that the Ascendants did not place any greenhide nests within the Barrier Mountains, and it beggars belief that a queen might have openly crossed the Plateau from Sanang without being observed. We asked Frostback and Halfclaw to patrol the area, and it was Halfclaw who first noticed one of these creatures from the air. He followed it, and he saw from where it had originated.'

'It is the Palace of the Almighty,' said the Empress. 'One of its walls has been breached, by whom or what we do not know.'

'This morning,' Naxor went on, 'Frostback and Halfclaw decided to ambush one of these creatures as it left the palace. They circled overhead, waiting, and then dived as soon as one appeared. They unleashed fire upon it, but the... greenhide, or whatever it was, emerged unscathed from the flames. Then, to our dismay, over two dozen flying beasts emerged from the same breach in the wall of the palace. They swarmed around Frostback and Halfclaw, dealing them several wounds, and forcing the dragons to withdraw to Colsbury. Now, Colsbury is a mere thirty miles from the location of the Palace of the Almighty. Fortunately, the flying creatures did not follow the dragons, but I am sure you can appreciate the risk to your two sisters.'

'Are both of my sisters living on Colsbury now?' said Corthie.

'They are,' said Naxor, 'but let us not be distracted. If dragons cannot defeat these creatures, then it is unlikely that the regular army will be able to deal with them.'

'We are calling upon you, Corthie,' said the Empress. 'Will you help us? If we cannot destroy these beasts, they will ravage over the Holdings, slaughtering the people of the villages and towns. What if they reach Holdings City? What if they attack Colsbury? We will give you whatever you need – soldiers, dragons, explosives, Quadrants – everything will be put at your disposal.'

'Karalyn can control greenhides, Your Majesty,' said Corthie. 'Can't she order them to kill themselves?'

'Your sister has tried,' said Naxor. 'The creatures were unaffected by her powers.'

'Karalyn told us some things that she had learned from Lord Bailey,' said the Empress. 'Do you know him?'

Corthie shook his head.

'Lord Bailey is an extremely old god,' said Naxor. 'So old, that he remembers events prior to the Ascendants arriving on Implacatus. He has also spent time imprisoned within the Palace of the Almighty, and he mentioned to Karalyn that there were beasts within that could prove deadly and dangerous. Karalyn suspects that these... creatures were perhaps the result of an experiment. As you know, Leksandr, the Sixth Ascendant, was responsible for creating greenhides. Karalyn has speculated that he may have also created these beasts, though why Edmond decided to keep some within his palace is unknown to us.'

'If you agree to help us, Corthie,' said the Empress, 'we will first dispatch you to Colsbury, so that you can learn from Karalyn and the dragons all that they know, and all that they have seen.'

'Is my sister expecting me, Your Majesty?'

'She is. It was Karalyn who suggested that we call upon you. I was reluctant, as I wished to honour my pledge to you, that I would never again ask you to serve, not unless the very fate of the Star Continent was at stake. It might be at stake, Corthie. We simply do not know what could be hidden inside the Palace of the Almighty. What else might Edmond have locked away within its dark depths?'

Corthie took a breath. 'I will kill these creatures for you, Your Majesty.'

Thorn smiled. She glanced at Brogan. 'Issue a statement to the public, my Herald. Inform them that greenhides have escaped from the Palace of the Almighty, and be sure to emphasise that Corthie Holdfast has volunteered to rid this world of them.'

Brogan bowed her head. 'Aye, Your Majesty.'

'Herald?' said Corthie. 'What happened to Kelsey?'

The members of the Imperial Court glanced at each other.

'Sometimes, Corthie,' said the Empress, 'we forget how long it takes for news to reach Kellach Brigdomin. Your sister has not been Herald for close to five thirds.'

'Did she resign, Your Majesty?'

'You will be seeing both of your sisters tomorrow,' said Thorn. 'I will let them tell you what occurred. For now, it is late, and I would like to invite you to eat with me this evening. I have missed your company, Corthie. Will you join me?'

Corthie tilted his head. 'I never say no to dinner, Your Majesty.'

# CHAPTER 5
# ULTIMATE GUARANTOR

**Plateau City, The Plateau – Year's End 544**

'In the City of Salve,' said Achan, 'every last tree was counted, every ounce of coal, every gallon of oil. Surrounded on all sides by greenhides and water, and enclosed by high walls, every single item of food was accounted for and recorded. The fresh water supply was carefully guarded, rationed and distributed according to need. In other words, the bureaucracy required to ensure the survival of millions within such a tight and restricted space was far more advanced than it is on the Star Continent, with its wide open lands and plentiful resources. Furthermore, the strict tribal system, which kept the Rosers and Gloamers at the top, and the Evaders, Hammers and Scythes at the bottom, was rigorously enforced. An enterprising Evader, for example, would always remain an Evader, no matter how intelligent they might be. Is it any wonder, therefore, that political consciousness achieved a far higher level of sophistication in the City, compared to the Star Continent? In order to keep the City functioning, the God-King, God-Queen and their immortal children depended upon repression. Violence was employed whenever their rule came under the slightest threat; Hammers and Scythes were kept in slavery, and any hint of resistance from the Evaders would be ruthlessly put down.'

Achan paced over the floor of the classroom, as the students listened and took notes.

'These conditions taught us the true nature of power,' he went on, 'and the extent to which those in authority will do anything to retain control over the masses. I am not trying to claim that the Empress is as murderous and evil as the God-King and God-Queen, but my experience in the City has left me able to see how the Empire is able to exploit its subjects. Without wishing to sound condescending, perhaps people brought up in the City are able to discern these matters better than those of you who have only known life in the Star Continent. We are able to see through imperial propaganda; we are able to see where the true power lies – in the hands of a small but exceptionally powerful and wealthy family – the Holdfasts.'

A few students turned to glance at Kyra, but she kept her gaze studiously on Achan.

'The Holdfasts are not the same as the family of gods and demigods who ruled the City for thousands of years,' Achan went on, 'but, there are some striking parallels. Karalyn Holdfast, for example, reminds me of the God-King. Both were obscenely powerful, and yet both stayed out of day-to-day politics, preferring to lurk in the background as the ultimate guarantor of overwhelming force. You may mock this analogy, pointing to the fact that the Holdfasts are mortal; but we all know that Karalyn herself has now achieved immortality. She, along with Sable Holdfast and Corthie Holdfast, are breeding a new generation of immortal children, who, in time, will come to inherit the Empire. If we do not act now to prevent this outcome, then I fear for the future – a future that looks uncomfortably similar to what was experienced in the City for long millennia.'

He came to a halt and faced the class.

'It is not too late to prevent the Holdfasts' grip on power from becoming too strong to overcome, but we are fast approaching that point. History will not be kind to your generation, if you allow this family to assume permanent control over the known worlds, for, make no mistake, that is precisely what they are working towards.' He smiled.

'It is almost noon, and when the bell rings, you will be leaving university for the New Year holiday. I wish you all a pleasant time at home with your families, but I have one small assignment that I would like you all to complete before you return for Spring Term. I need each of you to write a short answer to the following question – what, if anything, can be done to arrest the Empire's slide into repressive imperialism? One page will suffice.'

The noon bell rang, and the students began packing away their books.

'Have a wonderful New Year,' said Achan, 'and I will see you all upon your return.'

The students got to their feet and filed towards the door.

Kyra glanced at Dazi. 'Go on without me,' she said. 'I'll just be a minute.'

'I'm going to the canteen,' said Dazi; 'will I buy you a coffee?'

'Aye, thanks.'

Kyra slung her bag over her shoulder and waited until the rest of the class had left the room.

Achan smiled at her. 'Did you have a question for me, Kyra?'

'I don't think that was very fair, sir,' she said.

'No? Which part, in particular?'

'Comparing my mother to the God-King,' she said; 'and implying that she is deliberately raising immortal children in order to take over the Empire. You don't know my mother, sir.'

Achan sat down. 'I hesitated over including that section in my lecture, if I'm being honest,' he said; 'but I cannot shy away from the truth, even if it upsets people. The Holdfasts are building the necessary foundations to ensure that they rule the Empire for thousands of years. Do I include every Holdfast in this? No, of course not. I used to count Corthie as a good friend, and I know that he's a decent man at heart; but you cannot deny that he is raising a large family of demigods, who, no doubt, will inherit his battle-vision, along with powers passed down by their mother, who, if you will recall, is the granddaughter of God-King Malik and God-Queen Amalia.'

Kyra folded her arms across her chest.

'Do you know anything about Lady Aila's father?' said Achan.

She shook her head.

'Lady Aila has a tendency to glorify her father as a martyr, because he stood up to Prince Michael, and was then murdered by him. Perhaps it is true that his death was a noble one, but that should not blind us to the kind of man Prince Isra was. Aila's father was every inch as ruthless and violent as Prince Michael. He fathered twelve children by the means of holding innocent Reaper girls in his harem. Ask Aila if she knows the name of her mortal mother. She won't, because her father treated the poor women in his harem as little better than breeding stock, discarding them once they had served his purpose. Prince Isra joined Princess Yendra's rebellion, not because he pitied the mortals, but because he hated Prince Michael. Isra saw the rebellion as an opportunity to usurp his brother's power and, because he failed, he is treated as a hero. This is the bloodline that contaminates the children of Corthie. Wittingly or not, Kyra, your uncle is raising a new tribe of immortals who share their heritage with Malik, Amalia, Michael, Montieth and Isra. Can you not see this?'

'You cannot blame children for the crimes of their great-grandparents.'

'I agree. But we can warn others of their potential. This alliance between the two most ruthless and bloodthirsty families in history is one that should trigger a sense of fear in everyone who cares about the future. And what of Sable's daughter? I believe that she is also a demigod. What if she inherits her mother's callous disregard for life? What if, in the decades to come, the immortal Holdfasts take over the throne of the Empire? The time to act is now, Kyra, before this is allowed to happen.'

'Do you hate my family, sir?'

'I fear them, Kyra. They have come to believe that they are entitled to rule over the rest of us. History is repeating itself in front of our eyes and, if we are not careful, we will soon find ourselves in a position where resistance is impossible. As a Holdfast with a conscience, you are in an unenviable situation. Do you remain loyal to your family, or do you fight for those your family will trample upon? Only you can make that decision.'

Kyra said nothing.

'Are you going to Colsbury for New Year?' he said.

'Aye.'

'Then I hope that you keep an open mind. Observe and listen to what your family does and says. Make up your own mind about these matters; that is all I ask.'

Kyra nodded, then she walked out of the classroom. She ignored a few glances from the students in the corridor, and hurried down the stairs towards the university canteen. When she got there, Dazi was seated at a table with two coffees. Kyra joined her friend.

'Are you all right?' said Dazi.

'I feel humiliated,' she said. 'I didn't think my family would be portrayed as the embodiment of evil. My mother is nothing like the God-King, Dazi. And Uncle Corthie isn't trying to raise a family of gods to take over the Star Continent. I don't like the path the Empire is taking, but that lecture felt like a personal attack.'

'What are you going to write for your assignment?'

'I don't know. I can only imagine what the rest of the class will write; and I will have to hear it all when we get back after New Year. I wonder how many will call for my family to be rounded up and executed.'

'I don't think anyone will call for that,' said Dazi; 'but, at the same time, you can't deny that the Holdfasts are ridiculously rich and powerful. And some of Corthie's children might want to become Empress or Emperor when they're older. Who would be able to stop them?'

Kyra shook her head as she sipped her coffee.

'When are you leaving?' said Dazi.

'As soon as Arrosa and Cole get here.'

'Are you taking them to Colsbury?'

'Aye. Shit, Dazi – what if Achan is right? I grew up with Corthie, Thorn and Sable. What if I can't see the truth that is staring me in the face? I know my mother better than anyone else – I know how ruthless she can be, if someone angers her.'

Dazi nudged her with an elbow. Kyra glanced up, and saw Arrosa and Cole walking through the canteen towards them, each with a bag over their shoulder.

Kyra got to her feet. 'Thanks for the coffee, Dazi.'

'No problem. Have a great New Year.'

'I'll try.'

Kyra walked towards Cole and Arrosa, then a Kellach student from one of her classes stepped in front of her.

'Are you going home for the holiday, Kyra?' he said.

'Aye.'

'Do you want to meet up when you get back? We could go out for a drink.'

'No thanks.'

'Come on; just a drink or two. You won't regret it. I know some great taverns in the Kellach Quarter.'

She tried to ease past him, but he moved to block her way.

'I saw you at the protest a third ago,' he went on. 'Someone told me you're seeing Professor Achan; is that true? You should go out with someone your own age; someone like me. Why don't I come round for you when you get back to Plateau City and I'll take you out? One night. Try it.'

'I said no.'

'Aye, but I'm going to keep asking until you say yes.'

'Leave me alone,' she said.

Cole stepped forward. 'You heard her,' he said. 'Fuck off.'

The student shook his head and walked away.

Kyra's temper simmered over. 'I don't need you to stand up for me, Cole.'

'I was just trying to help.'

'Do you speak to all boys like that?' said Arrosa. 'No wonder you're single.'

'Shut up,' said Kyra. 'I'm not in the mood for your bullshit, Arrosa.'

'You've barely spoken one word to me or Cole this entire term,' said Arrosa. 'I've seen you walk past, pretending you haven't noticed us. It isn't me that's full of bullshit.'

'We are not friends, Arrosa. I was polite to you when we were younger, but I'm not going to act as though we have anything in common just because we're at university.'

'Fine,' said Arrosa. 'I wanted to give you a chance because you're Cael's sister, so you'll soon be my sister-in-law, but, to be honest, I couldn't give a shit if you don't like me.'

Kyra narrowed her eyes. 'My brother doesn't love you. He's confused, because you spent so much time together on his world. Was that a lie?'

'You don't think it's a lie, but that doesn't make it true.'

Kyra laughed. 'Poor little deluded Arrosa. I feel sorry for you. Cael is going to break your heart, just as he's broken the hearts of every other girl he's gone out with. It will be a useful lesson; it might teach you to grow up a bit.'

'Will you both stop it?' said Cole. 'We're going to Colsbury together; can we maybe pretend to get along?'

Kyra glanced at him. 'Why are *you* going to Colsbury? You've never shown any interest in Colsbury before. You never used to leave the Hold Fast Estate.'

'You might not want anything to do with us, Kyra,' he said, 'but Arrosa and Cael are my friends. I'll go back to the estate in summer, as I agreed with Aunty Celine.'

'You don't need Kyra's permission to go to Colsbury,' said Arrosa. 'Karalyn asked us all to come.'

'I'm looking forward to this holiday,' said Kyra; 'especially the part when my brother drops you.'

Arrosa pulled a necklace out from her shirt, and held the silver chain up in front of Kyra. 'Do you see this?' she said. 'It's pretty, isn't it? Cael sent it to me six days ago. I'm sorry to disappoint you, but he's not going to break up with me. We're getting married, and there's nothing you can do to stop us.'

A sudden rage gripped Kyra, and she turned and strode out of the canteen. She left the building through another door, and walked into the warm sunshine of the quad.

Why did she care if her brother was in love with Arrosa, when she had never been the slightest bit concerned about any of his previous girlfriends? Arrosa had been a near constant presence in her life for eight years, but not for one moment of that time had Kyra considered the possibility that her brother might grow to love the strange orphan girl that their mother had brought back from Athumia.

Arrosa and Cole walked out of the side of the university. They saw Kyra, and approached her.

'Wait here,' Kyra said, before either could speak.

She touched the Quadrant in her pocket.

*My room. Go.*

She appeared in her bedroom, and picked up the bag she had packed the previous evening.

*Go back.*

She re-appeared in front of Cole and Arrosa.

*Colsbury. Go.*

The air shimmered a third time, and then she, Arrosa and Cole found themselves standing in the forecourt of Colsbury Castle, between the Great Keep and the Summer Palace. Kyra shivered from the cold. The sky was a crisp blue, but the flagstones were glistening with frost. Halfclaw soared above the island, and the shadow of his wings passed over Kyra.

'Thanks for bringing us here,' said Cole.

Arrosa rolled her eyes. 'Yeah, thanks.'

Kyra glanced at them both, then she turned, and walked into the Summer Palace.

Half an hour later, Kyra was in her rooms in the palace. She had unpacked her clothes, and was lighting a fire in the hearth when her front door was knocked.

'Come in,' she said.

The door opened, and her mother entered the room.

'I thought I'd come and see you,' she said, 'as you haven't bothered to let anyone know that you're here.'

'What do you want, Mother?'

Karalyn frowned. 'Are you all right? I spoke to Arrosa and Cole – they are in the dining hall, having lunch with everyone else. Did you have an argument with them?'

Kyra glanced up from the hearth. 'Why do the Holdfasts rule the Empire?'

'Do we?' said Karalyn. 'Thorn is the Empress, and she is an adopted Holdfast, but she is the only member of the family in the Imperial Court. Are you counting Lucius? My husband married a Holdfast, but he has retained his family name. No other Holdfast has any position of power in the Empire.'

Kyra shook her head. 'The Holdfasts are the power behind the throne.'

Her mother laughed. 'What does that mean? Do you think Kelsey and I are secretly telling Thorn what to do? Do you think your Uncle Corthie and Aunty Sable hold meetings about government policy? I suppose you could say that we have the potential to be influential, if we wanted to be, but even the Holdfasts have to obey the same laws as everyone else.'

'But we have been involved with the Empire from the start. Granny Daphne was Herald for years, and then Aunty Kelsey.'

'My mother was a terrible Herald,' said Karalyn. 'She constantly fought with Bridget, or ignored her. I'm not sure which was worse. Kelsey, on the other hand, was a more effective Herald, but her clash with the Empress showed who really holds the power. It was Kelsey who had to give way, not Thorn. Part of the reason I knocked on your door was to tell you that your Uncle Corthie is here. Do you know why? Because the Empress summoned him. Corthie did not want to leave his family in Kell, but he was ordered to come here, and he obeyed. Does that sound like we are in charge?'

'Why was he summoned?'

'Come to the dining hall, and we'll talk about it.'

'Is Cael here?'

'He arrives tomorrow. Well, I'll be collecting him tomorrow, to be more accurate. I want to talk to you about that, too. Aren't you hungry? The kitchens have laid on a wide selection of food for us all; it would be a shame to let any go to waste.'

Kyra smiled. 'None will go to waste if Uncle Corthie is here.'

Karalyn smiled back at her. 'I've missed you. Have you thought about what you want to do this year, after you leave university?'

'I might stay on for a fourth year.'

'Aye? And study what?'

Kyra's smile slipped away. 'I have been ejected from Professor Nadia's class – permanently. That means I won't have enough points to qualify for a diploma. If I want to graduate, I will have to sit another course next year.'

Her mother nodded. 'And why were you ejected from Nadia's class? Or was that a silly question? Were you staging another protest against Thorn's government?'

'Aye.'

'There is a time and a place for everything, Kyra. Sometimes, you have to hold your tongue if you want something.'

'Is that what you do, Mother? You *hold your tongue* when you see the Empire carry out atrocities? How many civilians need to be slaughtered in Rahain and Rakana before you act?'

'Act? What is it that you think I should do? Do you wish me to prove that the Holdfasts really do control this world? Should I descend upon Plateau City like an avenging god and wipe out the government? We voted for Thorn, just as we voted for Bridget. When Thorn dies or abdicates, we shall vote for her successor.'

'This is exactly what I'm talking about – half of the Electors are Holdfasts; more than half – seven out of thirteen.'

'I will concede that,' said Karalyn. 'The Holdfasts do have some power – to be exercised at the time of choosing another Emperor or

Empress. But, once that decision has been made, our power evaporates. For good or ill, we are stuck with whomever we have chosen. We cannot, for example, vote to remove an Emperor or Empress from power. That would be true influence, but we lack that ability.'

'Professor Achan called you the *ultimate guarantor of overwhelming force*. That means that...'

'I can guess what it means. It means that if this world is invaded by a hostile force, then I will act to defend it. Forgive me for being so evil, daughter, that I would dare to protect the innocents of the allied worlds.'

'It also means that you intimidate all legitimate opposition aimed at the Empress. You frighten people into silence.'

'Do I? How do I do that – by merely existing? I take no interest in the politics of the Empire. Part of the reason for that is because I know I am powerful. So, I sit here in Colsbury with my husband, looking after our children, and I try not to influence the government in any way. Look; I'm hungry. Can we continue this conversation in the dining hall before Corthie eats everything?'

'All right.'

Kyra and her mother left the room and walked along a carpeted hallway. Kyra kept her gaze away from her mother, not wishing to catch her eye. What her mother had said sounded reasonable, but Achan's lecture had also felt true. There was a contradiction somewhere, a contradiction at the heart of the Holdfasts. Could it be true that they were as powerful as Achan had stated, but chose not to exercise that power, as her mother had insisted?

They entered the dining hall. A long table had been set out with a great variety of dishes, and the diners had loaded up their plates and were sitting round another table. Arrosa and Cole were there, seated next to Cardova, Carden and Caitlyn. Next to them were Shella, Olo'osso, Corthie and Kelsey, then Kelsey's two children.

Corthie got to his feet, smiled, and embraced his niece.

'Good to see you, Kyra,' he said. 'You're so tall now – like a proper Kellach. How's university?'

'It's all right,' said Kyra. 'Hello, everyone.'

'We'll get some food,' Karalyn said, 'and then I have a couple of announcements.'

Kyra followed her mother to the long table. They each picked up a plate, and chose from the selection on offer. Once their plates were full, they walked over to the other table. Karalyn sat down next to Cardova, and Kyra found a space between Corthie and Olo'osso.

'Now that we're all here,' said Karalyn, 'I want to talk about Cael, but, before we do that, we should let everyone know why Corthie is here. Unfortunately, we have a serious situation on our hands. A wall in the Palace of the Almighty has been breached, and beasts have been carrying out attacks on the local villages in Hold Stringer. So far, none of these creatures has ventured anywhere near Colsbury, but we are nevertheless going to evacuate the village, and bring everyone on to the island. The Empress has asked Corthie to investigate.'

'Well,' said Corthie, 'not so much investigate, as to kill the beasts that have been coming and going from Edmond's palace. Halfclaw and Frostback have been patrolling, but the last time they strayed too close to the palace, they were attacked by flying creatures.'

Cole frowned. 'Why don't we use death powers to kill them?'

'We've tried,' said Karalyn. 'Death powers and flow powers do not work against these beasts. They are similar to greenhides, but I am unable to control them. They have no eyes, so their minds are impenetrable, and we think their skin is too thick to allow our powers to kill them. Dragon fire has also proved useless against them.'

'They're going to have to be dispatched the old-fashioned way,' said Corthie; 'with the Clawhammer.'

'We're sitting here, eating and drinking, while these things are on the loose?' said Kyra.

'Frostback and Halfclaw will tell us if they see any beasts leaving the palace,' said Kelsey, 'and your mother is regularly sweeping the area with vision. If they try to attack another village, we'll be ready.'

'And if they don't come out,' said Corthie, 'I will go in. Your mother has already taken me, through her vision powers, to see the exterior of the palace. There is only one breach in the walls. If we had a stone mage, we could close it up.'

'We could ask Bailey,' said Kyra.

'Bailey has gone missing,' said Karalyn. 'You can draw your own conclusions from that.'

'What does that mean?' said Arrosa. 'What has Bailey done?'

'The last time I was on Zamata,' said Kelsey, 'Bailey asked me for permission to retrieve his sister's body from the Palace of the Almighty. I turned him down.'

'Bailey wouldn't have left an open breach in the wall of the palace,' said Arrosa. 'He's not like that. He's good at heart, I think.'

'I agree,' said Karalyn. 'Perhaps, if Bailey did enter the palace, then something went wrong with his plan. Bailey himself warned me that the palace has secret dungeons. Who knows what is hidden inside?'

'Then Bailey might be trapped in there,' said Arrosa.

'That's one of the reasons why I'll be going in,' said Corthie. 'If Bailey is there, I'll find him.'

Karalyn glanced at Kyra. 'Is this the power of the Holdfasts in action, daughter – working together to protect the civilians of the Holdings, and expecting nothing in return? Risking our lives to help others?'

Kyra said nothing.

'Let's move on to Cael,' Karalyn went on. 'Tomorrow, at noon, Cael and the other members of his officer cadet class will be commissioned as second lieutenants. My son's six thirds of training are at an end. Family members are invited to the ceremony, so I will be taking us all to the marine base of Pebble Strand, so we can watch Cael become a junior lieutenant. After that, we will bring him back here, and have a New Year's party. How does that sound?'

Kyra watched as everyone smiled and nodded in agreement. Arrosa, in particular, was beaming, and her new necklace was on display over the front of her dark green dress.

'I'm not going,' said Kyra.

The table stilled.

'I refuse to attend a ceremony that glorifies the oppressive militarism of the Empire,' Kyra went on. 'I don't blame my brother – he was forced to join the marines as a punishment, but I will not be lending my support to violent imperialism. The marines are part of the armed forces that slaughtered tens of thousands of Rahain and Rakanese over the last year; that is not something to celebrate.'

'But he's your brother,' said Arrosa.

'As I said, I don't blame him personally for what the marines have done. Not yet. If he serves in a war of aggression, my opinion may change.'

'You spoilt little brat,' said Shella. 'You say you loathe violence, but if we hadn't defended ourselves against the Ascendants, every one of us would be dead. The marines fought as hard as anyone else in that war, maybe harder. We owe them our lives.'

'Then it's a pity that they've been forced to act as Thorn's agents of colonial oppression,' said Kyra. 'I will not be going.'

A few people opened their mouths to speak, and Karalyn raised a hand.

'Let us respect my daughter's opinion,' she said, 'even if we disagree with it. We are all entitled to our views. I will take everyone; Kyra can remain here to look after the children.'

'May I tag along, my lady?' said Olo'osso. 'I'm not family, but I would be keen to show my support for Cael.'

'I will take you and Shella,' said Karalyn. 'I will also be bringing Sable from Dragon Eyre, as she has asked to attend. When we get back, I would be obliged if no one seeks out Kyra in order to lecture her or reprimand her for her behaviour. No one should be coerced into doing something that offends their moral code.'

A few people glared at Kyra, but no one said anything.

Kyra got to her feet. 'I'm not very hungry,' she said. 'I might go and rest for a while.'

Kyra walked to the door amid utter silence, the only sound coming from her heels as they tapped off the floor. She left the dining hall, and stopped to lean against a wall. She felt isolated, and alone, as though her entire family had turned against her. Did none of them understand that she was acting out of love? Her mother's philosophy of passive inaction amounted to nothing more than allowing Thorn to do whatever she liked. Corthie had been brought to Colsbury to fight monsters, but wasn't the real monster the one who sat upon the throne of the Empire?

A tear trickled down her cheek. Cael wouldn't understand. He would assume that she was being obtuse and awkward, when all she wanted to do was keep her hands clean.

She reached into her pocket.

*My room. Go.*

She appeared back in her quarters, on the floor above the Summer Palace's dining hall. She sat down on the bed, and wept.

# CHAPTER 6
# WEDDING PLANNERS

**Pebble Strand, The Plateau – New Year's Day 545**

'Second Lieutenant Cael Holdfast,' said the major.

Cael got to his feet and walked towards the centre of the podium. A large canopy had been erected over it, but the threatened rain had not appeared, despite the dark clouds in the sky.

The major shook his hand, then Cael saluted, and was handed his new insignia.

'Well done,' said the major.

'Thank you, sir.'

Cael glanced out at the large crowd of relatives and friends who were gathered close to the podium. He spotted his mother, who was seated next to the other Holdfasts who had come to see him. Cardova was wearing his uniform as commander-in-chief of the imperial armed forces, and, next to him, Arrosa was smiling. She waved, and Cael tilted his head slightly. He walked back to the other graduating officers, and the next name was read out.

Cael took his seat between Dodd and Audrey Longhold, who were both clutching their new lieutenant insignia. He smiled at them, then they waited as the last of the cadets went up to be congratulated.

'I would like to say a few words,' said the major, once all of the new officers were seated. 'Of the thirty-seven young men and women who joined the officer course at the beginning of autumn, only the twenty-three you see sitting behind me were able to successfully complete the training. I mean no disrespect to any of those who, for whatever reason, failed to finish the course. It is fit and proper that the officers who lead the Imperial Marines should undergo the most rigorous and demanding training regime yet devised by the Empire. For six thirds, they have been tested, challenged, and pushed to their limits; honed into leaders. The next stage of their journey will see them use the skills they have learned on an active commission. As second lieutenants, each will be in command of a single platoon of marines, and each will come under the tutelage and guidance of the first lieutenants who lead companies of four such platoons. If I may, I wish to impart a single piece of advice to our new officers, and it is this – never order your marines to do something that you are not willing to do yourself. Marines can sniff out bad leaders in an instant, but they will always listen to those who are willing to share their perils. Trust your sergeants, but do not expect them to make your decisions for you; lead from the front, and your sergeants will follow.'

The major smiled. 'And to the parents, families and friends of our new officers, before I let them go home for the New Year holiday, I say this – you can be very proud of what these young second lieutenants have achieved, for there is no better vocation in life than to fight to protect all that we hold dear. Our freedoms, our prosperity – none of it would exist without those who volunteer to serve the Empire, for strength is the only guarantee of peace.'

The major began to applaud the new officers. He was joined within seconds by the other senior officers on the podium, and then by the entire crowd. A colonel gestured for the new officers to stand, and they did, to a great cheer from those gathered.

Cael smiled, as he and the others basked in the applause.

Another colonel beckoned them towards the steps, and the new officers began to file off the podium. Each was handed a sealed envelope by an old sergeant major as they descended the steps.

'What's this?' said one of the graduates.

'Your orders, sir,' said the sergeant major.

A few of the new lieutenants smiled at hearing the veteran sergeant major refer to one of their number as *sir*. Cael reached the bottom of the stairs, and the sergeant major checked the names on the envelopes and passed him the correct one.

'Thank you, sergeant major,' said Cael.

The lieutenants were led to the front of the podium, where the crowd had got up from their seats. Arrosa was the first to greet him.

'Congratulations,' she said, then she kissed him.

'Thanks. It's good to see you here.'

'I wouldn't have missed it for anything. Your mother even had a tear in her eye.'

Cael saw several marines of all ranks stand to attention and salute as Cardova made his way through the crowd. Cael did the same, and Cardova saluted back.

'At ease, Lieutenant,' said Cardova; 'you are on leave.'

There were a few gasps from the crowd as Karalyn, Sable, Kelsey and Corthie approached.

'Well done, marine,' said Sable. 'You look very handsome in that uniform.'

'Thanks for coming.'

'I'm almost jealous,' said Corthie, 'though, in truth, I don't think I would have made a decent officer. I was never good at obeying orders.'

'We have that in common,' said Sable.

Kelsey laughed. 'That sounds about right.'

'Good lad,' said Olo'osso, slapping Cael on the back. 'Your first drink's on me.'

'We're all very proud of you,' said Shella. 'After watching that, I think even Cole might want to enlist.'

'Me?' said Cole. 'No chance. Cael's already told me about his training. It sounds like torture.'

Karalyn approached, and embraced Cael.

'I couldn't have asked for a better son,' she said, as a tear rolled down her cheek.

'Thanks, Mother.'

'I have a message from the Empress,' Karalyn went on. 'She asked me to pass on her congratulations, and she has also said that she releases you from your promise.'

Cael narrowed his eyes. 'What promise?'

'Your promise to serve at least three years. If you wish, she said, you can walk away from the marines now, with an honourable discharge.'

Cael stared at her, unable to think of what to say. He glanced at the expectant faces, as they waited for him to speak, then he turned to Arrosa.

'I want to stay in the marines,' he said to her, taking her hand, 'but, if you ask me to leave, then I will.'

'I would never ask you to leave,' she said. 'I'm patient. I want us to be together, but I understand that we might have to wait.'

'Then I'll stay,' he said. 'Thank you.'

Cardova put a hand on his shoulder. 'I think you've made the right decision, Cael. The marines need good young officers like you. Give it a few years, and apply for a staff posting. Preference is always given to those who are married.'

'Thank you, sir.'

'You should probably open your orders now,' said Cardova.

Cael unsealed the envelope, and pulled out a sheet of folded paper. He unfolded it, and read.

'I am to report to the marine garrison in Plateau City at noon on the fifth; five days from now.'

'I'll make sure you get there on time,' said Karalyn.

Cael stared at his orders. 'What does it mean, do you think?'

'It's difficult to say,' said Cardova. 'The new lieutenants will be receiving postings all over the Empire, and the garrison in Plateau City deals with multiple areas of jurisdiction. Whatever it is, it will most likely be a six-third posting.'

'I hope it isn't too dangerous,' said Arrosa.

'That cannot be guaranteed,' said Cardova.

'Aren't you going to get involved, Lucius?' said Sable. 'If you wanted to, you could easily get Cael posted to a comfortable position.'

'I'm going to pretend I never heard that,' said Cardova. 'I will not interfere. Cael shall be treated the same as any other lieutenant.'

'Will I be allowed to use my mage powers now, do you think, sir?' Cael said. 'For the last six thirds, I have been forbidden from using any type of vision abilities, so that I wouldn't have an unfair advantage over the other cadets.'

'That I can answer more easily,' said Cardova. 'Your powers will be extremely valuable to the marines, Cael. I have a feeling they will ask you to use them to communicate intelligence and orders; or perhaps they will ask you to become a scout. They certainly won't squander or neglect your abilities.'

Cael nodded. 'And now I have to ask – where is my sister?'

'She wouldn't come,' said Karalyn.

'I'm disappointed, but not surprised,' said Cael. 'Does she think I've become an imperialist oppressor?'

'She said that she doesn't blame you personally,' his mother went on, 'but that was when your service was a punishment. Her opinion may change when she learns that you are staying on voluntarily. Right now, she is looking after the children in Colsbury; shall we join her?'

'Give me a moment,' he said.

Cael gazed around at the training camp. He saw the other new officers surrounded by their friends and family, and it occurred to him that he might never see some of his classmates again. He walked through the crowd until he came to Dodd.

'Sorry to interrupt,' Cael said. 'I thought I should tell you that I'm going to Colsbury in a minute or two, and I wanted to say goodbye.'

Dodd extended his hand. Cael shook it, then he embraced the Kellach man.

'This is Cael Holdfast, Ma,' Dodd said to his mother.

'A Holdfast, eh?' said Dodd's mother.

'Aye, ma'am,' said Cael. He gestured over to where his family was standing. 'The rest of the Holdfasts are over there.'

'Pyre's arse,' muttered Dodd's father. 'Is that Corthie?'

'Aye, sir,' said Cael. 'He's my uncle.'

Audrey Longhold approached from the other side, and she embraced Dodd and Cael in turn.

'Good luck, boys,' she said.

'Aye, good luck, Audrey,' said Cael.

She nudged him, and drew in closer. 'Is that Arrosa I can see?'

Cael nodded.

'You've got yourself a good-looking girl, Cael,' she said. 'Make sure you treat her well.'

'I will.'

Cael walked back to his family.

'Who were they?' said Cole.

'My two best friends from the class,' said Cael. 'Dodd and Audrey.'

'And that little lady,' said Olo'osso; 'she is a marine, eh?'

'She has battle-vision,' said Cael. 'Most of the Holdings in the marines have that power. It's the only way they can keep up with the Kellach Brigdomin.'

'Eyes off her, Olo'osso,' said Shella, 'you old pervert.'

'Madam,' Olo'osso said; 'my fair princess, my Rakanese beauty – you know I have eyes only for you.'

Sable laughed.

'Stand together,' said Karalyn.

The air shimmered, and they appeared on the middle balcony of the Summer Palace on Colsbury. Kyra was there, sitting at a table with Caitlyn, Carden, Caelius and Calpurnia. She glanced up, and got to her feet. Cael walked over to her.

'Happy New Year, brother,' she said.

'Aye, and the same to you,' he said.

'How long will you be here for?'

'Until the fifth. I have to report to Plateau City then.'

Kyra nodded. 'I... I, uh...'

'It's all right,' he said. 'I understand. I don't agree, but I understand.'

'I don't blame you,' she said; 'please know that. You had to join the marines, because of what happened last summer. You had no choice.'

'And now I do have a choice,' he said. 'The Empress has given me permission to leave the marines, but I intend to stay.'

Kyra stared at him. 'Why?'

'I think it's the right thing to do. We can't neglect the hard work, hoping that someone else will do it.'

'Oh, Cael. That makes me so sad I don't know what to say.'

The others walked over, and Arrosa took Cael's hand.

'It was a beautiful ceremony,' Arrosa said.

Kyra burst into tears, and hurried off the balcony.

Arrosa's eyes widened. 'I only said it was a beautiful ceremony; I didn't say anything to upset her.'

'We know,' said Karalyn. 'Let's leave her be for a moment. Right now, I don't think she will listen to any of us.'

'Because no one else agrees with her,' said Cole.

'That is true, but remember what I said yesterday. I don't want anyone berating Kyra over her opinions. That will not help her be reconciled to Cael's decision; it will only push her further away.'

They gathered the young children, and walked into the palace. Karalyn led them to a small dining room that had been set out for lunch. They all sat, and began to eat. Cael's seat was between Arrosa and Kelsey, and his aunt poured him a glass of wine.

'Thanks,' said Cael. 'How is life on Colsbury, Aunty? Are you still writing your book?'

'Aye,' said Kelsey. 'I'm reaching the point when the Holdings and Rahain first contacted each other in the Plateau. Did you know that they fought a war for twenty years when that happened? Imagine that – you think you are the only people in the entire world, and then you come face to face with a foreign nation.'

'Who won?'

'Neither side. They divided the Plateau between them. The Holdings built Plateau City; the Rahain built Rainsby, and then they stared at each other across the Inner Sea for years.'

'Do you think I might get sent to Rahain, Aunty?'

Kelsey shrugged. 'It's possible. Of course, I have no way of knowing what the Empress is planning these days.'

'I could read her mind for you.'

Kelsey laughed. 'Advocating treason on the day of your graduation? A bold move.'

'You will do no such thing,' said Karalyn.

'I was joking,' said Cael.

Arrosa put a hand to her head. 'Ow!' Then she laughed.

'Have you been planning the wedding?' Cael said.

'Can we talk about that?' said Karalyn, before Arrosa could answer. 'We were thinking, son, that if you are on active duty for, say, two years, then what's the harm in waiting until then to get married?'

'We don't want to wait,' said Cael. 'As soon as I know where I'm being sent, I will ask for a three-day pass for the end of spring, right after Arrosa's birthday. I might not get it, of course, but I will put in the request.'

'If it's to get married,' said Cardova, 'then they will probably allow it. Be sure to mention that when you apply.'

Karalyn narrowed her eyes at her husband.

'I don't think we should try to stop them,' Cardova said. 'And, if we can't stop them, we should support them.'

'I don't see the harm in it,' said Sable. 'Let them marry, and good luck to them.'

'I agree,' said Corthie. 'I was eighteen when I first met Aila.'

'Aye, but you waited a few years before you got married,' said Karalyn.

'No, we didn't,' said Corthie. 'Mother married us as soon as we got back from Lostwell. I was nineteen.'

'You were almost twenty.'

'Nineteen and a half.'

'Right now,' said Karalyn, 'I would be happy if Cael waited until he was nineteen and a half. Eighteen is too young, in my opinion.'

'We're not going to change our minds,' said Arrosa. 'This is what we want. We would like the ceremony to take place in the gardens, here on Colsbury. Or, if it's pouring with rain, we could hold it in the ballroom downstairs.' Her cheeks flushed a little. 'I would also like, if it's all right, to be married by a Gunstian priest.'

Karalyn pursed her lips.

'Do you still believe in all that?' said Sable.

'I... well, I do, I guess,' said Arrosa. 'I understand that Chadura, or Theodora, whatever name you give her – I understand that she was not the god I once believed in; but, she still created Athumia. That part wasn't wrong. I suppose though, that it's more to do with tradition. I'm not asking Cael to believe in the same things as I do. I don't really know what I believe in any more; but this is what I would like, if it's possible.'

Sable shrugged. 'I can snatch a priest for you,' she said. 'I could visit Gunst, and be back in ten minutes. And then, after the ceremony, I can put him back and wipe his memories.'

'You don't speak Gunstian,' said Karalyn.

'Then I'll take the language out of Arrosa's mind first.'

Karalyn put a hand to her brow. 'Am I the only one here counselling a delay?'

'You're not the only one, sister,' said Kelsey. 'I didn't want to say anything, as it's none of my business.'

'Speak your mind,' said Karalyn.

'All right,' said Kelsey. 'My feelings on the subject of marriage have changed recently, as you might have guessed. I'm not opposed to the idea, but I do think a lot of careful consideration is needed before you jump into it. Where will you live, for example?'

'We want to live in the Holdfast townhouse in Plateau City,' said Cael.

Kelsey smiled. 'Then you will have to ask me for permission. As Holder Fast, I hold the papers for the townhouse.'

'Why are you Holder Fast?' said Corthie. 'I thought the title had reverted to Karalyn after she came back from Athumia, because she's the oldest.'

'I don't want it,' said Karalyn.

'Why not?'

'Because, brother, if I become Holder Fast, I will remain Holder Fast forever.'

Corthie puffed out his cheeks. 'I sometimes forget that you're immortal now. I'm not sure I'll ever get my head round it.'

'Nor I,' said Cardova.

'I'm still not used to it,' said Karalyn.

'Next question for our betrothed couple,' said Kelsey. 'Do you both want children?'

'Aye,' said Cael.

'Three or four,' said Arrosa.

'All right; here's a possible situation I want you to think about,' Kelsey went on. 'Imagine this, Arrosa – you have a young baby who isn't sleeping through the night, and you're pregnant again, while your husband is thousands of miles away on active duty with the marines. How are you going to cope?'

'The same way that every other woman in that position copes,' said Arrosa. 'I know it will be difficult.'

'But it wouldn't be difficult if you waited,' said Kelsey. 'If you delay until Cael gets a desk job, and then get married, you will be together.'

'She'll have help though, won't she?' said Sable. 'Nannies and servants. We're Holdfasts. She won't be doing it all on her own, especially if they stay on Colsbury, rather than in Plateau City. She will have her forever-young mother-in-law to assist her.'

Karalyn put her head in her hands.

'What's wrong?' said Sable.

'It just occurred to me that I might be a grandmother soon,' said Karalyn. 'Don't grow up too fast, Cael.'

'I'm an officer in the marines, Mother,' he said. 'It might be a little late for that.' He glanced at Arrosa. 'What if we lived on Colsbury until I finish active service, and then move to Plateau City?'

'All right,' said Arrosa. 'That probably makes more sense.'

'Well, Mother?' said Cael. 'You know what we want.'

Karalyn said nothing for a while, then she nodded. 'I will support your decision,' she said. 'You can marry at the end of spring.'

Cael and Arrosa smiled at each other.

The sound of slow clapping came from the doorway, and everyone turned.

'Well done, Mother,' said Kyra. 'You capitulated without a fight. In a few thirds, Arrosa will be living here as your daughter-in-law, and then you'll be changing her baby's nappies. And a Gunstian priest to conduct the ceremony? What bullshit is this? And shame on the rest of you for encouraging them; except you, Aunty Kelsey – at least you have some sense. What about Arrosa's education? Is she going to throw it all away to play housewife to Cael the marine? It's pathetic.'

'I am not a tyrant, Kyra,' said Karalyn. 'I will not try to control my children's lives. Their decisions, and their mistakes, are their own to make.'

'That's even worse,' said Kyra. 'You know it's a mistake, and yet you are going to let it happen. Tell them that you refuse to support them unless they wait. See? It's not that hard.'

'Why are you so angry?' said Cael.

'Because Arrosa is a silly little girl, and you are being a stupid boy,' she said. 'I love you dearly, brother, and it hurts me to see you destroy your life like this.'

'Do you remember what I was like this time last year?' said Cael, getting to his feet. 'I was so miserable, getting sent round the Star Continent every season; and I was angry all the time. I was angry with Mother and Aunty Kelsey, and I was even angry with Uncle Corthie, because I had to spend each winter down in Kell; even though he and Aunty Aila were nothing but kind to me. I stole the Sextant because I didn't know how else to escape. And now? The thirds I spent with Arrosa and Cole on World Three taught me what was important; what really matters – love, friendship, loyalty, and never giving up, no matter how bad things seem. You say you love me, sister; well, I love you, too.

We are twins, forever bound together, and I will always be there for you if you need me. I want you to be happy – don't you want the same for me?'

'Arrosa won't make you happy.'

'She already makes me happy. You talk about shame, but I look back at how I used to treat her, and that fills me with shame. I loved her back then, but I was too immature to know how to deal with it, so instead, I lashed out. Might you be lashing out now?'

Kyra stared at him. 'You've changed,' she said. 'I don't know you any more, Cael. What have the marines done to you?'

'They taught me self-respect.'

'If you had any self respect, Cael, you'd tell Arrosa to fuck off.'

Several people at the table started to talk at once, clearly angered by Kyra's words. Arrosa got to her feet, and Sable had to put a hand out to restrain her.

'I'm sorry you feel that way,' said Cael. 'I hope that, one day, you will realise that Arrosa and I are meant to be together, and you'll change your mind.'

Karalyn walked over to Cael's side. 'Kyra,' she said, 'when you decided to avoid Cael's graduation ceremony today, did anyone here condemn you? We disagreed with you, but we respected your decision. I want you to show your brother the same courtesy. Feel free to disagree with his decision, but respect it. As for the hostility you have shown towards Arrosa, I don't understand where it's coming from. Has Arrosa done something to offend you? Has she insulted you? Belittled you? Has she been ignoring you at university?'

Kyra said nothing.

'It's the other way around,' said Cole. 'Arrosa doesn't want to say anything about it, but Kyra has been ignoring her since autumn. She turns away if she sees Arrosa coming, and sometimes she has walked right past her without acknowledging her presence.'

'I told you not to mention that,' said Arrosa. 'I'm not a telltale.'

'I know,' said Cole; 'that's why I'm saying it, because you won't.'

'I don't want anyone to feel sorry for me,' said Arrosa. 'I have made new friends at university, and Cole has been great. He's been like a big brother to me.'

Kyra laughed, then she put a hand into her pocket. 'You're good, Arrosa; I will grant you that. Maybe no one else can see through your bullshit, but I can. You're a conniving, selfish little bitch, who has spent the last eight years leeching off the Holdfasts. You've become accustomed to living like a princess, and now that you're about to become an adult, you've decided that you want to maintain your lifestyle, this time as my brother's wife. Cael had a point, before you managed to bewitch him. Remember when Cael used to say that you stole our mother's love from us? He was right.' She raised her chin. 'I give this marriage two years at the most. Goodbye.'

The air shimmered, and Kyra vanished.

'Pyre's arse,' muttered Corthie. 'Where did all that come from?'

'I don't know,' said Cael. 'I had no idea she didn't like Arrosa.'

'This might make me unpopular,' said Kelsey, 'but let's not rush to condemn Kyra. She's having a hard time in Plateau City. She used to be the Empress's favourite, her chosen candidate to succeed to the throne and, in a matter of thirds, that's all fallen apart.'

'I think Professor Achan is trying to drive a wedge between her and the rest of the Holdfasts,' said Karalyn.

'Achan?' said Corthie. That wee Hammer guy?'

'He's a visiting professor at the university,' said Kelsey. 'You can blame me – I hired him.'

Cael glanced down at Arrosa. She looked forlorn, and close to tears.

'I want to spend some time alone with Arrosa,' he said. 'Give us an hour, and we'll come back to the party.'

'Take all the time you need, son,' said Karalyn.

Cael took Arrosa's hand, and they walked out of the hall. He led her upstairs to his quarters, and opened the door. The room had been thoroughly cleaned, and fresh blankets and cotton sheets were folded up on the mattress. He closed the door, and Arrosa started to cry.

'Why does she hate me, Cael?'

'I don't know.'

'For years, I thought you were the one who hated me,' she said, 'while Kyra was always civil. And now that you love me, she decides to turn on me?'

They sat on the bed.

'Maybe it has nothing to do with you,' said Cael. 'Maybe Aunty Kelsey's right, and it's everything else going on in her life that's making her act like this. She hates me being a marine, and perhaps she's hurting you to get to me. We've always been so close, but we're drifting apart. Her opinions about the Empire are now the exact opposite of mine.' He put his arm round her shoulder. 'Whatever the reason, it doesn't change my feelings towards you. I want you to be my wife, Arrosa. I want to have children with you, and grow old by your side. I am truly sorry about some of the things I said to you in the past.'

'I know you are.'

'I was a stupid little boy,' he said, 'but I'm not a boy any more.'

## CHAPTER 7
# RETURNING THE FAVOUR

**Yearning, Eastern Rim – 25th Arginch 5266 (18th Gylean Year 17)**

The harbour of Yearning was full to overflowing, with frigates, troopships and supply vessels filling the quayside and berthed at every available pier. Beyond the breakwaters, more ships were anchored out at sea, and smaller vessels were ferrying sailors and supplies back and forward between them and the docks. The quayside was heaving with soldiers, sailors, marines and harbour workers. Some of the soldiers had just arrived, brought over from the Star Continent by Quadrant, and were being guided to their temporary accommodation, while sailors were on shore leave or were trying to reach their vessels. Lord Sigum and the five dragons under his command were stationed a little to the west of the main harbour, upon a high ridge of cliffs that lined the edge of the bay, from where they had a perfect view of the military build up.

Lahnos was sitting with Efizel and the other riders at the top of the cliffs. Ora'lya was on his right, as they basked in the bright sunshine, and their hands were intertwined. On Lahnos's left sat his sergeant major, while the other Bullan were busy preparing their new quarters in a building at the rear of the small harbour town.

'A surprise attack right now would cripple the entire invasion,'

Lahnos said. 'All those ships and soldiers? If I was the enemy, I would strike hard, and incinerate the entire harbour.'

'That won't be happening, sir,' said Annu'tila, the rider of Gallantmorn.

'I thought Na Sun Ka was in range of Yearning?'

'It is, sir, but the two islands are over four hundred miles apart. Any dragon that flies that distance would need to rest for a night before being able to fly again.'

'Ah, I get it,' said Lahnos. 'So any attack would need to be a complete success, or there would be no way to retreat?'

'The same thing applies the other way round,' said Ora'lya. 'If or when we attack Na Sun Ka, we will have to secure a foothold on that island, and defend it until our dragons have recovered their strength. This is why the Eastern and Western Rims are separate, sir – because of the gap between Yearning and Na Sun Ka. There is a similar distance between Na Sun Ka and Gyle, which adds to the difficulties of any dragon-led invasion.'

'And yet,' said Annu'tila, 'a ship-borne invasion would not succeed without dragon support; not unless there were gods aboard the fleet – gods with death powers.'

'What about where the two rims meet on the northern side of the circle?' said Efizel.

'The distance between Alef and Wyst is too great for any dragon to cross,' said Ora'lya. 'It's better to think of the archipelagos as a long chain, rather than a circle, with Yearning at the centre of the chain. It's the midway point between the Eastern and Western Rims, and the only place where a dragon can cross from one side to the other.'

'Wait,' said Lahnos. 'I thought we were going to be fighting Wystians.'

'We are,' said Ora'lya.

'But you just said that Wyst is up by the northern edge of the circle. What are Wystians doing in Na Sun Ka?'

'Sable put them there,' said Annu'tila. 'She removed the entire dragon population from Wyst, and sent a few hundred to the Home

Islands, and the rest to an archipelago in the centre of the ocean called Rigga.'

'Rigga?' said Lahnos.

'Thousands of Wystians are stranded there,' said Ora'lya. 'Rigga is too far away from the other island groups for any dragon to be able to escape. I've never seen it, but Rigga has a reputation as a barren, treeless wasteland. I almost feel sorry for the trapped Wystians, even though they hate all humans.'

A single courtyard down in the harbour was being kept clear, with a few soldiers posted to ensure that no one entered the area. As Lahnos was watching, a black, swirling portal opened up in the middle of the courtyard, and a company of over a hundred Imperial Marines marched through, each weighed down by packs, weapons and equipment. Lahnos looked for the person holding a Quadrant, but couldn't locate them. An officer guided the arriving marines out through a gate in the harbour wall to a field filled with rows of tents. Lahnos's gaze lifted to the battlements of the wall protecting the harbour area. There were several towers that had been enlarged by the addition of stout wooden platforms at their summits. Lahnos narrowed his eyes. He had expected to see batteries of ballistae sited there, but instead, each platform had several strange-looking catapults, crewed by members of the Imperial Army.

'What else do you know about Na Sun Ka?' he said.

'None of us have ever been there,' said Ora'lya, 'but, in the old days before Implacatus invaded, people from all over Dragon Eyre would try to visit the city of Sun Ta at least once in their lives. There are twelve temples in Sun Ta – one for each of the island groups that make up Dragon Eyre – and people would go to pray to the dragon spirits.'

'It was the priests there,' Annu'tila went on, 'who formed the Unk Tannic. At first, they were a charitable organisation, opposed to violence, but as the invasion proceeded, they started attacking the Banner occupation forces.

'They evolved into fanatics,' said Ora'lya. 'They believe that all dragons are gods, and that humans exist only to serve them.'

Lahnos smiled. 'That sounds familiar. I think it was the religion of Na Sun Ka that filtered down to Athumia. A man by the name of Elbannon told me that the dragons who went to Athumia were all from Na Sun Ka.'

Ora'lya narrowed her eyes. 'Are you descended from Dragon Eyre people?'

'No. I'm a native of Athumia, just like the Bullan. The settlers who came with the dragons are called Aucterians, and they make up what's known as the Dragon Dominion; but I don't think they were from Dragon Eyre.'

'Look!' said one of the other riders, her right arm extended towards the open sea.

Lahnos turned. A few hundred yards beyond the harbour breakwaters, a huge portal was forming above the waves. It grew in size, towering over the ocean, then the bow of an enormous ship appeared through the black void. The ship slowly edged its way into the sea next to Yearning, the waters churning up by its flanks. Two great masts appeared, then a long, wide flight deck.

Lahnos and Efizel jumped to their feet.

'That's my dragon carrier,' Lahnos said. 'I was supposed to leave Zamata on that ship.'

The giant vessel kept coming, sailing though the tall, wide portal. There were sailors up on the vast flight deck, watching as they moved into the seas of Dragon Eyre. On the far side of the portal, through the swirling mist, Lahnos caught a brief glimpse of Handshore Naval Base, the main port facility on his home of Zamata.

At last, after several minutes, the rear masts appeared, and then the stern of the great ship moved onto Dragon Eyre. The portal collapsed with a loud crack, leaving the mighty dragon carrier drifting towards Yearning. There was a clatter of chains as the ship's anchors were released, and the vessel ground to halt.

'Look at the size of it!' cried Annu'tila.

Ora'lya stood. She glanced at Lahnos. 'I've heard you mention these ships before, but I had no idea they were so big. Did you say you recognised this one?'

'It's from Athumia,' Lahnos said. 'I don't just recognise it – I've been on it. I sailed across the ocean on that ship, from Aucteran to Zamata.'

'That enormous deck,' said Ora'lya; 'it's... for dragons?'

'It is. Athumia has a similar problem to Dragon Eyre – the ocean is too wide for dragons to cross; so, the Dominion designed and built these ships to transport dragons over the seas.' He eyed the five riders. 'They are big enough to accommodate six dragons at once. I think I can guess what the Empire is going to do.'

'I have a question,' said Efizel. 'Why did no one on Dragon Eyre think of building ships like that?'

The riders glanced at each other.

'If I had to guess,' said Ora'lya, 'it was because only the Sea Banner and the occupation forces from Implacatus had the resources and technology to construct such vessels, but they didn't want dragons to be able to cross the ocean.'

Lord Sigum soared overhead. He circled once, then he descended to the cliff face.

'My rider,' he said, 'do you see what has arrived? I could scarcely believe what I was witnessing.'

'I could see the Cyasarta through the portal,' Lahnos said, 'and Handshore.'

'I saw them, too,' said the dragon. 'Is Bauchlie in league with the Empire?'

'Maybe the Empire paid him a lot of money for the ship; Bauchlie would have no need for a dragon carrier.'

'Who's Bauchlie?' said Ora'lya.

'An old... acquaintance,' said Lahnos. 'When Sigum and I left Zamata, Bauchlie was its ruler. I have no idea if he is still in that position.'

The air shimmered above the dragon carrier, and Queen Blackrose appeared, along with two other dragons.

'The Queen!' cried Annu'tila. 'Queen Blackrose is here.'

They watched as Blackrose descended through the air, then she landed onto the wide flight deck of the anchored ship. The air shimmered again, a few yards to Lahnos's right, and Naxor and Brogan appeared on the top of the cliff.

'Herald, Chamberlain,' said Lahnos, tilting his head slightly.

'Greetings, Commander Laimos,' said Naxor. He gazed out over the harbour of Yearning. 'Ah, Dragon Eyre. Somehow, the air always feels sweeter, and the light brighter, than anywhere else in existence. And do you see how clear the waters of the ocean are, Lady Brogan?'

'I'm more interested in looking at the quayside,' said Brogan. 'I hadn't realised that the docks of Yearning were so small. The dragon carrier will never fit into the harbour. Will it be safe from storms?'

'It isn't the season for storms, ma'am,' said Annu'tila.

Brogan eyed him. 'And who are you?'

'I am Gallantmorn's rider, ma'am.'

'Gallantmorn?'

'He is one of the dragons under the command of Lord Sigum,' said Naxor. 'A most noble warrior.'

'Indeed, he is,' said Sigum. 'All of the dragons who fought by my side in Rakana are accomplished fighters, brave and honourable. Tell me – how do you intend to use this dragon carrier?'

Naxor smiled. 'Perhaps you would like to find out? A conference has been arranged to take place upon the large deck, and, as you can see, Queen Blackrose is already there. Herald Brogan and I are here to fetch you and Commander Laimos, so that you may take part in the discussions.'

The demigod took out a Quadrant.

'Might I fly there with Lahnos upon my shoulders?' said Sigum. 'I am well used to landing upon the flight decks of dragon carriers.'

'Of course you are,' said Naxor. 'I would guess that you have sailed upon a few of these mighty vessels, yes?'

'I have, and Lahnos happened to cross the ocean of Athumia upon that particular ship. I am familiar with every inch of a Dominion dragon carrier.'

Naxor tilted his head. 'Then we shall see you in a few minutes.'

He slid his slender fingers over the surface of the Quadrant, then he and Brogan vanished.

Lahnos faced Efizel and the other dragon riders. 'Sigum and I will let you know what's happening when we get back. If I were you, though, I'd start thinking about what supplies you will need to make your life comfortable on board that carrier for a few days. How long does it take to sail to Na Sun Ka?'

'What speed can a dragon carrier reach, sir?' said Annu'tila.

'About nine or ten knots,' said Lahnos, 'if the winds are favourable.'

'Then we should be able to make the crossing in four or five days,' said Ora'lya. 'Add on another two to reach the city of Sun Ta.'

'Climb up onto my shoulders, Lahnos,' said Sigum.

'We'll be back soon,' said Lahnos, then he gripped onto a rope hanging from the harness, and pulled himself up onto the dragon's back. He buckled the strap, and Sigum ascended into the air, his silvery-green wings sparkling in the sunshine. Lahnos felt the warm wind on his face as they soared up into the blue sky, and he looked down at the small island of Yearning. It looked no bigger than Zamata, but was dominated by high mountain peaks, their flanks carpeted in thick green rainforest.

'It is very beautiful here,' said Sigum, 'and Naxor was correct. The air does taste sweeter.'

He flew towards the dragon carrier, passing over the full harbour and the frigates anchored outside the breakwaters. Sigum descended when he reached the dragon carrier. He circled once, then his talons landed onto the wide, wooden deck.

Sigum laughed aloud as he pulled his wings in. 'I thought I would never again feel that sensation, my rider. Truly, these ships were the marvel of the Dominion.'

'Will one be enough to conquer Na Sun Ka?'

'Let us listen to what the Empire has to say about that. I can see Commander Lucius Cardova among those waiting for us. He is standing with Herald Brogan and Chamberlain Naxor. The Empire has sent its best to this conference.'

Lahnos released the buckles, then he climbed down Sigum's right flank. He jumped the last two feet, and his boots landed on the flight deck. He glanced at a few of the sailors, who were standing close by.

'Are you men from Zamata?' he said.

'No, we ain't,' said one. 'Every sailor on board is Irlanian. Are you Lahnos Laimos?'

'I am.'

'Ha! I knew it. What did I tell you, lads? The folks on Zamata told us that you might be here.'

Lahnos smiled. 'Do you know where *here* is?'

'Not exactly, but it ain't Athumia; that's for damn sure. We've been working in Zamata for over a year, re-commissioning this boat, and another one just like it. It's got a new name.'

'I don't know what its old name was,' said Lahnos.

'The Dominion didn't bother much with naming their warships,' said the sailor. 'Anyway, this boat is now called the *Horned God*, after you.'

Lahnos narrowed his eyes. 'After me? Is this a joke?'

'It ain't no joke, mate,' said the sailor. 'You saved Linnagatz from the Dominion, and we ain't forgotten that. Irlan is free now; just like Zamata.'

'And the Empire pays well,' said another sailor. 'By the time we get back home to Irlan, every sailor on board will be rich.'

'What've you been doing, then, Lahnos? It's been nine years since you left Athumia.'

'Lord Sigum and I have been working for the Empire,' he said. 'I'm surprised anyone remembers me.'

'Will you be our passenger?' said another. 'I heard we're taking dragons off to a battle.'

'That's what we're here to find out,' said Lahnos. 'I can see the officers beckoning me over. It's been good to talk to you, lads.'

Sigum and Lahnos walked away from the group of sailors, and

headed towards the centre of the deck, where Blackrose and the others were waiting.

'Irlanian sailors?' said Lahnos.

'It makes sense, my rider. They will know the vessel better than anyone.'

Blackrose cast a glance in Sigum's direction. Sigum returned her gaze, and the black dragon looked away, her red eyes burning. Maddie walked forward, with Sable Holdfast by her side.

'Hey, Lahnos,' said Maddie.

'I was expecting to see you here, Maddie,' said Lahnos. 'But you, Sable? Are you joining the invasion of Na Sun Ka?'

Sable laughed. 'Not a chance, Lahnos. Lara would kill me. I'm here as an advisor.'

Sigum took his place by the side of Blackrose and the other two dragons, while the humans sat down in a semi-circle of chairs facing them, with Brogan, Naxor and Cardova in the centre. To either side of the members of the Imperial Court were several naval, marine and army officers. Lahnos took a seat next to Sable, and Cardova got to his feet.

'Thank you all for coming to this conference,' Cardova said. 'A few days from now, the invasion of Na Sun Ka will commence. Before we discuss tactics, I want to speak about the reasons behind this military action. Over the last ten years, following the expulsion of the occupation forces, Dragon Eyre has been split into three separate regions. Queen Blackrose of Ulna has united the Eastern Rim under her authority, restoring peace and stability to every island from Wyst to Haurn. In the northern half of the Western Rim, Olkis has declared independence, and is ruling Alef. Olkis is not a threat. In fact, the Olkian government has expressed a willingness to enter into a defensive alliance with Queen Blackrose. However, logistically-speaking, such an alliance is meaningless, since the so-called Home Islands lie between Olkis and the Eastern Rim.'

He gazed at the watching officers. 'The Home Islands consist of Na Sun Ka, Gyle and Ectus, and, at present, they are governed by a mixture of dragons expelled from Wyst, and the fanatics of the Unk Tannic. Both the Wystians and the Unk Tannic would like to see humans enslaved to the will of dragons, and they are a grave threat to the security of this world. In order to counter this threat, Queen Blackrose has called upon the Empire of the Sapphire Throne. The Empire and the Eastern Rim are allies, and the Queen's enemies are our enemies. Your Majesty, would you like to say a few words about why you have requested imperial aid?'

Blackrose took a single step forward. 'Thank you, Constable Cardova,' she said. 'For many years, Unk Tannic agents based upon Na Sun Ka have been sending spies, saboteurs and assassins into the Eastern Rim. They have recovered the knowledge of building explosive devices, and have been sowing terror, death and destruction across my realm. The time has come to make them pay for this perfidy. In times past, my realm has provided aid to the Empire. When the Ascendants invaded the home of the Holdfasts, I sent my best warriors to assist them, and, though we emerged victorious, the price was high. The Empress has agreed to return the favour. This mighty fleet and army will punish the arrogance of the Unk Tannic, and push them out of Na Sun Ka, making safe our southern flank. I call upon Sable to speak, to tell the imperial officers what dangers lie ahead of them.'

Sable stood, and smiled at the assembled officers.

'I have some experience of Na Sun Ka,' she said. 'Sun Ta is its main settlement – a sprawling city on the northern coast with a large harbour. It is home to the twelve great temples, which, if the city is attacked, will almost certainly be used by the Unk Tannic as fortresses. Each temple is colossal, with thick walls and easily-guarded entrances. The Banner used to control a large, walled-off district close to the harbour; and that, too, is defensible. Also, even if Sun Ta is successfully taken, you must not forget that the Unk Tannic are accustomed to living out by the volcanoes that dominate the west of the island. They would burrow tunnels under the mountains and hide there, stockpiling weapons and supplies. I have no doubt that any surviving Unk Tannic agents will gather there if they are defeated in Sun Ta.

They will use their old bases to mount terror attacks upon the imperial forces.'

A marine captain raised his hand. 'What do the local population think about the Unk Tannic, ma'am?'

'There is a wide variety of opinions,' Sable said, 'as you might expect. Many people fear the Unk Tannic, but they are too cowed to resist them, as they are currently being supported by around three hundred exiled Wystian dragons. I wouldn't expect any support from the locals while the fighting is going on, but many will be relieved if the Unk Tannic forces are vanquished. You must also be careful about dealing with Unk Tannic agents who will remain behind, even if they are defeated. The Unk Tannic are masters at blending into a civilian population.'

'I concur with every word,' said Cardova. 'Members of the Unk Tannic would not hesitate to strap a bomb to their chests and walk into a busy tavern, destroying themselves and anyone else who happened to be inside. They are ruthless, and determined.' He shook his head. 'It has been a long time since I served on Dragon Eyre, but the memories will live with me forever. During the Banner occupation, one of our biggest difficulties was trying to distinguish between peaceful civilians and Unk Tannic infiltrators. We made many mistakes, and earned the hatred of the local population. We must learn from those mistakes, or any liberation of Na Sun Ka will soon start to feel like a second occupation to the native inhabitants.'

'Remember that there will be many settlers and former Banner soldiers from Implacatus living on Na Sun Ka,' said Sable. 'We removed the vast majority of the Banner soldiers years ago, but we didn't get them all, and we left the civilian settlers where they were. Many might have been enslaved by the Unk Tannic, or by the natives. After all, that is exactly what the settlers did to the natives when they ruled.' She glanced at Cardova. 'Are there any old Banner veterans among the invasion forces?'

'We have brought along a few,' said Cardova. 'They will act as guides, and they will liaise with anyone from Implacatus we find on the island.' He paused for a moment. 'Let us move on to the tactics we are going to employ.'

Sable sat back down, and lit a cigarette.

'This dragon carrier, the *Horned God*, will set sail for Na Sun Ka six days from now,' said Cardova, 'once it has been loaded with all of the supplies and munitions it needs. Lord Sigum and the five Eastern Rim dragons under his command, along with their riders, will be on board. Sailing with them shall be a dozen frigates, manned by sailors from the Eastern Rim, and six transport vessels, each of which will contain eight hundred imperial marines. The fleet shall anchor fifty miles north-east of Sun Ta and, from there, the six dragons will launch daily attacks upon the coastal military installations of Sun Ta: neutralising the harbour, and destroying the city's defensive capability. Once that has been achieved, the marines will land by the city, and secure a foothold upon the island. A portal shall then be opened, and divisions of the Imperial Army will march through from their bases on the Star Continent.'

Cardova paused again, to allow the information to settle over the assembled officers.

'Our forces shall be facing hostile Wystian dragons, regular Unk Tannic troops, and the more secretive agents mentioned by Sable. However, we have four advantages, which our enemies lack. Firstly, we have the *Horned God*, which will allow the dragons to stage attacks without having to land and seek shelter upon Na Sun Ka. Secondly, our fleet is equipped with the latest version of Forty-Eighters, able to repel any dragon counter attack. Thirdly, the marines will have an officer with them who has vision powers; and, finally, the commander leading the attacks possesses the Gift of Pain.'

All eyes turned to Lahnos.

'Commander Laimos,' said Cardova, 'would you please speak about the tactics you deem necessary to ensure success?'

Lahnos got to his feet. 'Thank you, sir,' he said. 'I have led similar attacks to the one being described. The Gift of Pain is effective against dragons. It doesn't kill them, but it will drive them away and keep them away. Care will be needed, as the Gift of Pain is a blunt weapon. There is no precision involved – anything in the way will be struck. The other five dragons will need to stay behind me and Sigum, or to our flanks, so that they are not inadvertently targeted. The same applies to the landings. If they get into difficulty, I can use the Gift of Pain to subdue the entire area, but I will hit our own marines as well as the enemy soldiers. They will recover, but I doubt any will thank me for the experience. Can I ask – what are Forty-Eighters?'

'I will have a word in private with you after this,' said Cardova.

'I also want a word with you, Lucius,' said Sable.

Lahnos glanced at the Holdfast woman. Her demeanour had completely changed, from relaxed to furious, and Lahnos raised an eyebrow.

'I would be happy to answer any of your questions in private, Sable,' said Cardova. 'Let us move on to logistics. I have a list of everything that will be loaded onto the fleet prior to departure, and I wish to go through it in some detail.'

Two hours later, Lahnos and Sable accompanied Cardova into the wardroom, which sat directly under the rear of the flight deck.

As Lahnos was about to ask Cardova a question, Sable pushed past him, and prodded a finger into Cardova's chest.

'How long have you known?' she said.

Cardova raised an eyebrow. 'Known what, Sable?'

'That you would be sending your stepson into the heat of battle? He only graduated a few days ago, and he's being deployed to Dragon Eyre?'

Cardova narrowed his eyes. 'That information was classified.'

'Don't give me that horseshit, Lucius. I read your mind, as soon as you mentioned the presence of a marine officer with vision powers. Cael is only eighteen.'

'So was Corthie when he fought at the Great Wall. So was I, for that matter, when I was first sent to Dragon Eyre. I told you, and Cael, that he would be treated no differently from any other officer. When the request came in from the commanders of the marines, what was I supposed to do? Refuse them? Should I have said, *No, sorry, you can't have Cael, because he's family*? I am ultimately responsible for over two hundred thousand men and women who serve in the imperial armed forces, Sable. I can't give any favours, not even to Cael.'

'Does his mother know?'

'Not yet. I only learned of this earlier today. I will tell Karalyn as soon as Naxor takes me back to Colsbury.'

'She is going to kill you.'

Cardova sat down. 'Yes. I know.'

'Is that why the Empress offered him the chance to leave?' Sable went on. 'Was it Thorn's idea to send Cael?'

'I don't know.'

'Now, no one can blame her if he dies. She can say, *Well, I gave him the opportunity to walk away. It's not my fault he was ripped to pieces by a Wystian dragon*.'

'I'll watch out for him,' said Lahnos. 'I will guard his back.'

Sable turned to him. 'Thank you, Lahnos.'

'I didn't know Cael had joined the marines.'

'He spent autumn and winter at Pebble Strand,' said Sable. 'Do you know it?'

'I've heard of it,' said Lahnos. 'Is he a junior lieutenant?'

'Yeah.'

Lahnos nodded. 'I'll find him as soon as we set sail. Unless... is he already on Yearning, sir?'

'He's still on leave in Colsbury Castle,' said Cardova. 'Karalyn is due to take him to Plateau City tomorrow.'

'Poor Arrosa,' said Sable.

'Why?' said Lahnos. 'Is she all right?'

'She's betrothed to Cael. They're getting married at the end of spring, if he's still alive.'

Lahnos smiled. 'Arrosa is going to marry Cael Holdfast? That's a wedding I'd like to attend.'

'Then I will make sure you get an invitation,' said Sable. She paced up and down. 'Maybe I should get involved in this invasion. Cael is my niece's son. If he gets killed while I'm sitting doing nothing on Ulna, I'd never forgive myself; and Karalyn would be unlikely to forgive me, either.'

'Stay out of it, Sable,' said Cardova. 'This is an imperial operation.'

Sable laughed. 'After all those years of begging me to come out of retirement, are you now telling me to stay at home with the children, Lucius? Do you know who you're talking to?'

Cardova said nothing.

'Can we change the name of the ship, sir?' said Lahnos. 'I'm uncomfortable with it.'

'No,' said Cardova. 'The Irlanians have honoured you for what you did for them, and they are the ones who will be sailing it. I'm not going to risk offending hundreds of sailors over a name.'

'And the Forty-Eighters, sir?'

'Stop changing the damn subject, Lahnos,' said Sable. 'I might keep a very close eye on this operation. I may even move back to Haurn for a while, so I can watch it unfold from there.'

'Don't get involved,' said Cardova.

Sable placed a hand on her hip. 'Or what, Lucius? Dragon Eyre is my home, and someone needs to make sure you don't ruin it.'

## CHAPTER 8
# IN THE FOOTHILLS

**Colsbury Castle, the Holdings – 5th Day, First Third Spring 545**

Corthie staggered into the kitchen in a pair of long shorts, his head pounding. He reached a table, picked up a jug of water, then he raised it to his lips and drank.

'Good morning, sir,' said a servant. 'Coffee?'

'Aye,' said Corthie, 'with lots of sugar. Thanks.'

'Certainly, sir.'

Corthie drank the rest of the water as the servant walked over to a stove.

'Rough night?'

He turned, and saw Karalyn standing by the kitchen door, with baby Caitlyn in her arms.

'Aye, sis,' said Corthie. 'Shella can still knock back the whisky, eh? I had a hard time keeping up with her.'

'How long did Arrosa and Cael stay up for?'

'They were with us until about midnight. Kelsey went to bed a little later. To be honest, I didn't stay up much longer than that. It's a pity you couldn't be with us; it was a good night.'

'Someone has to look after the children when Lucius is away.'

'Is he not back yet?'

'Not yet.'

'I wonder where he is.'

'There's a reason I never ask him about work, brother. I don't want to know what he's doing.'

The servant returned with a mug of steaming coffee, and passed it to Corthie.

'Thanks.'

'My pleasure, sir. Ma'am, would you also like a drink?'

'No, thanks,' said Karalyn. 'I had one when I got up.' She glanced at Corthie. 'Which was four hours ago. Remind me again, Corthie – are you on holiday?'

'It feels like a holiday,' he said. 'There hasn't been a single sighting of any greenhides since I got here.'

'I scanned the environs of the palace this morning.'

'And?'

She shrugged. 'Nothing.'

Corthie sipped from his mug.

'Let's get some fresh air,' said Karalyn. 'Carden is with his nanny, so we can go for a walk down to the gardens.'

'What about Cael and Arrosa?' he said. 'Aren't you due to take them to Plateau City soon?'

'Aye. They're both up, and they've packed. They're in the gardens just now.'

'I should probably put some more clothes on first,' said Corthie.

They walked to Corthie's quarters, and he went inside. He pulled on a shirt, and laced up his boots, then he went back outside, his half-drunk mug of coffee in his hand. They descended the stairs of the palace.

'How's Kyra?' Corthie said.

'Unhappy,' said Karalyn. 'I visited her in Plateau City yesterday, when I was dropping Cole off at the university, but she refused to come back to Colsbury to say goodbye to her brother. I don't understand what's going on with her.'

'Don't take this as an insult, sis,' he said, 'but she didn't exactly have a stable upbringing, did she? She was with Thorn, then you, then Thorn again, and then you came back from Athumia with Arrosa. Cael might have been the loudest with his complaints, but I think maybe that Kyra was just better at keeping her opinions to herself.'

'She used to tell me that she saw Thorn as her real mother.'

'And now she's lost that, too; and she's feeling alone and isolated. I don't think she hates Arrosa; she just doesn't want to lose her brother.'

'She hasn't been the same since Cael stole the Sextant last summer. I've often wondered why he took Arrosa and Cole with him, but left his sister here. As for Kyra losing him, I think the marines are responsible for that. Kyra hoped he would hate being a marine.'

'Could that be the real reason for her anger?'

'Maybe.'

'You know,' he said, 'if we don't see any greenhides soon, you could take me back to Clackenbaird for a few hours, so I could see Aila and the bairns.'

'I could,' said Karalyn, 'as long as we make it a short trip. We wouldn't want to get caught out.'

They emerged from the palace into the chill spring morning. The sun was high in the sky, but there were patches of glistening frost on the ground wherever the shadows lay.

'Are you not cold in those shorts?' said Karalyn.

He eyed her.

'This is like summer in Kell.'

They entered the tunnel that went under the two keeps, and emerged into the gardens of Colsbury. The first shoots were appearing on the branches of the apple trees, and Corthie savoured the fresh mountain air. They came across Cael and Arrosa sitting on one of the many benches arranged throughout the gardens, under the branches of an oak tree. Cael was in his uniform, while their packed bags lay by their feet. They were holding each other's hands and Arrosa was laughing at something Cael had said.

'Morning,' said Corthie.

They glanced up.

'I'm surprised to see you up,' said Arrosa. 'You were very drunk last night.'

'I wasn't that bad,' said Corthie.

'Shella was saying that you're out of practice,' she went on. 'She said that, in the old days, you would have drunk her under the table.'

'I don't drink so much in Kell these days,' he said, 'which is ironic, as I'm continually surrounded by whisky.'

'You have seven children, Uncle,' said Cael. 'That might have something to do with it.'

'You'd think it would drive me to drink,' he said.

'Are you ready to leave?' said Karalyn.

'There are two hours until noon,' said Cael. 'We have plenty of time.'

'Aye, but I was thinking of dropping you off early. That way, you could have some time together in the city before Arrosa goes to university, and you go to the marine base. I'll give you some spending money.'

'Thanks,' said Cael. 'Are you going to try to persuade us to delay again?'

Karalyn frowned. 'Would there be any point? You know my opinion. Waiting wouldn't mean that you were any less committed to each other, and betrothals of one or two years are common.'

'If we waited,' said Cael, 'then I think we'd look back on it and wonder why we didn't get married sooner.'

'I hope you aren't going to rush into having children.'

'I think we'll wait a couple of years for that,' said Arrosa. 'I'm in no hurry to push out a baby.'

'I am relieved to hear it, but I wish you would apply the same logic to marriage.'

'If Cael wasn't going back to the marines,' Arrosa said, 'then we might have been more likely to wait, because we could see each other every day. But with him going away, I want something tangible; something that will get me through until the next time he's back.'

Karalyn shook her head. 'No one is going to abandon you, Arrosa. You are not the lost little girl you were on Athumia – this is your family.'

'Kyra doesn't seem to think so. When I get back to university, I'm going to try to be her friend, whether she likes it or not. I'm not going to let her walk past without acknowledging me.'

'Corthie thinks it's Cael she's upset with, not you,' said Karalyn.

'It's just a theory,' said Corthie. 'If Cael had left the marines after training, then I doubt Kyra would have acted the way she did. That's what's making her angry; in my opinion.'

'Up you get,' said Karalyn.

Cael and Arrosa got to their feet.

'Take care, you two,' said Corthie. 'Good luck with whatever commission the marines give you, nephew; and work hard at university, soon-to-be niece.' He glanced at his sister. 'Do you want me to hold Caitlyn for you?'

'No, I'll be fine,' said Karalyn. 'I'll be back in a few minutes.'

Corthie embraced Cael and Arrosa in turn, then he stood back. The air shimmered, and Corthie was left alone in the gardens. He walked through the orchard, passing the well-tended gravestones, and made his way to the other side of the island, where the small harbour was situated. Olo'osso was working on his yacht, while Shella watched from a deckchair on the quayside, a thick blanket over her legs, and a stick of dreamweed dangling from her right hand.

Shella laughed when she saw Corthie approach. 'Here he is, Olo'osso,' she said; 'three whiskies and he was nearly unconscious.'

Corthie sat down on the quay next to her. 'I'm not eighteen any more.'

'Let's hope your battle-vision hasn't suffered as much as your tolerance for alcohol, eh?'

'You've made Shella very proud, lad,' said Olo'osso. 'I suspect Her Highness has been waiting years to be able to say that she out-drank the famous Corthie Holdfast.'

'I'm thinking of putting a plaque up on the wall,' said Shella, 'to mark the occasion.'

'You do that, Aunty,' said Corthie.

'Has Karalyn taken Cael and Arrosa to Plateau City?'

'Aye.'

'Oh, to be young and stupid again.'

'I think it's sweet.'

Shella shook her head at him. 'That's because you experienced love at first sight with that Aila woman. Real love rarely works that way, Corthie.'

'But they've known each other for years.'

'They're children.'

'I think the commanders of the marines might disagree with you. Cael is an officer.'

'The marines like to get them young, so they can mould them into killing machines. Not that I'm opposed to that, but it doesn't mean Cael is old enough to be wed.'

'And how will he ever be able to lie to her?' said Olo'osso. 'Has Cael taken that into consideration?'

Shella narrowed her eyes. 'Why would he want to lie to her?'

Olo'osso raised his palms. 'I can think of a thousand reasons, my fair princess. What if Arrosa asks him if he thinks she's beautiful, but he hates what she's wearing? What if she asks him what's wrong, but he doesn't want to say?' He grimaced. 'What if she asks him what he's thinking? The contents of a young man's mind should not always be revealed to his beloved, as she might not like what she hears.'

'What are you thinking right now?' she said.

'I'm thinking about carrying you up to our room, tearing off your clothes, and ravishing you, my sweet darling. But I'm an old man, and I have lost my inhibitions, if I ever had any to begin with.'

'You're an insatiable old pervert.'

He bowed. 'Only when it comes to you, my dear.'

Cardova walked on to the small quayside.

'She's gone,' said Shella. 'She's taking the kids to Plateau City.'

Cardova nodded, his eyes grim.

'Did Naxor drop you off?' said Corthie.

'Yes. Just a moment ago.'

Shella peered at him. 'Why do you look as though someone's farted in your face, Lucius?'

Cardova gazed out over the still waters of the lake. 'I know where Cael is going to be posted.'

'Aye?' said Corthie.

'Is he going to Rahain?' said Shella.

'Worse,' said Cardova. 'Dragon Eyre.'

'That doesn't sound too bad,' said Corthie. 'A bit of garrison duty on Yearning?' He noticed that Shella's face had paled. 'What am I missing?'

'The Empire is about to invade Na Sun Ka,' said Shella.

Corthie frowned. 'Why?'

'Good question,' said Shella. 'It was the Empress's idea.'

'Queen Blackrose requested imperial assistance,' said Cardova. 'We could hardly turn her down.'

'I don't think we should be fighting Blackrose's wars for her,' said Shella. 'If the Unk Tannic or the Wystians actually invaded the Eastern Rim, then sure, we should rush to her assistance; but this? I don't like it. The Empire is already over-stretched.'

'Why has Cael been picked to go?' said Corthie. 'Was it random?'

Cardova shook his head. 'It's because of his vision powers. The leaders of the marines want the tactical advantage Cael will bring.'

'That means he's going to be deep in the shit,' said Shella. She took a draw from the weedstick. 'If I were you, Corthie, I would find something to do for the rest of the day.'

'Why?'

'Because Karalyn is going to lose her fucking mind over this.'

An hour later, Corthie was in his rooms in the Summer Palace, strapping on pieces of his armour to check that they still fitted. He hadn't seen Karalyn return, but he had taken Shella's advice, and was staying out of her way. He lifted the blue-coloured breastplate, and ran his fingers over the compressed layers of stone. It still bore the scorch marks from the inferno that had nearly killed him in the Kell Pass, but it remained strong. He walked to the front door of his quarters, and opened it. A Holdings servant was walking down the hallway, and Corthie gestured to him.

'Could you help fasten the straps for me?' Corthie said.

'Of course, sir,' said the servant.

Corthie passed him the breastplate, and held his arms out. 'Do you know where my sister is?' he said. 'Kelsey, I mean.'

'I believe she is with Frostback and Halfclaw, sir,' he said. 'They are patrolling the skies over the Palace of the Almighty. Could you please place your hand on the front of the armour, sir?'

Corthie did so, and the servant fastened the straps on either side.

'There you are, sir,' he said. 'Would you like me to help you get the rest of the armour on?'

'Aye, thanks.'

They walked into the room, and Corthie stood motionless, as the servant fished various plates of armour out from the crates.

'It was Kelsey who used to do this for me,' Corthie said.

'You have no padding, sir, nor any mail.'

'I'm checking that it still fits. I'm not going into battle.'

'Very good, sir.'

Corthie caught his reflection as the servant decked his body with the full panoply. A mixture of melancholy and dread rose up within him as he stared back at the armoured man in the mirror. Was he really about to pick up the Clawhammer and go back to his old life? It seemed ridiculous. He was a father and a farmer, not a warrior. Those days had gone. He had fought many battles between the years of eighteen and twenty-three, but none since; would he still know what to do?

The servant stepped away, and regarded him. 'You look like a god, sir.'

'I was once the greatest mortal warrior who ever lived, or so they tell me.'

'You remain so, sir. You are unrivalled upon any world.'

'I don't like baseless flattery.'

'My apologies, sir, but it was far from baseless. Did you not strike down the Second Ascendant?'

'Aye, that was me.'

'And did you not hold the Kell Pass on your own, against thousands of greenhides?'

'That was a long time ago.'

Another servant appeared at the door. 'Sir? Mister Holdfast, sir?'

'Aye?'

'Frostback, Halfclaw and Miss Kelsey are requesting that you join them in the forecourt, with all speed, sir. A beast has been sighted.'

Corthie glanced at the servant who had helped him with the armour. 'You were right. I should have put some padding on first.'

'I can have you ready in twenty minutes, sir.'

'Miss Kelsey was insistent that you come as quickly as possible, sir,' said the servant by the door.

Corthie grabbed the handle of the Clawhammer in one hand, and his helmet in the other. He nodded to the servants, and walked out of his rooms. He hurried down the stairs of the palace, and emerged into the bright sunlight of the forecourt. The two dragons were there, while Kelsey was standing on the ground, her arms folded over her chest.

'You took your time,' she said.

Corthie laughed. 'I came as soon as word reached me.'

'Then why are you in armour?'

'I was trying it on.'

'That is fortuitous,' said Frostback, 'for we have found an enemy for you to fight.'

'Where?'

'In the foothills a few miles south of the Palace of the Almighty,' said the silver dragon. 'It appears to be alone.'

'About time,' said Corthie. 'I was starting to think they'd never leave the damn palace.'

'I will bear you,' said Halfclaw.

'Thank you,' said Corthie. He glanced at his sister. 'Where are your children?'

Kelsey rolled her eyes. 'You sound like my ex-husband. Calpurnia is having school lessons, and Caelius is with Carden's nanny. Is that all right with you, brother? Should I post up my childcare arrangements for the whole island to read?'

'I was only asking.'

'Would you have asked Van, if he was here?'

'Settle down, sis.'

She glared at him.

'I was asking,' said Corthie, 'because I was hoping that you and Frostback would come with me. I don't care if you have a damn nanny. We have a cook in Clackenbaird; does that mean Aila and I are bad parents?'

'You have a cook?'

'Aye, and he's damn good. Shall we go?'

They walked towards the two dragons.

'You were reeking last night, brother,' she said.

'Shella and Arrosa have already mentioned that. That's the most I've had to drink in ages.'

'You're still a good-natured drunk, though; a good laugh, but you don't half talk a load of shite after a couple of whiskies.'

They reached the dragons. Kelsey climbed up onto Frostback's shoulders, and Corthie pulled on the harness straps and clambered up onto Halfclaw's back.

'My thanks again for carrying me today, Halfclaw,' he said.

'It is my pleasure, Edmond-killer.'

The two dragons ascended into the sky above the island of Colsbury. They circled twice, then soared off towards the north.

'What kind of beast did you see?' said Corthie.

'One like, but unlike, a greenhide,' said Halfclaw. 'Eyeless. Bigger. Stronger.'

'Still green, though?'

'A deeper green. I suspect its skin is exceptionally thick, for they are impervious to dragon fire.'

'How does it move around without eyes?'

'I cannot answer that. Kelsey thinks it has the same ability to listen as a bat, and uses its hearing to find its way, but I cannot confirm that.'

'If we can kill one,' Kelsey shouted over, 'I want to send it to the university. I'm calling them *ironhides*.'

'Is that their name?' Corthie shouted back.

Kelsey shrugged. 'It's what I call them. If they move by echo-location, then the university professors might be able to come up with a way to confuse them.'

'Echo-what?'

'Like a bat, brother. Never mind.'

'If I'm quiet and still, will it be able to find me?'

'It has a nose. No offence, but it'll probably smell you.'

'There it is, my rider,' said Frostback.

Corthie glanced down at the wooded slopes of the foothills at the southern fringe of the Holdings plains, as the two dragons descended. A large creature was bounding along a track. After everything Corthie had heard, the creature was smaller than he had been expecting – its height somewhere between that of a normal greenhide and a junior queen. Its long arms were similar to a greenhide's, with talons that glistened in the sunlight. It came to a halt, and held its eyeless head at an incline, as though it could hear the two dragons approaching.

'Observe, Corthie,' said Halfclaw.

The blue and green dragon surged down, and opened his jaws. A burst of fire enveloped the large beast, which huddled down, letting its rounded back take the brunt of the flames. Halfclaw hovered over it for a few seconds, keeping his flames centred on the beast, then he closed his jaws.

The creature remained still, then it rose back to its feet, unharmed.

'Pyre's knackers,' said Corthie. 'Right. My turn.'

'Should I land close by?' said Halfclaw.

'Take us in a bit lower, and I'll jump.'

'As you will it.'

Halfclaw slowed, and swooped low over a grassy bank. Corthie unbuckled the harness straps, then he leapt over the side of the dragon.

He fell ten feet, and activated his battle-vision just before he landed. He glanced up, his hands gripping the Clawhammer, to see the beast racing up the slope towards him, moving far faster than Corthie had been expecting. He swung the Clawhammer, and the creature moved to the side.

'How did you get so fast, you big bastard?' Corthie cried.

Halfclaw pounced upon the beast from its rear, driving it back, and Corthie launched himself forward. He swung the Clawhammer again, and its three talons ripped through the flesh of the creature, spraying the ground in green blood. The beast roared out in pain, then its wounds began to heal themselves.

'Hey!' Corthie shouted. 'That's cheating!'

The ironhide launched its own attack, and Corthie threw himself to the side to avoid its claws. He struck the slope, and felt the pain from the unpadded armour jolt through his body. A claw came down, aiming for his head, and Corthie rolled out of the way. He lost himself to battle-vision, realising that he had a fight on his hands, and allowed his limbs to move without thinking. He struck the ironhide again, ripping great tears across its chest, but the wounds healed within seconds.

'Decapitate the bastard!' Kelsey shouted down to him from Frost-back's shoulders.

'What do think I'm trying to do?' he shouted back.

Halfclaw darted down from the sky and lunged out with his own claws, and Corthie charged. He ducked under the ironhide's talons while it was distracted by the dragon, and dealt the beast another fear-some injury. Corthie swung again before it could react, and the Clawhammer severed the end of its right forelimb, shearing off its claws.

The ironhide howled in agony, then it swiped its other limb through the air, and the claws ripped through Corthie's stone armour, and sent him flying backwards through the air. Corthie landed heavily against some rocks, winded and in pain. He saw blood coming from the ragged holes in his breastplate, as the beast raced towards him. Corthie gripped the Clawhammer as it approached, then Halfclaw swooped down and lifted Corthie from the ground. The ironhide roared in fury, and raised its uninjured limb in the air. The other had stopped bleeding, but there was no sign that its limb was re-growing. Corthie was borne away, as Halfclaw flew up to meet Frostback.

The blue and green dragon soared above Frostback, then he dropped Corthie onto the silver dragon's harness. Kelsey's hands reached out to grab hold of him.

'How bad is it?' Kelsey said. 'I saw you get hit.'

'You tell me,' he groaned.

'Your armour's ruined,' she said, as she peered at the wound on his chest, 'but it saved your life. I can't believe it – the ironhide got you. I thought...'

'You thought I was invincible.'

'Aye.'

Corthie sat up, his left hand gripping the harness straps, as his right held the Clawhammer.

'Did you know it could self-heal?'

Kelsey shook her head. 'I've never seen them get wounded before.'

'Set me back down,' he said. 'I'm not finished.'

'I don't know...'

'Come on, sis; what do you think the Empress is paying me for?'

'Are you getting paid?'

'It was a figure of speech.'

'I will set you down,' said Frostback, 'but if that creature endangers your life again, I will not hesitate to carry you back to Colsbury.'

Corthie glanced down. 'Where's it gone?'

'It is on the path that leads to the lake,' said Halfclaw. 'It is running at full speed.'

'I must have scared the big eejit,' said Corthie. 'Will its hand grow back?'

Kelsey shrugged.

'Get after it, Frostback; I'm not done.'

The two dragons banked, then they chased after the running ironhide. It was moving far quicker than any normal greenhide, but the dragons were faster, and they soon caught up with it. The beast roared its defiance into the sky, as both Frostback and Halfclaw sprayed it with fire. Corthie released his grip on the harness, and jumped to the ground. The ironhide turned, and Corthie charged at it. He ducked out of the way of a wild swing of its uninjured limb, and then he battered the Clawhammer down onto its head. The creature moved back, and the three talons tore its face off. Corthie entered a battle frenzy, the Clawhammer swinging in his arms. He delivered another great wound across the beast's chest, but the ironhide continued to heal itself. Frostback's claws raked down its back, and Corthie sliced off one of the beast's rear limbs. It barrelled towards him, and Corthie was flung back again by a vicious swipe. He rolled down the slope towards the banks of the lake, and the creature limped after him.

Corthie groaned, then he realised that the Clawhammer was lying a yard to his right. He reached out for it, but the ironhide was almost upon him. The air shimmered, and Karalyn appeared, a long black-bladed sword held in both hands. She drove the blade into the ironhide's bloody face, giving Corthie time to reach the Clawhammer. He sprang to his feet as the ironhide screamed, then he swung the Clawhammer, removing the beast's head in an explosion of green blood.

Corthie staggered, then he fell to his knees by the edge of the lake. Karalyn placed a hand on his brow, and he felt a giddy wave of power pass through his body. He swayed while his wounds healed, then he glanced up at his sister.

'What are you doing here?' he said.

'Is a thank you too much to expect?'

'Thank you.'

Karalyn walked up to the decapitated beast. She placed a boot against its severed head, and pulled the Weathervane free.

'Since when do you fight?' said Corthie.

'I don't,' she said, 'but I have battle-vision now, even if I rarely use it. And, after what Lucius told me, I was in the mood to kill something.'

The two dragons landed close by, and both sniffed the body of the ironhide. Kelsey jumped to the ground, and ran over to take a closer look.

'They can heal themselves,' she said.

'I know,' said Karalyn. 'I was watching.'

'I don't understand,' said Kelsey, as she peered at the remains of the creature. 'Why would the Ascendants make such a beast? It cannot be burned, it can heal itself, it's immune to death, flow and vision powers... It's too powerful.'

'Maybe that's why it was imprisoned within the Palace of the Almighty,' said Karalyn.

'How many more are there?' said Corthie, as he got to his feet.

'Maybe a few dozen?' said Kelsey. 'We don't know if every one of them has left the palace at the same time.' She took out her Quadrant. 'I'm taking the body to the basement under the university, while it's still warm. I'll be back in a minute.'

The air shimmered, and Kelsey disappeared, along with the remains of the ironhide.

'We need an army,' said Corthie. 'If I can barely fight one, what will I do if I come up against several?'

'I have an idea that involves a few tons of explosives,' said Karalyn.

'To close up the breach?'

Karalyn nodded. 'If we can seal the hole in the wall of the palace, then no more of these... things will be able to escape.'

'But they would still be alive. Use the Sextant to get rid of the entire palace, sis.'

'I wish I could. The Sextant refuses to move it. It claims it cannot determine the layout of the interior.'

'But Edmond was able to bring it here.'

'Edmond designed the Palace of the Almighty. Bailey told me that he built it after Nathaniel had raided his old palace and stolen the Sextant. Presumably, Edmond didn't want his rival to be able to transport his new palace into the middle of a volcano. Regardless, it can't be moved by the Sextant.'

Corthie glanced at his sister. 'So, Cael?'

Her eyes darkened.

'I assume Lucius told you?' Corthie went on. 'Is... Lucius still alive?'

'It wasn't Lucius's fault. The marines want Cael, and there was nothing Lucius could do about it. That doesn't mean I'm happy with the idea of my son fighting a war for Blackrose. I'm furious.'

'It was Cael's decision to stay in the marines.'

Kelsey reappeared next to them. 'Poor old Gallea was in the basement when I arrived with the dead ironhide,' she said. 'I think I gave her a bit of a fright.'

Karalyn nodded, then the air crackled, and Corthie found himself standing in the forecourt on Colsbury, with Karalyn, Kelsey and the two dragons next to him.

Cardova and Shella approached.

'We got it,' said Kelsey. 'Well, Corthie and Karalyn got it, with some help from Frostback and Halfclaw.'

'It took two dragons and three Holdfasts to kill one of them?' said Shella. She narrowed her eyes. 'Guys, I think we might be in trouble.'

# CHAPTER 9
# ASSISTANT SECRETARY

**Plateau City, The Plateau – 8th Day, First Third Spring 545**

Professor Achan knocked on the door, and opened it. He walked into the room, with Kyra a pace behind, and a dozen students sitting around a table glanced up.

'Good morning,' said Achan; 'sorry to disturb you. This is the student I was telling you about. Her name is Kyra Holdfast.'

'I recognise her,' said a Holdings student. 'We know who she is.'

'Excellent,' said Achan. 'What was it that we agreed – that the Student Council would take her on as a junior assistant until summer? Is that right?'

'We would like to ask her a few questions before we take a vote,' said another student.

'By all means,' said Achan. 'I will leave her here with you.'

Achan tilted his head slightly, then he left the room, closing the door behind him. Kyra glanced at the dozen students sitting by the table.

'We have heard a lot about you, Kyra,' said the Holdings student at the head of the table. She leaned back in her seat. 'Not all of it was good. You have been participating in the protests against the Empress, even though, this time last year, you were allowed to attend meetings of the Imperial Court.'

'Some of us feel that you might be a little too disruptive to sit on the Student Council,' said a Rahain student. 'You were expelled from Professor's Nadia's class, were you not?'

'I was asked to leave for expressing my opinions,' said Kyra. 'I was exercising my right to free speech.'

'Professor Nadia had warned you what would happen if you continued to disrupt her lessons.'

'That class is complicit in the subjugation of Rahain,' said Kyra. 'The students on that course are helping the occupation forces, whether they like it or not. It's not right. A university shouldn't be encouraging imperialism; it should be opposing it.'

'It is not the place of the Student Council to take any political side,' said the Holdings student.

'But that is exactly what Professor Nadia is doing,' said Kyra. 'She is actively supporting the invasion of Rahain, and she is forcing her students to apply their skills and knowledge to help the occupation forces – the same occupation forces who slaughtered tens of thousands of civilians. My only crime was to point this out. If anyone should be punished, it should be Professor Nadia, for bringing the university into disrepute.'

The members of the Student Council glanced at each other.

'It's only a junior position,' said a tall Kellach student. 'If Kyra promises to remain apolitical while doing her job, then we shouldn't refuse her application.'

'You're only saying that because you agree with her,' said the Rahain student. She glanced at Kyra. 'Would you remain apolitical if we offered you the position?'

'What would I be doing?' said Kyra.

'You would be running a few small committees,' the student said, 'and acting as assistant secretary to the council. It's a voluntary position, so there would be no remuneration.'

'She's a Holdfast,' said someone else. 'She has plenty of money; she doesn't need to be paid.'

'I say we refuse her,' said the Holdings student. 'How will it look to the university faculty and administrators, if we take on someone who's been kicked out of a class for being a troublemaker? The faculty might decide to cut our funding.'

'The faculty can't dictate to us who to hire,' said the Kellach student. 'And isn't Professor Achan a member of the faculty?'

'A temporary member. He's leaving at the end of spring.'

'Even so, he supports her application.'

'We should vote on it,' said the Rahain student. 'But only if we hear her say that she will keep her politics out of her role.'

'I will be apolitical if you give me the job,' said Kyra. 'You have my word.'

'Then step outside,' said the Rahain student. 'We'll let you know our decision in a few minutes.'

Kyra walked to the door and left the room. There was a window in the corridor that overlooked the quad, and she gazed down at the students milling around in the spring sunshine. She wondered if she even wanted to work for the Student Council. As far as she knew, they were responsible for organising the various dances that took place throughout the year, along with helping students find accommodation. In her two and a half years at university, she had barely had any contact with the council and, after meeting with them, it seemed as though they were too weak-willed and reliant on faculty funding to ever oppose the Empire's savage policies. She had lied about remaining apolitical. If chosen, she would have access to the university printing press, and she intended to put it to good use.

The Kellach student walked out of the room.

Kyra turned to him.

'You're in,' he said. 'Seven votes to five.'

She nodded.

'You don't seem very pleased,' he said.

'I wasn't very impressed with what I heard in there, if I'm honest,' she said. 'The council members don't seem to care that Nadia is an accomplice to war crimes. They're frightened of upsetting the faculty, when they should be organising protests and walk-outs. What is the point of the Student Council if it tamely submits to the will of the establishment?'

The Kellach man smiled and extended his hand. 'My name is Larron. I'm vice-president of the council, and I think we might have a lot in common.'

She shook his hand.

'It was Professor Achan who got me selected on to the council, back at the beginning of autumn,' Larron went on. 'Do you take his class on Politics and Industry?'

'I do,' she said.

'Achan is a genius, in my opinion,' Larron said. 'He is exactly what this university needs, to shake it out of its apathy.'

'I couldn't agree more.'

'People like you and I – we have to be careful when we're doing official business for the council. We can't be seen to be too political. Keep your head down for the first few days, and watch out for Avril.'

'Who?'

'Avril of Hold Cane. She's the Holdings woman who opposed your selection. She's pro-Empire, but she also happens to be the president of the council. She's losing influence, and she knows it. After all, she could only rustle up five votes against you.'

Kyra nodded. 'Why haven't I seen you in any of my classes?'

'I'm not taking any classes this year. I interrupted my studies to devote all of my time to the council. What say we get a coffee this evening, and we can discuss our tactics?'

Kyra smiled. 'All right.'

'It's not a date, I'd like to add,' he went on.

'I know,' she said, a little too quickly.

He smiled at her. 'I'll see you in the canteen after the final bell.'

Larron walked back into the room, and Kyra suppressed the stupid grin that was about to appear on her face.

. . .

'And I'm meeting him here this evening,' Kyra said, as she picked up her mug of coffee.

Dazi narrowed her large eyes. 'You said yes to a boy asking you out?'

'It's not a date; we're going to be discussing council business.'

'Is that what he told you? What does he look like?'

'He's Kellach. Tall, dark hair.'

'Handsome?'

'I didn't notice.'

'You liar. His name – does that mean he's a Lach?'

'Aye.'

'Like your father?'

'So?'

'Nothing. Just saying.'

'My father died when I was a baby. I have no memory of him.'

Dazi tilted her head to the left. 'Here comes Arrosa.'

Kyra sighed.

'How are you doing, Kyra?' said Arrosa, as she reached the table.

'Fine,' said Kyra.

'Do you mind if I sit here?'

'There are no rules against it.'

Arrosa sat. 'I've been meaning to speak to you for a few days,' she said. 'Do you want to talk about what happened on Colsbury?'

'No.'

'You said some cruel things to me.'

'What do you want – an apology?'

'That would be a good place to start.'

'You're too young to marry my brother. I haven't changed my mind.'

'You called me a leech. Do you hate me?'

Kyra frowned, knowing that Arrosa would be able to tell if she was lying.

'I don't hate you,' she said. 'I was angry.'

'With Cael?'

'With both of you. I don't understand how you can want to marry him, not after he was so mean to you for years.'

'Normally,' Arrosa said, 'I'd agree with you, but you didn't see your brother on World Three. I watched him change in front of my eyes. He was like a different person by the time we got back.'

'And now the marines have got hold of him. Do you want your husband to be a trained killer?'

'The marines have turned him into a man.'

Kyra snorted. 'Comments like that only prove that you're too young to get married. How will you be able to look Cael in the eye after he's killed for the Empress?'

'Cael killed people on World Three, to defend us.'

'What? No, that was Cole. It was Cole who burned the village.'

'But Cael had already killed several of those who were hunting us, before that. I'm also friends with Lahnos, and he's a killer. And what about your mother? And your Aunty Sable? Corthie? The Holdfasts are full of people who have killed others. I have killed people, too. I once turned a dragon into glass.'

'I was... hoping Cael would be different.'

'Is that why you're so angry? I'm not stealing Cael from you. Even without me, you would be drifting apart from each other.'

Kyra glanced down at the table.

'I hope you come to the wedding,' Arrosa said.

Kyra said nothing.

'I love your brother,' Arrosa went on.

'If you loved him, you would ask him to leave the marines. He would do it. He would do anything you asked him to do. Use your influence over him, Arrosa. If a few thirds on World Three changed Cael, imagine what he'll be like after he's fought in a war. I know what war can do to people.'

'So do I,' said Arrosa. 'We both had violent childhoods. We were both looked after by someone who wasn't our real mother. We have both lost our fathers. The marines and the army protect us from these things happening again. We live in peace because of what they do for us. I'm proud of Cael for wanting to be a part of that, and I will never ask him to give it up. Nor should you.'

'We are not at peace. We are fighting wars in Rahain and Rakana – wars of conquest and slaughter. How does that protect us? Do you feel safer because our army has massacred tens of thousands of innocent civilians? And there will be more wars to come; believe me – the Empress is just getting started.'

'What a load of rubbish,' said Arrosa. 'What new wars? Where?'

'I don't know,' said Kyra, 'but I do know that the Empress won't stop until she's tried to bring all of the known worlds into the Empire.'

Arrosa laughed. 'Do you think she's interested in Athumia?'

'The Empire is already on Athumia. There's a garrison guarding the Tempest mine – land we stole from the Dragon Dominion; and we're supplying Zamata with ships and weapons. What will you do if Cael is sent there?'

'He won't be sent there.'

'Maybe you're right; maybe he'll be sent to kill civilians in Rahain. I will go to the wedding if Cael leaves the marines. You were right before; I don't hate you. I think you're being naïve, but I don't hate you; I never have. It's Cael. He's breaking my heart. Every time I see him in uniform is like a punch in the guts.'

'Your father was a marine.'

'We were being invaded,' she cried. 'I have no objections to self-defence, but what the Empire is doing is not that. Cael isn't protecting us; he's fighting for a cause I hate. He's fighting to bring other nations under the control of the Empress. Can't you see the difference?'

Arrosa said nothing.

'I'm sorry I called you a leech,' said Kyra. 'I shouldn't have done that. And I'm sorry that I've been avoiding you.'

'Thank you.'

'I have a class soon.'

Arrosa nodded and got to her feet. 'I'll see you later, Kyra.'

She walked away, and Kyra shook her head.

'Wow,' said Dazi. 'I can see why you don't want her to marry your brother.'

'She's not that bad,' Kyra said. 'In some ways, she's well suited to Cael – they share the same stupid opinions. She's young, though. She might change her mind about the Empress once Cael has been deployed.'

'Do you think there's going to be another war?'

'I have no doubt about that. I'd better go. I have Elbannon next, and you know what he's like if I'm late.'

Two hours later, Kyra walked into her bedroom within the university's accommodation block. She closed the door, and put her bag down onto her unmade bed. She had an hour to pass before she was due to meet Larron, but she had an idea of how to spend the time. She sat facing the room's only window, and allowed her vision powers to drift out into the skies above the university. She turned towards the Ministry of the Plateau, and raced her vision there, passing over the tall rooftops of the New Town.

She was on a hunt for information – information that she might reveal to Larron, to let him know how useful she could be. Dropping a few choice pieces of information into their conversation would no doubt impress him, and she wanted his support on the council.

Her vision entered the ministry building, and she guided it to the Empress's audience chambers. The larger of the two was empty, apart from a few soldiers guarding it, so she went to the smaller chamber. Inside, the Empress was talking to Naxor, Brogan and Slaeon, the Imperial Treasurer. Kyra went into Brogan's mind, and remained still.

'I recommend the following cuts to the costs of occupying Rahain, Your Majesty,' said Slaeon, passing the Empress a document.

Thorn glanced over the pages. 'This covers all infrastructure projects – tunnels, lighting, heating and so on.'

'Yes, Your Majesty,' said Slaeon.

'But the purpose of annexing Rahain was to allow it to prosper. If we do not repair and rebuild the cities, then the people there will continue to live in dire conditions.'

'That cannot be helped, Your Majesty. The only way to fund these projects would be to cancel all operations on Dragon Eyre.'

'That is out of the question,' said the Empress. 'We have given our word to Queen Blackrose.'

'Those are our choices, Your Majesty. We cannot spend what we do not have.'

'Aren't we raising taxes?'

Slaeon passed the Empress another document. 'This lists all of the taxes that are due to rise in the coming days, Your Majesty. Everything from custom duties to imperial levies – all are to rise. However, this will not cover the shortfall in expenditure; the only way to do that is to postpone the projects in Rahain and Rakana.'

'Rakana, too?' said Naxor.

Slaeon handed the chamberlain another document.

'I see,' said Naxor. 'This will bring chaos back to Rakana. We have told the local administration that we will cover the wages of their staff, and invest in fixing the sea walls and canals. What will we tell them if all of that is to be cancelled?'

'One should not promise what one cannot deliver,' said Slaeon.

Naxor narrowed his eyes, then Kyra felt the demigod send out his vision powers. He entered the mind of the Imperial Treasurer, then did the same to Brogan. Kyra remained still and quiet, as Naxor ransacked the Herald's memories.

'What if we were to postpone the capture of the four Rahain cities that remain outwith our control?' said the Empress.

'That would certainly relieve some of the pressure on the treasury, Your Majesty,' said Slaeon.

'I fail to see the point in conquering the entirety of Rahain if we cannot afford to fund its reconstruction. Could the money saved be diverted to Rakana, to pay the staff of the new government there?'

'It would cover some of the costs, Your Majesty.'

'Have you spoken to the banks and lending houses?'

'I have, Your Majesty,' said Slaeon; 'as you requested. Their terms are quite reasonable, given the circumstances. Their interest has been set at twenty parts for every hundred borrowed, repayable within five years.'

'You call that reasonable?' said Brogan.

'I do, Madam Herald. If the banks were aware of the true nature of the financial crisis we are facing, their demands would have been far greater.'

'Take out a loan to cover the full costs of the Rakanese administration,' said the Empress, 'once the money from Rahain has been subtracted. We cannot allow Rakana to sink back into anarchy.'

Slaeon bowed her head. 'It shall be done, Your Majesty.'

'We will consolidate our position within the three Rahain cities under our control,' said the Empress. 'Naxor, think up some clever ways to complete as many of the unfinished infrastructure projects as possible.'

'We could employ forced labour, Your Majesty,' the demigod said. 'For criminals, naturally. We could sentence them to work on the rebuilding projects. We could also squeeze more out of the university. Professor's Nadia's class has been very helpful with offering advice on repairing the heating systems of Tahrana City and the Rahain Capital, but I feel they could do more.'

'Should we trim back our expenses on Athumia, Your Majesty?' said Brogan.

'In what way?' said the Empress.

'Perhaps we have supplied Zamata with everything it needs to defend itself. If we stopped funding the regime there, and cut back on the garrison based at the Tempest mine, that would save a considerable sum. For eight years, we have stationed several full regiments at the Tempest mine, and not once in that time has the Dominion attempted to take the place by force.'

'Look into it,' said the Empress. 'Our priority is to ensure that the operation on Dragon Eyre is conducted rapidly and smoothly.'

Naxor had left Brogan's mind, so Kyra took the opportunity to raid the Herald's memories herself, keen to find out more about the operation on Dragon Eyre that they had been discussing. Kyra didn't have far to go, as the operation was bubbling away near the surface of Brogan's thoughts. Kyra read through everything, until she recoiled in horror. Na Sun Ka was about to be invaded by a huge imperial force that included dragons, the Sanang divisions, ships, soldiers, and marines.

Kyra had been right. When she had predicted to Arrosa that another war was coming, she had been basing that on guesswork, and now she had proof.

She cut the connection with Brogan's mind, and her vision snapped back to her body.

'Remind me,' said Achan. 'Na Sun Ka is what – an island?'

'Aye,' said Kyra. 'A large island on Dragon Eyre, and we're about to invade it with a massive army. We have to let everyone know, sir. We could post up pamphlets and organise a demonstration. The money that was supposed to be spent repairing the Rahain cities is going to be used for another war. It's outrageous. The Empire is almost bankrupt, and yet Thorn is dragging us into another conflict.'

'As much as I agree with you,' said Achan, 'if we advertised the fact that we know about this, the Imperial Court will suspect that a spy is at work. You are too valuable to the cause to get yourself arrested, Kyra.'

'But hundreds of officials must know about the impending invasion, sir. They couldn't have moved all those soldiers and ships to Dragon Eyre without people finding out.'

'But would those people also know about the Empire's financial problems? Only someone with access to the Imperial Court would know all of that, and you would become a possible suspect. Let us play this more carefully. All we have to do is wait until the invasion becomes public knowledge, and by then, we shall be ready to act. You have bought us time, Kyra; time to make our preparations.' He rubbed the side of his head. 'Tell me – what persuaded you to reach out to the Imperial Court? I thought you weren't going to do that again.'

Kyra's features flushed a little. 'I'm meeting Larron in ten minutes, sir. I wanted to have some information to give him.'

Achan chuckled. 'I see. Trying to impress him, eh? I met with him after the council voted to accept you as an assistant secretary. He has been my eyes and ears on the council for some time. He mentioned that he was going to be speaking to you this evening.'

'I learned something else, sir. Naxor is reading the minds of Brogan and Slaeon.'

'Of course he is,' said Achan. 'Why do you think he was so keen to see your aunt resign from her post? Kelsey Holdfast had been preventing him from reading the thoughts of his colleagues for years. Naxor is now free to discover exactly what the other members of the Imperial Court are thinking, and what they are plotting. It will give him an unassailable advantage over them. Some things may change, but Lord Naxor doesn't; he's as slippery now as he has always been. Do you know Rosie Jackdaw? She has been conducting a few small classes on salve.'

'I have taken one of those classes, sir.'

'Ask her about Lord Naxor. Ask her what Naxor did to her and Lady Jade, when he was holding them captive by the salve mine. It was a long time ago, but the passing of years means very little to demigods. The Empress should be ashamed to have such a person as her Imperial Chamberlain. Lord Naxor should be in prison; instead, he occupies one of the most powerful positions in the Empire. Anyway, enough about him. You don't want to be late to meet Larron. Give him my regards.'

Kyra nodded and got to her feet. She left the professor's rooms, and walked to the stairs. The final bell of the academic day rang at that moment, and the hallways and corridors filled with students leaving their classrooms. Kyra joined the crowds making their way down to the quad, then she turned for the canteen. A long queue was forming by the kitchen counter, from where food and coffee were being served. Kyra frowned.

'We could go somewhere else,' said a voice.

She turned, and saw Larron standing close by, his gaze on the queue.

'Where should we go?' she said.

'My parents own a tavern,' Larron went on, 'but it's in the Kellach Quarter – a forty-minute walk from here.'

Kyra almost mentioned her Quadrant, but she reined in her enthusiasm. Larron seemed decent enough, but she didn't know him.

'How about the Old Town?' he said. 'I know a few good places that are only five minutes away.'

'All right,' she said.

They walked out into the busy quad, and made for the arched entrance leading to the streets of the New Town.

'Your parents have a tavern?' she said, as they passed under the tall archway.

'Aye. They arrived in this city as children; refugees fleeing Kellach Brigdomin after the Rahain invaded. My younger siblings live there, and my twin brother works behind the bar. You also have a twin, aye?'

'Aye.'

'Professor Achan told me that he had joined the marines.'

Kyra glanced down at the smooth cobbles.

'Too many Kellach join the armed forces, in my opinion,' Larron said. 'Instead of fighting imperialism, they help prop it up. It's tragic, but we mustn't blame those who choose that life. They are misguided, rather than wicked.'

'My brother thinks he is defending our freedom.'

'That used to be the case. Back when the Ascendants invaded, the entire Star Continent was engaged in a life or death struggle; but those times are over. We won, and entered a new era of peace. That should have warranted a large reduction in the numbers filling our armed forces, but no – the Empress chose to retain a massive army. Why does the Empire need two hundred thousand men and women in uniform? All those soldiers, and marines, for what? The temptation to use them must be overwhelming, which is why I think another foreign conflict is inevitable.'

Kyra nodded. She wanted to tell him about Dragon Eyre, but managed to restrain herself. They came to a set of gates in the walls of the Old Town, and passed through. The street layout changed from wide, neat boulevards, to narrow, winding alleyways. Larron stopped at an old tavern, and they went inside. The interior was thick with smoke from the cigarettes of the patrons, and Kyra detected a faint trace of dreamweed among the tobacco. The tables were filled with a mixture of Holdings, Kellach and Rakanese customers, but none of them glanced up at Kyra and Larron. They went to the bar.

'What would you like?' Larron said. 'I'm going to order a coffee and a whisky.'

'I'll have the same,' said Kyra.

'They have Lachellan here,' Larron said. 'Lach whisky. Have you heard of it?'

Kyra nodded, resisting the urge to tell him that the distillery was owned by her Aunty Aila. The barman served their drinks, and Larron paid for them. He and Kyra walked over to a small alcove and sat down.

'So,' said Larron; 'what's it like being the daughter of the most powerful mage in existence?'

She shrugged. 'My childhood wasn't very conventional. I spent the first five years of my life with the Empress acting as my mother; well, she wasn't the Empress back then. Then my mother came back, then she went away again. Then she came back.'

'The Empress adopted you, didn't she?'

'Aye. Legally, I was her daughter for about two years. That was torn up when my mother returned from Athumia.'

'Your two mothers are the most important women on the Star Continent. What about your father? What happened to him?'

'He died in Agatha's war, when I was a baby.'

'My parents told me that they had to evacuate Plateau City when Agatha's army arrived. They took me and my brother into the mountains, along with thousands of other civilians. And then, when they were allowed to go home, they told me that the streets were filled with dead Rahain soldiers. None of them had any wounds, and they looked like they were sleeping. My parents remember it vividly.'

Kyra nodded. 'My father had just died, and my mother was... very angry.'

'Is your mother upset by your political stance? You are taking a risk, by opposing your own kin.'

'She refuses to get involved in politics. I think she secretly agrees with many of my opinions, but she doesn't want to stamp her will onto the world. I think we're lucky, in a way. If the most powerful mage happened to be a power-hungry tyrant, then that mage could conquer us all. Instead, my mother spends her time at home, looking after her new children. As for the rest of the Holdfasts, I don't think they approve of me. My brother, my uncle, my aunts, my cousin – they all think I've lost my mind.'

Larron sipped his whisky and smiled. 'I know it's irrational,' he said, 'but I love the fact that this whisky comes from Lach, the homeland of my parents. I'd like to visit Kellach Brigdomin one day, but it's such a long journey.'

Kyra said nothing.

'As for the Student Council,' Larron went on, 'I'm glad that you have been voted on as an assistant secretary. I happen to know that Avril of Hold Cane will be stepping down as president soon. When that happens, I was considering standing for the position. If I become president, I intend to abandon the council's apolitical stance, and directly challenge the university authorities over their support for the Empress's wars. Professor Nadia should be forced to resign, along with every other lecturer and member of staff who has failed to criticise the appalling atrocities that have been carried out in our name.'

'I would like to see that happen,' said Kyra.

'As president,' he went on, 'I will promote you to council secretary, and kick out the useless Rahain woman who currently holds that position. That will give you the power to organise mass protests. Imagine if the students took over the entire university - we could bring its work to an abrupt and complete halt. The authorities could then bow to our demands, or use force to evict us from the premises. We win either way. What do you think of this approach?'

'I think it could work.'

'Then, sorry to sound crass, but can I depend upon your vote, when Avril steps down?'

'I will vote for you, Larron.'

'Thanks. You know, Kyra, I think we are going to do great things together.'

Kyra smiled, and sipped her whisky.

# CHAPTER 10
# IN DEMAND

**Plateau City, The Plateau – 10$^{th}$ Day, First Third Spring 545**

The old cavalry base in Plateau City sat on the southern bank of the river, its wide acres flanked by the Rahain Quarter to the east, and the Rakanese Quarter to the west. The old stable buildings, first built by Guilliam when he was King of the Holdings, had been converted to army barracks, while the marines occupied the north-western corner of the large complex. A bridge crossed the river by the western end of the base, linking the headquarters of the imperial armed forces to the Old Town, and the vast building site of the new palace was visible from there, as its twin towers rose up over the demolished remains of the Great Fortress.

For five days, Cael had been waiting to be deployed. He had been introduced to the platoon he would be leading, which consisted of two squads, each containing twelve marines, and each led by a sergeant. He had also met the three other second lieutenants of his new company, and the first lieutenant, from whom Cael would be taking orders. One of the other second lieutenants was a fresh-faced Holdings graduate, who had been in the same class as Cael in Pebble Strand, while the other two had served in the Rahain campaign of the previous year.

Cael and the four other lieutenants of his company walked into a large room on the ground floor of the marine base. The major in charge of the entire battalion was there, along with every captain and lieutenant under his command. Cael and his colleagues saluted as they joined the others.

'At ease,' said the Holdings major. He glanced over his officers. 'For the last few days, we have been preparing for our next deployment, and I have gathered you here today to tell you that this battalion has received its orders.' He paused for a moment, as he glanced at the group of captains and lieutenants. 'We are going to Dragon Eyre.'

Cael smiled. He had heard about the battalion-strength garrison on the island of Yearning. Marines who had returned from that posting had told him about the endless sunshine, and the opportunities for swimming in the clear ocean. From their descriptions, it had sounded more like a holiday than an active operation.

'I can guess what you are all thinking,' said the major. 'The marine garrison on the island of Yearning amounts to possibly the cushiest posting of anywhere on the allied worlds; however, you are wrong. We are not going to Dragon Eyre to garrison a small island. Instead, we shall be joining five other marine battalions as part of a full invasion of Na Sun Ka. The army will also be involved, but Her Imperial Majesty has chosen the marines to lead the assault. We are to establish a foothold on Na Sun Ka, to allow a portal to be opened for the main force to move onto the island. Six troopships are currently anchored in the harbour of Yearning, and each one shall carry a single battalion to a position off the northern coast of Na Sun Ka. From there, allied dragons shall neutralise the enemy defences, prior to the marines forcing a landing.'

He paused again, to allow the officers to absorb the news.

'Normally,' he went on, 'we would have a few days' notice of any such operation; however, in this case, due to the secrecy with which this deployment is being shrouded, we shall be travelling to Yearning today. A portal shall open two hours from now, and all six battalions shall be transferred to their destination. Once there, each battalion shall board their designated troopship, and the fleet shall set sail at dusk, this evening. Not a word of this must leave the base. Do not inform any of the marines under your command of the location or nature of this operation until you see the portal open. Any questions, thus far?'

'Who will we be fighting, sir?' said a first lieutenant.

'Dragons,' said the major, 'and their fanatical dragon-worshipping followers – a sect known as the Unk Tannic. Each troopship shall also contain a few veterans from the Banner of the Sapphire Throne. They have extensive experience of Dragon Eyre, and they will be available to provide local information during the voyage from Yearning to Na Sun Ka. I recommend that you listen to what they have to say. Commander Laimos and Lord Sigum shall be leading the allied dragons; some of you may remember them from the Rahain campaign last year. We shall wait on the troopships until Commander Laimos has cleared the coastal defences, and then all eight battalions will effect landings to the east of the city of Sun Ta.'

The major looked around for more questions, but no one spoke.

'Now,' he said, 'where is Second Lieutenant Holdfast?'

'Here, sir,' said Cael.

'Come up here, Lieutenant.'

Cael walked to the front of the room, and saluted the major.

'Face the others.'

Cael turned, so that he was looking at the group of officers.

'Second Lieutenant Holdfast has vision powers,' said the major. 'This will give our battalion a crucial advantage; so much, in fact, that we have been selected to be the first battalion ashore. Lieutenant Holdfast will be responsible for communicating intelligence back to the command ship, the *Horned God*. I had to fight to keep him in our battalion, as the staff officers from the marine group command are desperate to poach him for themselves.' He glanced at Cael. 'These extra responsibilities will not affect your primary duty, which is to lead your platoon into battle. Are you up for it, lad?'

'Aye, sir.'

'While you are on the troopship,' the major went on, 'I have no doubt that the staff officers will take full advantage of your abilities, to communicate messages between the vessels of the fleet, and to scan the skies for any possible attack from hostile dragons. Some of these staff officers believe that a vision mage should not be in the front line of a battle, and they may try to persuade you to defect to them. I trust you will know what to say to them, Lieutenant?'

'Aye, sir.'

The major gestured to an aide, who unrolled a large map onto the surface of a table.

'Gather round,' said the major.

The officers clustered round the map. On it was depicted the island of Na Sun Ka.

'The island is two hundred and ten miles from east to west,' the major said, 'and it averages fifty miles from north to south, However, in the central part of the island, where the city of Sun Ta is located, that narrows to a distance of only eight miles. The vast majority of the population lives in this narrow central region. To the east, the island is covered in forested mountains, while, to the west, are clusters of active volcanoes. The fleet shall approach from the north-east, and anchor fifty miles off the coast.'

'Where is Yearning, sir?' said a captain. 'I don't see it on the map.'

'Yearning lies four hundred miles to the east,' said the major.

The captain frowned. 'Then, sir, how will the dragons under Commander Laimos be able to assault the defences? Wouldn't they have to land and take shelter upon Na Sun Ka to do so?'

The major smiled. 'We have a secret weapon. I mentioned the *Horned God* earlier; the command ship of the fleet. This vessel is unlike any other you have seen in your lives. It was built to carry up to six dragons across the oceans of Athumia, and Commander Laimos will be using it as his forward base. It is from the flight deck of that ship that the raids will be carried out. Frigates will be picketed around it in a circle, and their Forty-Eighters should prevent any hostile forces from damaging the dragon carrier.'

'A ship that can carry six dragons, sir?' said the captain.

'It is a marvel of engineering,' said the major, 'and this will be its first operation since being fully refitted on Athumia. The vessel is already on Dragon Eyre, and the six dragons under Commander Laimos are ready to depart. All they need now are the marines. Get your companies organised in the marshalling yard. Our battalion shall be first to pass through the portal. Dismissed.'

The officers dispersed. Cael and the others from his company left through a side door, and walked back out into the open air of the Plateau City base.

'Holdfast,' said his Kellach first lieutenant, 'why did you never mention that you had vision powers?'

'I was told not to, sir,' said Cael.

'I'm going to have to rearrange the entire fucking company around you. It was bad enough having a damn Holdfast to look after, now I have the fleet's only vision mage to protect as well.'

'I don't want any special treatment, sir.'

'That's not up to you. If you get killed, it'll be me who has to answer to the Holdfasts. Tell your sergeants what you can do. From now on, their main duty will be to watch your back.' He shook his head. 'I don't get it. Your stepfather is commander in chief of the entire armed forces – and yet he's allowing you to be posted to the front lines of an invasion?'

'I will speak to my sergeants, sir.'

'Good lad. Make sure your platoon is ready to leave one hour from now.'

Cael made his way to the small barracks where the marines of his platoon were based. He entered the front door and walked into the common room. At once, seven marines jumped to their feet and saluted.

'At ease,' said Cael. 'I need to speak to both sergeants.'

The two sergeants approached, and Cael led them outside.

'Feel free to have a smoke while I tell you something,' Cael said.

'Thank you, sir,' said one, as the two sergeants, one Kellach, the other Holdings, lit up cigarettes.

Cael glanced at the two older men. They had both fought in the

Rahain campaign, and had given Cael a wary welcome when he had arrived to take over the platoon.

'I have vision powers,' he said.

'Sir?' said one.

'I was forbidden from using them in Pebble Strand, or even mentioning that I had them.'

'What can you do, sir?' said the Holdings sergeant.

'Everything except battle-vision,' he said. 'I have a few other tricks as well. Watch.'

*You cannot see me.*

The two sergeants cried out, and one dropped his cigarette.

*You can see me.*

The Kellach sergeant started to laugh. 'That's quite a talent, sir.'

'I can make up to four other people invisible at the same time,' Cael said, 'as long as they're close by.'

'You ain't going to be a second lieutenant for long, sir,' said the Holdings sergeant. 'As soon as the senior officers of the marines find out what you can do, they'll whisk you away to a specialist scout unit, or promote you into the staff.'

'They already know. The battalion major has managed to hold on to me for now, and I'd rather stay with the platoon.'

'I can't say I'm too surprised by your powers, sir,' the Holdings sergeant went on. 'I mean, you're a Holdfast. But, I thought you'd brought us out here to tell us that we were being deployed somewhere.'

'We are being deployed. We have an hour to get everyone packed up and in the marshalling yard.'

'Where are we going, sir?' said the Kellach sergeant.

'I will tell you as soon as the portal opens. Get the two squads ready to leave.'

'Aye, sir.'

'I'll be back here before the hour is out to lead you to the yard. Let the squads know that I have vision powers, but keep the invisibility thing quiet for now. Carry on.'

The two sergeants saluted, then they disappeared back into the building. Cael walked to the officer's block, where he had been given a tiny room, which he shared with another second lieutenant. The room was empty when he arrived, and Cael quickly packed away his clothes and equipment. He laid his pack on the bed when he had finished, and sat down.

Dragon Eyre. For years, he had listened to Cardova tell stories about how awful the wars on that world had been, but he was glad that his stepfather hadn't tried to interfere in Cael's deployment. He wondered what his mother had said when she had heard where he was going. His thoughts went to Arrosa, who was just a few miles away, in the university. He felt an urge to use his powers to tell her that he was leaving the Star Continent, but then he remembered what the major had said about secrecy. He felt a ripple of nervous anticipation run through him. He had been to Dragon Eyre before, when he had been younger, but only to the safe island of Ulna; and he wondered why the Empire was getting involved in a new war with the Western Rim. Kyra would no doubt have a view about that. He hadn't spoken to his sister since she had stormed away on New Year's Day, but he knew from his frequent vision-talks with Arrosa that his desire to stay in the marines was the reason why she had been so upset.

Cael scanned the room to make sure he hadn't left anything behind, then he picked up his pack and walked back out into the fresh air.

When the portal opened, almost five thousand marines were lined up in the marshalling yard. Herald Brogan was standing with a Quadrant in her left hand, controlling the Plateau City end of the portal. Through the swirling air, Cael could see a harbour on the other side of the portal, with dozens of masts poking up into the blue sky. Wagons weighed down with equipment and supplies were also scheduled to pass through the portal, and they were sitting in rows next to the marines.

Cael's two sergeants glanced at him.

'Dragon Eyre,' he said. 'We're invading the Western Rim.'

'Why, sir?' said the Holdings sergeant.

Cael smiled. 'I have no idea. We're being loaded onto a troopship as soon as we cross over.'

The major of Cael's battalion gestured to his captains, and the first marines began to march through, their boots crossing the paving slabs of the large yard. Cael's company started marching, and he led his platoon towards the hole in the sky.

He stepped through the portal, and felt the warm sunshine hit his face.

'Keep moving,' shouted an old sergeant major. 'Don't block the portal.'

Cael's company marched down the quayside, and were directed towards a long pier, where two of the troopships were berthed. Someone pointed out to sea, and Cael turned. In the distance, the largest ship he had ever seen was anchored beyond the breakwaters of the harbour.

'Look at that!' cried a corporal.

'It's a dragon carrier,' said Cael. 'The *Horned God*.'

The first marines of the battalion began walking up a broad gangway, and onto the deck of a troopship. Cael glanced over his shoulder. Marines were continuing to march through the portal, and they were filling the quayside. Overhead, a small green dragon soared through the air, banking over the harbour to watch the marines arrive. A larger, silvery-green dragon approached, and they circled each other above the bay.

Cael glanced up, and saw Lahnos sitting on Sigum's shoulders, his horns unmistakable. The two dragons circled again, then they flew off towards the carrier. Cael's platoon queued by the base of the gangway, then they ascended, and stepped onto the deck of the troopship.

'Go below,' said a sailor. 'All marines are to go below.'

Cael joined another queue, at the head of a set of steep stairs that descended into the bowels of the troopship. The marines around him looked relaxed, and happy to be on the move, and many were staring at the packed harbour, or out at the dragon carrier.

A naval officer approached. 'Second Lieutenant Holdfast?' he said.

'Aye, sir?'

'Please remain here.'

Cael glanced at his sergeants. 'Get the platoon down to their quarters, and I'll catch up with you later.'

'Yes, sir,' said the Holdings sergeant. 'Shall I take your pack, sir?'

Cael handed the sergeant his luggage. 'Thank you.'

He stepped out of the queue, and watched as his platoon disappeared from sight.

The naval officer spoke to a few sailors, who hurried to the stern of the ship, where they raised a large green flag. Moments later, Lord Sigum appeared again, flying towards the pier.

'The commander wishes to have a word with you, Lieutenant,' said the naval officer.

Cael's first lieutenant walked up the gangway. 'Why are you still on deck, Holdfast?' he said.

'Commander Laimos wishes to speak to him,' said the naval officer.

The first lieutenant rolled his eyes. 'No special treatment, eh?'

Cael said nothing.

The Kellach lieutenant joined the queue of those heading towards the stairs, and Cael turned to watch Lord Sigum descend over the harbour. The silvery-green dragon flew towards the ship that had hoisted the flag, then his eyes went over the deck, until they fell upon Cael.

'Greetings, young Holdfast,' said the dragon, as the marines on the deck stared up at him.

'Lord Sigum,' said Cael, tilting his head.

'Get up here,' said Lahnos, from the dragon's back. 'Can you climb up?'

'If you are leaving the ship, Lieutenant,' said the naval officer, 'I shall inform your superiors. We are due to depart at sunset, so make sure you are back on board by then.'

'Aye, sir,' said Cael.

Sigum manoeuvred himself so that his right flank was parallel to the troopship, then Cael stepped up onto the railings, grabbed hold of a dangling rope, and climbed up the side of the dragon, as several marines laughed and cheered. Cael reached the harness, then he strapped himself in next to Lahnos.

Sigum rose into the air. He circled over the packed harbour, then sped off in the direction of the *Horned God.*

'The carrier has a strange name,' said Cael.

Lahnos eyed him.

'It reminds me of someone,' Cael went on. 'Can't think who, though.'

'Yes, very funny, Cael,' said Lahnos. 'The Irlanian sailors are responsible. They mean well, but it's embarrassing.'

'When did you get here?'

'About twenty days ago,' said Lahnos. 'All we've done is watch as more and more soldiers and supplies have arrived. And today, it's the marines.'

'How did you know I was here?'

'Lucius Cardova told me. We had a conference to discuss the battle plans and, afterwards, he told me and Sable that you were being sent here. Sable was pretty angry. She reckoned that Lucius should have used his influence to get you posted elsewhere. Of course, Lucius disagreed. Personally, I think Lucius did the right thing. You can't be giving out favours to family members; it would lower the morale of everyone else.'

'I completely agree. This is what I signed up for.'

'I did tell Sable that I would watch your back, though,' Lahnos said; 'but that also makes sense, as it would be wise to protect our vision mage. When the invasion starts, I want you to be my far-seeing eyes.'

'Are you asking me as a friend, or as my commander?'

Lahnos smiled. 'Both.'

'Then I will do as you command, sir.'

Sigum descended over the mighty dragon carrier, then he landed, his claws digging into the thick wooden beams. The green dragon that Cael had seen earlier was also on the crowded flight deck, along with four others. Lahnos and Cael unbuckled their straps, and then they climbed down to the deck.

'I want to introduce you to the other dragons, and their riders,' said Lahnos. 'Your part in the invasion is going to be crucial to our success.'

'My battalion is going to be the first to land on Na Sun Ka.'

'I'm not just talking about the landings; I'm talking about the raids that will happen prior to that. Do you know about the raids?'

'Only what I was told by my battalion major earlier today.'

Lahnos smiled. 'I almost forgot – congratulations.'

'What for?'

'I hear you and Arrosa are getting married.'

Cael smiled back at him. 'Aye. At the end of spring.'

'When she's eighteen, in other words?'

'Are you going to lecture me about how young we are?'

'No. I hope you'll both be very happy. Sable said she's going to arrange an invitation for me.'

'Well, sir, if you are the overall commander of the invasion, I guess you will have to approve my request for leave. Then, we could both go to my wedding.'

'I'll see what I can do. I suppose I should give you the whole talk about what will happen if you hurt Arrosa. She's like a little sister to me, Cael, and I don't want you messing her around.'

'I am also very fond of little Arrosa,' said Sigum. 'Do I need to say any more, Cael?'

'I have no intention of ever hurting Arrosa,' he said.

'You have been pretty mean to her over the years,' said Lahnos.

Cael glanced down. 'I know. It was wrong of me. I like to think I've grown up a bit since then.'

'You're an officer in the marines, Cael. If they don't make you grow up, no one will. Come on; let's speak to the others in my team.'

They walked over the packed flight deck, with Sigum following them. The five other dragons were taking up an entire half of the deck, with their riders standing by their forelimbs, while the Bullan stood off to the side.

'Everyone,' said Lahnos, 'this is Second Lieutenant Cael Holdfast of the Imperial Marines. He's the one I mentioned before; he has the ability to see far into the distance, and the ability to read minds. For the first phase of the invasion, while we are raiding the coast of Na Sun Ka, I want Cael up on the back of Lord Sigum, sitting next to me. From there, he will be able to spot hostile forces coming from miles away. He will also be able to communicate messages between us, and send messages back to this ship.'

Cael narrowed his eyes, but said nothing.

'Is he related to Sable?' said one of the riders, as they approached to get a better look at him.

'He's one of Karalyn's twins,' said Lahnos, 'so, yes. Sable and Cael are members of the same family. He's just graduated from the marine training facility on the Star Continent, and this will be his first active operation.'

'I will need to ask permission if I am to be seconded to your team, sir,' said Cael.

'I've already cleared it with the marine commanders,' said Lahnos. 'They had no objections. Come the actual landings, however, you will be back with your usual battalion. This is the way it's going to be, Cael – your abilities are too useful to be confined to leading a small platoon.'

'Understood, sir.'

'What's your vision range?'

'The furthest I've ever visioned was about two hundred miles, sir. It's about the same range as my mother. And I'm really a dream mage, rather than a vision mage. I can do other things, if you're interested.'

'Such as?'

'I can make myself invisible,' Cael said, 'and I can also make the dragon I am riding on invisible. Would that be useful?'

Lahnos laughed. 'All right; change of plan. The first time Lord Sigum and I fly over Na Sun Ka, we will go with Cael, but no one else, and we'll thoroughly survey the area. Anything else?'

'I can persuade people.'

Lahnos narrowed his eyes. 'Like Sable can?'

'I'm better at it than Sable, sir. Sable's persuasive skills usually wear off after a while. I can implant them for life. If I have access to a dragon's eyes, I can scour its mind, or order it to attack its own side; or I could send it to sleep.'

Lahnos puffed out his cheeks. 'I should have you permanently reassigned to my team.'

'But, sir, I'm a marine. I want to be with my platoon. Please allow me to lead them in the landings; it's what I have been trained to do. I can't abandon them.'

'He would be of far more use to the invasion if he were by your side, sir,' said one of the Bullan.

'But he wants to fight,' said a young woman.

'I know he does, Ora'lya,' said Lahnos, 'and I respect that.'

'I have already agreed with Arrosa that I will seek out a staff job after a couple of years, sir,' Cael said. 'This might be the only active operation I get to go on. Please don't deprive me of the opportunity.'

Lahnos frowned. 'Here's my compromise,' he said: 'you're mine until the landings commence, then you can return to your platoon. However, as soon as the portal has been opened to allow the army to come through, you're mine again. Deal?'

'Aye, sir.'

'Could I see some proof of this boy's abilities?' said a large, dark orange dragon.

'Certainly,' said Cael; 'but will you be insulted if I do so?'

'I shall not be insulted, young pup,' said the dragon, 'not after I requested it.'

'Might I know your name?' said Cael.

'It is Gallantmorn, little Holdfast.'

Cael nodded, then he glanced into the orange dragon's eyes.

*Sleep.*

The orange dragon collapsed to the deck, his limbs folding under him, then his eyes closed, and he began to snore. The other dragons stared for a while, and some of the riders edged back a step from Cael.

Ora'lya laughed. 'I've heard about Sable doing tricks like that, but that's the first time I've ever seen it.'

Cael noted the way that Lahnos looked at the young woman, but said nothing.

'Will Gallantmorn be all right?' said another rider.

'I shall awaken him,' said Cael. 'Please open one of his eyes a fraction.'

The rider ran to Gallantmorn's head, and prised open one of his eyes.

*You are not angry at having been sent to sleep, Gallantmorn; you think it's humorous, and don't take any offence. Awaken.*

Gallantmorn opened his eyes. A few of the riders and other dragons tensed, then Gallantmorn began to laugh.

'That was most amusing,' he said, as he got back to his feet. 'Well played, young pup. Commander, with your Gift of Pain, and this lad's mage skills, we should have an unassailable advantage over our foes on Na Sun Ka.'

'I agree,' said Lahnos. 'However, we should remember that the Wystian dragons on Na Sun Ka will heavily outnumber us. We are but six dragons with their riders, and we shall be fighting dozens of Wystians. We must use our tactical advantages with great care.' He turned to Cael. 'Shall Sigum and I take you back to your troopship?'

Cael nodded. 'Thank you, sir.'

Lahnos and Cael climbed up onto the shoulders of the silvery-green dragon, and they flew back to the harbour. As Sigum was hovering over the troopship, Lahnos dipped into a pocket and handed Cael an envelope.

'What's this?' said Cael.

'Give it to your immediate superior,' said Lahnos. 'It's my orders to have you detailed to my team during the raids.'

Cael stuffed it into a pocket. 'Aye, sir.'

'We'll come and collect you during the voyage,' Lahnos said, 'so we can pore over some maps and plan out our raiding strategy.'

'I will be available at your command, sir.'

Lahnos smiled. 'It was good to see you again, Cael.'

'And you, Lahnos.'

Cael climbed down the straps, then he jumped the last few feet and landed on the deck of the ship. A few sailors gazed at him in surprise, then they stared up at the dragon. Cael descended the aft stairs, and was given directions to his company's sleeping quarters. The hold of the ship was filled with hammocks, trunks, crates and marines, and Cael had to weave his way through them to reach his platoon. His sergeants got to their feet, and showed him where his hammock had been positioned, then his first lieutenant walked over.

'Enjoy your little trip, did you, Holdfast?' the Kellach officer said.

'Aye, sir. I have a letter for you.'

He handed the first lieutenant the envelope. The officer ripped open the seal, and pulled out the letter, his eyes narrowing as he read it.

'I might have guessed,' he said. 'Just as the major predicted.'

'I insisted that I be allowed to lead my platoon ashore, sir, and the commander agreed.'

'We should be thankful for that, I suppose,' said the first lieutenant. 'The commander isn't the only one who will be needing your vision skills. How does it feel to be in such demand?'

'I'd rather be on the front line with my platoon, sir.'

The Kellach officer nodded. 'Good answer, lad. Carry on. We sail at dusk.'

# CHAPTER 11
# A DISPLAY OF POWER

**Off Na Sun Ka, Western Rim – 7th Nethinch 5266 (18th Gylean Year 17)**

Lahnos glanced along either side of the ship's passageway, but no one was there. He crouched down, picked up the tray, and walked back into his cabin, using a foot to ease the door shut behind him. Ora'lya was getting dressed in the dim light of a solitary oil lamp, and he laid the tray down on the bed next to her and sat.

He poured coffee from a pot into two mugs, then he picked up a piece of bread, dipped it into a shallow dish of honey, and began to eat.

Ora'lya tied her hair back, then she took hold of her mug. She looked out of the small window. A dim light was growing through the salt-glazed glass.

'We don't have long to wait,' he said.

'Let's not talk about that,' she said. 'I want to pretend that this is just another morning while I eat breakfast. Is it true that there are two dragon carriers?'

'There were two berthed in Zamata.'

'Then where is the other one? I heard the sailors say that both were being refurbished. Is it on Dragon Eyre?'

'It might be. Maybe it's being kept in reserve, or maybe the Empire has found another purpose for it. Perhaps Blackrose is using it as her personal yacht. Despite what you may think, the Empress doesn't keep me informed of her every decision.'

'She should,' said Ora'lya. 'If you were more ambitious, you could achieve anything. Are you happy serving the Empire?'

'Happy enough.'

'I don't understand what motivates you. You have spent the last few years fighting on worlds that are foreign to you, for causes that are not your own. Do you owe the Empress a personal debt?'

'I'm grateful for everything the Holdfasts have done for me, but I'm not beholden to them. And I wouldn't fight for the Empire if I thought it was evil. They've made mistakes – who hasn't? – but, at heart, I think they want to bring peace and prosperity to the allied worlds. Besides, it gives me something to do while I try to absorb the fact that I cannot die.'

'You *can* die,' she said. 'A ballista bolt through the back of the head would do it. Dragon Eyre is the grave of many gods who thought they would never die. You still need to be careful.'

'I'm too busy worrying about you and the other riders to think about being careful. You are all so… fragile. And I have Cael Holdfast to watch out for, too. He has a great range of powers, but he's as mortal as you.'

'He looks as though he can handle himself.'

'He's certainly toughened up since the last time I knew him.'

'The entire fleet knows that a Holdfast is serving in the marines,' she said.

He eyed her. 'What is everyone saying about it? You hear things that no one says to me.'

'Some are surprised that Karalyn is allowing her son to be put into danger,' she said; 'but most are pleased – pleased that the Empress is willing to have members of her own family fight alongside us ordinary folk. A few of the more excitable ones are saying that Cael is going to become a new Sable.'

'He's not devious enough.'

'Hey! Don't insult the liberator of Dragon Eyre.'

'I wasn't. Deviousness is one of her weapons. That, ruthlessness, and a complete disregard for her own safety. Cael isn't like that. All the same, I can sense something in him; something that, if nurtured and allowed to flourish, may give rise to greatness. Don't tell him I said that. He needs to keep his feet on the ground.'

'Not literally, I assume?'

'Let's see how he copes with today, and then I'll have a better idea of what he might become.'

'I think Idali'rona is developing a crush on him. Every time Lord Sigum brings him over to the dragon carrier, I see her eyes widen.'

'Tell Idali'rona that he's taken.'

'Maybe we shouldn't. Maybe we should allow her to flirt with him, to see how he reacts. If he's going to marry that friend of yours, then you want to be sure that he won't betray her.'

'Who's being devious now? Let's not try to trick the lad, not when we're about to go to war. And remember that he can read our minds. Are you going to eat that apple?'

'You can have it.'

'Thanks.'

He picked it up and took a large bite. He leaned back, and rested his bare feet on the bed. 'We should take some leave after this.'

She smiled. 'Are you in a rush to meet my parents?'

'Who said anything about meeting your parents? I was thinking of a quiet, deserted island; just the two of us for a few days.'

'I haven't been home for eight months, Lahnos.'

'All right; we visit your people for a day, and then we go to our deserted island.'

She kissed him. 'Thanks. There are several small islands near Enna where no one lives. We could sail a little boat out to one. Do you know how to sail?'

'I thought I did, but Olo'osso disabused me of that notion when I went sailing with him on Colsbury lake.'

'You've been sailing with Olo'osso? I didn't think that old pirate was still alive.'

'Alive, well, and living like a prince on the Star Continent. And I mean that literally – his girlfriend is an actual princess.'

Someone knocked on their cabin door.

'Who is it?' said Lahnos.

'Second Lieutenant Cael Holdfast, sir.'

Lahnos smiled. 'Come in, Second Lieutenant Cael Holdfast.'

The door opened and Cael walked in. He eyed Ora'lya for a moment, then turned to Lahnos.

'I have conducted a survey of the coastal installations, sir.'

'Take a seat,' said Lahnos. 'Coffee?'

'Thank you, sir,' said Cael, as he sat.

Lahnos filled a mug and passed it to him. 'What did you see?'

'It might be easier if I imprinted it into your mind, sir.'

'Quit the *sir* talk when we're alone, Cael.'

Cael smiled. 'But we're not alone, sir. While I was on my way here from the flight deck, three different officers and your Bullan sergeant major all warned me that Miss Ora'lya would be in your cabin.'

'And yet you came here anyway.'

Cael shrugged. 'I knocked.'

'Are you missing Arrosa?' said Ora'lya.

'Aye, ma'am,' he said, 'but I knew what I was getting into.'

'How long did you spend scanning the coast?' said Lahnos.

'An hour, sir. Lord Sigum fetched me long before the sun had started to lighten the sky. I saw the city of Sun Ta, and the ships in the harbour. The old Banner base is now full of soldiers working for the Unk Tannic. The great majority of them were still sleeping when I saw them, but a few were on duty. There is also a slave compound, where the former settlers of Sun Ta are being corralled. I hope freeing them will be part of our objectives.'

'The slaves were once the occupiers of this world,' said Ora'lya. 'If we free them, what would happen to them afterwards?'

'I have no specific orders regarding the ex-settlers of Na Sun Ka,' said Lahnos, 'but we will refrain from destroying the slave compound when we attack. Describe to me where it lies, Cael.'

'It would be far quicker if I implanted the scene into your mind, sir. You will see exactly what I saw.'

Lahnos nodded. 'All right.'

Cael looked into his eyes, and Lahnos's vision clouded over. When it cleared, he saw a vast, dark coast appear in his mind, punctuated by the streetlamps of Sun Ta. The waves were glistening white as they crashed against the shore and the breakwaters of the harbour. He saw the masts of the merchant ships tied up alongside the piers and quayside, then, beyond, he saw the huge temples spread out along the southern edge of the city centre – massive buildings that rose into the night sky. His vision then focussed on the harbour defences, and the military base to the east of the harbour. Five dragons were sleeping in a large plaza, but there were no harnesses upon their shoulders. Lahnos noted the layout of the base, and the positions of the anti-dragon defences – ballistae and net-throwing catapults, all pointed towards the sea.

His vision faded, and he blinked.

'Did it work?' said Ora'lya.

'Yes,' said Lahnos.

'Did you see the temples? Are they all still standing?'

'I saw them. Sable was right; they could be easily fortified and held against us. Dragon fire won't do much against them, and the Gift of Pain won't penetrate their walls.' He glanced at Cael. 'Taking them will fall to the ground forces. The good news is that I can see where the marines might be able to make a landing – the coast to the east has a long, flat beach – but that will come after we've destroyed the city's defences. That was very helpful, Cael; thank you. Now, go back up to the flight deck, and tell my Bullan sergeant major to summon the other dragons and their riders. We shall depart when the whistle blows to signal the end of the night watch.'

Cael got to his feet. 'Aye, sir.'

The young marine officer left the cabin and closed the door. Lahnos reached down and pulled on his boots. He heard Ora'lya whisper something, turned, and watched as she mumbled a few words, her eyes closed.

'What are you doing?' he said.

'Praying to the dragon spirits,' she said.

'I thought you didn't believe in that.'

'I'm not Unk Tannic; I don't believe that the dragons are our masters, but we're about to attack the most sacred place on Dragon Eyre. If the dragon spirits are real, then I want them to forgive us. Does that sound stupid?'

'Your beliefs are your own,' he said.

'Don't you believe in anything?'

'I used to, before I grew horns and was told I had no soul. Now I believe that this life is all we have. Dragons are powerful, but they aren't gods. There are no real gods.'

'You seem very sure about that.'

'Faith is nothing but an admission that there's no evidence for your beliefs. If there was evidence, it would be knowledge, not faith. But I don't care if others have faith; people are free to believe whatever they like. Arrosa believes that the Ascendant who created Athumia is a real god, but I don't think there's any point in disagreeing with her. The same goes for other religions. As long as no one tries to force me to believe in their god, or tries to make me live according to their beliefs, then there's room enough for all of us.'

Ora'lya smiled. 'I guess I'd better ask the dragon spirits to forgive you, too.'

He laughed. 'You do that.'

They got ready, blew out the lamp, and left the cabin. They walked along a long corridor that stretched down the port side of the huge ship, and passed the closed entrance to the enormous hold where the dragons on board slept. It had room for four, so there were always two dragons who had to sleep up on the flight deck each night. They came to the rear of the ship, where several large capstans were situated next to the lift that brought the dragons down from the flight deck. They climbed a set of steep steps next to the lift, and came out into the open air. To the east, the sky was beginning to brighten a little, and a warm breeze was gusting off the wide deck.

Efizel saluted him. 'Sir, orders have been sent down to the members of your team to assemble on the flight deck.'

'Thank you,' said Lahnos, 'and thanks for breakfast. Is Lieutenant Holdfast up here?'

'Yes, sir. He is talking to Lady Quicklime by the bow.'

Lahnos, Efizel and Ora'lya began to walk towards the front of the ship.

'I wonder what my dragon is doing up so early,' Ora'lya said.

'She probably misses you.'

'I feel a little guilty about that. The other riders sleep on the dragon deck, and I'm the only one who doesn't. I've never brought this up before, but I'm breaking a lot of rules by being with you, Lahnos.'

He frowned. 'Riders have rules?'

'We have dozens of rules. Always being available for your dragon is one of the most important. Does Lord Sigum not mind if you spend time away from him?'

'I love Sigum, but he and I occasionally need our own space. He likes to fly off on his own sometimes, and I would never begrudge him that. Kelsey and Frostback have a similar arrangement; they aren't always together.'

'Then, according to the strict interpretation of the Dragon Eyre code, neither you nor Kelsey Holdfast are genuine dragon riders. Another rule states that we are not to enter into any serious, long term relationships with other people.'

Lahnos narrowed his eyes.

'Casual relationships are permitted,' she went on, 'but dragons can get jealous if their riders show love and affection towards someone else.'

Lahnos shook his head. 'Is that why the other riders disapprove of us? I thought it was because they didn't like me; or perhaps because I'm a foreigner.'

'It is my behaviour that they dislike,' she said. 'They think I am betraying Quicklime.'

'They don't think I'm betraying Sigum?'

'They don't perceive you to be a genuine rider, so they are holding you to a lower standard.'

They reached Cael and Quicklime, then Sigum soared overhead and landed on the flight deck next to them.

'Greetings,' said Sigum, as he pulled his wings in. 'I have patrolled the immediate vicinity; there are no hostile dragons close by.'

Quicklime eyed Ora'lya. 'Good morning, my rider.'

'Good morning, Quicklime,' she said. 'Did you sleep well?

'I slept badly.'

Ora'lya lowered her gaze. 'I am sorry to hear that.'

The green dragon eyed her. 'I wish to speak to you, rider – alone.'

Lahnos watched as Quicklime and Ora'lya walked away to the far side of the flight deck.

'Are you coming between them?' said Sigum.

'Apparently so,' said Lahnos.

'The dragons of this world seem very possessive of their riders,' Sigum went on.

'Aren't you?' said Cael.

Sigum regarded the young Holdfast officer. 'I dearly love Lahnos, and I would die to protect him. However, that does not mean I wish to spend every waking moment in his company, nor do I require him to sleep by my side each night.'

'When I was a captive on Athumia,' Lahnos said, 'Sigum spent months searching for me.'

'And I would do so again,' said the silvery-green dragon. 'We are bonded, no matter what the other dragons here may imply. Furthermore, I do not envy the other friendships that Lahnos has developed. I wish him to be happy; I hope that he finds a mate, and has children that I can dote on. I do not wish to keep him all for myself.'

'Nor I, you,' said Lahnos. 'I still hope that you will find a lady dragon to love.'

'I fear my time has passed, rider. My father saw to that.'

A sound came from the stern of the ship as the great lift was raised. Upon it stood Gallantmorn and Annu'tila, his rider, and the dark orange dragon stretched his wings as soon as he stepped onto the flight deck. Behind him, the lift was lowered again, and Gallantmorn strode forwards. Within ten minutes, all of the dragons had gathered on the flight deck in the dim pre-dawn light. Around the dragon carrier, the lanterns of their twelve frigate escorts could be seen in the distance, forming an outer perimeter; while the six marine troopships were making up an inner circle, closer to the protective shadow of the carrier. Every vessel had lowered their anchors, and all were riding up and down on the ocean swell.

Lahnos spoke to the group for a few minutes, then he gave the order for the riders to climb up onto the shoulders of their dragons, as he and Cael clambered up into Sigum's harness.

'We are fifty miles from the coast of Na Sun Ka,' Lord Sigum said to the other dragons. 'Lahnos and I shall lead, and the Holdfast will give warning of any approaching foe. Your job will be to destroy the military targets within the town and port of Sun Ta, while I will protect us from the air.'

'Good luck, sir,' said Efizel.

'Thanks,' said Lahnos. He glanced over in the direction of Quicklime. Ora'lya was up on the green dragon's shoulders, but she looked unhappy about something.

Sigum extended his wings and soared up into the dark sky, and the other five dragons followed him. They formed themselves into a column, then Sigum raced off for the south, keeping low above the waves.

'Cael did something to my mind earlier,' Lahnos said, as they raced over the line of frigates. He put an image of the coast in there, so I could see it. Should he do the same for you, Sigum?'

'He has already done so, my rider,' said the silvery-green dragon. 'Are you going to end your relationship with Ora'lya?'

'Why would I do that?'

'Because of the stress you are placing upon her bond with Quicklime.'

Lahnos said nothing.

Cael glanced at him. 'Maddie has a husband. If Queen Blackrose can cope, then I don't see why Quicklime can't.'

'Their bond is also... unorthodox,' said Sigum. 'It seems that only those raised with the traditional Dragon Eyre customs see a problem with their riders forming other relationships. Tread carefully, my rider, for I do not wish to see dissension within our team.'

'It's a little late for that,' said Lahnos. 'No one warned me about their rules.'

'I was also ignorant of them,' said Sigum.

'This can wait,' said Lahnos. 'Let's focus on what we're doing, and making sure we all return to the carrier alive.'

They flew for an hour, as the sky steadily brightened into another beautiful day on Dragon Eyre. The coast came into view, just as the sun was appearing on the eastern horizon to their left.

'Three dragons have seen us and are ascending into the air,' said Cael; 'from the vicinity of the temples.'

A lone bell began to peal in the distance.

'I see the dragons,' said Sigum. 'I also see humans running towards the harbour ballistae.'

The first bolt was loosed at them, but it fell short and landed in the ocean. Lahnos glanced up, and saw the three dragons that Cael had mentioned. More were starting to ascend into the air, and he readied his Gifts. He aimed first at the line of ballistae stationed by the harbour walls, and unleashed the Gift of Pain. Swathes of men fell screaming, some falling into the waters of the harbour, others writhing on the stone walls.

'Tell Gallantmorn to attack the defences, Cael,' Lahnos said. 'Sigum, take us over to where those dragons are coming from.'

Cael's eyes hazed over, and Sigum ascended sharply, rising high above the range of the ballistae and into the path of the first approaching dragons.

'Miserable traitors of the Eastern Rim,' cried one of the enemy dragons. 'Blackrose has sent you to your deaths.'

Lahnos waited until Sigum was close to the three dragons, then he battered them with the Gift of Pain. One dropped in silence, crashing into a line of vessels berthed by a pier, while the other two screamed in agony. One managed to retreat in panic, losing altitude as he made his escape, while the other lost consciousness, and plummeted from the sky. Down below, Gallantmorn was leading the other dragons over the harbour defences, burning the unattended ballista batteries. More bells began to peal, as the town awoke to the peril. Sigum dived towards the military compound, where another four enemy dragons were ascending into the air, and Lahnos struck them down with the Gift of Pain, sending them crashing into the buildings of the base.

'Tell Gallantmorn to commence the complete destruction of the base, Cael,' he said.

Cael glanced at him.

'Except the slave area,' Lahnos added; 'tell him to spare that.'

'Aye, sir,' said Cael, then his eyes glazed over again.

Three hours later, all six dragons landed back on the deck of the carrier, to a roar of cheers and applause from the crew and officers who had been watching for their return. Lahnos unbuckled himself from the harness and climbed down to the deck. He saw the captain of the ship, and strode through the cheering sailors towards him.

'A complete success, Captain,' Lahnos said. 'No casualties, and the military base next to the harbour of Sun Ta has been burned to the ground.'

'Excellent work, Commander,' said the captain. 'Did you encounter much resistance?'

'The Wystian dragons tried to fend us off, but they couldn't get close enough to attack.'

'However,' said Sigum, who had also approached, 'they saw the direction in which we flew away. They will suspect that we have somewhere other than land upon which to rest; even if they do not yet understand it.'

'I do not believe there is any cause for concern,' said Gallantmorn. 'The Wystians will believe we have veered round to the east. They have no conception that we possess a ship such as this.' He laughed. 'They will be searching for us upon the eastern coasts of Na Sun Ka, but they will find us not.'

'Were any hostile dragons slain?' said the ship's captain.

'Possibly one or two who were rendered unconscious by the Gift of Pain,' said Lahnos, 'but we can't confirm that.'

'Do you wish me to remain on duty, sir?' said Cael. 'I can watch the coastline of Na Sun Ka from here, and I will see if any dragons attempt to search for us in this direction.'

'Don't you need some rest, Lieutenant?' said Lahnos.

'Not if there's a risk that the fleet might be attacked, sir.'

'I don't want to rely too much upon you,' said Lahnos. 'I don't want you to get exhausted; I'll need you again for tomorrow's raid.'

'I'm feeling fresh, sir. If I near exhaustion, I will let you know.'

Lahnos smiled. 'All right. I accept your offer. Get something to eat and drink, and remain on duty.' He turned to the dragons and their riders. 'Well done. Go below, and get some rest. We'll be doing it all again tomorrow.'

The dragons and their riders moved off towards the lift at the rear of the ship, where the Bullan were waiting for them. Lahnos caught up with Ora'lya as they walked towards a hatch that had stairs leading down to the dragon deck.

'Do you want to get some dinner?' he said.

She shook her head. 'I need to spend more time with my dragon, Lahnos. She... she thinks I've been neglecting her. I'll be sleeping on the dragon deck tonight.'

'All right.'

They descended the stairs, then Lahnos watched as Ora'lya and the other riders walked towards the large hold reserved for the dragons, then he made his way back to his cabin, alone.

He was dozing when he heard a voice appear in his mind.

*Lahnos. It's Cael. Dragons are approaching from the south.*

Lahnos opened his eyes. 'How many?' he said.

*Around four dozen.*

'Alert the duty officers. I'm on my way.'

Lahnos got to his feet in the dark cabin. He glanced out of the window. The light of the day was fading, and the sky to the west was a deep and glorious red. He left his cabin and ran along the corridor. He was at the bottom of the stairs when the ship's whistle let out three short blasts. Lahnos raced up the stairs, taking two at a time, and emerged onto the flight deck. Sigum was waiting for him, along with Gallantmorn and his rider.

The ship's whistle blasted again, and signal flags were raised, alerting the rest of the fleet. Sailors and officers were hurrying onto the deck, and the lift at the stern began to lower, ready to fetch the first dragon from the hold.

'Do you see them?' said Lahnos. 'Where's Cael?'

'I'm here,' said the young lieutenant, stepping out from Sigum's shadow. 'There are fifty Wystian dragons coming this way. I've sent messages to the duty officers on board the four frigates along our southern flank.'

'Fifty? We didn't see that many dragons the entire time we were over Sun Ta. How did they find us?'

'I don't know,' said Cael. 'It's possible that I might have missed the presence of a single scout. I don't think so, but it's possible.'

'You missed them?' said Gallantmorn.

'I can't look in every direction at the same time,' said Cael. 'I was focussed on the south, but if a scout approached from the east or west...'

'You did well to warn us at all,' said Lahnos. 'Sigum, Gallantmorn, we shall ascend. The frigates will prevent most of the attackers getting through the perimeter, but any that manage will assault the troopships. Defending them is our priority.'

He glanced at Efizel, who was hurrying towards him. 'Order the other dragons to take off as soon as they get up to the flight deck.'

The Bullan nodded. 'Yes, sir.'

'Do the frigates have enough ballistae to down fifty dragons?' said Gallantmorn.

'The frigates don't have any ballistae,' said Lahnos. 'Whatever you do, do not fly out to meet the attackers. Stay within the perimeter. Cael, you're with me.'

Lahnos climbed up Sigum's flank, and Cael followed him up into the harness.

'For one who has never seen these fabled Forty-Eighters in operation,' said Sigum, 'you seem very confident that they will succeed.'

'I didn't want Gallantmorn to panic,' said Lahnos. 'I have no idea if the Forty-Eighters work. Have you seen them, Cael?'

'I've heard of them, sir,' he said, 'but I've never seen them in action. The army and navy have them, but not the marines.'

Sigum and Gallantmorn ascended into the darkening sky. They circled together over the dragon carrier, then Sigum broke off to the east, and Gallantmorn the west, and they took up positions over the six troopships.

Lahnos watched as the fifty Wystian dragons approached. Four frigates lay directly in their path, but those to either side were beginning to shift their positions, so that their port flanks were facing the wave of attackers.

'This is like the invasion of Gunst,' said Lahnos, 'except, that time, we were on the side of the dragons.'

The fifty attackers were staying tightly pressed together as they soared towards the thin line of frigates, their wings glowing in the last rays of sunset.

'Quicklime is on the flight deck, sir,' said Cael.

'Send her up,' said Lahnos. 'Tell her to support Gallantmorn.'

'Aye, sir.'

Lahnos turned his head, and saw the green dragon take off from the carrier. As always, Ora'Lya was on her back, as the dragon banked towards Gallantmorn. He turned back to the view of the approaching Wystians.

'Why aren't the frigates doing anything?' he said.

'The Forty-Eighters have an effective range of around one hundred yards,' said Cael. 'They're waiting until the attackers are closer.'

Sigum beat his wings, hovering over the troopships as they watched. The closest frigate to the Wystians raised a red flag, then a hailstorm of small projectiles was launched from the Forty-Eighters fixed along the ship's port flank. The other three frigates also loosed, and the sky filled with a cloud of tiny black dots. The Wystians flew straight into them, and the explosions rippled through the air, lighting up the sky as the first row of dragons was torn to shreds. The frigates nearest the four on the southern side also loosed, their small projectiles striking the flanks of the Wystians. Screams echoed over the ocean as dragons began to fall from the sky. The explosives were tearing great holes in their wings, or sending shrapnel into their flesh, piercing the thick scales. A cloud of smoke began to hover over the ocean, as the frigates loosed another barrage, then another. Dragons began to peel off from the main cluster, soaring out to the east and west, and the other frigates in the perimeter loosed. Flying out from the midst of the carnage, a few injured dragons soared over the line of frigates, their wings ragged, and their flanks pierced in several places.

Lahnos raised his hand, and unleashed the Gift of Pain. The injured dragons screamed, and fell into the ocean, creating waves that bucked the troopships up and down. Two approached from the flank where Gallantmorn and Quicklime were positioned, and Lahnos hesitated. Gallantmorn lunged out, and ripped the throat from an injured red dragon, then the other one collided with Quicklime. Gallantmorn went to her aid, but the dragon he had killed fell, and struck one of the troopships by its main mast, splitting its hull in two. Another falling dragon smashed into the bow of a frigate, and it began to sink.

The Forty-Eighters loosed again, and again, and the Wystians turned and fled, leaving over thirty of their number dead, their corpses swallowed up by the ocean waves. Gallantmorn helped Quicklime kill the last of the dragons who had made it through the perimeter, and the fleet fell back into silence.

'Take us down to where the troopship was hit,' Lahnos said. 'Search for survivors.'

Sigum banked, and soared down. Where the struck troopship had been, scattered flotsam and debris were floating upon the surface of the ocean. Sigum went in low, and picked up two marines who had been clinging onto the fragments of a mast, plucking them from the water. Gallantmorn saw what he was doing, and came down to assist, while Quicklime flew to the site of the sunken frigate. The three other Eastern Rim dragons joined the search and, for twenty minutes, they scoured the ocean, pulling any surviving sailor and marine out of the water and depositing them onto the flight deck of the dragon carrier, as Cael sat on Sigum's shoulders in silence, his eyes dark.

The dragons returned to the carrier when the last of the survivors from both losses had been collected, and they landed, their claws digging into the wooden beams of the deck.

Lahnos turned to Cael. 'Was that your troopship?'

Cael shook his head. 'No, sir.'

'This is not your fault,' said Lahnos.

'I must have missed a scout, sir. How else could they have found us?'

'You gave us enough warning to get prepared,' said Lahnos. 'I can't ask for any more. You can't do the impossible. If you hadn't notified the captains of the frigates, the Wystians would have swept through them.'

'There were eight hundred marines on that troopship, sir. An entire battalion.'

'War is brutal, Cael, but if the Wystians decide that they cannot afford the losses of another attack, then the marines won't have died for nothing. We killed more than half of the Wystians. Three dozen dragons in fifteen minutes. Come on; I think you need a whisky.'

'What about Ora'lya?'

'Ora'lya will be spending time with her dragon,' said Lahnos.

He and Cael climbed down to the deck. Around seventy marines and forty sailors had been pulled from the ocean, and the crew of the *Horned God* were giving them blankets and mugs of steaming coffee.

Gallantmorn approached.

'I have never witnessed a spectacle like that in my entire life,' said the dark orange dragon. 'What godlike power these humans possess, to bring down such a mighty swarm of dragons.'

'And with power like that,' said Sigum, 'is there anything the Empire cannot achieve?'

## CHAPTER 12
## INTO THE BREACH

**Hold Stringer, Republic of the Holdings – 17th Day, First Third Spring 545**

The air shimmered, and Corthie, Karalyn and Kelsey appeared on a grassy slope, surrounded by soldiers from the Imperial Army. More soldiers were crouching by the edge of a low, rocky ridge, keeping their heads down as they peered over the summit. Corthie glanced around, looking for signs of danger, but there were none, so he slung the Clawhammer over his shoulder. He was wearing his blue, stone armour, but with a borrowed steel breastplate, to replace the one that had been torn apart by the ironhide. Corthie and the others approached the ridge, and looked over. Sitting on the edge of the great plains of the Holdings was the enormous Palace of the Almighty. Its weight had caused the gargantuan structure to sink a few feet into the ground, and its featureless outer wall was glimmering a pale grey in the sunlight.

'There it is,' said Kelsey; 'exactly where I last saw it.'

'And there's the breach in the wall,' said Karalyn.

Corthie had seen the breach before, through the vision powers of his elder sister, but it looked smaller when confronted with it face to face. The opening was perhaps twelve feet high, and around ten feet wide, and beyond was a smooth-walled hallway or cavern, made out of the same grey granite as the rest of the structure. Next to the breach were tracks leading away from the building, but nothing was moving that he could see.

Kelsey signalled to the soldiers. 'Get the explosives into place, but retreat if anything emerges from the breach. Go.'

The soldiers hurried off down the slope, carrying ladders and crates with them as they made their way towards Edmond's palace.

'Listen to her,' said Karalyn. 'She thinks she's still the Herald.'

'You can give the orders, if you prefer,' said Kelsey.

'I'm here to observe,' said Karalyn, 'and to get us out of here in a hurry, if needed.'

'Then shut up, sis, and leave it to me.'

'It's as big as the Great Racecourse in Medio,' said Corthie.

'It's bigger,' said Kelsey. 'I surveyed it, years ago, when I was Herald. I came up here with a team of engineers, and we examined every inch of the exterior, to make sure nothing could get in or out. Do you see how the edges of the breach are smooth?'

'Aye,' said Corthie.

'A stone mage created that hole, or a god with stone powers. And, they knew exactly where to open it up.'

'I can see a few windows, high up on those towers,' said Corthie. 'Couldn't something get in or out through them?'

'They aren't windows,' said Karalyn; 'they are ventilation shafts, and they're blocked by grilles, and are too narrow to climb. The interior is riddled with tunnels and chambers, but most of the palace is solid granite.'

'Don't the damn ironhides have to eat or drink?' he said. 'We've been waiting for more to emerge for days, and nothing.'

'If you were Edmond,' said Kelsey, 'wouldn't you have laid by tons of supplies, just in case? That's what I reckon. The ironhides will be eating their way through old Edmond's stores.'

The soldiers reached the corner of the palace, and set down the crates on the grass by the open breach. They began to carry large explosive devices over to the side of the building, and affixed them to the edges of the breach.

'Will it be enough?' said Corthie.

'That quantity of explosives would level the entire island of Colsbury,' said Kelsey. 'If it's not enough, then... I'm out of ideas.'

'Maybe I should go in first.'

'Why?'

'Well, what if Bailey is trapped inside?'

'Then it's his own stupid fault.'

Karalyn eyed her sister.

'What?' said Kelsey. 'If it was Bailey who opened up that breach, after I explicitly told him not to, then it'll be his own fault if he ends up trapped inside. His meddling has already killed a few hundred folk from Hold Stringer, along with several soldiers. If we can seal up the breach, even temporarily, that will buy us time to find a stone mage.'

'Killing the ironhides was supposed to be my job,' said Corthie.

'Aye, well, that was before you actually fought one, brother. No offence, but if two or three attack you at the same time, I'll be sending flowers to Aila.'

'Does the Empress know you're involved in this?' said Karalyn.

Kelsey shrugged. 'I couldn't give a shit.'

Two dragons soared overhead, then Frostback and Halfclaw landed behind the ridge.

'I loathe the sight of that grotesque building,' said Frostback.

'We have done nothing but patrol the skies over it for days,' said Halfclaw. 'I, too, despise it. For a palace, it is unremittingly ugly.'

'Unlike the Blue Palace that is being built in Plateau City,' said Frostback, 'which is a beauteous wonder to behold.'

'It occurs to me,' said Corthie, 'that the Empress is building a palace that will have half of its area reserved for dragons, aye? A home for you and Halfclaw. But that was when Kelsey was the Herald. Will you still live there if Brogan remains Herald?'

'Is the Empress stupid, Corthie?' said Frostback.

'Eh, no?'

'Then it is only a matter of time before she realises her grave mistake and reinstates Kelsey in her rightful post,' said the silver dragon.

'Who says I want the job back?' said Kelsey.

Frostback stared at her. 'I have eyes, rider. I have ears. You try to remain busy by scribbling countless words onto the blank pages of your manuscript, or by organising outings to the Palace of the Almighty, but I know the truth.'

'Aye?' said Corthie. 'What truth?'

'My rider is bored,' said Frostback. 'She misses juggling three dozen emergencies at the same time. She misses being able to give orders to all and sundry, and she misses being close to power. She is especially restless on days like today, when the idiot Van has the children. Rider, how did you ever manage to fall in love with such a worthless creature?'

'You know why,' said Kelsey. 'I had a prophecy that we would be together and, well… it became self-fulfilling. I doubt I would have loved him, if I hadn't seen it in a damn vision first. But I can hardly regret it, not when I have Calpurnia and little Caelius.'

'When will you find a new mate?'

Kelsey shook her head. 'I'm divorced with two children; I doubt I'll ever find someone else.'

'I did,' said Karalyn. 'Lucius knows dozens of officers your age. Any time you want to meet one of them, all you have to do is ask.'

'Aye, right,' said Kelsey. 'I am never going with another soldier again; that's for damn certain.'

'You might like my cook,' said Corthie. 'He's a couple of years older than you, and he's unattached to anyone. And, obviously, he makes a fine meal.'

'Stop it, both of you,' said Kelsey. 'I'm not interested. Just let me write my damn book in peace. Look; the soldiers are finishing up.'

Karalyn tensed, as though she was ready to whisk everyone out of trouble at any moment. The soldiers had laid down one of Ravi's new fuse wires, and they rolled it out over the grass as they backed away from the corner of the huge palace. They reached the ridge and climbed over it, to where the two dragons and the three Holdfasts were standing.

'All devices are in position, ma'am,' their officer said to Kelsey.

'Take cover, everyone,' said Kelsey. The dragons ascended into the sky, and the humans took shelter behind the ridge. Corthie peered over the top, as one of the soldiers lit a match.

'The fuse is lit,' the soldier said, as he touched the flame to the end of the wire.

The wire sizzled and burnt, and a small flame raced across the grass towards the palace. Halfway, it fizzled out.

'Fucking Ravi,' muttered Kelsey.

'He told you it was experimental,' said Karalyn.

'Should I go down and re-light it, ma'am?' said the officer.

'No,' said Kelsey. 'You'd be too close to the explosion when it went off.'

Corthie picked up a palm-sized stone. 'Tell me what to aim for.'

'I don't know anything about the design of these new explosives,' said Kelsey. 'I don't know if they even have detonators.'

'Professor Ravi told us that they required the fuse wire, ma'am,' said the officer.

Karalyn glanced at the palace. 'I have fire powers, thanks to Albany,' she said. 'Will a burst of flames set them off?'

'It should, I guess,' said Kelsey.

'Pile up the crates and start a fire,' Karalyn said.

The soldiers broke up the crates that had carried the explosives, and heaped them into a small stack. The officer lit a few matches to get a fire started, then flames took hold of the wood. Karalyn stood next to the fire as the others took shelter again, then she lifted her right hand, and the flames were pulled from the burning wood, until a fireball was hovering in the air next to her. Kelsey put her hands over her ears, then Corthie did the same. Karalyn swung her arm, and the fireball shot through the air. It went over the top of the ridge, and smacked into a cluster of explosives fixed to the left-hand side of the breach. A series of huge explosions went off in quick succession, and Karalyn was blown off her feet, sent flying back a dozen yards until she landed on the grass. A cloud of dust rose as the air stilled. Corthie and Kelsey joined the soldiers as they peered over the ridge.

'I can't see anything,' said Kelsey. 'Did it work?'

'It did not, my rider,' said Frostback, as she came in lower. 'The breach remains exactly the same as before.'

The dust began to clear, and Corthie frowned. The dragon was right. Apart from a few dark scorch marks on the surface of the granite, the breach was unchanged.

'Bollocks,' said Kelsey.

'I'm fine, by the way,' said Karalyn, as she walked up to them. 'Thanks for asking.'

'Why is the palace unaffected by explosives?' said Corthie. 'How can that be possible?'

'It was built by Edmond's stone powers,' said Karalyn. 'The granite must be compressed, or somehow strengthened. He had a long time to think about its design.'

'I'm going down to take a closer look,' said Corthie.

He took the Clawhammer from where it had been slung over his shoulder, then he climbed over the ridge and walked down the slope towards the palace. The ground by the corner of the palace had suffered more than the structure had, and a deep crater had formed. Because of that, the breach was harder to access, being almost too high to reach. Corthie gazed up, and looked inside. The chamber beyond was empty, but its floor was covered in sods of earth and pieces of ripped-up turf from the explosion.

Corthie powered his battle-vision, then he leapt up. He grabbed the lip of the floor with his free hand, and pulled himself up into the breach. He got to his feet, his Clawhammer ready. There were two passageways leading off from the empty cavern, both with identical, smooth granite floors, walls and ceilings. Corthie peered down them, but they were in darkness.

'Don't go far,' Karalyn cried from the ridge. 'It's easy to get lost in there.'

'I'll need a lamp before I can go any further,' Corthie shouted back.

He heard a low, droning sound coming from the left-hand passageway. It reminded him of a swarm of bees, and he narrowed his eyes. The sound increased, then several large shapes burst out from the passageway. They were flying at head-height, and their bodies were clad in the same dark green skin as the ironhide he had killed. Corthie braced his feet and lifted his Clawhammer, and one of the flying beasts flew straight into the path of the three talons. Its body was ripped apart by the Clawhammer, and green blood and gore fell onto Corthie. Another flying beast battered into his chest, and Corthie was knocked off his feet as the chamber filled with the creatures. Corthie rolled on the floor as they flew over him, then, as soon as the flying beasts were out of the palace, they extended their long forelimbs, each terminating in a set of claws.

Corthie got to his feet. He glanced down at the dismembered creature on the floor of the chamber. Like the ironhides, it had no eyes, and seemed to consist almost entirely of muscle and its thick, green protective hide. Down by the ridge, Karalyn had raised her arm, but the flying beasts seemed unaffected by any powers she was trying to send their way. At length, one of the creatures exploded into a thousand pieces, which rained down onto the soldiers, but there were dozens remaining. Halfclaw opened his jaws and emitted a thick blast of flames, but the flying beasts flew through the cloud of fire, and began to swarm around the two dragons. They attacked the flanks of Frostback and Halfclaw, as the dragons attempted to ascend out of their reach. One of the beasts ripped a hole down Frostback's left wing. The silver dragon snatched the beast from the air with her forelimbs, and tore it in two, but others were fastening their claws on to her shoulders and sides.

'Get them out of here!' cried Kelsey.

Karalyn glanced at her sister, then she nodded. A moment later, Karalyn and the two dragons vanished, along with four of the flying beasts that had been attached to Frostback or Halfclaw at the time. The other flying creatures buzzed low over Kelsey and the soldiers. One of them picked up a soldier, and tore off his head with its claws. The other soldiers formed up around Kelsey, as the creatures dived towards them again.

Corthie jumped down into the crater, and ran up the slope towards his sister. He cleaved through a flying beast that was tearing another soldier to shreds, then Kelsey swiped her fingers over her Quadrant.

The air shimmered, and they appeared in the forecourt of Colsbury, the surviving soldiers standing next to them. Over to their left, Frostback, Halfclaw and Karalyn were killing the creatures they had brought along with them when they had fled. One of the flying beasts avoided a swipe from Halfclaw's claws, and then it soared away over the lake towards the mountains. Karalyn pointed at the last of the beasts remaining in the forecourt and, after a few moments, it exploded, coating the flagstones in a layer of green blood.

'They aren't completely immune to flow powers,' Karalyn said, 'but I can only concentrate on one at a time, and they require a lot of effort to kill.'

'We lost three soldiers,' said Kelsey.

Karalyn glanced up. She gazed at the soldiers Kelsey had brought back, and then at the dragons, and raised her hand again. The wounds down the flanks and wings of the dragons closed and healed.

'Thank you, Karalyn,' said Halfclaw. 'I curse those vile creatures – that is twice now that Frostback and I have been driven away by their claws.'

Corthie frowned at Karalyn. 'Why are you able to use flow and healing powers while Kelsey is standing here? Didn't you get those powers from a normal god?'

Karalyn looked down at her hands. 'You're right. I hadn't even noticed.'

'Neither did I, to be honest.' said Kelsey. 'I guess I'm used to seeing you use your powers in my presence.'

'But that was the first time I've used flow or healing next to you.'

'I need to go back to the palace,' said Corthie. 'More of those things could be escaping. I think the explosion might have woken them up.'

'Either that,' said Karalyn, 'or someone inside sent them out to chase us away.'

'Will you take me back?'

Karalyn narrowed her eyes. 'Kelsey, the soldiers and the dragons should remain here.'

'I will see if I can rustle up a few Forty-Eighters,' said Kelsey. 'I think they might be effective against those green, flying things. Greenflies; that's what I'm going to call them.'

'You don't have any authority to requisition military supplies,' said Karalyn.

Kelsey smiled. 'No, but your husband does. I assume he's working in his office? He isn't going to say no if we need some ordnance to defend Colsbury. If he writes up his orders, I can travel to Plateau City and collect the equipment.' She glanced down at the bodies of the dead creatures. 'I'll even take one of these back for the university to look at, to go along with the body of the ironhide they already have.'

'We shall resume our patrols,' said Frostback. 'I think that one of us should remain aloft over Colsbury, in case any more of these greenflies attacks the island, while the other will watch over Karalyn and Corthie by the entrance to the Palace of the Almighty.'

'I shall go,' said Halfclaw. 'You should stay here with your rider, my beloved.'

Frostback tilted her silver head.

'Wait here,' said Karalyn. She vanished, then returned a few moments later with a lantern in her left hand. She nodded to Corthie.

'Get ready,' she said.

The air shimmered, and Corthie found himself back at the ridge in front of the breach in the wall of the palace. Above the heads of Corthie and Karalyn, Halfclaw had also appeared, and he ascended over the palace to keep watch.

'How many did you kill?' said Karalyn.

'Two,' said Corthie. 'They die easier than the ironhides, that's for sure. Are they another of Leksandr's failed experiments, do you think?'

'They don't seem like failures to me,' said Karalyn. 'Perhaps, like the ironhides, they were too good at what they did, and the gods couldn't control them.' She walked over to the bodies of the three dead soldiers and placed the lantern on the ground. 'Stay here. I won't be long.'

She vanished, along with the three bodies. Corthie gazed down at the breach, then he scanned the skies for any flying beasts. All he saw was Halfclaw, circling overhead. Karalyn re-appeared by Corthie's side. She picked up the lantern, and they walked down the slope towards the corner of the colossal palace.

'Where have those flying bastards gone, do you think?' he said.

'I don't know,' said Karalyn. 'If someone is controlling them, then they might have gone back inside.'

'Either that, or they've flown away,' said Corthie. 'Maybe we should call in the army. They could wall off the entire area around the breach, and have a thousand soldiers guard it day and night.'

Karalyn said nothing.

'Or maybe you should try to move it with the Sextant again,' Corthie went on. 'Now that there's a great big hole in the wall, maybe the Sextant would let you send the palace to the bottom of the ocean.'

'I could try, but the Sextant is no longer in Colsbury.'

Corthie frowned. 'Where is it?'

'I've hidden it somewhere safe.'

'Why?'

'To avoid placing temptation in Cael's way. No one knows where it is apart from me, and that's how it's going to stay.'

'But can you get to it quickly, if you need to?'

'That depends on how you define *quickly*. Let me try something.'

The air shimmered again, and they appeared in the breached chamber.

'I can transport us as far as here,' Karalyn went on, 'because I could see it, but the rest of the interior is still impenetrable to my powers. My guess is that the same thing would happen if I tried to use the Sextant to shift the entire building.' She broke off. 'Did you hear that?'

Corthie glanced at the two passageways. 'I didn't hear anything.'

Karalyn crouched by the lantern, and lit it with a match. She adjusted the flow of oil, until the lamp was at its brightest, then she stood and held it up. They approached the passageway on the left, and Karalyn shone the light down the long, featureless corridor.

'Do you remember much about the last time you were in here?' said Corthie.

'There's not much to remember,' she said. 'Every hallway and staircase looks the same. I survived by remaining invisible and hiding in the network of ventilation shafts.'

They moved to the other passageway. It looked identical to the first they had gazed down, then Corthie heard a soft groan. He gripped the Clawhammer and glanced at his sister, who nodded. They crept up the passageway, towards a corner where it swung to the right. They reached the corner, and Corthie peered round. Another passageway stretched away into the distance, but there was a doorway on the right. They edged up to it, and looked into a square-cut chamber. Three bodies had been nailed to the opposite wall, the nails driven through their foreheads. The body on the right was a withered old corpse, while the one in the middle was an old woman, whose mouth was opening and closing voicelessly as she hung from the nail.

Corthie stared at the body on the left. It was a man, wearing a restrainer mask that was leaking blood and pus down his face. His legs were jerking, and his hands had been severed.

'Bailey,' Karalyn whispered.

Corthie kept watch by the door, as Karalyn set the lantern down and hurried forward. She leaned up, and ripped the nail from Bailey's forehead. His body fell to the floor, and he groaned aloud, while flailing his handless arms around as though he was trying to protect himself. Karalyn released the other two bodies, pulling the nails from the granite wall. The withered old corpse dropped to the floor, but the old woman landed on her feet. She stared around with lifeless eyes, then began to walk away. Karalyn raised her hand, and the old woman toppled over, falling down next to the withered corpse.

'I'll carry Bailey,' Karalyn said. 'Corthie – you bring the other two.'

'Eh?' he said, as he looked down at the corpse and the old woman. 'Who are they?'

'I'll explain later. Hurry.'

Corthie shouldered the Clawhammer then, with a grimace, he slung the withered corpse over his free shoulder. He then picked up the old woman with both arms, as Karalyn dragged Bailey by his feet along the floor, leaving blood smearing the smooth granite. They retreated back along the passageway, then, as soon as they were in sight of the breach, the air shimmered, and Corthie found himself in a reception chamber within the Summer Palace on Colsbury. Karalyn released Bailey's legs, and ran off through a door. Corthie frowned, then he lay the bodies of the old woman and the withered old man down on the floor. Bailey gasped and choked, and blood spurted from his lips. Corthie crouched down next to the wounded god, and gazed at the restrainer mask. He felt for the buckle at the back of Bailey's head, feeling through his matted hair.

'Not yet,' said Karalyn, as she hurried back into the room with Cardova, Shella and several soldiers.

Karalyn rushed to Corthie's side as the others stared down at the bodies.

'I'm ready,' she said. 'Unfasten the buckle, and I'll fill his body with healing.'

Corthie nodded, then he loosened the buckle at the back of Bailey's head. He brought his hands round to the god's face, and prised off the restrainer mask. Bailey's impaled eyeballs were still attached to the long nails on the inside of the mask, and he screamed in agony. Karalyn reached out, and slid each eyeball off its nail, and Corthie pulled the mask free and set it down on the floor. Bailey began to convulse, and Karalyn laid a hand onto his brow. The god settled, then seemed to fall into unconsciousness. Some of his wounds closed up, but the holes in his eyes remained, and Karalyn shut his eyelids with her fingers.

'It will take a while for Bailey to heal properly,' Karalyn said, 'and I can't read his thoughts and memories until his eyes have recovered.'

'We have a few vials of salve locked up somewhere,' said Cardova.

'That will help,' said Karalyn.

'And he was inside the Palace of the Almighty?' said Shella.

'Nailed to a wall next to the other two.'

Shella and Cardova peered down at the two other bodies.

Karalyn gestured towards the old woman. 'This is Theodora, the First Ascendant. Edmond killed her millennia ago while she was creating Athumia; then he brought her back, to exist in a kind of half-life. The other body belongs to Nathaniel, the Fourth Ascendant.'

'Eh?' said Shella. 'The rest of you are too young to remember this, but I watched Nathaniel's body being burned on the roof of the Great Fortress.'

'That was Guilliam's body,' said Karalyn. 'It was occupied by Nathaniel's consciousness, but his real body was still in Lostwell. Keira did kill him, though. Nathaniel died when Keira cut off Guilliam's head.'

'And all three were nailed to a wall?' said Cardova. 'By whom?'

'By someone with the power to subdue Bailey,' said Karalyn. 'Whoever it was, they also knew the significance of Nathaniel and Theodora. I think they were left there for us to find.'

'I authorised Kelsey's request to arm Colsbury with a few batteries of Forty-Eighters,' Cardova went on. 'She's gone to Plateau City with the requisition papers to fetch them. We can have them placed on the roofs of the gatehouse and the two keeps, to defend the island if those flying... things return. Did you see any more when you went back to the palace?'

Karalyn shook her head.

'We didn't see any beasts,' said Corthie. 'What will we do with Theodora? If she's... half-alive, should we try to heal her, or is it too late?'

'It's much too late for that,' said Karalyn. 'Her mind is a void.'

'Then shouldn't we put her out of her misery?'

'Not until Bailey has recovered. If anyone should do it, it should be him. She's the reason he was in there.'

'And he's the reason all those creatures have escaped,' said Shella. 'Idiot god.'

'We'll have to go back into the palace,' said Corthie. 'We can clear it, one room at a time.'

'An ironhide ripped through your stone armour,' said Karalyn. 'What will happen if we come up against six of the beasts?' She narrowed her eyes and glanced at her husband. 'Tempest,' she said. 'Could we get my brother a new suit of armour, made from Tempest?'

Cardova nodded. 'It will take a few days to prepare, but I don't see why not. If you are going in there with him, then I will order you a set, too.'

'Do we have enough stocks of Tempest?' said Shella.

'A large consignment has recently been brought over from Athumia,' said Cardova. 'After Elbannon's admission that he had sabotaged the previous experiments, I ordered the army to start creating Tempest weapons. They're meant for the front-line soldiers and marines, but there is more than enough for two suits of armour. Leave it with me, Karalyn.'

'Is Tempest any good?' said Corthie. 'Is it better than stone armour?'

'It is the strongest material in existence,' said Karalyn.

'Then why didn't the Ascendants wear it?'

'Because, brother, it can only be found on Athumia, and that world was lost to the gods thousands of years ago.' She glanced at the three bodies. 'We will move Bailey to the infirmary, and keep the bodies of the two Ascendants safe until he recovers enough to tell us what happened to him. And then, when our new armour is ready, we shall enter the Palace of the Almighty again.'

She caught Corthie's gaze.

'If we can't seal up the breach,' she said, 'then we have no choice – we shall have to hunt down whatever lurks inside.'

## CHAPTER 13
# MARCHBRAE AULD DEER

**Plateau City, The Plateau – 20th Day, First Third Spring 545**

Kyra remained behind, as the other students filed out of Professor Gallea's lecture room. She picked up her bag, and tried to catch Gallea's eye.

'Was there something you wanted to ask, Kyra?' said the old professor.

'Aye, ma'am,' she said. 'You mentioned that someone in the city is attempting to build a steam-powered printing press?'

'That's right. An enterprising little business located in the Rakanese Quarter, if my memory serves me well.'

'Why don't we make one here, in the university? If it works, then we could produce thousands of books in the time it takes us to print a few dozen. Books would become cheap and plentiful, and every household would be able to afford them.'

'These things will happen with or without the university building a new printing press,' said Gallea. 'Our job is to impart knowledge. The students who come here are then free to use that knowledge to build the designs found within the Aurelian Papers, and to improve them. For example, I also know of three small businesses who are all trying to be the first to develop a working steam locomotive. The men and women behind these businesses first studied here, and they are using what they learned to benefit themselves and, I hope, the wider public.' She walked towards the door. 'If you will excuse me, I am going to meet Professor Elbannon for tea.'

Gallea left the room, and Kyra followed her out.

'I still think the university should also be trying to build these things, ma'am,' she said, as she followed the professor along the corridor. 'Whoever invents these steam machines first is going to become extremely rich.'

'Then why don't you invest in some of these small businesses, Kyra? I am sure they will be very happy to receive some extra capital to further their ambitions.'

'But it should be the university that leads the way. The profits shouldn't be concentrated in the hands of a few lucky businessmen, who are probably already rich to begin with.'

Gallea smiled. 'We are a house of learning, Kyra, not a mercantile enterprise. We have a charter to follow; a charter that was written by your aunt Kelsey Holdfast. She remains the patron of the university, despite her stepping down as Herald. We disseminate knowledge, and bring together the best young minds from across the allied worlds. A time of rapid change is nearly upon us, or so I would like to believe, and that change shall be powered by coal and steam. Tell me; are the Holdfasts investing in these new technologies?'

Kyra narrowed her eyes. 'I don't know.'

They came to a halt by an open doorway, from where laughter was emanating. Kyra gazed into the classroom.

'They were a complete success, I tell you,' Ravi was saying to an unimpressed-looking Elbannon, 'and I have orders to build as many as possible. We're going to be expanding into bigger premises; but, do you know my problem?'

Elbannon raised an eyebrow. 'I am sure you are about to tell me.'

'Production cannot keep up with design,' said Ravi. 'Every model we build is already obsolete by the time it has been finished, because the improvements we are making far outpace the manufacturing process.'

Elbannon sighed and turned to Gallea. 'Professor Ravi would like to talk to you about steam.'

'I do, indeed,' said Ravi, his eyes glowing with enthusiasm. 'I was wondering, Gallea, how your steam contraptions might be used to speed up production of my... my designs.'

'Your killing machines?' said Kyra.

Ravi blinked, as he noticed Kyra standing next to Gallea.

'What was a complete success?' Kyra went on. 'Your Forty-Eighters? Where have they been used?'

'That information is confidential,' said Ravi, 'and you, I'm afraid, no longer have permission to access the work I do.'

Kyra smiled, and went into his mind. She delved through his recent memories, and found the news he had been told by Herald Brogan that morning. The Herald had returned from Dragon Eyre, to report that the imperial fleet had wiped out three dozen dragons in fifteen minutes, blowing them out of the sky in a hailstorm of explosions. The Herald had also ordered Ravi's department to step up production of his latest designs, making Ravi almost giddy with pride and excitement.

'How sad,' said Kyra, 'that you take such pleasure in death and destruction, Professor Ravi.'

Ravi glared at her. 'The work I do protects the men and women, and dragons, of the imperial armed forces. My work saves lives.'

'Your devices slaughtered three dozen dragons.'

'Those dragons were about to sink the imperial fleet,' said Ravi, getting angry. 'They would have killed hundreds... no, thousands of sailors and marines, including your brother, Miss Holdfast. Would you rather he had died?'

Kyra frowned. 'What are you talking about?'

'Your brother,' Ravi went on. 'Cael Holdfast was posted to Dragon Eyre, to join the invasion of Na Sun Ka. Didn't you know that?'

Kyra said nothing.

'Commander Laimos reported that your brother assisted his team in the raids upon the coast,' Ravi said. 'His powers have come in very useful. It was Cael who alerted the fleet to the presence of the attacking dragons, giving the crews of the ships enough time to prepare the Forty-Eighters. I hear he is in line for a commendation from the Empress.'

Elbannon chuckled. 'The poor girl seems a little lost for words.'

'Leave her be,' said Gallea. 'She is clearly in shock at the thought of her brother's life being in peril.'

'She should be proud,' said Ravi. 'Cael's actions saved a good portion of the fleet.'

Kyra turned without a word, and walked away from the classroom, her heart troubled and her mind racing. She remembered reading Brogan's mind, when she had discovered that the Empire was about to attack Na Sun Ka. She had been so excited to learn the news that she hadn't stayed to find out which marines were being sent.

She hurried down the stairs, and saw Dazi waiting for her at the bottom.

'How was Professor Gallea's class?' the Rakanese student said.

'My brother is on Dragon Eyre,' Kyra said. 'He's with the marines taking part in the invasion.'

Dazi glanced around. 'Are we allowed to talk about that? I thought Professor Achan told us to keep it quiet until it had been officially announced.'

'I don't care,' said Kyra. 'My brother... he's using his powers to help the Empire slaughter the inhabitants of Na Sun Ka.'

'Do you want to sit down and talk about it?' said Dazi. 'We could go to the canteen.'

Kyra shook her head. 'I'm meeting Larron. We're going to his parents' tavern for dinner.'

Dazi laughed. 'Meeting his parents, eh?' she said. 'It must be serious.'

'I'm not in the mood for jokes.'

'I didn't mean anything by it. I'm sure your brother will be all right.'

Kyra nodded. 'I'll catch up with you later.'

She walked out of the building and entered the quad, which was full of students who had finished their lessons for the day. Larron was standing by the archway that led out on to the main street that ran by the university.

'Hi, Larron,' she said, as she glanced around. 'Are we taking a carriage to the Kellach Quarter?'

'I thought we'd walk,' he said. 'It's a beautiful spring afternoon and the flowers are out; but, if you like, we can hail a carriage.'

'No. We can walk.'

Larron narrowed his eyes at her. 'Is everything all right? You seem upset about something.'

'Let's start walking,' she said.

They went under the archway and left the grounds of the university. They took the road leading to the Old Town, while Larron remained silent, waiting for her to speak.

'You know that my brother is in the marines, aye?' Kyra said, as they passed through the open gates into the narrow streets of the Old Town.

'Aye,' said Larron.

'He's been sent to Dragon Eyre for his first commission.'

Larron puffed out his cheeks. 'That's a tough one. He'll have veterans around him, though, to give him advice. I hope he has decent sergeants.'

'I think you might be missing the point,' said Kyra. 'My brother is just another killer in uniform, doing the bidding of the imperialists who run the Empire.'

Larron glanced at her. 'Who else but imperialists would run an Empire? We shouldn't blame the ordinary men and women who enlist, but. Listen; before we get to my parents' tavern, you should know that they both served in the armed forces. They met while they were in the army, then my father went on to become one of the first marines. He joined as soon as the marine division was founded, twenty years ago, just after I was born. You might have to temper your language in their presence.'

Kyra glared at him. 'I thought you loathed everything the Empire stands for?'

'I do, but that's because I believe the nature of the Empire has changed over the last decade. It wasn't always so aggressive and expansionist. My parents are proud of serving under Empress Bridget, and they both have a soft spot for Empress Thorn. They know that I am opposed to the annexation of Rahain and Rakana, but I have to tread a careful line not to offend them. Does that make me sound like a hypocrite? Maybe I am, but I don't believe we will change the minds of the older generation by ranting to them about the wickedness of imperialism.'

Kyra glanced away, then she noticed the angry expressions on a group of people gathered around a newspaper seller, who was standing on a street corner. The mixture of Holdings, Rakanese and Kellach were staring down at the newspapers they had bought, and were complaining bitterly about something.

'What's going on?' Kyra said.

Larron stepped down from the pavement. 'Let's find out.'

They walked over to the seller, and bought a newspaper for a few pennies. It was a late edition, and consisted of a single sheet, printed on both sides. Larron and Kyra walked to a quieter part of the street, and then they both glanced down at the headline on the front page.

*Marines on Dragon Eyre*, it stated, in large, bold letters.

*Imperial forces go to the aid of Queen Blackrose*, the line underneath read.

'Is that why everyone's angry?' said Kyra. 'Are the people finally realising how corrupt and evil the Empire has become?'

Larron looked doubtful, and he turned the sheet over to glance at the back page.

*All Taxes Rise*, said the headline.

'I think this might be the source of their rage,' Larron said. 'Custom duties, taxes on alcohol, food and clothing, shipping dues, land taxes, the imperial levy – all of it is going up. This will hurt the people more than any announcement of war on a foreign world. Are we really on the verge of bankruptcy?'

'I told you that a while ago.'

'Aye, but now they're admitting it in public. Nothing gets printed in the official newspaper without it having been sanctioned by the Imperial Chamberlain. I wonder why they decided to print both pieces of news in the same edition.'

'The taxes will distract people from the war,' she said.

He nodded. 'I think you might be right.'

'But can't people see that the two are connected? The taxes are to pay for the damn war on Dragon Eyre.'

Larron turned the sheet back over, and they read what had been printed about the war.

'It only mentions a few thousand marines being sent,' Larron said. 'That wouldn't drain the treasury dry. And look – your brother's name has been printed. *Lieutenant Cael Holdfast of the Imperial Marines, son of Karalyn Holdfast, is proud to serve in Her Majesty's armed forces, having recently graduated from the Pebble Strand training facility.* They want people to know that a Holdfast is in uniform.'

'They are using my brother as propaganda.'

'We'll take the newspaper to the tavern,' Larron said. 'Let's see what my parents make of it.'

Larron folded the newspaper and placed it into a pocket of his outer coat, then they set off again.

They walked for thirty minutes, passing through the Old Peasant District, and entering the Kellach Quarter. On their left, the huge construction site of the new palace loomed up above the horizon, dominating the centre of the city. Dozens of workers could be seen high up on the wooden scaffolding, as the building slowly took shape. Down on the streets, the atmosphere among the citizens was angry, as small clusters of people gathered round whoever had bought a copy of that afternoon's special edition.

Larron guided Kyra through the wide streets of the Kellach Quarter until they came to a large, three-storey stone tavern, with an extensive walled garden to its rear, which was full of people eating and drinking among the trellises in the sunshine.

'This is it,' said Larron. 'The *One-Eared Goat*; don't ask. Come on; I'll take you inside.'

Kyra followed him through a gate and into the walled garden. Long tables stretched under the trellises of vines and roses, and several young waiters and waitresses were delivering huge trays of ale and food to the customers. Almost everyone was Kellach, but there were a few Holdings seated among the others, and two Sanang men were sitting by themselves in a corner, smoking dreamweed while they ate their dinner. Larron led Kyra to the back of the building, and they entered a packed bar area.

'It's so busy,' said Kyra.

'Business is good,' said Larron. 'My brother is behind the bar; we'll tell him we've arrived.'

They walked up to the long bar, and Larron shouted for attention. A Kellach man who looked a lot like Larron saw him, smiled, and approached.

'Kyra,' said Larron, 'this is Larig, my twin. Larig, this is Kyra.'

'Good afternoon, gorgeous,' said Larig. 'I refuse to believe that my idiot brother is friends with a girl as beautiful as you are, especially when everyone knows that I'm the more handsome twin. Ale?'

'We're supposed to be meeting Ma and Da for dinner,' Larron said.

'They're upstairs,' said Larig. 'Go up, and I'll bring food and ale in a few minutes.'

Larig winked at Kyra, then he laughed as Larron led her towards the stairs.

'Is your brother always like that?' she said.

'Aye. You get used to it.'

They climbed the stairs, and entered a small, private dining room, where two middle-aged Kellach were sitting, a copy of that afternoon's newspaper laid out in front of them.

They looked up, and the woman stood.

'Our boy is here,' she said, kissing her son on the cheek.

'Hi, Ma,' he said.

'Did ye walk?' said his father.

'Aye.'

'Good lad,' he said. 'And this must be Kyra Holdfast, aye?'

'These are my parents, Kyra,' said Larron said.

Kyra tried to master her awkwardness. She had never met the parents of a potential boyfriend before, mostly because she had never had a boyfriend. She recalled the training in etiquette given by the Empress when she had adopted her and her brother.

'It is very nice to meet you both,' said Kyra, tilting her head.

'And so polite,' said Larron's father. 'Get yerselves seated.'

Kyra and Larron sat by the table.

'Larig told us he'd be bringing dinner up here soon,' said Larron.

'About time,' said Larron's father; 'I'm starving. What do ye think of the *Goat*, Kyra, hen?'

'It's wonderful,' said Kyra. 'So busy.'

'It'll no' be that way for long, but,' he said, gesturing to the newspaper. 'These tax rises are gonnae cripple us. What's the Empress up to, eh?'

'Dinnae talk about that,' said Larron's mother. 'We're no' here to discuss politics. Once Larron gets started on that, he never shuts up.'

'Aye, right enough.' The man glanced at Kyra. 'I hear yer brother's a marine, hen.'

'Aye,' said Kyra.

'Good on the lad, I say. The marines are the hardest bastards around, and I should know. I spent the best years of my life in the marines.'

'And ye've never stopped talking about it,' said Larron's mother. 'I couldnae join the marines, Kyra. I had just given birth to Larron and Larig when Herald Dyam founded them. She issued a call for veterans, and Lorrie here jumped at the chance.'

'I fought in Rainsby during the long siege, and in Stretton Sands,'

Lorrie said. 'Once, I saw Thorn healing a whole crowd of wounded marines, way back before she was Empress. Pyre's arsehole, we loved that lassie; we would have burned the world for her.'

'And now she's raised every tax in existence,' said Larron.

'More importantly, she has invaded Dragon Eyre,' said Kyra.

Lorrie shrugged. 'Queen Blackrose is our ally, hen. We cannae ignore that. She sent dragons to help us when the Ascendants invaded eight years ago. What kind of friend would we be if we turned her down when she needed us, eh?'

Larig appeared at the doorway, carrying a large tray. He walked into the dining room, followed by a young woman who was holding another tray. They set down dishes, plates, mugs, bottles and a tall jug of ale.

Larig smiled, as he took the lids off a few plates. 'Has Larron been droning on about politics yet?'

'He looked like he was just about to start, son,' said Lorrie.

Larron laughed. 'Someone in this family needs to pay attention to what's going on in the Empire.'

'That university has given ye some strange ideas, but,' his mother said.

'What do ye think of his pretty new friend?' said Larig.

Lorrie laughed. 'Time will tell.'

'Kyra is on the Student Council with me,' said Larron.

'Is that where ye met her?' said Larig. 'Have ye got a boyfriend, Kyra?'

Kyra shook her head.

'In that case,' said Larig, 'do ye fancy going out with me? I'm free tomorrow night.'

'Dinnae embarrass the lassie,' said his mother. 'Ye've already got about a dozen girlfriends, Larig.'

'There's no harm in playing the field, Ma. I'm keeping ma options open. Let me know if yer interested, Kyra. I'll show ye a far better time than ma eejit of a brother.'

Larig and the young woman left the dining room, and Lorrie began to fill four large mugs with ale.

'Dig in,' said Larron's mother.

They took plates and began to eat. Kyra tried to relax, but she was conscious that Larron's parents were attempting to discreetly study her.

'How many years have ye been at the university, hen?' said his mother.

'This is my third year,' she said, 'but I'll probably go back for a fourth.'

'And yer Karalyn's daughter, aye?'

'Aye.'

'She used to be the adopted daughter of the Empress,' said Larron, 'when Karalyn was missing.'

'Is that right?' said Lorrie. 'Pyre's tits.'

'Lorrie,' said his wife. 'That's enough of the language.'

'I was officially the Empress's daughter for almost two years,' said Kyra.

'Are ye still close to her?' said Lorrie.

'Not as close as we used to be.'

'That's an awful shame. If ye were still close, then ye could tell her what we think of her stupid bloody palace. It's nae wonder taxes are going up; they're all to pay for that big blue monstrosity she's building. Who needs to live in a house that big, eh? And who wants dragons living in the middle of a city? She hasnae thought it through.'

Kyra frowned. The cost of constructing the massive new Blue Palace took up a miniscule portion of the overall budget; a tiny amount compared to what was being spent on the military. She bit her tongue, resisting the temptation to point out Lorrie's mistake.

'Bridget managed with a tiny, wee palace,' Lorrie went on. 'Ye know, sometimes I think power might have gone to Thorn's head.'

'Bridget lived in the Great Fortress,' said Larron. 'That was hardly tiny, Da.'

'I was talking about before that, son. Bridget had a townhouse close to the Ministry of the Plateau; that was her first palace. Do ye mind it, Lena?'

'Aye,' said Larron's mother. 'It was an ordinary house. Bigger than most, but ye wouldnae call it a palace.'

Lorrie picked up another bottle from the table. 'I have a wee treat for ye. This has come all the way from Lach. After decades, the auld country is making whisky again.'

'Kyra knows about Lach whisky, Da,' said Larron. 'They serve it in a wee tavern in the Old Town.'

'Oh. Well, this is *Marchbrae Auld Deer*, a blend of four different Lach whiskies. Have ye tried it before, Kyra?'

'No,' she said.

Lorrie smiled, then he set down four glasses, opened the bottle, and poured out small measures into each. Kyra glanced at the bottle. She was aware that her Aunty Aila had created various blends for the market in the Plateau, and she also knew that *Auld Deer* was among the cheapest. They picked up their glasses.

'To Lach,' said Lorrie, raising his glass.

They drank, and Kyra suppressed a grimace at the harsh taste. It was stuff that Shella would have flushed down the toilet in Colsbury, and Kyra realised that she had only ever drunk the most expensive whiskies produced at Clackenbaird and Severton.

'What do ye think?' said Lorrie.

'I think it's fabulous,' said Kyra, taking a swig of ale to remove the taste from her mouth.

They ate, drank and talked for a couple of hours, and Kyra could feel herself getting drunker by the minute. At one point, when Larron and Lorrie left the room to visit the toilets, Larron's mother leaned over the table towards her.

'So, what's going on, then?' Lena said.

Kyra raised an eyebrow, as she tried to assemble her whisky-addled thoughts.

'Between you and ma son?' said the woman. 'Do ye... like him?'

Kyra laughed, then she realised that Lena wasn't joking. 'Uh, aye. I like him.'

'Do ye know much about him, hen?'

'Aye. Larron helped me get voted onto the Student Council, and we've met up every day since; but just to talk, or get a coffee; or go for a walk. He hasn't asked me out.'

'Aye, well, I wouldnae hold yer breath waiting for that to happen, hen.'

Kyra frowned, unable to grasp what she was being told.

'Ye seem like a nice enough lassie,' Lena said, 'even if ye are a wee bit quiet; but yer family is... well, everyone knows that the Holdfasts are the richest and most powerful folk on the Star Continent. Why would ye be interested in being friends with the son of a tavern-owner?'

'I, uh...'

'Ye know,' Lena went on, 'I cannae work out if yer just shy, or if maybe yer a wee bit stuck up. I saw yer face when ye drank ma husband's whisky. Whatever ye thought of it, it certainly wasnae *fabulous*.'

Kyra said nothing.

'Maybe you need to be a wee bit more honest with us, and with yerself, hen,' said Lena. 'Yer a Holdfast, aye? Act like one.'

She closed her mouth as Larron and his father returned to the table. Lorrie belched as he sat, then he reached for the bottle of whisky.

Larron eyed Kyra. 'Are you all right? What was my Ma saying to you?'

'She's just a wee bit drunk, son,' said Lena. 'She's no' used to gulping down whisky at this hour of the day.'

'I, uh... I have a confession to make,' Kyra said.

The others fell silent and waited for her to speak.

'My aunt and uncle own Marchbrae,' Kyra went on. 'I didn't want to say anything, because it sounds like I'm bragging, but my aunt and uncle own several Lach distilleries, including the four that make the whisky that goes into *Auld Deer*. Marchbrae is the name of the hill next to where they live, in a place called Clackenbaird. Have you heard of my Uncle Corthie?'

Lorrie stared at her, then Larron began to laugh.

'Corthie makes whisky?' said Lorrie, his eyes wide.

'Well, his wife does,' said Kyra, her speech becoming slurred. 'No, she doesn't actually make it. She blends it, stores it, and sells it to the Plateau. I could take you there to visit the distilleries.'

'It takes six thirds to get to Kellach Brigdomin and back, hen.'

Kyra glanced down. 'Not if, eh... not if you have a Quadrant.'

Lena narrowed her eyes. 'Now ye sound like yer bragging, hen.'

'I'm not,' she said. 'I'm trying to be honest. I grew up in palaces – on Colsbury, the Hold Fast estate, and here in Plateau City; but now I'm trying to live a normal life. The Empress doesn't speak to me any more because I disagreed with her, but I'll always be a Holdfast. Nothing I ever do will change that.'

The others said nothing, and Kyra worried that she had said too much. Her mood turned again, and she began to feel sorry for herself.

'I envy what you have,' she went on. 'My life has been filled with violence and fighting, from the day I was born. My father, my Aunt Jemma and Uncle Keir, my grandparents – they were all murdered by gods, and my mother has spent half of my life elsewhere. I would swap all of the palaces and wealth to have had a loving family when I was growing up; to have what you have.'

Lorrie and Lena glanced at each other.

'Sorry,' said Kyra. 'I didn't mean to bring everyone down. Maybe I've had too much to drink.'

'The whisky making ye melancholy, eh?' said Lorrie. 'Not to worry, hen. Yer among friends here.' He smiled at her. 'I might take ye up on yer offer, though. A wee trip to Kell and Lach? I've never been, not once in ma life. Could ye really take us?'

'Aye,' said Kyra. 'Do ye want to go now?'

'Maybe another time, hen,' said Lena. 'Larron, I think ye should take Kyra home. She shouldnae be drinking any more. Take her home and make her a strong coffee.'

Larron gazed at Kyra. 'Do you want to go back to the university?'

Kyra nodded.

'I'll call ye a carriage,' said Lena.

'No need,' said Kyra. She got to her feet, and swayed. 'It was lovely to meet you both,' she said. 'Thanks for all the food and drink.'

'Yer welcome here any time,' said Lorrie.

Kyra glanced down at Larron. 'You'd better stand up.'

Larron frowned, then he rose to his feet. 'Why?'

Kyra touched the surface of the Quadrant through the hole in her pocket.

*My room, the university. Go.*

The air shimmered, then she and Larron appeared in her bedroom in the accommodation block of the university.

Larron blinked. 'Pyre's arse; where are we? Wait – is this your room?' He walked to a window and gazed out. 'We're back at the university.'

Kyra sat down on the bed, her head swimming.

Larron turned to look at her. 'You weren't joking about having a Quadrant, then,' he said.

She shrugged. 'Why do you want to be my friend?' she said. 'I'm a drunken mess.'

'I happen to think that you're wonderful, Kyra. Your family, on the other hand...'

'Most of them are mass murderers. Even my mother. And now my brother is about to join their ranks. I can't stand it, Larron. I thought Cael was better than that. The Empire will use him to kill. If you had any sense, you'd stay away from me. The Holdfasts are a poison.'

He sat down on the bed next to her. 'Whatever your family has done, Kyra, that doesn't mean you will turn out to be the same as the rest of them. You're intelligent, beautiful, confident – you could be anyone you wanted to be.'

She stared at him, then she reached out, pulled his face towards her, and kissed him. Their lips came together for a few moments, then he got back to his feet, and gently pushed her arm away.

'I don't think this is a good idea, Kyra,' he said. 'You're too drunk to know what you're doing. I should go. Will you be all right?'

Kyra said nothing, as humiliation spread over her.

He walked to the door, his gaze still on her.

'I'll find Dazi,' he said. 'I'll find her and ask her to come up to see you.' He attempted a smile. 'The next time we go out, we probably shouldn't drink so much.'

He left the room and closed the door. Kyra lay down on the bed, curled up, and began to weep, for the embarrassment, for her family, but, most of all, for her brother.

# CHAPTER 14
# BOOTS ON THE GROUND

**Off Na Sun Ka, Western Rim – 11th Nethinch 5266 (18th Gylean Year 17)**

Cael's vision snapped back to his head, and he turned to face the large group of officers from the navy and marines who had assembled on the carrier's long flight deck.

'The landing site to the east of Sun Ta is clear, Captain,' he said, 'as is the harbour area. The Unk Tannic appear to have retreated to the district where the twelve temples are located.'

The senior officers nodded.

'Thank you, Lieutenant,' said the captain of the dragon carrier.

'What about the Wystian dragons?' said a major from the marines.

'They have also retreated, sir,' said Cael. 'They have gathered on the southern edge of the city.'

'Lord Sigum and I will keep them there,' said Lahnos. 'I recommend that the landing goes ahead.'

'I tend to agree,' said the colonel in overall command of the marines; 'however, the raids have been more successful than we had been anticipating, and so I want our plans to be more ambitious. Instead of landing all five battalions on the beach to the east of the city,

I intend to send two of them directly to the harbour, to capture the waterfront defences, and to secure the area so that we can start landing supplies. This is an opportunity we cannot afford to miss.'

'Should we be dividing our forces, Colonel?' said the captain of the dragon carrier. 'The objective of the landings is to secure a site to open a portal, which will allow the army to enter Na Sun Ka.'

'Then we risk the harbour being overrun with fleeing Unk Tannic soldiers,' said the colonel. 'If the enemy is in disarray, there is no need to be so cautious. By sunset, both the portal site and the harbour will be in our hands.' He glanced at Lahnos. 'Would you be willing to divide your dragon team, Commander? Three dragons could be assigned to each landing group – one to cover the beaches, and the other to cover the harbour.'

'I can do it,' said Lahnos, 'but I will be able to use the Gift of Pain in only one of those two locations.'

Cael glanced at the faint line of lights coming from the large city of Sun Ta. Over to the east, the dawn was still an hour away, while, to the south of the carrier, the troopships and their escort of frigates were ready to sail.

'If you and Lord Sigum were to cover the beaches, Commander,' said the colonel, 'then Lieutenant Holdfast's battalion should be one of those sent to the harbour. If they encounter serious opposition, he can contact you to request assistance.'

'I think we should keep to the original plan,' said the captain of the carrier.

The colonel smiled. 'The marines are trained to adapt to changing circumstances, Captain,' he said. 'This is one of those times, and I am the operational commander. I'm giving the order – Battalions One and Two shall sail for the harbour, and secure the quayside and piers; while Battalions Four, Five and Six shall land at the beach, then move west to the designated portal site.' He turned to his majors. 'See to it at once.' He glanced at the captain of the carrier. 'And if you could order the escort of frigates to also divide, Captain, I would be much obliged.'

'I will give the orders, Colonel,' said the captain.

The officers dispersed, and Cael and a few others followed the major of their battalion as he made his way below decks. They went to an open hatch near the water line, and boarded one of the small launches that the carrier had brought along. The other majors were doing the same thing, each returning to their troopships to begin the landings, and several launches set sail under the dark sky.

The major glanced at Cael as their vessel sailed towards their anchored troopship.

'The colonel is taking a risk,' the major said, 'but I am confident that we shall succeed. I am giving you the responsibility of alerting me if enemy forces concentrate against us in the harbour area, Lieutenant. If that occurs, you will also alert Commander Laimos, and request his immediate assistance. Is that clear?'

'Aye, sir,' said Cael.

'It's a lot to place upon the shoulders of a newly-graduated officer,' the major went on. 'Try not to get yourself killed.'

The major walked away to speak to a few of his other officers, leaving Cael alone to stare out at the calm sea.

The troopships raised their anchors one hour later. A breeze was coming from the north-east, and the ships' sails filled as they began to move off towards the coast of Na Sun Ka. Cael had been ordered to remain up on deck, so that he could use his powers to keep watch on the harbour area of the city of Sun Ta. Over to the east, three of the troopships separated from the other two, and sailed away in the direction of the long beaches, taking two frigates with them to act as escorts. Cael's Kellach first lieutenant saw him standing by the railings, and approached.

'I hear there's been a change of plan, Holdfast,' he said. 'Are we going to the harbour?'

'Aye, sir.'

The first lieutenant shook his head. 'After we'd been preparing for a beach landing for days. Bloody typical. Did the senior officers say why?'

'The colonel thinks it would be a wasted opportunity if we don't, sir.'

'Do you know what I think? The colonel wants to save the harbour from the mess the fucking Sanang are going to make of the city.'

'The Sanang, sir?'

'You heard me. Have you served with the Sanang before?'

'No, sir.'

'They're the best assault troops in the Empire,' he said. 'Utterly fearless, and extremely aggressive. They are also undisciplined and savage. I saw what they did to Tahrana City a while back. As soon as they emerge from the portal, they're going to sweep through Sun Ta in a hailstorm of blood and destruction; and I reckon the colonel intends to make sure that the harbour is in our hands, to prevent the Sanang from burning it to the ground. Of course, this is between me and you, Holdfast. Don't be gossiping this to your sergeants.'

'My sergeants have also served with the Sanang before, sir. They might have already reached the same conclusion.'

'Aye; they might.'

'Why does the Empire employ the Sanang, sir, if they have no discipline?'

'Because, lad, no one can stand up to them. Well, no one except the marines. They're all criminals; did you know that? The bloody Matriarch of Sanang sends the murderers of that country off to join the army, rather than keep them in prison. And the Empress, well, she's Sanang, isn't she? She doesn't want to upset her own people.'

'Will it definitely be Sanang who come through the portal, sir?'

'That's my bet. If I'm wrong, I'll buy you a beer when the harbour is ours.'

They watched as the harbour walls drew closer. The other troopship heading to the harbour was on their starboard side, and their two frigate escorts were sailing on either flank, their Forty-Eighters aimed up at the sky, where two dragons from Lord Sigum's team were patrolling.

'I'm going to do one last scan of the harbour before we dock, sir,' said Cael.

The first lieutenant nodded, then he leaned against the railings of the troopship.

Cael allowed his vision to rise up from his body. The sun had yet to make its appearance on the horizon to their left, and the piers and quayside were shrouded in darkness. Most of the ships in the basin had been sunk by the repeated dragon raids, and the entire area looked abandoned. Several of the harbour front buildings had also been damaged in the raids, and smoke was still rising from one large warehouse. To the left of the harbour, the military base had been razed to the ground, and appeared to be deserted.

Cael pulled back his vision, and blinked.

'Anything?' said the first lieutenant.

'No, sir,' said Cael. 'If any Unk Tannic are still in the harbour, they're keeping themselves well hidden.'

'Then get back to your platoon, before they forget who you are. When you hear the whistle, disembark from the port side. Our company will be among the first to land.'

'Aye, sir.'

Cael went to a hatch, and descended into the lamp-lit interior of the vessel. He walked through the tight press of marines until he found his platoon. The two sergeants saluted as he approached.

'Five minutes,' said Cael, as he gazed at the marines he would be leading. Each one of them was standing, and they all had their equipment, armour and weapons ready. There were two Holdings marines with battle-vision, but the rest were all Kellach Brigdomin.

'What are our objectives, sir?' said a sergeant.

'We are to occupy and secure the entire harbour area,' said Cael. 'We'll be assigned to our positions as we disembark. The harbour looks empty, but there might be Unk Tannic hiding among the buildings, or in the narrow lanes behind the waterfront.'

A marine captain appeared on the stairs. 'First Company!' he cried. 'Make your way to the port side of the main deck. We are about to land.'

Cael nodded to his platoon, and they joined the others from First Company, as they made their way up the stairs and onto the main deck of the troopship. The vessel had entered the deserted harbour, and was edging towards a long pier. The hundred marines of the company waited until the troopship bumped against the pier, then a whistle blasted, and they clambered off the ship and onto the wooden beams of the pier.

The marine captain gestured to Cael's immediate superior. 'Lieutenant, take your company to the edge of the quayside and secure the base of the pier.'

'Aye, sir,' said the Kellach first lieutenant. He nodded to his junior officers, and the marines moved off at a slow run, heading down the pier towards the solid, stone quayside.

The company fanned out at the base of the pier, and took up positions by the warehouses and buildings that lined the quayside, as the other companies disembarked from the two troopships.

'So far, so good,' muttered one of Cael's sergeants, as he peered over a low wall.

A squad of twelve marines to their right entered one of the large harbourside buildings, and, a moment later, a huge explosion blew out its doors and windows, followed by a great cloud of dust. Four wounded marines staggered back out through the shattered doorway, then one fell to the cobbles.

'Stay where you are!' cried the first lieutenant. 'The Unk Tannic have set traps. Do not enter the buildings.'

The company settled down, as the wounded were pulled out of the damaged structure. By then, every marine from the two troopships had disembarked, and the entire quayside was occupied. A few senior officers came to look at the building where the bomb had gone off, then fresh orders were issued.

'We're going into the alleyways,' said the first lieutenant, as he returned to his company. 'We're going to push into the city until we reach a large, circular plaza, and then we'll form a perimeter and hold our ground. Go.'

The company divided into its four platoons, and they set off, with each platoon taking a different alleyway. Cael led his platoon into the narrow lane, the thick shadows making it difficult to see anything.

A crossbow bolt skittered off the cobbles a few yards to his left, and the marines in his platoon looked up.

'Take cover,' said Cael.

'The bastards are loosing from the roof of that warehouse, sir,' said a sergeant.

Cael gazed up at the warehouse roof, and saw a few figures aiming crossbows down into the alleyway.

'I'll deal with them,' said Cael.

He powered his vision, and soared it up to the flat roof. He entered the minds of the three Unk Tannic soldiers.

*Sleep.*

The three men toppled over. One had been standing too close to the edge of the roof, and he plummeted down into the alleyway, his body striking a low wall and then the cobbles.

A few of the marines stared at the body, then at Cael.

The platoon moved on, and they reached the end of the alleyway, where it opened out onto the large plaza. The trees that had stood there had been burned in the fires caused by the dragon raids, and their blackened stumps were poking up into the slowly-brightening sky.

'This is where we stop,' said Cael, as he gazed over the open space of the plaza. 'Shields to the front; form a barrier.'

The four marines who were carrying large shields made their way through the platoon. They stopped at the end of the alleyway, and raised their shields to block most of its width. Cael used his vision to check on the locations of the other three platoons of his company. They, too, had reached the ends of their respective alleys, and all four were occupied. On either flank of the company, more marines were moving into position, sealing off the streets that led to the harbour. One of the frigates had weighed anchor in the middle of the harbour basin, its Forty-Eighters aimed over the city. Cael moved his vision several miles to the east, and saw the three other troopships unloading their marines onto the long, flat beach, next to rows of swaying palm trees. Above them, Lahnos and Sigum were circling over the beaches, guarding the marines as they landed.

Cael brought his vision back, and peered out into the plaza, searching for movement from the streets and buildings on the other side. Nothing.

'The Wystian dragons must know we're here by now,' said a corporal. 'Where are they?'

'The Gift of Pain has scared them all away,' said a sergeant.

The other sergeant narrowed his eyes. 'The last time you said everything was fine, a bomb took out half a squad.'

The first sergeant shrugged. 'I'm going to be right one of these times.'

The platoon remained in position as the sun rose over the city of Sun Ta. As the hours passed, Cael made use of his powers to relay the locations of the other marine battalions to the marine commanders based in the harbour. Over to the east, the landings on the beach had been completed, and the three battalions were making their way to the edge of the city, where the twelve huge temples lay. By the harbour, the two battalions that had landed by the pier were blocking every route that led to the quayside, where the colonel in command had set up his forward headquarters.

When the sun reached its zenith, Cael sent out his powers again, to see if he could locate the Wystian dragons. He was moving his vision over the buildings and streets on the far side of the plaza, when he saw dozens of Unk Tannic soldiers clustered around five open-topped wagons, upon which small catapults had been fixed. The soldiers were placing cylindrical ceramic containers onto the arms of the catapults, while others were loading crossbows.

'Pull back,' Cael cried to the platoon. 'The Unk Tannic are about to loose explosives at us. Move.'

Several objects flew through the air, over the roofs of the buildings. They soared above the plaza then dropped into the alleyways where the marines were positioned. Explosions rocked the ground, as Cael's platoon scrambled back. A bomb landed a few yards away, tearing through a shop front that lay next to their alleyway, sending fragments of rubble in all directions. There was a guttural cry, and then Unk Tannic soldiers flooded across the plaza, loosing their bows into the defences of the marines, as more bombs landed.

A bomb exploded in the alleyway twenty yards to their rear, and the platoon took cover by the low walls. Above them, the air filled with small projectiles, hurled from the direction of the harbour.

'The Forty-Eighters have opened up,' cried a marine.

The projectiles rained down into the plaza, each one exploding upon impact, blowing dozens of the Unk Tannic to pieces. The range of one of the Forty-Eighters fell short, and several projectiles landed by the entrance to the alleyway, sending shrapnel into the air.

'We'll be cut to pieces if we stay here, sir,' shouted a sergeant.

Cael gazed up and down the alleyway. His platoon was pinned down, caught between the bombs coming from both directions. He looked at the sergeant, not knowing what to do.

As he stared at the sergeant, his vision clouded over. It was sunset, and he saw Lahnos shaking his hand; and Cael realised he was looking out from the sergeant's eyes at events that had yet to pass. The sergeant gazed around, and Cael saw every member of his platoon lined up, bar one. The only one missing was a young Kellach marine by the name of Batham.

Cael's vision cleared, and he knew exactly what to do.

'We're going to take out the enemy catapults,' he said to his platoon. 'If we don't, we'll be cut down in this alleyway.'

'But, sir,' said a sergeant, 'that would mean charging through the plaza, in range of the Unk Tannic and the Forty-Eighters.'

'I know,' said Cael, 'but we're going to do it anyway.' He glanced at the unsure faces, and saw Batham crouching close by, his loaded crossbow cradled in his arms.

'Follow me,' said Cael.

Batham was the first to obey. The young marine got to his feet, then a projectile from the Forty-Eighters struck his head and blew it off, showering the rest of the platoon in his blood. The headless body fell to the ground, and Cael stared at it.

'Follow me!' Cael shouted again. 'Kill anything that fucking moves.'

Cael drew his sword and ran into the circular plaza, powered by the knowledge that, no matter what he did, no more of his platoon would be dying that day. The sergeants led the rest of his platoon out, and they sprinted across the plaza as explosions went off on either side. Crossbow bolts flew past their heads, then over a dozen Unk Tannic soldiers emerged from a building, and charged into the platoon's flank. The marines loosed once, then they dropped their crossbows and drew their swords and maces. An Unk Tannic soldier swung an axe at Cael's head. Cael laughed as he dodged the blow, then he rammed the tip of his own sword into the soldier's face.

'With me!' Cael cried, raising his bloody sword amid the smoke, screams and explosions.

He charged into one of the streets leading away from the plaza, his platoon racing alongside, and they ran into the first wagon. Its catapult was being operated by four Unk Tannic soldiers, and the marines pulled them down from the wagon and butchered them on the cobbles, then they destroyed the catapult, smashing it to pieces. Cael sent his vision toward the harbour, and slammed it into the mind of the naval officer in charge of the Forty-Eighters on the frigate.

'Stop loosing!' Cael cried in the officer's mind. 'We are securing the Unk Tannic artillery. Cease loosing.'

'Who is this?' said the officer.

'Second Lieutenant Cael Holdfast, sir. We have destroyed one catapult, and we will do the same to the others within a few minutes, but not if your damn Forty-Eighters blow us to pieces.'

Cael withdrew from the officer's mind.

'There are four more wagons,' he said, as his platoon stared at him. 'I want them all.'

'You heard the Holdfast!' shouted a sergeant.

Cael led the platoon further into the streets of the city, until they reached a wide tree-lined avenue where the other four wagons were located. The marines were seen by the Unk Tannic soldiers guarding the wagons, and the two sides clashed in the street, the marines setting upon them before they could reload their crossbows. The Kellach marines, and the two Holdings marines with battle-vision, cut their way through the Unk Tannic, their maces and swords cleaving them to pieces. Cael leapt up onto the back of a wagon, heedless of any risk, and drove his sword into the chest of a soldier. More marines joined him, and they turned the catapult to face the three other wagons. Cael sliced through the tension ropes, and the catapult loosed, hurling its ceramic canister through the air towards the Unk Tannic. It landed in the midst of the three wagons, and the explosion set off the stockpile of bombs that had been sitting next to them.

The marines stayed back as smoke and flames belched up from the site where the three wagons had been, and Cael jumped down to the cobbles. A single, black-robed man with a canister strapped to his chest ran out from a side street and charged towards Cael.

'For the dragon spirits!' he cried, then one of the Holdings marines picked up a loaded crossbow. He aimed, and loosed. The bolt struck the canister, and the body of the Unk Tannic soldier was blown into a thousand pieces.

Another marine platoon charged into the street, then they came to a halt and gazed around at the carnage.

The first lieutenant strode through the drifting smoke.

'Holdfast,' he shouted; 'what the fuck did you think you were doing?'

Cael saluted. 'My platoon was destroying the Unk Tannic artillery, sir. All five catapults have been neutralised.'

The first Lieutenant shook his head. 'You are one lucky bastard,' he said. 'This is now the edge of our new perimeter.' He pointed. 'Seal off that street with what's left of the wagons, and get behind the barricade. Hold your lines, and no more running off without orders.'

'Aye, sir,' said Cael.

The Kellach first lieutenant shook his head again, then he half-smiled. 'Good job, though, lad.'

'Thank you, sir.'

The first lieutenant walked away, and the two platoons got to work. They dragged the undamaged wagon to the end of the road and pushed it onto its side, then they took up positions on the street leading back to the plaza.

When the barricade was ready, Cael took an offered water skin, and drank.

'That was... a little reckless, sir,' said one of his sergeants.

'It was worthy of Sable fucking Holdfast,' said the other. 'He's either going to get us all killed, or he's going to win the war on his own.'

The two platoons settled down. Sentries were posted by the barricade, while the others rested, sorted out their equipment, or ate a few of their rations. Two marines were sent back to the alleyway to recover Batham's body and take it to the harbour, while Cael used his powers to watch the progress of the three battalions that had landed by the beach.

As the sun was lowering in the western sky, Cael watched as the three battalions neared the first of the twelve huge temples. It was occupied by hundreds of Urok Tannic soldiers, who had taken up position behind its thick walls, and who were aiming their crossbows through the narrow, slit-like windows. The marine battalions came to a halt, remaining out of range, then Cael saw the air shimmer. A man in uniform appeared next to the marines, and spoke to their officers for a moment, then the man swiped his Quadrant, and a portal began to open in the wide square next to the first temple. The air in the portal darkened and swirled, then, as it cleared, armoured Sanang soldiers began charging through. The marines stood aside, while their officers gestured to the Sanang, showing them where to attack.

The Sanang soldiers formed up in the square, as hundreds poured through the portal, then they roared out a battle cry, and charged towards the temple.

Cael severed his vision connection, and glanced at the marines in his platoon.

'It's done,' he said. 'The portal is open, and the Sanang are here.'

Screams, smoke and flames billowed up from the southern edge of the city centre, from the location of the great temples, as the Sanang cut their way through Sun Ta. For the marines by the barricade, there had been nothing to do for hours except keep watch on the street ahead of them, but no Wystians or Unk Tannic had made any appearance.

As the sun began to set, Sigum flew overhead. He circled over Cael's position, then descended into the large, circular plaza. Cael got to his feet, and walked out from the barricade to meet the dragon. Lahnos climbed down from Sigum's shoulders. He raised an eyebrow at Cael, and approached.

'I've been hearing a few stories about your conduct today, Lieutenant,' Lahnos said. 'You scolded a senior officer on the frigate in the harbour, and you led a platoon that single-handedly destroyed five Unk Tannic catapults. Are you trying to get yourself court-martialled or killed?'

'Neither, sir.'

'Fortunately for you,' Lahnos went on, 'the marines are so happy with what you did, that the naval officer has decided not to press charges. I would suggest a small apology might not go amiss, though.'

'The only casualty in my platoon was caused by a Forty-Eighter, sir.'

'Is that right?'

'We were being hit by both sides, sir. There was nothing else I could have done.'

'It was a pity that we were not here to witness your deeds, Cael,' said Sigum, 'but Lahnos's Gift of Pain was needed to disperse the Unk Tannic by the portal site.'

'Thanks to you, Lieutenant,' said Lahnos, 'the colonel's ill-judged plan to divide his forces has paid off handsomely. The marines are in full control of the harbour, while the Sanang are storming through the rest of the city.'

'And the Wystians, sir?'

'I scattered them when they tried to attack the three battalions landing on the beaches. Look, Cael; while every marine is singing your praises, it falls to me to keep your feet on the ground. What am I supposed to tell your family if you get yourself killed through your own recklessness? You were exceptionally lucky today; will your luck always hold?'

'I will try to be more careful in future, sir.'

'There's a thin line between courage and stupidity; try to remember that. I want to speak to your platoon. Line them up.'

Cael led Lahnos to the side of the barricade, and he ordered his platoon to line up in their squads. Lahnos eyed them all, as the sun set to the west over the burning city, then he shook Cael's hand.

'Well done,' he said to the marines. 'Your courageous actions this day in the face of fierce resistance have secured the harbour's southern flank, and saved the lives of many of your comrades. The senior command wishes to express its thanks, and they want you to know that your destruction of the five catapults will be mentioned in the official report being sent to the Empress.'

The marines smiled.

'Thank you, Commander,' said Cael.

'You're being pulled back to the harbour for the night,' Lahnos went on, 'but you will be back on duty first thing in the morning. Dismissed.'

Cael nodded to his sergeants. 'Lead the platoon back to the harbour,' he said. 'I will join you in a moment.'

'Aye, sir,' said one.

Cael watched as the two sergeants led the marines away from the barricade, then he saluted as Lahnos walked back to Lord Sigum. Cael gazed down at his hands, but they were steady. People had kept saying that he had been lucky, but he knew that luck had played no part in his success. His vision had told him exactly who would, and who wouldn't survive from his platoon that day, but the sun had set, and the prophecy had been fulfilled. Cael realised that, for the first time in his life, one of his visions of the future had turned out to be useful rather than a curse. What if he had seen his entire platoon lying dead in their own blood? He shivered at the thought, and knew he would be unable to rely upon his visions. It would be better if no more appeared; better by far – they were too unpredictable, too uncertain.

He began to make his way along the road towards the harbour, trailing after the marines from his platoon.

One thing was certain, though – no matter what occurred in the future, no one would ever question his courage.

# CHAPTER 15
# BATTLE OF SUN TA

**Sun Ta, Na Sun Ka, Western Rim – 15th Nethinch 5266 (18th Gylean Year 17)**

Four Wystian dragons soared over the burning city of Sun Ta, flying straight towards Lord Sigum and his team. Two moved within Lahnos's range, and he gripped the harness on Sigum's shoulders with his left hand, while he raised the other and unleashed a long blast of the Gift of Pain. The two Wystians screamed and banked, retreating away from the temple district of the city. The other two dragons stayed out of Lahnos's reach, instead choosing to send fire down onto a convoy of wagons that was trying to reach the temples. The wagons exploded into flames, and Gallantmorn howled in frustration.

'We must stay together,' said Sigum. 'The Wystians are trying to distract us.'

Lahnos glanced down. The Sanang divisions were besieging three of the twelve huge temples, while another two had been gutted by fire. The Unk Tannic defenders inside the Temples of Haurn, Gyle and Geist were loosing bolts from high, narrow windows, while battering rams were being hauled over the large plaza that sat in front of the enormous structures. Thousands of Sanang had been trying to get into the last of the temples for four days, but the ancient and mighty walls had been keeping them out.

'More Wystians are coming,' bellowed Gallantmorn.

'Dozens of them!' cried Quicklime.

Sigum and the five dragons in his team circled over the besieged temples, protecting the Sanang soldiers, as a large wave of Wystians approached from the south. When they were still three hundred yards away, the Wystians began to disperse into smaller formations until they were approaching along a wide front.

'Their tactics have improved,' said Lahnos. 'They know the Gift of Pain can only be in one place at a time.'

Four formations, each containing three Wystian dragons, peeled off to the east, and soared down towards the harbour district, where the marines were still in control. The first formation swooped in low, spraying flames over the marines' strong points, before banking and retreating quickly. A hail of small projectiles hurtled up into the sky, loosed from the navy's Forty-Eighters, but the Wystians had fled, and the bombs fell into the streets of the city, setting off dozens of small explosions. The other three formations began blasting fire down at any imperial forces the Wystians could see. A roadblock burst into flames, killing several Holdings soldiers who had been there, then another convoy of wagons was targeted. The dragons swooped down at will, taking their time to ensure that every wagon was destroyed.

'They are trying to draw us away from the temples,' Lahnos shouted to the dragons in Sigum's team. 'Hold your positions! Defend the Sanang!'

Over a dozen Wystians grouped together into a tight cluster and surged towards Sigum's team in a blur of speed. Lahnos hit them with the Gift of Pain. Five Wystians screamed and pulled away, but the ones in the centre of the cluster reached Ochretail, a dragon from Ulna who had been on the edge of the group. The Wystians surrounded Ochretail, their teeth and claws ripping and slashing, then they scattered as Lahnos concentrated his Gift of Pain at them. One of the Wystians plucked Ochretail's rider from the red dragon's harness as they fled, then, as soon as they were out of Lahnos's range, they turned, and the dragon tore the rider to pieces.

Ochretail, his flanks covered in blood, and his wings ripped, screamed in rage at the sight, and charged at the Wystians. Ochretail slammed into a large green dragon, then the others were upon him again, and the green dragon ripped out his throat. Ochretail fell, lifeless, and crashed into the streets to the rear of the temples.

Sigum bellowed in anger, and his cries were taken up by Gallantmorn, Quicklime, and the other two from Sigum's team, as they gazed down at the body of their fallen comrade.

'Avenge brave Ochretail's death!' Sigum cried, before Lahnos could counsel restraint.

The five dragons protecting the Sanang soared off as one, charging into the Wystians, who scattered at their approach. Lahnos glanced around, but the Wystians were doing everything in their power to stay out of his range, wheeling back and forth, and fleeing if Sigum got too close. Unable to come to close quarters with the enemy, the five dragons banked, and Lahnos saw that four Wystians had taken advantage of their absence, and were pouring flames down onto the Sanang soldiers assaulting the three temples. Sigum raced back to the temples, and the four Wystians turned and fled.

In the plaza below them, dozens of Sanang soldiers were dead, their bodies smouldering, as the living gazed up and hurled insults and abuse at their defenders.

'What shall we do, Lahnos?' said Sigum. 'The tactics of the Wystians shall see us defeated this day. If we stay here, the Wystians shall pick us off one by one, and if we leave, the Imperial Army will be annihilated.'

'We do our job,' said Lahnos. 'We stay until the Sanang break into the last three temples.'

'The Temple of Geist looks set to fall any moment, said Sigum, 'but the other two could hold out for days.'

Lahnos glanced down again. The pink marble of the Temple of Geist was resplendent in the bright sunshine, but smoke was pouring from its shattered windows. Fierce fighting was going on by the temple's main entrance, which had been breached by a battering ram. The Sanang ranks charged, and began streaming into the entrance, driving through the barricades, and sweeping resistance aside. Lahnos turned his gaze to the two temples still in the hands of the Unk Tannic. The huge grey structure of the Temple of Haurn looked impregnable, but it was dwarfed in size by the enormous Temple of Gyle, with its three white towers.

The Wystians approached again. They had split into small, dispersed formations, and were attacking the supply routes that led from the harbour to the besieging Sanang divisions.

'They are mocking us!' cried Gallantmorn.

'And more are coming,' shouted Quicklime. 'Look!'

Lahnos turned, and saw a large group of over three dozen dragons soaring in from the mountains in the east of Na Sun Ka. He cursed under his breath, then he realised that the dragon leading the new group was huge, almost as large as Sigum, and she was black from tail to head.

'Queen Blackrose!' roared Gallantmorn. 'The queen is here!'

Blackrose led her dragons into the flank of the unsuspecting Wystians, and tore through their ranks, sending them fleeing in all directions. Two Wystians who were burning a roadblock were attacked from behind, and were ripped to shreds, their throats torn out. A few Wystians resisted the attack of Blackrose's forces, but they were overwhelmed, and the retreat turned into a rout, as the Wystians made their escape to the west.

Blackrose and her dragons roared out in triumph, then the great black dragon issued her orders. Most of her force split off, and took up positions circling over the edges of the city, while the others approached Sigum and the four remaining members of his team.

'Your Majesty!' cried Gallantmorn. 'You have saved us.'

Blackrose gazed down at the Sanang soldiers fighting in the plaza below them, then she looked at the Temple of Geist, from which flames were rising into the sky.

'Thank you for coming to our aid, Your Majesty,' said Sigum.

'It seems it was necessary,' said Blackrose. 'Eight dragons I lent to the Empire, and now, under your command, Sigum of Athumia, only four remain.'

'Three fell to a flow mage during the conflict on the Rakanese border, Your Majesty,' said Sigum, 'while Ochretail fell this day, to the Wystians.'

'Did the Empress believe six dragons would be enough to conquer Sun Ta?' said Blackrose. 'My kin and I have flown all the way from Ulna to be here. We imagined we would be attending a victory celebration, and instead we find three of the great temples in ruins, and a further two besieged.'

'The Wystians are fleeing to the west, Your Majesty,' said Gallantmorn. 'Should we pursue them?'

'No,' said Blackrose. 'Let them go. I do not wish to leave the city unprotected while the Unk Tannic are still occupying the Temples of Haurn and Gyle.'

'The Unk Tannic are also fleeing,' said Lahnos. He pointed towards the roads leading west out of the city, where columns of soldiers were streaming away.

'The sight of the Wystians abandoning them has snuffed out their spirits,' said Sigum.

'The Wystians will likely flee to Gyle,' said Gallantmorn, 'the next island of the Western Rim.'

There was a great crashing sound from below, followed by a roar. Lahnos looked down, and saw Sanang soldiers storming into the Temple of Haurn, its huge doors broken. Hundreds of Sanang charged into the interior amid screams and smoke. A few explosions went off inside the huge building, and a grey tower fell, crashing into a row of houses that sat to the rear of the temple.

The dragons from the Eastern Rim said nothing as they watched.

'That leaves none but the Temple of Gyle still holding out,' said Sigum. 'The battle for Sun Ta is drawing to a close.'

Blackrose glanced at her kin. 'Remain aloft and keep watch, in case any of the Wystians return. I shall descend into the harbour district, and speak to the leaders of the imperial forces.'

'I should go with you, Your Majesty,' said Sigum, 'to ensure that the naval officers in command of the imperial artillery do not mistake you for an enemy.'

Blackrose ignored Sigum, and soared off to the north.

'Stay here,' Sigum said to his team, then he flew after Blackrose.

Lahnos glanced to his left at the fleeing columns of defeated Unk Tannic soldiers filling the roads out of the city.

'The Wystians might retreat to Gyle,' he said, 'but the Unk Tannic will be trapped on Na Sun Ka.'

'I suspect the marines will be sent into the volcanic wilderness to hunt them down, my rider,' said Sigum.

'We've given the Empress what she wanted – a quick victory. Now, somehow, we have to restore law and order, and bring peace back to the island.'

'Will the Empress covet Gyle next, do you think?' said the dragon.

'Who knows?' said Lahnos. 'Doesn't it depend upon what Blackrose wants? With the Unk Tannic and the Wystians kicked out of Na Sun Ka, the Queen of the Eastern Rim might consider her southern border to be secure.'

'But who will rule Na Sun Ka?'

'That's another good question, Sigum, but it's one for the politicians.'

The silvery-green dragon descended in the warm sunshine, and followed Blackrose over the sprawling, ancient city of Sun Ta. Much of it had been reduced to rubble by the ferocity of the Sanang assault, and lines of bewildered civilians were queuing up in the dusty streets to receive handouts of food from the imperial army. To the north, the fleet had docked in the harbour of Sun Ta, which had remained in the tight grip of the marines, but the dragon carrier was too large to squeeze into the basin, and had remained anchored beyond the breakwaters, where it was being protected by four frigates.

'We should visit Cael,' said Sigum, as he flew towards the harbour, 'once our business with Blackrose is over.'

Lahnos frowned. 'I'm still annoyed with him for what he did when the marines landed. It was either the stupidest or the bravest thing I've heard of. What possessed him to lead a single platoon into the midst of the Unk Tannic?'

'He has the courage of the Holdfasts running through his veins.'

'Apart from one marine who got his head blown off before they had started their charge, not a single member of his platoon got so much as a scratch. How is that possible? And he's handed a wonderful piece of propaganda to the Empress. Her former adopted son, her nephew – the glorious hero of Sun Ta.'

'You sound a little envious, rider.'

'I'm not envious. I'm not serving the Empire for praise or medals; but I'm concerned about him. He acted without any consideration for his own safety, or the safety of his platoon. Do you remember what he was like when we knew him on Colsbury; did he strike you as reckless? I'm worried that all the adulation he's receiving will go to his head.'

'He was a young teenager when we knew him, Lahnos,' said the dragon. 'Clearly, he has changed.'

They caught up with Blackrose as she was about to descend over the quayside, and the two dragons landed side by side next to the docks. A company of marines was guarding the harbour front, and their officer approached Blackrose and Sigum.

'Lord Sigum,' said the lieutenant, 'have the Wystians departed?'

'They have,' said Sigum, 'thanks to the timely intervention of Queen Blackrose, who also stands before you.'

The officer eyed the black dragon, then he bowed his head. 'My apologies, Your Majesty; I had not recognised you.'

'Where are your commanders?' said Blackrose. 'My kin and I flew the great distance from Yearning yesterday, in order to observe what progress had been made by the Empress's armies. We did not realise that we would have to take part in a battle to rescue Sun Ta from Sigum's incompetence.'

The lieutenant glanced from Blackrose to Sigum, saying nothing.

'Lord Sigum had five dragons to oppose dozens of Wystians,' said Lahnos, his temper rising. 'Over the past ten days, he has achieved great things, despite being heavily outnumbered. It is a pity that your irrational dislike of him has blinded you to that simple truth, Queen Blackrose.'

Blackrose's eyes glowed red. 'Once again, horned wretch, you cast words of disrespect against me, when it was I who has just saved your miserable life.'

'Remind me why we are here,' said Lahnos. 'Was it not because you were unable to defend your own borders?'

'Remember that you are speaking to a queen, my rider,' said Sigum. 'I would be obliged if you showed Her Majesty some respect.' He turned to Blackrose. 'I would also ask that you, Your Noble Majesty, refrain from calling my rider a *horned wretch*. Lahnos has fought for days to defeat the Unk Tannic and the Wystians. If the pacification of Na Sun Ka was your objective, then you owe him an apology, and your gratitude.'

Blackrose bellowed with rage, and a few of the neighbouring buildings shook. More marines spilled out onto the quayside at the sound, and several senior officers approached from the structure being used as the marine headquarters. Among them were Lord Naxor, Lady Brogan and another man that Lahnos had seen a few times before – the Adjutant of the Empire, Martius Claudian.

'Honourable Blackrose,' said Naxor, bowing with a flourish. 'It is so good to see you here, great Queen of the Eastern Rim. Herald Brogan and I have arrived in time to discuss the future of this island.' He frowned. 'Do you need a moment to regain your composure?'

'Do not provoke me, demigod,' Blackrose said. 'When Brogan visited me on Ulna, she assured me that the city of Sun Ta would be in our hands by now. Why is there still fighting going on in the temple district?'

'The ancient dragon temples of Sun Ta are each as strong as a mighty fortress, Your Majesty,' said Naxor, 'and the last one shall fall by this evening, I can assure you of that. I see that you have already met Lord Sigum and Commander Lahnos, who have been instrumental in our success. Might some congratulations be in order, Your Majesty? Were it not for Lord Sigum and his team of Eastern Rim dragons, and Commander Laimos's Gift of Pain, the island of Na Sun Ka would still belong to your mortal enemies.'

Blackrose said nothing for a few long moments, then she glared at Naxor. 'Congratulations,' she said.

'I am honoured to be of service, Your Majesty,' said Sigum.

'Might I suggest,' said Naxor, 'that we retire somewhere to discuss the future of this island? Would the flight deck of the dragon carrier be a suitable location? There is a lovely cooling breeze up there.'

'That is acceptable,' said Blackrose.

'Do you wish to fly, or should I transport us all by Quadrant, Your Majesty?'

'I shall fly,' said Blackrose. 'I wish to land upon the carrier. You may use the Quadrant.'

Naxor bowed again, then he brushed his fingers down the surface of the Quadrant. The air shimmered, then he, Brogan, Claudian and the senior officers of the marines vanished.

'I will escort you to the carrier, Your Majesty,' said Sigum.

'If you must,' said Blackrose.

The two dragons took off from the quayside. They circled once over the harbour basin, then flew in the direction of the anchored carrier.

'Your world is extremely beautiful, Your Majesty,' Sigum said, as they passed the breakwaters.

'I know.'

'Have I offended you in some way, Your Majesty?'

'Your very presence offends me, Sigum of Athumia,' said the black dragon. 'And to think that the Empress placed you in charge of decent Eastern Rim dragons; what ignominy.'

'I am sorry you feel that way.'

'You should be sorry about a great many things, Athumian.'

The two dragons landed on the wooden beams of the dragon

carrier. Blackrose gazed down at the waiting Bullan, who were standing amid the sailors, and her red eyes burned.

'Is this the first time you have seen our Bullan support team, Your Majesty?' said Sigum.

'It is.'

'They have proved to be of great service to the dragons under my authority, Your Majesty.'

'I am sure they have,' said Blackrose.

Lahnos resisted the urge to say something as he unfastened the buckles and climbed down to the deck.

He nodded towards the Bullan. 'Lord Sigum and the Queen of the Eastern Rim are here to talk to the imperial staff,' he said. 'They do not require any assistance at the moment.'

'Congratulations on your victory, sir,' said Efizel. 'We watched the Wystians break and flee from here. It was a marvellous sight.'

Maddie Jackdaw clambered down from Blackrose's shoulders. She joined Lahnos, then they followed the two dragons as they walked towards the end of the deck, where Naxor, Brogan, Claudian and the officers were sitting in a wide semi-circle.

'How are you, Maddie?' said Lahnos.

'Me?' she said. 'I'm fine, and don't worry about old grumpy chops; she's still embarrassed that she called Sigum a liar back in Colsbury. And she won't admit it, but she's really impressed by these dragon carrier ships. They are amazing, eh? I didn't think it was possible to build a boat this big. Anyway, how are you? Has the fighting been hard?'

'It was easy at first,' he said. 'The raids went well, and the landings were successful, but the Wystians changed their tactics when they learned more about the Gift of Pain. At first, it confused them, as they didn't understand where it was coming from. As soon as they realised I was responsible, they avoided Sigum, and attacked everywhere else.'

'The Empire has made a right mess of the city,' said Maddie. 'Half the buildings are destroyed, and the temples are... well, you know. That will upset a lot of people. The temples are sacred, and five of them are now ruined.'

'I wish there could have been another way to take Sun Ta,' said Lahnos, 'but the Unk Tannic barricaded themselves inside the temples. Any damage to them is their responsibility.'

They reached the curved line of chairs, and a marine officer gestured to a couple of free seats that were close to the dragons, who were standing by the open end of the semi-circle. Lahnos glanced down the line of officers and officials, as he and Maddie sat. He nodded his greetings at a few, then he noticed Cael Holdfast sitting among them. Brogan got to her feet.

'Greetings, Queen Blackrose,' she said. 'The Empire has done as you requested, Your Majesty. We have driven your enemies from Sun Ta, and eliminated the threat to your realm that they represented.'

'You have not quite driven all of my enemies away,' said Blackrose. 'The Temple of Gyle remains in the hands of the Unk Tannic, despite your earlier assurances, Herald of the Empire.'

Cael Holdfast got to his feet. 'Your Majesty,' he said, 'I am pleased to announce that the Imperial Army has just broken into the Temple of Gyle. The last of the enemy redoubts in Sun Ta has fallen.'

There was a smattering of applause, but Blackrose looked almost put out by the news.

'Thank you, Lieutenant Holdfast,' said Brogan, as Cael sat again. 'Those are indeed welcome tidings. I would be obliged if you kept watch on the movements of the Wystian dragons who have fled to the west. They may decide to continue onwards to Gyle.'

'I will, ma'am,' said Cael.

'And what about the Unk Tannic?' said Blackrose. 'The Empire's work upon Na Sun Ka will not be finished until the last of those robed fanatics has been put to death.'

'The task of eliminating the remnants of the Unk Tannic will be carried out by the Imperial Marines,' said Brogan. 'As soon as hostilities upon Na Sun Ka are at an end, the Empire will withdraw the Sanang divisions and the marine battalions back to the Star Continent.'

'Then who will be left here to garrison the island, Herald?' said Blackrose.

'We will be handing Na Sun Ka over to your authority, Your Majesty,' said Brogan. 'Our job was to defeat your enemies, not to maintain a permanent occupation.'

Blackrose tilted her head. 'No.'

Brogan frowned. 'Excuse me, Your Majesty?'

'I do not want Na Sun Ka, Herald,' said Blackrose. 'This island is part of the Western Rim, and I am Queen of the Eastern Rim. If my forces occupy Na Sun Ka, the rest of Dragon Eyre will assume that I am attempting to become ruler of the entire world. That is not my desire, and the resources available to me do not allow me to undertake such a stance. Perhaps the Empress might reconsider? I suggest that your Empire takes this island under its protection. If you do not, then the Wystians shall return, and so will their Unk Tannic followers.'

'Are you serious?' said Naxor.

'Of course I am serious, demigod,' said Blackrose. 'While I am happy to see my enemies defeated and in disarray, my realm cannot afford to send soldiers, dragons and gold to Na Sun Ka. The Empire has won this island by force, so let the Empire deal with the consequences, and the fruits, of that conquest.'

Brogan's features hardened, and she opened her mouth to speak.

'Wait just a moment,' said Naxor. 'Your Majesty, might the members of the Imperial Court – myself, Herald Brogan and Adjutant Claudian, withdraw in private for a few minutes to discuss this alteration of circumstances? A proposal of such magnitude should be brought to the ears of the Empress.'

Blackrose tilted her head again. 'You may do so.'

Naxor swiped his Quadrant, and the three members of the Imperial Court disappeared from the flight deck.

'I shall order some refreshments while we await their return,' said the ship's captain, standing. He spoke to a couple of aides, who hurried away.

Lahnos leaned over towards Maddie. 'Did you know this was going to happen?'

Maddie half-smiled, half-grimaced. 'Would you be angry with me if I said yes?'

'Was this Blackrose's plan the whole time?' he said. 'Lure the Empire in to fight her enemies, and then leave us in charge of Na Sun Ka, to act as a buffer between her realm and the Wystians?'

Maddie turned away and stared at the deck. 'I try not to get involved in politics. What, eh... what do you think the Empress will say?'

'I haven't the slightest idea. But, if we abandon Na Sun Ka, after all we went through to conquer it, it will be overrun with Wystians and Unk Tannic within days.'

'I feel we have been deceived, my rider,' said Sigum.

Blackrose's eyes burned a deep red. 'Are you accusing me of double-dealing, serpent of Athumia? I will tear your head from your shoulders.'

Sigum regarded her. 'For all the great respect I bear towards you, Your Majesty,' he said, 'you do not frighten me. I have defied stronger dragons than you and survived. However, in this case, could it be true that, without actually uttering an outright falsehood, you might have misled the imperial delegates when you struck this bargain? I would be obliged if you answered this question in simple terms, without any obfuscation. If you do not, then I, and the officers assembled here, will be forced to draw our own conclusions.'

Sparks rolled over Blackrose's jaws as she stared at Sigum, her claws gouging through the beams of the flight deck.

'I see,' said Sigum. 'I am disappointed, but at least we all know where we stand.'

Maddie groaned. 'Malik's sweaty ass,' she muttered.

The air shimmered, and Naxor, Brogan and Claudian reappeared on the flight deck.

'We have spoken to Her Imperial Majesty the Empress,' said Brogan. The Herald stopped, and narrowed her eyes as she saw the fury on Blackrose's face.

'And?' cried Blackrose. 'Don't just stand there, Herald; tell me what the Empress said.'

'The Empress has decreed,' Brogan went on, 'that Her Imperial

Majesty will accept Na Sun Ka as a protectorate realm of the Empire. It shall be garrisoned by imperial forces, and rebuilt with imperial gold. In time, it will be annexed into the Empire, as an equal member of the family of nations.'

'There is one condition, Your Majesty,' said Naxor.

'Name it,' said Blackrose.

'Yearning is also ours,' said Naxor. 'If you accept these terms, Your Majesty, Yearning will be absorbed into the Empire with immediate effect, and in perpetuity. You will resign all claims to the island. Do you accept?'

'And if I do not?' said Blackrose.

'Then the Empire will have withdrawn all of its forces from Na Sun Ka by the time the sun sets tomorrow, Your Majesty.'

Blackrose gazed out at the ocean. 'I accept.'

Sigum banked over the Temple of Gyle. Victorious units of the Sanang division were celebrating in the plaza in front of the ruined temples, while the bodies of slain Unk Tannic soldiers were being carried out by natives conscripted for that purpose. Two hours had passed since the conference on the dragon carrier, and Lahnos and Sigum had left as soon as it was polite to do so.

'I enjoyed hearing your words to Blackrose,' said Lahnos.

'It needed to be said, my rider. Queen Blackrose prides herself on never lying, and yet it was clear to me that she had been less than honest while negotiating the deal that brought imperial forces to Na Sun Ka.'

Lahnos looked down at the half-ruined city. 'And now this place is part of the damn Empire, even though we didn't want it.'

'Queen Blackrose must have guessed how the Empress would react towards her proposal, my rider. It was an astute chance to take; dishonest, but astute. The Empire will now protect the southern flank of the Eastern Rim, at no cost to Queen Blackrose, except for the loss of Yearning. The Eastern Rim can now live in peace and security, while we defend her borders.'

Lahnos saw the other dragons from Sigum's team. They were on the ground, gathered in the half-ruined streets around the broken body of Ochretail. Sigum also saw them, and he started to descend. He landed close to the others, then he walked across the rubble towards them.

'Ochretail was a most noble and courageous dragon,' said Sigum, 'and I mourn his loss. We shall be the keepers of his memory, and I will honour his name until the day I take my last breath.'

The other dragons stared at the body of the red dragon, saying nothing. Lahnos saw the other riders gathered together by the side of a ruined building, and he climbed down to the street. He walked up to them, and the other riders bowed their heads in his direction.

'Well done, everyone,' he said. 'Might I speak to you alone, Ora'lya?'

'Yes, Commander,' she said.

They walked away from the others.

'I'm sorry about Ochretail's rider,' he said.

'At least it was quick.'

'I just wanted to ask,' he said; 'is it over between us? You have been avoiding me for days.'

She lowered her gaze.

'Should I give up all hope?' he went on. 'I thought we had something. I thought we were good together. I want to go back to that, but if you don't, then tell me.'

'I've missed being with you,' she said.

'And I've missed being with you.'

'But we have no future, Lahnos. Quicklime has made it very clear that she doesn't want me to have any kind of relationship with you. It's nothing personal. She doesn't care if I have casual relationships, but she could see that we were starting to get serious, and so she wants me to end it.'

'What if it was up to you?'

Ora'lya glanced up at him. 'You know the answer to that, Lahnos. I...

I think I might love you, but what's the use? Quicklime has forbidden it.'

'So you are destined to never find someone to love?'

'I love Quicklime. She will have to be enough for me.'

'Should we allow her jealousy to keep us apart?'

'I swore an oath when I became her rider.'

He took her hand. 'I want to fight for you. I don't want to lose you, Ora'lya.'

'There's nothing I can do, Lahnos. I'm sorry.'

She pulled her hand away, and walked back to the other riders. Lahnos narrowed his eyes, then he saw Quicklime staring at him, a look of anger and mistrust in her eyes. Lahnos wanted to say something to the green dragon, to tell her exactly how he felt about her possessive treatment of Ora'lya, but he restrained his rage, and turned away to gaze out over the smoking ruins of Sun Ta.

# CHAPTER 16
# FROM A FORGOTTEN TIME

**Colsbury Castle, the Holdings – 28th Day, First Third Spring 545**

Corthie ran around the balcony, growling like a bear, as the three children shrieked and laughed. Kelsey was watching from a chair, with Karalyn's daughter Caitlyn balanced on her knee.

'I'm getting dizzy just watching you,' said Kelsey.

Corthie laughed. 'I have a lot of battle-vision energy I need to use up.'

'Your coffee's getting cold, but.'

Corthie walked over to the table, and sat down. Calpurnia ran up to him, and took a seat to his left, leaving the two younger boys playing on a rug that had been brought out from the Summer Palace.

'What a beautiful day,' said Kelsey, as she held Caitlyn. 'It makes me glad I moved to Colsbury.'

Corthie nodded. He picked up his mug of coffee and gazed out at the view of the mountains and the lake. The trees in the island gardens were growing their annual covering of leaves, and a few had pink and white blossom.

'It's nice,' he said, 'but it might be time for another short trip to Clackenbaird.'

'Are you missing Kell again already?' said Kelsey. 'You were only there a couple of days ago.'

'I know, but each visit only lasts a few hours, and I miss the family,' he said. 'It's good to spend time with you and Karalyn's bairns, but; it reminds me of home. When is Van next getting Calpurnia and Caelius?'

'We're going to Daddy's house tomorrow,' said Calpurnia.

'The arrangement's changed again,' said Kelsey. 'Van needs to travel back to the City more often, and so he's asked me to take the children for seven days, then he'll have them for three; then back to me for seven, and so on.'

'It seems that you're getting more and more of them,' said Corthie, 'and he's getting less and less.'

'It was his idea,' she said, 'and it suits me fine. Now that we're divorced, he can't complain about me hiring a nanny. Well, he can complain, but there's nothing he can do about it.'

Corthie glanced at Calpurnia. 'Do you like your nanny?'

'She's all right,' said the eight-year-old girl, 'but she spends most of her time looking after the little ones.'

Kelsey leaned over and glanced at the sundial down in the forecourt. 'Can you read that from here, Corthie?'

Corthie peered over the edge of the balcony. 'It's an hour after noon.'

'It's time for your writing lesson, Calpurnia,' she said. 'Go inside and get your books. Your tutor should be in the library.'

'Do I have to go?' said the girl.

'Aye, you do. If you work hard, you can go swimming in the lake afterwards.'

Calpurnia got to her feet and trudged away.

Kelsey turned back to Corthie. 'Who teaches your children down in Kell?'

'They go to the local school in Marchside with all the bairns from the village,' Corthie said.

Kelsey frowned. 'Marchside has a school?'

'Aye. We paid for its construction, but Chief Kallie hires the teachers and is responsible for their wages. It's free for any child in the area who wants to attend.'

'You mean for any parents who want their children to attend?'

'Aye. The Empire should do the same thing, in my opinion, although on a much larger scale. Every town should have a school.'

'You're talking to the wrong woman about that, brother,' she said. 'If you had asked me this a year ago, I might have been able to do something about it.'

'Would you have agreed?'

'I don't know. Why should the Empire pay for every child's school lessons?'

'It's an investment. Better educated citizens.'

'It's bloody expensive, that's what it is.'

Karalyn walked out on to the balcony. She glanced at her two children, then turned to Corthie.

'He's awake,' she said.

Corthie rolled his eyes. 'About time. I thought that stupid god was going to be sleeping all year. What took him so long?'

'I asked him that. He said that he's trained his body to go into a deep hibernation whenever he's been badly injured. His hands had been cut off, his eyes gouged out; a nail had been rammed through his head, he had multiple stab wounds all over his abdomen, and he had a hundred other injuries. Even his toes had been cut off. Whoever did all that to him wanted him to be out of action for a while.'

'Simon once had his hand cut off, and an eye removed,' said Kelsey, 'and he was up and about not long afterwards.'

'Aye,' said Corthie, 'and I cut off Amalia's arm, and it didn't seem to slow her down for long.'

'What can I say?' said Karalyn. 'Maybe thousands of years in a restrainer mask have weakened Bailey's self-healing. Anyway, it's time he answered some of our questions. Are you coming?'

Corthie got to his feet.

'I want to come, too,' said Kelsey.

Karalyn glanced at the one-year-old girl sitting on Kelsey's knee.

'Bring all the children inside,' she said, 'and your nanny can watch them while we speak to Bailey.'

Kelsey stood, and passed Caitlyn to her mother, while Corthie herded the two boys into the palace. They took the children into the main living room of Kelsey's quarters, and left them with the middle-aged Kellach nanny; then they ascended a flight of stairs, and went to the apartment shared by Karalyn, Cardova and their children. Karalyn opened the door to their spare bedroom, and they walked in.

Bailey was sitting up in bed, a weak smile on his lips.

'Thank you all for rescuing me,' he said.

Corthie frowned. 'Your hands have grown back already.'

'Yes,' said Bailey. 'Did Karalyn tell you about my hibernation? It's a technique I picked up many centuries ago, after Edmond released me from the restrainer mask. It means I remain unconscious for longer than is strictly necessary, but I am fully healed when I awaken.'

Karalyn, Corthie and Kelsey each took a seat by the bed. Karalyn passed Bailey a tray filled with food, and the god started to eat.

'We need to know exactly what happened to you in the Palace of the Almighty,' she said.

'I thought you might,' said Bailey. 'Let me begin by apologising. I broke into the palace despite being ordered not to. This is not an attempt to justify my actions, but I felt I had to at least try to find the body of my sister. The worst thing is, I was unsuccessful. I searched everywhere, but I found no sign of Theodora.'

'Your sister's body is downstairs,' said Karalyn, 'next to that of Nathaniel. The three of you were nailed up together.'

Bailey stared at her. 'My sister... is here? Does she remain...? What condition is she...?'

'Theodora remains exactly as Edmond left her,' said Karalyn. 'We brought all three of you back to Colsbury, and I placed your sister's body into a deep sleep.'

'Forget about your reasons for entering the palace,' said Kelsey. 'Tell us what happened.'

'Of course,' he said. 'I created a breach in the corner of the palace wall, as I am sure you know. I opened it in a location with which I was familiar, and then I began my search for Theodora. Due to the nature of the palace's interior, I was forced to open up many hidden doorways with my stone powers, doorways that had been sealed for a very long time. Unable to find Theodora in any of the places where I had imagined she might be, I began to delve deeper, into the basement levels. I saw all manner of beasts during my search of the lower chambers, but I stayed clear of them, and left them where they were. I also came across a few prisoners.'

'How many?' said Kelsey.

'Several dozen. Some were skeletons by that point, while others had wasted away into an irredeemable state; terrible it was to see them. There weren't many still alive and capable of being healed. I even recognised a few of them.'

'Did you release any of them?' said Corthie.

'I released none of the ones I found in the main dungeons.'

'Why not?'

'Because I knew the awful things that some of them had done over the millennia. Edmond had locked up some of the worst criminals in history inside his palace.'

Corthie frowned. 'If they were so terrible, then why didn't Edmond execute them?'

Bailey smiled. 'Edmond executed many, many thousands of criminals over the long years of his rule; he spared only those who were close family members. His sons; a few grandchildren, and a daughter who had once flooded a new world, drowning seventeen million humans who had moved there... Edmond found it hard to kill those who were closely related to either him or Theodora – a fact which saved my life when he turned against me.' He frowned. 'And then I found someone I had not been expecting to see. A friend. An old friend from a forgotten time. I had thought him dead for millennia, because Edmond had announced his death to all and sundry.'

'Who?' said Kelsey.

'Edgar. Edmond's younger brother.'

'An Ascendant?'

Bailey shook his head. 'No, not an Ascendant. Edgar belonged to the same generation of gods as I did. Each of us had an Ascendant as a father, and a mortal woman as a mother. Edgar and Edmond shared the same Ascendant father – Edward. Edgar and I were friends for a very, very long time. I remember exploring Implacatus with him, back when that world was green and fertile. He was my dearest companion for millennia.'

'Why was he imprisoned?' said Kelsey.

'I still don't know that,' said Bailey. 'Remember, I thought he was dead.'

'Did you free him?' said Karalyn.

'I did. He was in a restrainer mask, and I used my healing powers to nurse him back to health. He was incoherent and rambling for several days; but then, so had I been, when I was first released from the mask after spending thousands of years locked within its cruel embrace. I gave him some salve, which helped. It also restored his youth, and he looked the same as when I had known him all those years before. I wept at the sight; I will not lie to you. And then he attacked me. It was sudden, and I was taken by surprise. That's... that's all I can remember.'

Karalyn narrowed her eyes. 'Are you certain that you didn't accidentally release any of the greenhide beasts from captivity?'

'Absolutely not; I swear it. I saw them through the bars of the cages within which they had been imprisoned. Like me, they know how to hibernate, and all were in a deep sleep. I left them exactly where they were, and sealed up the stone doorways that led to them.'

Karalyn glanced at Corthie and Kelsey. 'Then it was Edgar who released them.'

'Leksandr's monstrosities have been released?' said Bailey.

'Aye,' said Karalyn. 'They have killed over a hundred Holdings folk.'

Bailey blinked. 'Only a hundred? That can't be right. Are we talking about the same beasts? Eyeless, huge greenhides, impervious to fire and vision powers? Flying beasts with razor-sharp claws? Believe me, if they had been released, there would be thousands of corpses all over the Star Continent by now.'

'We are talking about the same beasts,' said Kelsey. 'We call them ironhides and greenflies. They have emerged from the palace on a small number of occasions, and then they seem to return there again.'

'Could they be under Edgar's control?' said Karalyn.

'They cannot be directly controlled,' said Bailey. 'That was a flaw Theodora insisted that Leksandr fix for his next iteration, and so he created what we all now know as greenhides. The previous batches were too powerful, and far too hard to kill. The only safety mechanism Leksandr included was their inability to kill any of the Ascendants or their close relatives. I am safe from them, for example, as is Edgar, but we most certainly cannot control them.'

'Do they have a queen, like normal greenhides?' said Corthie.

'No,' said Bailey. 'The ant-like characteristics were only introduced when Leksandr was ordered to try again. He was also told to remove their self-healing abilities, for obvious reasons. He kept their green skin, though, as it can convert light from the sun into energy, in the same way that a leaf does. Each beast is autonomous, and there is no leader or queen to whom it will listen. When Leksandr first created them, Edmond, Theodora and the others immediately demanded that they be wiped out, as a danger not only to the mortals under their rule, but to ordinary gods and demigods, too. Edmond must have hidden a few away, in case he... decided to use them for something. Have the undead dragons also been released?'

'Not that we've seen,' said Karalyn. 'Give us some numbers. How many beasts are in the palace?'

'I can only comment on the ones I have seen with my own eyes,' he said; 'there might be more hidden away in regions of the palace I didn't enter. As far as I know, there are two dozen beasts that you call ironhides, and perhaps four dozen greenflies, along with a few dozen undead dragons. There used to be a lot more, but I didn't see them.'

'We killed many during the battle for the Kell Pass,' said Karalyn. 'Anything else?'

'Undead gods,' said Bailey. 'There were rumours of greenhides designed to swim underwater, but I saw no sign of any. And, of course, there were the other prisoners – the ones I left chained up in their restrainer masks. There were also huge deposits of stores – food, fresh water, weapons; everything you would expect Edmond to stockpile. There was salve, too. Edmond's personal supply, I would imagine. Broken Quadrants. Treasure. An excellent cellar of wine...'

'I don't understand,' said Kelsey.

'Edmond was very fond of wine,' said Bailey.

Kelsey narrowed her eyes. 'Not about that, you numpty; about how and why the ironhides have been coming and going from the palace. If Edgar released them, then why haven't they been rampaging over the Holdings?'

'Edgar cannot control their actions,' said Bailey, 'but he can control where they go within the palace. Let's say that he wanted a single ironhide to roam free. He could use his stone powers to open and close certain doors and passageways, leading them towards the breach, while keeping the others constrained within their prison.'

'All right,' said Kelsey; 'I can see how that could happen, but why would they return to the palace?'

'Food is their main motivator,' said Bailey. 'If they know there is a guaranteed supply of food inside the palace, they would build a nest around the stores and supplies, and it would become their new home until it ran out. The location where Edmond placed the palace might also be significant. The flat plains of Hold Stringer contain very few animals, and it is sparsely populated by humans. If the palace had been placed in the middle of a cattle-rearing region, for example, then I imagine that things might be very different. What crops are grown in Hold Stringer?'

'Tobacco,' said Karalyn.

'Ah. That would not interest the beasts, not when there are tons of preserved meat in barrels hidden within the depths of the palace.'

'One more question,' said Karalyn, 'and then we will leave you to eat and rest. Can you think of any reason why Edgar betrayed you?'

Bailey exhaled slowly. 'No.'

'What were the events that led up to Edmond announcing his death?'

'I would have to rummage through my memories to provide an answer for you. I will get started, but it may take some time.'

Karalyn got to her feet, and then Corthie and Kelsey did the same.

'I will be up and about within a few hours,' said Bailey, 'and then... ah...'

'Aye?' said Karalyn.

'And then, I wonder if one of you would be so good as to take me and my sister's body back to Zamata? I want to give Theodora a proper burial on the world she created, but my, uh... my Quadrant has gone.'

'Edgar took your Quadrant?' said Corthie.

'I must assume so, as it is no longer in my possession.'

Kelsey's features flashed with anger. 'Do you see? This is exactly why I told you not enter the damn Palace of the Almighty, you dozy god! You not only unleashed Edmond's brother onto the Star Continent, you gifted him your fucking Quadrant, too.'

Bailey edged back a little. 'My humble apologies, Miss Holdfast.'

They left the room, and Corthie closed the door.

'What now?' he said. 'What's our plan?'

'Come with me,' said Karalyn. 'I have something I want to show you.'

They went into another room within Karalyn's quarters, and she gestured towards a large pile of crates.

'What's in there?' said Corthie.

'Open one and see.'

Corthie went to the closest crate and lifted the lid. Nestled among heaps of loose straw were several plates of gleaming black armour.

'Is this Tempest?' he said. 'When did it arrive?'

'Two days ago,' said Karalyn, 'while you were in Clackenbaird.'

'Why didn't you tell me?'

'What would have been the point, brother?' she said. 'We couldn't do anything with it until we'd spoken to Bailey.'

'And now?'

'Now, we're ready,' said Karalyn. 'We'll unpack the crates, try on our new armour, and then we'll look for Edgar.'

'This reminds me of the old days,' said Corthie, as Kelsey helped buckle on his armour.

'Aye?' she said. 'Don't get used to it.'

Corthie glanced at Karalyn, who was already wearing her full set of black armour over a padded layer of linen and mail. She was hefting a war axe with a Tempest blade, while her helm sat on a chair next to her.

'You look like Arete,' he said.

'Did you ever meet her?' said Karalyn.

'It was her and Leksandr who killed me in Yoneath,' he said. 'So, aye – I remember her pretty well.'

'Edgar might think you're Arete, or Albany,' said Kelsey, as she strapped armour round Corthie's right leg.

'I doubt that,' said Karalyn. 'We can be fairly confident that Edgar would have thoroughly read Bailey's mind. He had plenty of days in which to do it, while we sat out here waiting for beasts to leave the palace.'

'That means he'll know about the Holdfasts,' said Kelsey.

'And the death of Edmond and the other Ascendants,' said Karalyn. 'We should assume he knows everything Bailey knows.'

Kelsey stood. 'Right, Corthie; you're done.'

'Thanks, sis,' he said. He glanced at his reflection in the full-length mirror. 'I prefer the blue stone armour,' he said. 'This makes me look like a villain. Does Tempest only come in black?'

'You won't be complaining when you see how strong it is,' said Karalyn.

'Are you taking the Weathervane?'

'I'm going to leave it here. The imperial armourers have sent us several weapons to choose from, and I don't want to risk losing a sword that works in the Sextant.'

Corthie walked over to another crate, feeling the weight of the close-fitting armour pressing against his body. He peered down, and saw an array of black-bladed weaponry. He picked up a long pike, with a vicious-looking blade at one end. The shaft had been coated in a thin layer of Tempest, but the weight was easy for Corthie to handle.

'A halberd?' said Kelsey.

'Is that what it's called?' said Corthie.

'I can't picture you without the Clawhammer.'

'Will Edgar have any Tempest in the palace?' said Corthie.

'I shouldn't think so,' said Karalyn.

'Then I'm taking the Clawhammer. I worry that the greenhide talons won't be able to get through Tempest, but they'll tear anything else to pieces.' He picked up a Tempest-edged war axe. 'I might take this, too, in case of emergencies.'

Karalyn strapped a Tempest sword to her waist, and slung a war axe of her own over one shoulder. Corthie picked up his gauntlets. He glanced at the sharp-studded knuckles on each glove.

'If you punch something with them,' said Karalyn, 'your fist will go through anything.'

'You sound as though you're enjoying this, sister,' said Kelsey. 'What happened to *all violence is wrong, wah wah*?'

Karalyn narrowed her eyes, as Corthie chuckled.

'I want to be prepared,' said Karalyn. 'My principles haven't changed. There is a high probability that we are going to be attacked by someone, or something, and, since I happen to like this body, I intend to walk back out of the palace still in it.' She glanced at Corthie. 'Are you ready?'

'Aye, sis.'

Karalyn turned to Kelsey. 'Look after Carden and Caitlyn for me until we get back.'

'And when will that be?' said Kelsey.

'A couple of hours, at the most.'

Corthie placed his broad helmet over his head, and Karalyn did the same. She rolled her shoulders, picked up a lantern, then the air shimmered, and the two of them appeared in the chamber next to the breach in the wall of the Palace of the Almighty. They peered down the two passageways, but saw nothing, then Corthie turned, and scanned the area outside the palace.

'We are going to do this methodically,' said Karalyn. 'Chamber by chamber, passageway by passageway. This first trip will be to survey the nearest rooms and corridors, and then we will return to Colsbury. Do not wander off, brother. If you do, then I might not be able to find you for several days.' She crouched and lit the lantern. 'Left or right?'

Corthie turned back to look at the two passageways. 'Right, because that's where we found Bailey.'

Karalyn nodded as she stood, the lit lantern in her left hand. They walked towards the right-hand corridor, and Karalyn shone the lamp down it. They saw nothing but the same featureless grey granite that seemed to exist everywhere within the palace, then they glanced at each other, and entered the corridor. They came to the turn, and the chamber where they had discovered the three bodies nailed to a wall. Corthie remained by the entrance as Karalyn looked around within the chamber. She shook her head, and they carried on. They reached a flight of stairs that went down, and they descended, the lantern the only light visible.

'We're making a racket,' Corthie whispered. 'We should have oiled our armour before setting off.'

'We'll do it when we get back to Colsbury,' said Karalyn.

They explored the passageways and chambers close to the breach for over an hour, pausing every few minutes so that Karalyn could sketch out a rough map on a sheet of paper she had brought along with her.

'I wonder how many hidden doorways we've passed,' Corthie said. 'We should have brought Bailey.'

'He'll be fully recovered by tomorrow,' Karalyn said, as she added to her map in the light of the lantern. 'I can take him to Zamata, and then, once he's laid his sister to rest, I can bring him back into the palace, if he's willing.'

'What will we do with Nathaniel's body?' said Corthie. 'Should we bury him on this world, seeing as he created it?'

'I think Kelsey wants him sent to the university,' said Karalyn.

'Why, so that students can chop him up? Maybe we should put him in the crypt of the Great Fortress, and then he can lie alongside Bridget and Laodoc.'

'The Great Fortress has been demolished to make way for Thorn's new palace.'

'Aye, but the basement levels are still intact, or so I've heard.'

They walked on, and Karalyn shone the lantern down another long passageway. They followed it for a few moments, then the wall at the end of the corridor moved aside, as if of its own accord, revealing a huge, lamp-lit chamber at the end of another passageway. Two ironhides were waiting by the newly-created entrance, and they charged at Corthie and Karalyn.

Corthie raised his Clawhammer, as the two beasts roared in rage, their claws out. Next to him, Karalyn set the lantern down, and drew her Tempest sword. The ironhides reached the siblings, and Corthie lunged out, swinging the Clawhammer with both hands. The greenhide talons cleaved through the chest of the first ironhide, spraying the walls with green blood, then Karalyn leapt up, and drove her sword deep into the face of the beast. The black blade went through the ironhide's head without any resistance, and Corthie swung his Clawhammer at the second beast. Its claws raked out, scraping over Corthie's black breastplate, scoring its surface, but not penetrating the Tempest armour. To his left, Karalyn decapitated the first beast, as the second came to close quarters with Corthie. He clenched a fist and rammed it into the side of the ironhide's head, the Tempest studs on the gauntlet's knuckles going straight through the beast's skull. It fell to the floor of the corridor, and Karalyn severed its head from its shoulders.

Corthie stepped back, his eyes on the two dead beasts. 'That was a lot easier than last time.'

'There are two of us,' said Karalyn. She glanced at the dents and marks running down her brother's armour. 'The new breastplate saved you. Those claws would have torn your stone armour to pieces.'

'It's going to take a while to get used to seeing you fight like that,' he said. 'You were utterly fearless.'

'What is there to be frightened of?' she said. 'If I die, I will take a new body.'

Corthie raised an eyebrow. 'Oh aye? Whose body? Don't you have to kill someone to get a new body? And what happens if you go into the body of a normal mortal – will you lose Albany's powers, and her self-healing?'

'I can be patient,' she said. 'I will remain incorporeal until a suitable body becomes available.'

Corthie grimaced, then they turned, and saw that the way they had come had been sealed off by a smooth slab of grey granite. Corthie narrowed his eyes.

'I thought I felt something,' said Karalyn. 'The same power that opened the door where the ironhides were hiding must have closed up this entrance.'

'Shit,' muttered Corthie. 'What do we do now? Are we trapped?'

'There will be other ways out,' said Karalyn; 'other ways to the breach, or, if that fails, we can look for the main gates. And, even if that fails, we can find one of those ventilation shafts I was talking about. All I need is a glimpse of the sky, and we'll be free.'

They clambered over the corpses of the two slain ironhides, and walked up to the doorway leading to the large chamber. Inside were stacked-up crates and barrels, many of which had been ripped open, their contents gone. A rank odour of stale urine was pervading the air, and Corthie crinkled his nose.

'This might have been where the ironhides were nesting,' said Karalyn.

'Do they piss in their own nests?' said Corthie.

'Perhaps they were sealed inside, and couldn't get out.'

'Does this mean Edgar knows we're here? Has he led us to this place?'

They stepped inside the large chamber. As soon as they had passed the threshold, a granite door formed in place behind them; then another one opened up, twenty feet high along the wall opposite them.

A young man gazed down at them from the opening. He was clad in a full set of shining white and grey stone armour, and he stood as tall and as broad as Corthie.

'I was expecting a far harder challenge from the Holdfasts,' the man said. 'Was Bailey wrong about you?'

'Edgar?' said Karalyn.

'That... is my name,' he said, 'but I feel as though I have been born anew. Did Bailey tell you that I was in here? Has he recovered?'

'What do you want?' said Karalyn.

'To be free,' said Edgar. 'Free of pain, free of fear.'

'We don't need to be enemies, Edgar,' Karalyn said. 'Let's talk; we can come to a peaceful arrangement.'

'I spent ten days reading the mind of my oldest friend,' said Edgar, 'and I learned what the Holdfasts do to gods like me. You, Karalyn, and you, Corthie, are the strongest Holdfasts. How can I be free, if you are free to hunt me down? Do you think I am stupid?'

'You have been in a restrainer mask for a very long time,' said Karalyn. 'There is no need to fear us.'

Edgar smiled. 'There are a thousand reasons to fear you, Karalyn, and no way to kill you. Therefore, I shall not even try. Instead, you will remain here, while I make my escape. I will be taking Leksandr's creations with me, along with the other gods I have freed from their confinement. You and your brother will be quite alone within this palace, hemmed in by unbreakable walls, entombed.'

Karalyn raised her hand, and Edgar did the same.

'The death powers you stole from Albany are strong, Karalyn,' said Edgar, 'but mine are stronger. You cannot harm me.'

Corthie pulled the war axe from his belt, aimed, and threw it at the man, who reached out and caught it with his left hand.

Edgar gazed at the weapon. 'I was eager to obtain one of these new Tempest weapons. Thank you for the gift, Corthie. In exchange, you may eat and drink all that you can find within this chamber. My brother had an excellent selection of wine, and now it is yours.'

'Scour his mind,' Corthie cried.

'He's wearing eye-shields,' said Karalyn.

'Edmond had everything I needed,' said the man. 'Eye-guards, salve; and Bailey was kind enough to donate his Quadrant. Farewell.'

The stone doorway vanished, replaced by a solid granite wall. Corthie ran to the wall, and tried to climb it, but there was nothing to grip, and he slid back down to the granite floor.

He turned to his sister. 'Do something.'

Karalyn sat down on a crate.

'You have to do something,' Corthie repeated.

'I have no stone powers,' she said, 'and I cannot transport us anywhere, not while we are buried deep within the palace.'

'Then what do we do?'

'Edgar lured us into this trap,' she said. 'There is nothing I can do, brother.'

'Bailey and Kelsey know where we are,' Corthie said. 'They'll find us. Won't they?'

'It depends on what Edgar does next,' said Karalyn. She lowered her gaze. 'Colsbury might be in danger. The entire Star Continent might be in danger. We failed, Corthie. Edgar can do whatever he chooses while we are trapped in here, and there's nothing we can do about it.'

# CHAPTER 17
# THE CALENDAR POLE

**Plateau City, The Plateau – 6$^{th}$ Day, Second Third Spring 545**

Kyra waited in the corridor outside the office of Professor Achan. He had asked her to meet him, but his room had been occupied when she had arrived, and she had been standing in the corridor for over twenty minutes. She glanced out of the window at the students walking across the university quad. The sun was out, and the morning was developing into another beautiful spring day by the banks of the Inner Sea.

Achan's door opened, and Kyra turned to see a procession of people walk out of his office – Rakanese, Kellach, Holdings, and even one Rahain man. They filed past Kyra towards the stairs, then Achan appeared at the door.

'Sorry about the wait, Kyra,' he said. 'I've had a lot to do this morning. Come in.'

'Who were all those people, sir?' she said, as she entered his office.

'Representatives of the different communities living in Plateau City,' he said, closing the door behind them. 'They were here to discuss what action to take over the outrageous increases in the levels of taxation.' He smiled. 'The Empress is in for a surprise if she thinks that the ordinary folk of this city are not going to make their voices heard.'

'Are you helping them to organise a demonstration?'

'We were planning something more substantial than that, Kyra,' he said. 'We were discussing the practicalities of a general strike to take place across the entire city – from the docks, to the wagon-drivers, to the rubbish collectors. Between us, we are going to bring Plateau City to a complete standstill.'

'Forgive me for asking, but why did they want to talk to you, sir?'

'For several reasons, but mainly because I have access to the university printing press, which will be vital in disseminating information about the planned strike. They knew that I have planned protests regarding the illegal wars being carried out by the Empire, and they need our organisational expertise.' He smiled at her. 'I have a surprise for you this day. But first, I wanted to ask you something – why have you been avoiding Larron?'

Kyra's cheeks flushed. 'I don't really want to talk about it.'

'Neither does he,' said Achan. 'I must presume that you have had a falling out. A pity, as today's surprise also involves him. Tell me – would you rather not come with me if you knew he was going to be there?'

'Where are we going?' she said.

'Answer me first, and then I will tell you.'

'If it's related to the anti-war effort, then how can I object, sir?'

'Please tell me what happened. Perhaps I can help.'

'There's not a lot to say, sir. I drank too much and made a fool of myself. I'm so embarrassed.'

'I have never seen you indulge in alcohol.'

'Maybe that's the problem. I'm not used to it, and Larron's parents kept handing me whisky and ale. I should have politely refused, but I didn't. I… I tried to kiss him.'

Achan nodded. 'These things happen, Kyra. I have spoken to Larron several times recently, and he doesn't seem to bear any ill will towards you. I asked him if your presence today would be a problem, and he told me that he would be happy to be your friend.'

'All right. I'll come with you, even if he's there. I will apologise to him, and then try to pretend that nothing happened.'

'Excellent. Here is my surprise – we are going to the City.'

'The City of Salve?'

'Indeed. I received word yesterday that Freshmist has ended a few days earlier than usual, and summer has begun. I have a whole day planned out, but our main reason for going is so that I can introduce you and Larron to a few of my old political activist friends in Hammer territory. When was the last time you were in the City?'

Kyra thought back. 'I was there a few times when we were fighting the Ascendants, but I haven't been back since.'

'The last invasion by the Ascendants almost completely wiped out the Rosers as a tribe, did you know that? They are now a shadow tribe, like the Scythes. Reapers now live in Tara, and the Aurelians are one of only a tiny handful of aristocratic Roser families remaining. Anyway, I digress. Let's go downstairs. Larron is waiting for us.'

Achan picked up a bag, and then they left the office. The professor locked the door, and they descended the stairs to the ground floor. Larron was standing by the doorway leading to the quad, and he nodded at Kyra.

'Hello,' she said, keeping her glance lowered.

'Good morning, Kyra,' he said.

'I'm sorry about what happened,' she said.

'Please, Kyra, think nothing of it. I should have guessed that my parents would ply you with too much drink; it's my fault.' He glanced at Achan. 'Good morning, sir. I've been hearing a few strange rumours about some rogue greenhides that might be roaming the plains of the Holdings. Have you heard anything?'

Achan shrugged. 'Nothing. I suppose it's possible that a few greenhides are still alive on the Star Continent.'

'But in the Holdings, sir? I didn't think the Ascendants placed any nests in the Holdings.'

'They didn't,' said Kyra.

'Perhaps they migrated in search for food,' said Achan. 'It's best to leave it to the local Holdings militia to deal with.' He glanced at Kyra. 'You see? I'm not universally opposed to having an armed force in service of the state, not if their job is to keep the ordinary folk safe from greenhides.'

He walked out into the quad, and Kyra and Larron followed him.

'Shall we walk to the Ministry of the Plateau, or take a carriage?' Achan said.

'A carriage, on a sunny day like today?' said Larron. 'I would much rather walk.'

'Then we shall walk,' said Achan.

Kyra said nothing, and she wondered if Larron had mentioned her ownership of a Quadrant to Achan.

They left the university, and selected a street that ran close to the Holdfast townhouse.

'Have your parents mentioned my drunken behaviour?' Kyra asked Larron.

Larron half-smiled. 'I'd be lying if I said no. My mother is annoyed with my father for giving you too much whisky. And my brother is being his usual self.'

'I'm so embarrassed about what I said and did. Did you tell anyone about...?'

'I haven't said a thing to anyone. It's nobody's business but ours. I hope that we can pick up from where we left off. I don't want this to come between us.'

'It's good to see you friends again,' said Achan. 'I need you both, and that's the truth.'

They walked along the main streets of the New Town, until they reached a plaza in front of the Ministry of the Plateau, where a mixture of people had gathered.

'I assume this is the first time you have visited the designated portal site?' said Achan.

Kyra nodded. 'How does it work?'

'Every morning, an hour before the noon bell, someone from the Ministry comes down and opens up a portal to Ooste, in the City. Then, people are free to travel back and forward for ten minutes.' He pointed at a large pillar. 'That is the Calendar Pole. Let's take a closer look.'

They walked through the small crowd until they reached the stone, square-sided pillar.

'The four calendars of the Allied Worlds are inscribed into the surface of the stone,' said Achan, as they gazed up at the western flank of the square pillar. 'On this side, you can see the Holdings Calendar. Today is the Sixth Day of the Second Third of Spring, and if you follow the line round to the next side...' They walked to the south-facing flank. 'Here you can see the equivalent date in the City – the twenty-sixth of Amalan.' They walked to the east-facing side. 'On Dragon Eyre,' Achan went on, 'and upon all worlds that use the Divine Calendar, today's date is the twenty-sixth of Nethinch. Malik and Amalia based their City Calendar on the Divine Calendar; they only changed the names of the months. That's why the dates correspond; in other words, Amalan in the City is the same month as Nethinch on Dragon Eyre.' They walked round to the last side, which faced north. 'And finally,' Achan said, 'upon Athumia, today is the third of Duninch, which is quite confusing. Athumia uses the same months as the Divine Calendar, but each month is only twenty-eight days in length, and there is a thirteenth month, named after King Gahad. The purpose of this pillar, if it weren't obvious, is to allow travellers to quickly ascertain the date on the world they are about to travel to. There are other pillars at the portal site in Ooste, and on Ulna, on Dragon Eyre.'

'Is there a portal site on Athumia?' said Larron.

'There isn't,' said Achan. 'Not yet, at any rate. The occupied Tempest mine on Inopei is a military compound, and access is restricted.'

'Yearning and Na Sun Ka might need their own portal sites soon,' said Kyra, 'now that the Empire has annexed them.'

'Indeed,' said Achan. 'What brazen theft, to steal land upon Dragon Eyre. It's yet another example of the Empress's compulsive imperialism. She just can't help herself. It is clear to me that the Empress will not stop until all lands of the Allied Worlds are absorbed into the Empire.'

'I heard about your brother's feats on Na Sun Ka,' said Larron.

Kyra frowned.

'Whatever else you might say about Cael Holdfast,' Larron went on, 'it's clear that he has courage.'

'What he did was utterly reckless,' said Kyra. 'Doesn't he care if he gets killed? And for what? So that the Empire can claim another foreign territory? So much for going to Queen Blackrose's aid. This must have been the Empress's plan from the beginning.'

A side door in the Ministry of the Plateau opened, and Herald Brogan walked out, followed by Ambassador Van Logos and a few courtiers. They walked up to the Calendar Pole, then Brogan took out a Quadrant, and glanced at a sundial.

'Good morning, Kyra,' said Van. 'Are you travelling to the City today?'

Kyra nodded. 'Aye.'

'I'm giving her a tour, Ambassador,' said Achan.

Van smiled. 'I hope you have a wonderful time.'

Kyra frowned as Van turned and began talking to the courtiers.

Achan eyed her. 'I sense that perhaps you found it difficult to be polite to the City's Ambassador,' he whispered.

'I haven't forgiven him for the way he treated my aunt,' she said. 'He practically forced her out of her role as Herald.'

'But you thought Kelsey was a warmonger,' said Larron.

'She was, but at least I had some influence with her. Brogan is... well, I know she's the daughter of Bridget, but she's too obedient to the Empress to be a useful Herald. Heralds are supposed to understand when to say *no* to the Empress, but I doubt Brogan has ever refused her anything.'

At that moment, Brogan nodded to a courtier.

'The portal to Ooste is about to be opened,' the courtier exclaimed. 'Please allow everyone from the City to travel to the Star Continent before taking your turn to pass through to Ooste.'

Brogan swiped her fingers over the Quadrant, and the portal appeared. It began as a small swirling mass of black, then it expanded until it was twelve feet high, and the same distance in width. The swirling air cleared, and then a red sky became visible through the portal, followed by a large square that sat in front of an enormous building with a white façade. A group of around a hundred people were waiting in the large square, next to a man in a Banner uniform, who was holding the Quadrant on the City side of the portal. The group moved through, entering Plateau City.

'This is a wonder of civilisation,' said Achan, as they watched the people pass into the Star Continent.

Larron eyed him. 'Is it not a benefit of the City joining the Empire, sir?'

Achan shook his head. 'What was to stop the Empire doing this years ago? They refused to do so, until the City signed the annexation papers. They withheld it from us, so that they could call it a benefit.'

A courtier gestured towards the portal. 'You are now free to pass over into Ooste.'

Van was the first to step through the portal, where he was met by a carriage and a group of soldiers from the Banner of the Lostwell Exiles; then the others walked through. Kyra felt the temperature lower a little as she entered the City, then she gazed up at the red, pink and peach sky, and smiled. Achan led her and Larron across the plaza, then he came to a halt. He pointed at the building with the white façade.

'That is the Royal Palace,' he said, 'where the God-King Malik lived for many long centuries. It was burned by dragons during Simon's short reign of terror, and has been abandoned ever since.' He turned to face the bay. 'Over there is Pella, and then Tara. Do you see the gargantuan statue of the tyrant Prince Michael? That is a good example of the priorities of the old ruling gods of the City. While Evaders were starving, the City decided to spend its money on that monstrosity, to celebrate the life of an evil autocrat.'

'What is that huge black building on the hill behind the statue, sir?' said Larron.

'That is Maeladh Palace, where the God-Queen lived after she and Malik separated. It, too, was burned by dragon fire. Greylin Palace in Dalrig suffered the same fate, and, can you see the tall cranes at the construction site by the waterfront in Pella? That is

Cuidrach Palace, which was also burned, but by Simon, not by the dragons. It will take several decades to rebuild it, and the Aurelian government now sits in what used to be the Royal Academy, here in Ooste. The City suffered terribly during those days, what with greenhide incursions, and the rule of mad Simon. All the same, the Aurelians are building a better, fairer place from the ruins. There is no more slavery, for example, and the tribes are no longer restricted to certain regions. Hammers and Evaders are free to enter Auldan, which was unheard of in the days of Malik and Amalia. All of this, to be honest, is thanks to King Daniel Aurelian. He was prevented from passing his new constitutional laws around a decade ago, so His Majesty has been introducing them piece-by-piece ever since. Land reform, voting rights, freedom of speech and freedom of movement. It sounds terrible to say this aloud, but if Simon hadn't almost annihilated the entire Roser aristocracy, then many of these reforms wouldn't have been passed.'

'I have a question, sir,' said Larron. 'Why are you so opposed to the Empress, if you are in favour of the Aurelian monarchy?'

'You will laugh at me if I tell you,' said Achan. 'It is because of a very old legend that goes back to the last mortal prince of Tara. The legend stated that an Aurelian would arise again, defeat the gods who ruled the City, and free the mortals from servitude. And so it came to pass. Come; let us take a carriage to the Bulwark.'

Several carriages were lined up by the side of the large square in front of the Royal Palace, waiting to be hired by those who had walked through the portal from the Star Continent.

'And this happens every day?' said Kyra. 'Without any checks or customs?'

'Yes,' said Achan. 'If one wished, one could travel from here to the Star Continent and then on to Dragon Eyre within the course of a single day; though I believe that there are guards on Ulna who do check all new arrivals.'

'But there are none here, because the City is in the Empire?'

Achan nodded, though he looked a little annoyed by the question.

They walked up to the line of carriages, and a driver helped them board one.

'Where to?' said the driver.

'Hammer territory, if you please,' said Achan.

The driver closed the side door, mounted the bench, and got the ponies underway. Inside, Achan, Kyra and Larron settled down on the comfortable benches.

Achan pointed out all the sights, giving a commentary on each, as the carriage made its way across Auldan and Medio. They skirted to the north of the Circuit, avoiding its twisting lanes and alleys, and passed through the Middle Walls. Larron stared out at the position of the sun for much of the journey, while Kyra tried to recall everything she had seen on her previous trips to the City. They reached the old wall that encircled Hammer territory, and Kyra noticed that several large breaches had been opened in it, to allow free movement.

'Those walls ensured the Hammers were kept inside a vast prison,' Achan said, as he saw where she was looking. 'Despite being able to leave, the great majority of Hammers still live within the walls, along with several thousand who came over from Lostwell. The rest, of course, became what is known as the Brigades. They live in Jezra, on the Western Bank of the Straits.' He smiled as the carriage pulled into the streets of Hammer territory. 'This is where I truly belong; this is home.'

They paid the driver and walked the rest of the way. Smoke was rising from dozens of chimneys, and the red brick houses, workshops and factories were stained black by the soot.

'This is the industrial heartland of the City,' Achan said. 'A few years from now, when the fruits of Prince Aurelian's Papers have become widespread, Plateau City will be full of factories like the ones you can see here – steel foundries, mills, ironworks – and they will be powered by coal and steam.'

'I don't know if I like that idea,' said Kyra.

'It's progress,' said Achan. 'If done properly, it will benefit the workers more than the rich. This is why I have brought you here, Kyra, so that you can glimpse the future.'

Kyra frowned as she glanced at the smoke and the dirt.

'The gods, of course,' Achan went on, 'will do everything they can to stop this from happening. Why do you think they have been trying to keep mortals in rustic ignorance for so long? Progress hands power to the ordinary man and woman, and takes it away from the immortal gods.'

They came to a large concrete and brick building. 'This is the Metallurgical Institute,' Achan went on, 'where I have worked for many years. Come inside, and I will introduce you to my colleagues.'

Six hours later, Kyra and Larron emerged from the building. Kyra was exhausted after meeting countless engineers and technicians, who all appeared to be wearing the same nondescript overalls; and she was exhausted after having to listen to hours of lectures about industrial policy. She sat on a low brick wall, and exhaled.

Larron laughed. 'Of all the ways we could have spent a day in the City,' he said. 'There are dozens of sights to see, and we end up stuck in a concrete building talking about collectivisation and why it should be a crime to own property.'

'You told me you thought Achan was a genius,' she said.

'He is, about some things,' he said, 'but what has industrial policy got to do with trying to stop the Empress from embarking upon foreign wars? I don't think it's wrong for my parents to own a tavern; they've worked hard for it. I want to abolish the Empire, so that all nations can rule themselves, and live side by side in peace; I'm not interested in Hammer political philosophy.'

'Praise Pyre for that,' she said. 'I was worried you might walk out of there a convert. You were right, though; there are far more interesting places to see in the City. Do you want to visit the Great Wall?'

Larron turned, and squinted at the eastern horizon. 'I think I can see it from here.'

Kyra got to her feet. She sent out her vision, and crossed the distance to the Great Wall in a few moments. Imperial officers were up on the battlements with the full complement of Blades for the start of summer. She looked around until she found an empty turret, then she severed the connection and placed a hand in her pocket.

*That turret. Go.*

The air shimmered, and they appeared inside the turret, on the battlements of the Outer Wall. Larron's eyes widened, then Kyra gestured for him to look out of an opening in the side of the wall. They walked up to it, and gazed down on a vast, empty plain. Mile after mile of barren wasteland stretched out, reaching right up to the full moat.

Larron gazed out at the view.

'It's hard to imagine what this used to look like,' said Kyra. 'It's been fourteen years since Blackrose destroyed the greenhide nest in the Eastern Mountains.'

'Did there used to be greenhides down there?' said Larron.

'Millions of them. An unending sea of greenhides.'

A cry rang out from another turret, and Kyra watched as a solitary greenhide bounded into view, its long limbs carrying it across the plain in the direction of the City defences. Over to Kyra and Larron's left, a tall platform loosed a yard-long steel bolt from a ballista. The bolt shot out, impaling the greenhide through the chest. The beast tumbled forwards, then skidded to a halt on the barren ground; and a cheer rose up from the Blades on the battlements.

'Does this mean that, one day, there will be no greenhides left upon this world?' said Larron.

'Unfortunately not,' said Kyra. 'There are dozens of other nests on this world, and the one by the Eastern Mountains that Blackrose destroyed might have already been replaced; or another one established close by. The salve mine is located near to its location. Do you want to see it?'

Larron nodded.

Kyra put her hand in her pocket again.

*Salve Mine. Go.*

The air shimmered again, and they found themselves standing in a beautiful green valley, high up in the Eastern Mountains. A few imperial soldiers were sitting around, as workers sorted out piles of salve near the entrance to a cave. A Kellach soldier saw them, and got to her feet.

'What are you doing here?' she cried. 'This is a restricted area.'

'She's a Holdfast,' said Larron, gesturing towards Kyra.

The soldiers all got to their feet.

'A Holdfast?' said a Holdings sergeant.

'Which one?' came a woman's voice.

Kyra turned, and saw Jade walking towards them. The demigod squinted at Kyra, and narrowed her eyes.

'I'm Kyra,' she said.

Jade peered at her. 'You're the one who fixed my head. I thought you were a little girl.'

'I was. I'm eighteen now.'

Jade shook her head. 'Mortals.' She glanced at the soldiers. 'She's with me. Do you want to see my house, Kyra?'

Kyra nodded, then she and Larron followed Jade to the bottom of the valley, where a large stone cottage had been built by the banks of the stream. Jade stopped, then she eyed Larron.

'Why is there a boy following us? Is that Cael?'

'This is my friend Larron,' said Kyra.

'Do you like cats, Larron?'

'Aye,' he said.

Jade nodded, then she opened the door to her cottage and they went inside. At least six cats were sitting in the living room, where a fire was burning in the hearth.

'I live here now,' said Jade, 'and Dawnflame comes to visit me every day to take me flying. The soldiers built the cottage for me; it was my price for letting them take over the salve mine.'

They sat.

'I had a class with Rosie Jackdaw last year,' Kyra said.

'She was living here for a while,' said Jade. 'I hope she comes back. Have you... have you seen Naxor?'

Kyra nodded.

'I heard the Empress had given him an important job.'

'That's right,' said Kyra. 'He is the Imperial Chamberlain.'

'And what do they do?'

'All sorts of things.'

'Will you kill him for me?'

Kyra hesitated.

'It's not just for me,' said Jade. 'If you kill him now, then he won't be able to betray you later.'

'Naxor has been loyal to the Empress for years, Jade.'

The demigod smiled. 'Of course he has. That's what he does. He clings on to those with power, just like he did with Simon, but, as soon as something goes wrong, he breaks his vows and stabs his old friends in the back. When you next see him, tell him I haven't forgotten what he did, and tell him that I will never forgive him. Tea?'

It was late evening by the time Kyra, Achan and Larron emerged through the portal back onto the Star Continent. The streetlamps outside the Ministry of the Plateau had been lit, and the seven stars were shining down from the cloudless sky. Achan had been a little upset with Kyra and Larron for absconding from outside the Metallurgical Institute, but they had placated him by telling him how fascinating they had found the visit. Kyra was working up the courage to ask Larron if he wanted to walk back to the university with her, when she noticed her Aunt Kelsey shoving her way through the crowd towards her.

'Aunty?' she said.

Kelsey eyed Larron for a moment, then she ushered Kyra away to a quiet corner of the plaza.

'We have a problem, Kyra,' she said.

'What kind of problem?'

'A family problem. Your mother and Corthie... they're trapped inside the Palace of the Almighty.'

'What? Why would they go in there?'

'Hush. Hardly anyone knows, and I need you to stay calm,' said Kelsey. 'Bailey opened a big hole in the side of the palace, to search for Theodora, but he found someone else. Karalyn and Corthie went in to look, and they haven't come back out.'

'When did they enter the palace?'

'Uh, eight days ago.'

Kyra stared at her aunt. 'Eight days? And you're only telling me now?'

'That's right. And I'm only telling you for one reason.'

'What reason?'

'We need you to go in and look for them.'

# CHAPTER 18
# THE BAIT

**Na Sun Ka, Western Rim – 3rd Duninch 5266 (18th Gylean Year 17)**

The dry, baked ground rumbled, but no one in the marine encampment paid any attention. Small earth tremors were so common in the volcanic wastelands of western Na Sun Ka that the marines had learned to live with them. A plume of smoke was rising from one of the volcanoes a few miles to the south of the large camp, and ash had fallen overnight, coating the lines of tents in a thin grey film.

Cael was sitting with a few of the other junior officers from his brigade, and they were studying a large map held to the ground with a stone in each corner, as they planned out which routes they would sweep that coming evening.

'My platoon was the bait last night,' said a second lieutenant. 'It's someone else's turn.'

'I'll do it,' said Cael.

'You can't be the bait, Holdfast,' said a first lieutenant. 'We need you to coordinate the others if the advance platoon gets attacked.'

'I hear what you're saying, sir,' said Cael, 'but my platoon is beginning to be resented by the others. We need to take our fair share of the shit jobs. Let us do it this once, sir; the chances are it'll be another quiet night, but at least my platoon will be able to say that they've done it.'

The first lieutenant glanced at the brigade captain, who nodded.

'All right, Holdfast,' said the first lieutenant, pointing at the map with a stick. 'Take your platoon out along this ridge, and try to draw the Unk Tannic from their positions in the cliffs. The two companies will be covering your location from here, and here. If you get hit, send me a signal, and we'll come to your rescue.' He pointed again. 'I'll be here, where the two dried-up rivers meet.'

'I hope the bastards come out to play tonight,' said another first lieutenant. 'I'm sick of sending out marines to try to lure them from their caves. I mean, we all fucking know where the Unk Tannic rats are hiding.'

'There are miles of tunnels under those cliffs,' said the captain. 'Any platoon that goes in to look for the Unk Tannic will not be coming out again. Find the cave entrances, plant your explosives, and seal the bastards up inside the mountain. That way, your marines will be going home alive.'

'Understood, sir,' said the first lieutenant; 'but part of me wishes we could send the whole battalion in. We could start at one end of the ridge, and clean those bastards out in one long push. It would work, sir. We'd get the whole damn lot of them.'

'I agree,' said the captain, 'but we'd lose half the battalion in the process. I know it's frustrating, but we have to do this the slow way. Try to be patient. Lieutenant Holdfast, inform your platoon that they will be the advance team tonight. Have them check their equipment, and then make sure they get some rest.'

Cael got to his feet. 'Aye, sir.'

He walked away from the officers, and followed a path that led between two long rows of large tents. He reached the tent where his platoon slept, and saw one of his sergeants sitting by the entrance with a couple of marines, as they heated some water on a low fire.

They glanced up at him.

'We're the bait tonight,' said Cael.

The sergeant nodded. 'Did you have to beg the captain, sir?'

'He agreed without too much need for persuasion. This will probably be our only time, though.'

The sergeant glanced at one of the marines. 'Go inside and tell everyone, lad.'

The Holdings marine got to his feet, then he walked into the tent, and the sergeant turned back to Cael.

'Any day now, sir,' he said, 'and I'm expecting a new second lieutenant to be put in charge of this platoon.'

'I'm that bad, am I?' said Cael.

The sergeant chuckled. 'You're too useful to be leading a platoon, sir. I'm surprised the major hasn't personally requisitioned you as his own vision assistant. Planning, tactics, communications – that's where you belong.'

Cael sat by the dwindling fire. 'I'd rather lead from the front.'

'Aye, sir. We all saw you do that in Sun Ta, and it's a miracle we only had one casualty that day. You don't want to ride your luck, sir. If they offer you a staff role, you should snatch it out of their sweaty palms before they change their minds. Well, that's my opinion.'

'Duly noted.'

A few marines walked out of the tent, accompanied by the other sergeant.

'Is it true, sir?' the other sergeant said. 'Are we tonight's advance platoon?'

'Aye,' said Cael. 'We'll be going up by Salt Ridge, right under the eaves of the cliffs. There will be no requirement to keep silent; we want to draw the Unk Tannic out of their caves.'

The sergeant smiled. 'Just wait until I tell the eejits in Third Company. They've been taking the piss for days, telling us we're too precious to be risked.'

'It ain't us who's precious,' said the other sergeant. 'They just want to stop Lieutenant Holdfast from doing anything crazy or reckless again.'

One of the marines gazed up into the blue sky. 'Dragon.'

The others peered up. A solitary dragon was flying to the east, above the valley where the road to Sun Ta lay. Cael raised a hand to shield his eyes from the sun, and recognised the green dragon from Sigum's team.

'It's Quicklime,' he said.

'There must be another supply convoy coming up the hill,' said a sergeant.

Cael got to his feet. 'Have everyone double check their kit, and then I want the platoon to get some rest before we head out this evening.'

'Aye, sir,' said a sergeant.

Cael walked away from his platoon, and headed towards the tent for the junior officers of the company. Several marines nodded to him, or saluted as he walked. It was partly because of his famous name, but also because of what he had done in Sun Ta. Many of the marines seemed to believe that his actions had saved the lives of dozens of their comrades, while several of the sergeants and corporals disapproved of his seemingly reckless behaviour. Cael hadn't told anyone the truth, that he had been acting on the knowledge granted to him by his glimpse of the future. No visions had occurred since that day, and for that he was grateful. The chances of having such a positive vision again were tiny, if not impossible. He had been lucky, though not in the way that many others assumed.

The tent was empty when he reached it. He went inside, found his bunk, and stretched out. The ground rumbled again, and the unlit oil lamps inside the tent swayed back and forth. Cael closed his eyes and, despite the heat, fell asleep within a few seconds.

'Lieutenant Holdfast? Sir?'

Cael opened his eyes and squinted in the gloom. Standing two yards away was a Kellach staff sergeant from the logistics division.

'Aye?' said Cael.

'Are you leading the advance platoon tonight, sir?' said the staff sergeant.

'Aye.'

'Then the convoy has new equipment for your marines to try out,' she said. 'It arrived in Sun Ta two days ago, and was sent up here. The captain said it should go to your platoon, as you'll be the ones walking right under the noses of the Unk Tannic.'

Cael swung his legs off the bunk, and rubbed his face. He got to his feet and followed the staff sergeant out of the tent. The day had cooled, and the sun was lying low over the western horizon. The camp was bustling, as the hundreds of marines in the battalion were getting ready to eat their evening meal, before setting off on that night's operation. Cael and the staff sergeant walked to the stores depot, and Cael was escorted inside. They were directed to a pile of crates sitting close to the entrance of the large tent. The staff sergeant picked up a crowbar and opened one. She removed the lid, and Cael peered inside. Among the straw were new breastplates of black metal.

'There are two dozen of them, sir,' said the staff sergeant, reading from a document. 'There are also greaves, helms and short swords – all of the same black metal. Tempest, it says here. Have you used Tempest equipment before, sir?'

Cael shook his head. 'No, but I've heard of it. Is there more coming for the rest of the battalion?'

'Apparently so, sir. This is just the first batch. Do you need a hand carrying it to your platoon?'

'Aye, thanks.'

The staff sergeant handed him the document and a small pencil. 'Sign at the bottom, sir.'

Cael scrawled his name on the document, and handed it back. The staff sergeant summoned six marines, and they began carrying the crates out of the tent. Cael led them to his platoon, and the crates were set down outside their tent, as a few marines watched. His two sergeants emerged from the shadows of the tent.

'New armour and weapons,' said Cael. 'Tempest.'

The rest of the platoon was called out of the tent, and the marines unpacked the crates, then they began fitting the new breastplates to each other, and trying on their new helmets.

'Why are we getting all this fancy armour, sir?' said a marine.

'We're getting the first batch because we're the advance platoon tonight,' said Cael. 'The rest of the battalion will be getting theirs later. It's made of a metal called Tempest – the strongest material on the Allied Worlds. Make sure everyone has their own breastplate, greaves, helm and short sword, and practise moving with them. They'll be heavier than your old leathers, but you'll be grateful if you're hit in the chest with a crossbow bolt.' He glanced at a corporal. 'Have you still got that pot of white paint that you used to mark our platoon number on the side of the tent?'

'Aye, sir. I'll get it for you.'

The corporal went into the tent, as Cael selected a helm for himself from an open crate. When the corporal returned, Cael took the paint, and daubed a small stripe along the front and rear of his black helm.

'You should be able to see these stripes in the dark,' he said to the platoon. He glanced at the position of the sun. 'Get something to eat, and I'll be back when it's time to go.'

He picked up his armour and his short Tempest sword, and walked back to his tent.

Three hours later, Cael's platoon set off. They left the encampment by a narrow track, and walked for an hour in the darkness, the only light coming from the half moon in the eastern sky. They reached the edge of Salt Ridge, and came to a halt. Cael summoned the two sergeants, and they glanced down at Cael's map.

'We're going to traverse the entire ridge,' Cael said; 'all seven miles, under the shadows of the cliffs where we know the Unk Tannic are burrowed. Be quiet, but not silent. We want the Unk Tannic to know we're here. I'll be using my vision to keep an eye on the caves dotted along the side of the cliff, but I won't be able to see everywhere at the same time. If we are engaged by the enemy, we will take shelter while I call for assistance. Every cave entrance that we see being used by the Unk Tannic must be noted, and the explosives teams will seal them up later.'

The ground rumbled under their feet, and a brief flare of flowing lava lit up the volcanoes to their left. Cael glanced away from the red light, to preserve his night vision, then he led the platoon down the side of the ridge and into the narrow gorge that ran under the tall, overhanging cliffs. The surface of the cliff face was riddled with caves, and the cliffs ran into the flank of a mountain, beneath which the Unk Tannic were hiding in their tunnels and caverns.

Cael remained in front as the platoon began to walk along the floor of the valley. There was no talking, but the marines had been instructed to refrain from being silent, and Cael could hear their new armour creak and rattle, and their boots scuffing off the dusty ground. Cael sent out his vision, and used it to scan a handful of cave entrances. Some were shallow dead-ends, while others extended deeper into the side of the mountain, and were lost in the darkness.

They walked for three miles, but heard nothing coming from the cliffs, and saw no sign of the Unk Tannic, apart from a few old tracks in the dirt. Cael brought the platoon to a halt, and crouched as he sent his vision out again. He rushed his sight up over the ridge, and crossed a mile of barren terrain, until he found where that night's reserve companies were located, waiting for a signal to go to the aid of the advance platoon. Cael looked around until he recognised the first lieutenant on duty, and entered his mind.

*Second Lieutenant Holdfast reporting, sir.*

The officer frowned. *See anything, Holdfast?*

*No, sir; not so far. We are three miles along the ridge.*

*Stay where you are. We have a problem here. A squad from Fourth Company has failed to join us at the meeting point, and we think they've either got lost or have been captured by an Unk Tannic snatch team.*

*Shall I look for them, sir?*

*Do so. Report back in twenty minutes, or sooner if you see anything; but do not move from your current location. Do you get me, Holdfast? Stay exactly where you are.*

*Aye, sir.*

Cael severed the connection and turned to his platoon. 'We'll be staying here for a while. A squad's gone missing.'

'Whose, sir?' said a sergeant.

'I don't know. From Fourth Company. I'm going to look for them. Break me out of the vision trance if anything happens.'

Cael released his vision again, and lifted it high above the valley. He shot it back down the long slope towards the marine encampment, then he began to search among the wastelands in the moonlight. For ten minutes, he scanned the ground, following the tracks that criss-crossed the barren landscape, until he came across the body of a marine, lying on the ground with three crossbow bolts in his back. The body had been pushed off the side of a track, but was visible from above. Cael moved his vision back up the slope. He saw more tracks, which looked as though they had been made by someone being dragged along the ground, and then, after more minutes of searching, he found what he had been looking for. A team of Unk Tannic dressed in black were hauling ten disarmed and bound prisoners along a path that snaked up the sides of the cliff. They were pushed into a cave, then the Unk Tannic went in after them. Cael pulled back, and glanced at the location of the cave entrance – it was a quarter of a mile from his platoon's position.

Cael cut off his vision powers, and looked back along the valley. In the distance, he could just make out the rough position of the cave entrance.

'The Unk Tannic has taken ten marines prisoner,' he said to his platoon. 'They're in the tunnels.'

'Should we call for reinforcements, sir?' said a sergeant.

'If hundreds of marines assault that tunnel entrance, the captives will be killed,' said Cael. 'I need four volunteers.'

'For what, sir?'

Cael exhaled. 'I'm going in. If we leave now, we could be inside the tunnels within a few minutes, right behind the prisoners. We kill the Unk Tannic, and get the marines out alive.'

The others in the platoon stared at him.

'Is this another one of your reckless ideas, sir?' said the sergeant.

'Once I'm in the tunnels,' Cael said, 'I can use my vision powers to find the prisoners.'

'It's estimated that there are up to a thousand Unk Tannic sheltering in those caverns, sir. You'll never get out alive.'

'I need four volunteers,' he repeated.

'I'm in, sir,' said a Kellach marine.

'And me, sir,' said a Holdings woman with battle-vision.

'Pyre's fucking cock,' said a sergeant. 'I suppose I'd better go along, too.'

'Thank you,' said Cael. 'One more?'

A corporal nodded. 'Me, sir.'

Cael glanced at the other sergeant. 'Follow us after a few minutes, but remain out in the valley. We might need your help when we break out of the tunnels.'

'Aye, sir.'

Cael stood, and the four volunteers gathered round him. He glanced down at the rest of the platoon, then he gestured to his volunteers and began running along the valley. He heard the four others follow him, and they sprinted down the track, the high cliffs to their right. They slowed to a silent walk as they approached the cave entrance, and Cael pointed it out for the others, then he ordered them to crouch by a huge boulder.

'I'm going to make us all appear invisible,' Cael said to them. 'The Unk Tannic will not be able to see us, even in the strongest lamplight.'

The marines stared at him.

'Sorry, sir,' said the Holdings marine, 'but are you out of your mind?'

Cael glanced at the sergeant. 'I told you I could do this – did you let the rest of the platoon know?'

'No, sir,' said the sergeant. 'You told me to keep it a secret.'

'Well, it isn't a secret any more,' said Cael. 'Watch this.'

*You cannot see me.*

The marines' eyes widened, and the corporal edged away.

*You can see me again.*

'I'm going to do the same thing,' he said, 'but it will cover all of us. Do not stray too far from me, or you will become visible again. Understood?'

*You cannot see us.*

'Let's go.'

They edged their way up the slope, joining the snake-like path that the Unk Tannic had taken. Two of them were crouching by the cave entrance, keeping watch over the valley, but they looked right through the approaching marines. Cael drew his short sword, and the other volunteers did the same. They crept up the hillside, then the sergeant and the corporal rammed their swords into the throats of the two guards. They dragged the bodies to the side, and Cael led them into the tunnel. It was in pitch darkness for the first twenty yards, and the marines had to feel their way forward through the cramped, narrow shaft. It turned sharply to the right, and a faint glow appeared. Cael followed the dim light, and the tunnel turned again. Ahead was a small, lamplit cavern, where six Unk Tannic soldiers were surrounding four of the captured marines. Cael nodded to his volunteers, and they ran forwards, their swords out. The marines cut down the bewildered Unk Tannic soldiers in seconds, their invisible Tempest swords slicing clean through limbs and chests. The four captured marines dived to the ground, as the Unk Tannic bodies fell around them.

*The marines can see us.*

The captured marines gasped as their rescuers became visible to their eyes. Cael crouched, and cut the cords tied to the wrists of one.

'Where have the others been taken?' he said, as his volunteers released the remaining three captives from their bonds.

'For interrogation, sir,' said one of the marines. 'They were going to execute us four, and roll our bodies down into the valley where the advance platoon could find them.'

Cael smiled. 'Don't be distracted by our new armour; we are the advance platoon.'

'How did you lot get caught?' said Cael's sergeant.

'We were ambushed, sergeant. We were the last squad to climb the hill, and the bastards were waiting for us. They killed two of us on the way up here.'

'That leaves six,' said Cael.

One of the Unk Tannic soldiers groaned from the floor of the cavern.

'This one's still alive, sir,' said a marine, lifting his sword.

'Wait,' said Cael.

He walked over to the wounded soldier. Without help, he would likely die within a few minutes, so Cael kneeled by his side, and prised open one of the man's eyes. He entered the mind of the Unk Tannic soldier, ignoring the shock and agony passing through his mind. He sought out rough directions of the layout of the tunnel complex, and imprinted them into his own mind; then he nodded to the marine.

'I've got what I need. Cut his throat.'

'Aye, sir.'

The marine ran his Tempest blade along the soldier's neck, and opened up his throat. Cael stood, and eyed the four they had rescued.

'Go back along the tunnel and down the hill. The rest of the advance platoon will be there by now.'

'Aye, sir. Thank you, sir.

'Volunteers,' said Cael; 'with me.'

Cael felt a ripple of excitement and a feeling verging on joy as he led the four volunteers deeper into the cavern network. Once again, he was appearing reckless and stupidly courageous to the other marines, and he found it hard to admit that he was enjoying himself. His mother had always told him how awful violence was, and his Uncle Corthie had said that his own life had been scarred by death and fighting; of all his relatives, only Granny Daphne and Aunty Sable had relished the thrill of danger, and the intoxicating feeling of being good at killing. Cael wondered if he had found something he had in common with his grandmother and aunt, as he followed the map in his mind through the twisting tunnels, deeper into the flank of the mountain. They passed two Unk Tannic soldiers guarding a wide junction of tunnels, and cut them down with their Tempest swords, then they came to the entrance of a large cavern, where over sixty Unk Tannic had gathered. Crates of supplies, weapons and explosives lined one rough wall of the cavern, while the six captured marines were being beaten by soldiers, and questioned by three men in long black robes.

Cael brought his invisible volunteers to a halt by the entrance, and they gazed into the cavern. Cael went in to the mind of his sergeant.

*Upon my signal, sergeant, lead the others into the cavern. Go straight to the captives, and get them out. Do you remember the way back?*

*Aye, sir, but where will you be?*

*I'll be dealing with the rest of the Unk Tannic. Do you see those explosives by the far wall? There are enough to destroy half of the mountain stockpiled down here. Make sure you're back outside before I set them off.*

*Forgive me, sir, but you are a crazy bastard.*

*Someone has to keep up the good name of the Holdfasts, sergeant. Get ready for my signal.*

Cael withdrew from the sergeant's mind, and shot his vision into the eyes of a well-armed Unk Tannic soldier, who was standing close to where the three robed men were shouting questions about troop movements at the six captives.

Cael filled the heart of the soldier with hate and loathing.

*You despise the Unk Tannic. Draw your sword and kill them all! Do it! Kill them – kill them all!*

The soldier swayed, his eyes glazing over, then he drew the sword from its scabbard, and brought it down onto the neck of another Unk Tannic. In a frenzy, the soldier began swinging his sword two-handed, cleaving his way towards the robed men. Cael went into another soldier's mind, and did the same thing, then he did it to another, until all three were cutting down their comrades, and the cavern was in chaos.

'Now, sergeant,' Cael said.

Cael led his volunteers into the cavern. They were still invisible to all, and their black blades slashed out. Cael headed for the three robed men. He plunged his sword into the back of one, as the others stared around in panic and confusion. Screams arose, as many of the Unk Tannic tried to flee from the cavern, jostling each other, and bunching together as they were attacked from two sides. From their left, the three rogue Unk Tannic were still charging into their comrades; while, from the right, the five invisible marines were cutting their way towards their captured colleagues. The sergeant was the first to reach them. He sliced through their bonds, as Cael made themselves visible to the marines. The volunteers freed the others, and they began to retreat back towards the tunnel. Cael went into the mind of a robed man.

*You are now under my command. You can see me.*

The robed man screamed as Cael appeared in front of him.

'Come with me,' Cael said, driving his powers of persuasion into the robed man's mind.

Cael ran after the fleeing marines, and the robed man followed him. When the two of them were halfway to the outside, Cael came to a halt, and the robed man stopped alongside him, his hands shaking. Cael gazed into his eyes.

'Go back to the cavern, and open a box of explosives. Pick one up, then drop it onto the cavern floor, nose down. Do it.'

The robed man shuddered, then he turned, and ran back towards the cavern. Cael went in the opposite direction, sprinting as fast as he could along the twisting tunnels. He was within a few feet of the outside when an enormous explosion roared out. The force threw Cael forwards, through the cave entrance, and out into the night sky, followed a moment later by a huge cloud of dust and debris. Cael flew through the air, then he hit the side of the slope and tumbled and rolled to the bottom. For a few moments he could see nothing. His ears were ringing and bleeding, and he was coated in dust.

'Sir!' cried a sergeant, as Cael felt hands grab his shoulders.

'Is he dead?' said someone else.

Cael choked and gasped.

'Pyre's tits, lad,' shouted the sergeant. 'Platoon – get the freed captives and the lieutenant back down the hill. Go.'

Cael felt himself being picked up, then he fell into unconsciousness.

'I'm sorry, sir,' said the voice, 'but he is a danger to himself and to the marines under his command.'

'I beg to differ, Lieutenant,' said another voice. 'Did he not rescue ten captured marines, and destroy one of the largest Unk Tannic compounds yet discovered in this region? The bodies of over a hundred Unk Tannic soldiers have been pulled from the side of the mountain so far.'

Cael opened his eyes. He was expecting to feel nothing but agony, but he had no wounds, and his sight and hearing were working perfectly.

A marine nurse glanced down at him. 'How are you feeling, Lieutenant?'

'Fine,' Cael said.

The other officers in the hospital room turned to look down at him.

'You had a dose of salve,' the nurse went on. 'Without it, you might not have made it through the night.'

'Please leave us for a moment, nurse,' said the brigade captain.

The nurse saluted, and left the room. Cael watched as the officers approached. Among them stood the battalion major, and the colonel in command of the entire operation to hunt down the Unk Tannic in the west of Na Sun Ka.

'You disregarded orders, Second Lieutenant Holdfast,' said the captain. 'Your commanding officer told you to remain where you were, and to report any findings to him. You neglected those instructions. What do you have to say for yourself?'

Cael leaned up on an elbow. 'I was of the opinion, sir,' he said, 'that time was the critical factor. I watched the Unk Tannic bundle the captured marines into a cave entrance, and knew the only way to save them was to act with all the speed I could muster. Are all ten captives alive, sir? And my platoon?'

The captain allowed a small smile to flit across his lips. 'The freed captives are already back with their company, and your platoon suffered no casualties in the explosion.'

The colonel stepped forward. 'If I felt you were trying to show off, Lieutenant Holdfast, I would have no hesitation in stripping you of your commission. The marines are the pride of the Empire – they are not the place for those who recklessly place their comrades into danger.'

'I wasn't showing off, sir,' said Cael. 'I was doing my best to save the captured marines.'

'And the explosion?'

'That was designed to stop the Unk Tannic from following us, sir.'

'Once again, Holdfast,' said his first lieutenant, 'you were exceptionally lucky. You risked the lives of your marines, doing what should have been impossible. How did you find the captives? How did you get out alive?'

'I used my vision powers to locate the prisoners, sir.'

The first lieutenant shook his head. 'This boy should be packed off to the staff department. He was lucky in Sun Ta, and even luckier yesterday. I cannot work with a second lieutenant who so blatantly and continually disregards orders.'

'And how would we explain that to the rest of the battalion, Lieutenant?' said the major. 'They would think we were being petty, throwing away an asset like that. I recommend we overlook any regulations he might have broken, in order to preserve morale.'

'There is an elite marine company being formed in Sun Ta for seaborne operations,' said the colonel. 'Perhaps they would be a better place for Lieutenant Holdfast's abilities. They are running a training programme in the harbour – he could be there within a few days.'

'I would rather keep him in the battalion, sir,' said the major.

'We cannot ignore the fact that he disobeyed orders, Major,' said the colonel; 'however, there will be no charges, and no court martial. Announce his transfer to the battalion.'

The major frowned. 'Aye, sir.'

The colonel glanced at Lieutenant Holdfast. 'You can leave for Sun Ta at dawn tomorrow, when the supply convoy travels back to the coast. If I hear any more instances of you disregarding orders, I will not be so merciful.'

'Understood, sir,' said Cael.

The officers filed out of the room, with only the major lingering. He waited until the others had gone, then he nodded at Cael.

'Damn fine work, lad. The battalion is going to miss you.'

'Thank you, sir.'

The major walked out, and the nurse came back in.

'I am discharging you from the hospital, now, sir,' the nurse said. 'A fresh uniform is hanging up in the wardrobe.'

Cael nodded, and the nurse left. He got out of bed, opened the wardrobe, and pulled on the clean Number Three uniform. He laced up his boots, then walked out of the room. He went to the end of the corridor, and stepped outside into the bright sunshine, where his platoon was waiting for him.

'There he is!' cried a corporal. 'The luckiest bastard alive!'

Cael laughed, as the marines of his platoon crowded round him.

'You're getting yourself quite a reputation, sir,' said a sergeant. He leaned in close. 'And, just so you know, none of your volunteers has leaked your little secret to anyone outside the platoon. Your invisibility trick might come in handy again, eh, sir?'

'If I do use it again,' Cael said, 'it won't be with this platoon. I'm being transferred for disregarding orders.'

The faces of his platoon fell.

'But,' Cael went on, 'I'm not being hauled before a court martial. They could have kicked me out of the marines for what I did.'

'For saving ten prisoners, sir?' said a corporal.

'I might have neglected to tell you that I was ordered to stay in the valley.'

'Where are you being sent, sir?' said a sergeant.

'To a new company that's being trained in Sun Ta harbour. Seaborne operations.'

'Well, sir,' said the sergeant, 'life will be duller without you. Safer, but duller.'

'I'm leaving at dawn,' Cael said, 'which gives me time to buy you all a beer tonight.'

'You heard the lieutenant,' said the sergeant. 'Let's give the lad a proper send off.'

# CHAPTER 19
# THE STEPPING STONE

**Sun Ta, Na Sun Ka, Western Rim – 9th Duninch 5266 (18th Gylean Year 17)**

Sigum extended his wings and took off from the roof of the Temple of Throscala. Lahnos looked down from the shoulders of the dragon, his gaze on the streets of Sun Ta. Sanang soldiers were still occupying the city, along with a few regular regiments of the Imperial Army, and an uneasy peace hung over the neighbourhoods. After days of friction between the natives of Dragon Eyre and the former settlers and soldiers from Implacatus, the two peoples had been moved into separate districts of the city, and imperial forces were patrolling the line that kept them apart. Under Implacatus rule, the natives had been enslaved, and then, during the Unk Tannic regime, the situation had been reversed. With the advent of the Empire, official policy stated that both sides were to be treated equally, and the Sanang soldiers were enforcing that rule, dealing with the natives and the settlers with the same level of contempt.

The streets had been cleared of rubble, and the harbour and marketplaces had reopened to trade, but legal squabbles over who owned the fertile farmland to the south of the city were delaying the planting of new crops. Both settlers and natives had claims to the land that each insisted were legally valid, and an imperial commission had been established to work through the cases. In the meantime, Sun Ta remained dependent upon aid arriving from the Star Continent, and huge quantities of food were being brought through a portal every day.

Sigum soared towards the harbour. Most of the marines had been pulled out at the beginning of Duninch, in order to hunt down the remnants of the Unk Tannic in the volcanic wastelands in the western third of Na Sun Ka, and regiments of Holdings soldiers were helping to occupy the port district of the city. Beyond the breakwater, the dragon carrier remained anchored, a visible symbol of the power of the Empire, while the frigates and troopships were berthed along several of the harbour's long piers. Sigum swooped down, and landed on an area of the quayside kept clear for dragons.

Lahnos unbuckled the straps holding him to the harness and climbed down to the worn flagstones.

'I should be an hour or so,' he said to the dragon.

'Very well, my rider,' said Sigum. 'Do not be too hard on the boy.'

Lahnos gave the dragon a wry smile. 'I will try to restrain myself.'

'I will come back for you at noon,' said Sigum. 'Farewell.'

Sigum took to the skies, and Lahnos lifted a hand to his eyes as a wash of warm air and dust came down from his wings. Lahnos turned, and gazed over the harbour. Next to the warships of the Empire, several merchant galleys had docked, bringing goods from Queen Blackrose's realm of the Eastern Rim. One small pier had been sealed off from the others, and Lahnos made his way towards it, passing battle-damaged buildings and piles of supplies being offloaded from the ships. As always, his horns marked him out, and he received many glances, salutes and nods as he crossed the quayside.

He approached the sealed-off pier. Four marines were preventing civilians and unauthorised personnel from getting onto the wooden structure, and Lahnos greeted them.

'Commander Laimos,' said one of the marines, 'how can we help you?'

'I'm looking for Second Lieutenant Holdfast,' he said. 'I believe he has been assigned to Captain Doune's Seaborne Company.'

'He got here four days ago, Commander,' said the marine. 'The lieutenant is currently taking part in an exercise, along with the rest of the company.' He gestured towards one of the imperial frigates.

Lahnos looked out towards the frigate. A cluster of small boats were gathered by its port flank, and marines were scaling the side of the larger vessel with ropes, while bemused sailors watched from the main deck.

'Can I ask,' said Lahnos; 'is Captain Doune's company where those who disobey orders are usually sent?'

The marines looked a little offended by his words.

'No, sir,' said one. 'Lieutenant Holdfast is the only one. The others are all veterans and volunteers.'

'Thank you,' said Lahnos. 'Do I have your permission to enter the pier?'

'Aye, sir.'

The marines stood aside, and Lahnos eased past the small barricade of stacked barrels. He walked down the pier, which was loaded with dozens of crates. Six small, single-sailed craft were berthed down the left-hand side of the pier, but only a handful of marines was present, and they were all watching what was happening by the frigate. Lahnos joined them, and the marines saluted.

'What are they doing?' said Lahnos.

'They've been practising boarding vessels all morning, sir,' said a marine. 'They should be back in a few minutes.'

'Who is in command here?'

'That would be me, sir,' said a junior lieutenant. 'Captain Doune is leading the exercise in person.'

'How long have you been based down here?'

'The company was formed twelve days ago, sir. Marine command felt that a unit specialising in ship-to-ship tactics might be useful in the environs of Dragon Eyre. There is a fear that piracy may be on the increase following our takeover of the island.'

Lahnos watched as the marines clambered up the side of the frigate. A few reached the railings, and a light-hearted cheer arose from the sailors on board. A whistle sounded, and the marines began to return to the small vessels bobbing on the gentle swell by the side of the frigate. As soon as every marine was back on board their craft, the sails were raised and they turned towards the pier. A few minutes later, they berthed alongside where Lahnos was standing, and the marines on the pier helped secure the ropes and affix the gangways to the small craft.

The arriving marines crowded the pier. Many were soaking wet from having fallen into the waters of the harbour, and none were wearing any form of heavy armour. A tall Kellach officer with blond hair started issuing orders, and the marines obeyed, packing up the sails of the craft, and clearing away their equipment. Lahnos walked through the marines towards the officer, who turned and caught his glance.

'Commander Laimos?' the officer said. 'To what do we owe this singular pleasure?'

'Captain Doune?'

'Aye, sir. That's me, sir.'

'I would be obliged, Captain, if I could take Lieutenant Holdfast aside for a short while.'

'Is that an order, sir?'

'If that's what it takes, then yes.'

'Very well, sir.' Doune turned his head. 'Holdfast! Get yer arse up here.'

Cael looked up from where he was working on the deck of one of the small craft, then he climbed onto the pier and made his way through the marines to stand in front of Doune and Lahnos. He saluted.

'Commander Laimos wants you,' Doune said. He glanced at Lahnos. 'When will you be bringing him back, sir?'

'I'll have him returned to you in an hour or so, Captain. Thank you for your cooperation.'

Lahnos gestured to Cael, and they set off towards the quayside. They passed the barricade, and walked to the harbour front.

'Am I in trouble, sir?' said Cael. 'Are you here to reprimand me?'

'I'm here to take you to lunch,' said Lahnos, 'but there may be some scolding involved.'

They reached one of the few waterfront taverns that had reopened, and Lahnos selected an outside table, in the shade of the building. They sat, and a waiter approached.

'Two ales, a jug of water, and whatever you have for lunch,' said Lahnos.

The waiter bowed his head, and walked away.

'How are you settling in to your new position?' Lahnos said to Cael.

'I miss my old platoon,' said Cael, 'but I'm enjoying it here.'

'Are you leading a squad?'

'No, sir. Captain Doune told me that my rank was meaningless in the Seaborne Company. I'm currently taking orders from a corporal, who has nine years of service behind him. The captain gives out authority based on merit, he says, not rank.'

'That seems a little unorthodox.'

'Captain Doune reports directly to the colonel in command of all marines on Na Sun Ka. He claims he is outside the official chain of command.'

Their ale and water arrived, and the waiter set them down on to the table.

'Today's lunch is tuna steak with garlic sauce,' he said.

Lahnos nodded. 'Two portions, please.'

The waiter walked away again.

Lahnos eyed Cael, as he filled two mugs with ale. 'You are very fortunate.'

'So I am constantly being reminded, sir.'

'Drop the *sir*. This is just us talking, Cael. Why did you disregard orders?'

Cael sighed, as though he had answered the same question many times before. 'In my opinion, entering the caverns quickly was the only way to save the ten captured marines. If I had waited until reinforcements had arrived, then at least four of the captives would have been executed.' He looked into Lahnos's eyes. 'We stopped those executions from happening.'

'There are many rumours swirling around,' Lahnos said; 'stories claiming that you have a whole range of secret abilities. Can I assume that you used your powers of invisibility to get out of the caverns alive?'

Cael nodded. 'Aye, but the real reason I'm still alive is salve. The explosion would have killed me if they hadn't given me a dose in the field hospital. But I don't regret what I did. Ten marines are alive because we rescued them.'

'The explosion killed over three hundred Unk Tannic,' Lahnos said 'You eliminated one of their largest mountain strongholds.'

'And yet I am being punished.'

Lahnos narrowed his eyes, then he laughed. 'You call this punishment? No charges were laid against you, Cael. You ignored orders and got away with it. How did Captain Doune react to you being transferred here?'

'He was... dubious, at first. He asked if I was a glory-hunter, or a troublemaker.'

'I'm not surprised. Your behaviour is exhibiting a pattern, Cael – a pattern of reckless decisions that have, so far, turned out in your favour. If you keep this up, the marines will have no choice but to kick you out.'

'Captain Doune has warned me of this,' said Cael. 'He told me that this is my last chance.'

Lahnos took a swig of cool ale. 'Are you going to tell me why?'

'I have already told you,' said Cael. 'I acted because I thought it was the only way to save those marines.'

'And earlier, in Sun Ta? What explains that behaviour?'

Cael opened his mouth to speak, then the waiter returned. He set down several dishes next to them, bowed and walked away.

Lahnos pulled his lunch towards him, and picked up some bread from a bowl. They ate in silence for a few minutes, then Lahnos glanced at Cael.

'You were about to say something,' he said.

Cael kept his attention on his lunch.

'I have sway with the commanders of the marines, Cael,' Lahnos went on. 'If you have any sort of decent explanation, then I can help you.'

Cael glanced down. 'I...'

'Yes?'

Cael lowered his voice. 'Did you know that my mother has the ability to catch glimpses of the future?'

Lahnos puffed out his cheeks. 'Are you saying that you share this power?'

'Aye. I had a vision that day in Sun Ta. A vision that showed me shaking hands with you as the sun set. All but one of my platoon was in the vision. Do you understand what I am telling you? I *knew* that none of them would die that day. I knew we would be invincible.'

They carried on eating for a few minutes, as Lahnos tried to digest what Cael had told him. He remembered hearing about Karalyn's strange ability to occasionally see things that were yet to occur. At the time, he had dismissed it and, as Karalyn would never speak of any visions she had seen, he had almost forgotten that she possessed the power.

'I guess that makes sense,' he said. 'These visions, how often do you get them?'

'They're rare,' said Cael, 'and most of them are either useless or incredibly frustrating. The most common vision is of something that will happen within the next few moments, but sometimes I get visions of things I don't understand until they happen. The vision I saw in Sun Ta was the first useful one I have ever had. I knew exactly what kind of power it gave me, and I took full advantage of it. What I didn't consider at the time was how everyone else would react. I haven't told anyone about this vision, not until now. Is it any wonder that the marines think I'm reckless?'

'I will protect you from your officers,' said Lahnos. 'I will make it clear to them that you are not to be discharged from the service without my authority. And, if the worst happens, I will bring you into my own team, if, that is, you would be happy taking orders from me.'

'Thank you,' said Cael. 'Right now, I want to settle in to my new company. As I said, I'm enjoying it so far.'

'You might be hunting pirates soon.'

Cael smiled. 'Aye.' His smile faded a little. 'What date is it on the Star Continent?'

'Why?'

'Arrosa's birthday must be getting closer, but I lost track of the dates a while ago.'

'On Athumia, her birthday was on the eighteenth of Tradinch,' said Lahnos, 'which corresponds to the Nineteenth Day of the Last Third of Spring on the Star Continent.'

'I know, but what date is that on Dragon Eyre?'

'It'll be Tradinch, I think, so, next month? The differences between the Divine Calendar and the one we used on Athumia confuse me. They use the same names for the months, but the dates don't line up. I'll ask Adjutant Claudian when I next see him. He'll probably know.'

Their eyes went to the harbour, as a sleek merchant vessel entered, bearing the flag of Olkis from its main mast. It berthed by the side of the quay, and dockworkers tied its ropes to the iron cleats.

'That might be the first ship from Olkis to get here since we arrived,' said Lahnos.

Several sailors hurried down the gangway from the ship as soon as it was put in place. They went up to an imperial soldier, and started talking to him, their arms gesticulating. Within seconds, the soldier led them to an officer, and more gathered as the sailors spoke.

Lahnos glanced at Cael. 'Could you use your powers to persuade one of the Olkian sailors to come over here? I want to know what news they're bringing.'

Cael nodded, then he glanced over at the next batch of sailors who were coming down the gangway. One of them halted on the quayside, then he turned, and walked towards the tavern. The sailor approached the table where Cael and Lahnos were sitting, then he took a seat, and blinked.

'Tell us what your colleagues are telling that officer,' said Cael.

The sailor nodded. 'We sailed across the ocean in a straight line from Olkis to here,' he said, 'to avoid the dragons of Gyle and Ectus. When we were passing the midway point of the voyage, we saw the largest ship we've ever seen. The *Wondrous Light*, it was called.' He pointed at the dragon carrier anchored beyond the breakwaters. 'It looked just like that.'

'You saw the other dragon carrier?' said Lahnos.

'If that's what it is,' said the sailor. 'Five days ago, it was.'

'What was the dragon carrier doing?' said Lahnos.

'Nothing,' said the sailor. 'It was anchored.'

'In the middle of the ocean?'

'Aye. All alone in the middle of the ocean. Its big deck was crowded with dragons. We'd heard that the Empire had sent ships to Dragon Eyre, so we sailed closer to take a look. The dragons attacked us. They sank the two vessels we had set sail with, and we barely escaped. The dragons – they were Wystians.'

'Wystians were on board the dragon carrier? What about the crew?'

'We saw no sign of any humans on board,' said the sailor. 'Not one. The only reason we managed to escape was that the dragons were near exhaustion, as if they'd flown a great distance. We were able to outpace them.'

Lahnos frowned. 'The *Wondrous Light* was due to arrive in Olkis over twenty days ago. Two dragons from Ulna were on board. They were supposed to be arranging an alliance between Olkis and the Eastern Rim.'

'Well, they never made it to Olkis,' said the sailor. 'My guess is that they sailed too close to Rigga, and were attacked by the exiled Wystians who live there.'

'Rigga?' said Lahnos. 'Shit. The carrier was anchored close to Rigga?'

'No. It was halfway between Rigga and Gyle.'

'Then, a dragon could fly onto it from Rigga, rest a day, and then reach Gyle?'

'That's about right, sir.'

Lahnos got to his feet. 'I need to speak to the officers.' He threw some money onto the table. 'Finish your lunch, Cael, and buy this sailor an ale. Then get yourself back to the pier.'

Cael nodded.

Lahnos hurried away in the direction of the marine headquarters along the harbour front. Several Olkian sailors were standing outside, talking to a large group of army and marine officers, and Lahnos walked into their midst.

'Have you heard the news, Commander?' said an army major.

'I have,' said Lahnos. 'The trapped Wystians on Rigga are using the second dragon carrier as a stepping stone to reach Gyle. How many could fly over every day?'

'Perhaps ten?' said a colonel. 'We need to inform the Adjutant.'

Lahnos followed a dozen senior officers into the building. A few Olkians went with them, and they entered a grand meeting room on the ground floor, where Adjutant Claudian was based whenever he was on Dragon Eyre. The Adjutant was on his feet when they walked in, speaking to three aides.

'Adjutant Claudian,' said the marine colonel.

'I know,' said Claudian, his features stern. 'I have just heard the details from these men.' He strode over to a large map of Dragon Eyre hanging from a wall, and gazed up at it in silence, as the others clustered round him. He raised a long pointer, and tapped the area of the ocean between Rigga and Gyle.

'If the *Wondrous Light* is roughly here,' he said, 'then the distance between the ship and land is around four hundred and fifty miles in each direction. A fit adult dragon could fly that distance in around eight to ten hours. Assuming that they rest on board overnight, they could fly the same distance the following day. The carrier could act as a small island, allowing the Wystians on Rigga to escape their captivity.'

'How many Wystians are on Rigga, sir?' said Lahnos.

The Adjutant glanced at him. 'Sable Holdfast transported approximately seven thousand dragons from Wyst to Rigga over ten years ago. We don't have a precise number of how many live there now.' He turned to one of the Olkians. 'It has been five days since you saw the *Wondrous Light*, yes?'

'Aye,' said the sailor.

'That carrier set sail from Ulna forty days ago,' said the Adjutant, 'which means that they might have been in their current location for around twenty days, perhaps longer. But how did the Wystians on Rigga know where it would be? Any ideas? Anyone?'

'Maybe they sailed too close to the Riggan shore,' said one of the Olkians, 'and were seen by Wystians out flying from Rigga. They might have killed the two dragons on board, and forced the crew to sail to its current location.'

The Adjutant shook his head. 'Strange coincidences can happen, but long experience has taught me to look for the hand of others in disasters such as these. I served on Dragon Eyre when I was part of the Banner forces here. In those days, we would have ascribed such an ambush to the work of the gods. Could there still be a few gods upon this world? Did Sable Holdfast perhaps force a few into hiding during her infamous rampage?'

'There has been no sign of any gods here for years,' said an Olkian sailor.

'Maybe Sable's presence on Ulna has kept them hidden among the mortal population, and it was the arrival of the Empire that has emboldened them to take action. But why then would they assist the Wystians; and why would the Wystians trust any god of Implacatus?'

'Should we be taking practical steps, sir?' said Lahnos. 'The exiled Wystians will be arriving in Gyle at a rate of ten every day.'

The Adjutant of the Empire drew his gaze away from the map. He stared at the floor for a moment, then nodded.

'We shall send the fleet to intercept and liberate the second dragon carrier,' said Claudian. 'Lord Sigum's team, under Commander Lahnos, will be aboard the *Horned God*, and four frigates will accompany them.

We will also need a detachment of marines, who will board the *Wondrous Light* and take it back under our control. Assuming that the Wystians have eliminated some or all of the Irlanian sailors crewing the second carrier, spare crew will also be on board the *Horned God*. Once liberated, both carriers will return to Sun Ta.' He glanced at the marine colonel. 'I would also recommend that the fleet takes Second Lieutenant Holdfast with them. I hear that he has been reassigned to the harbour?'

'Yes, sir,' said the colonel.

'It is critical that we stop the Wystians from migrating to Gyle in large numbers,' Claudian said to the assembled officers. I would rather the *Wondrous Light* be sunk than it continue to be used as a stepping stone. If possible, bring the carrier back in one piece. If not, send it to the bottom of the ocean.' He glanced at the captain of the *Horned God*. 'When will your carrier be ready to sail?'

'We shall need to load supplies, recall some of the crew, and rustle up a detachment of marines, sir,' the captain said. 'We could leave Sun Ta at dawn two days from now, if the marines can be found at such short notice.'

'Lieutenant Holdfast is part of a company-strength detachment conducting ship-boarding exercises in the harbour,' said the marine colonel.

'Ship-boarding exercises?' said the Adjutant. 'That sounds perfect.'

'Unfortunately, sir,' the colonel said, 'the company was only formed some twelve days ago. They are still lacking in expertise.'

'But they are all experienced marines?' said the Adjutant.

'Yes, sir.'

'Send them,' said the Adjutant. 'That will be far quicker than trying to recall companies from the west of Na Sun Ka.'

'Is there a risk that we might be leaving Na Sun Ka vulnerable to a counter-attack from Gyle, sir?' said Lahnos. 'If I go with Lord Sigum's team, and Cael Holdfast is also on board, we would have little warning if the Wystians return from the west.'

'We have twenty thousand Sanang soldiers based in Sun Ta,

Commander,' said Claudian, 'along with fifteen thousand regular army infantry, as well as the five thousand marines in the west of the island. We also have several dozen batteries of Forty-Eighters to protect us from aerial assault. We shall be able to hold Na Sun Ka until the fleet returns.' He nodded. 'You have your orders. Get to work.'

The officers left the room, and Lahnos pulled the captain of the *Horned God* and the colonel in charge of the marines aside in the wide corridor.

'I will speak to Lord Sigum's dragons and the Bullan support team,' he said, 'and have them all on board the *Horned God* by tomorrow evening, ready to sail the following dawn.'

'And I will ensure Captain Doune's Seaborne Company is on board at the same time,' said the colonel.

'We shall need Cael Holdfast to begin scouting the ocean as soon as we set sail,' said the captain. 'Is the lad up to it? I heard he had got himself into some trouble.'

'There is no denying his courage,' said the colonel, 'but I worry about his ability to follow orders.'

'Would you be willing to temporarily transfer Captain Doune's company into my authority for the duration of the operation, Colonel?' said Lahnos. 'Cael will listen to me.'

The colonel nodded. 'That is acceptable to me but be warned, Commander; Captain Doune can be prickly to deal with, which is why I moved him to his own company.'

'Shall we meet tomorrow morning, to discuss progress?' said Lahnos.

The two other officers nodded, then they went their separate ways. Lahnos walked back to the tavern where he had been eating lunch, but Cael had gone. He glanced up, and saw Sigum circling overhead. Lahnos walked on to the cleared area of the quayside, and Sigum landed.

'I have been waiting for you for several minutes, my rider,' the silvery-green dragon said.

'Sorry about that,' said Lahnos, as he climbed up into the harness.

'We have a new crisis to deal with. We shall need to summon the whole team together, so I can brief them.'

'As you will, rider,' Sigum said, then he raised his wings, and ascended into the bright blue sky.

Five hours later, Lahnos was relaxing in his new quarters. He had been given a small apartment close to the harbour of Sun Ta, and he had a view of the piers and ships from his balcony. Small launches were ferrying crew and supplies out to the *Horned God*, while four of the frigates inside the harbour basin were also being loaded with food and fresh water. Efizel and the rest of the Bullan had already sailed to the dragon carrier on one of the launches, and were preparing the ship to take the five dragons back out to sea.

Lahnos sipped from a glass of white wine that had come from a vineyard on Haurn, as someone knocked on his front door. He frowned and got to his feet. It was the first time he had been able to relax all day, and he had only made it as far as one sip. He walked to the door and opened it.

Ora'lya was standing in the hallway outside.

'Am I interrupting anything, sir?' she said.

'No. It's fine. Have you spoken to Quicklime? I told her and the rest of the team everything I know, if you're here for more information about the operation.'

Ora'lya nodded and glanced down. 'I shouldn't have come here,' she said. 'It was a mistake. I should go.'

'Wait,' said Lahnos. 'Why did you come?'

Ora'lya said nothing, not meeting his gaze.

'Do you want to come inside?' he said. 'I've just opened a bottle of wine, and I have an excellent view from the balcony.'

'Quicklime would disown me if she knew I was here,' she said, 'but I had to come. I had to see you.'

Lahnos moved to the side and gestured towards the balcony. Ora'lya muttered something under her breath and walked into his apartment.

He led her out onto the balcony and they sat. Lahnos reached for a spare glass and filled it with wine, as Ora'lya remained silent.

'I usually prefer red,' he said to her, 'but white is all we're getting at the moment. It's from Haurn.'

Ora'lya remained silent.

'I can keep talking about nothing in particular until you're ready to tell me why you're here,' he went on. 'I met Cael Holdfast for lunch today. We had tuna in a garlic sauce. It was a bit odd, if I'm honest. I had never heard of tuna until I got here.'

'It's a big fish,' she said.

'So I gather. Why anyone thinks it should go with garlic is beyond me. I assume it's a Na Sun Ka delicacy.'

'I was wrong,' she said.

'About what?'

'I shouldn't have allowed Quicklime to destroy what we had. I should have stood up to her.'

'I would take you back without a moment's hesitation.'

'You would?'

'I have missed you so much, Ora'lya. It has pained me to see you every day on Quicklime's shoulders, knowing that I would never hold you again. As far as I'm concerned, my feelings haven't changed. I still want to be with you.'

'Then why haven't you said anything?'

'Because I'm immortal. I wanted you to be free to... I didn't want to put any pressure on you. Did you know that I turned thirty a few days ago?'

She shook her head.

'If we get back together,' he went on, 'then at some point in the future, we will cause each other a lot of pain. You will age, but I won't; and I still don't want to have any children. Knowing all that, are you sure you made a mistake breaking it off?'

'I can't bear to be without you,' she said. 'You made me happy when we were together, Lahnos, and I want to feel that again.'

'It will be difficult to hide this from Quicklime,' he said, 'seeing as how we'll all be on the dragon carrier together for several days.'

'I know, and yet – here I am.'

Lahnos got to his feet. He walked up to her, and reached out a hand. She took it, and stood. He put his hands on her waist and pulled her closer to him.

'This is probably a mistake,' he said.

'I know,' she said, as she draped her hands around his neck, 'but I don't care.'

They kissed, as the sun began to set in the western sky.

# CHAPTER 20
# A MATTER OF TIME

**Hold Stringer, Republic of the Holdings – 21st Day, Second Third Spring 545**

Corthie threw the empty bottle over his shoulder, and it shattered against the smooth granite wall.

'I hate wine,' he said. 'It tastes like vinegar.'

'Then why are you drinking it?' said Karalyn.

'Because there's nothing else here. Why couldn't Edmond have liked whisky or brandy, instead? Even gin would do, and I never thought I'd say that.'

Up on the wall to their left, an oil lamp sputtered and went out, and a thin tendril of dark smoke drifted up to the ceiling.

'We're running out of oil,' Karalyn said. 'In a few days, we'll be sitting in darkness.'

Corthie pulled another bottle of vintage wine from the rack. He found the corkscrew, and opened the bottle.

'Are you sure you don't want some?' he said.

'Aye, I'm sure,' she said.

'Why didn't Edgar kill me?' he said.

'Perhaps he thinks you will die of old age trapped in here.'

'But he also spared Bailey, and Bailey has stone powers. He must have realised that there was a risk Bailey would come back into the palace to look for us.'

'Put yourself in Edgar's position. The last thing he knew was Edmond putting him into a restrainer mask. A few millennia of agony pass, and then, when the mask is removed, he finds that everything he once knew has gone forever. Implacatus has been destroyed. The Ascendants are all dead.'

'Not all of them,' said Corthie.

'All right; not all – but the one who remains has had his mind completely wiped and his powers blocked. Effectively, as far as Edgar knows, he's dead. If I were Edgar, I would need a considerable amount of time to work out what I should be doing. Perhaps Edgar spared us because he is not completely sure if we can be trusted, or if we are his enemies. We need to know why Edmond put his own brother in a restrainer mask. Maybe Edgar was one of the rebels. Maybe he was helping Belinda and Nathaniel's revolt against Edmond. If that's the case, then he might consider us to be his enemy's enemy.'

'I'm too drunk to follow all that,' said Corthie. 'Pyre's arse, I miss the bairns.' A tear sprang from an eye and trickled down his cheek. 'I missed Clova's birthday. She was five. And, in a few days, Cairney will be turning nine. And I know that you also missed wee Caitlyn's second birthday, too.'

Karalyn rolled her eyes. 'I prefer you on whisky,' she said. 'Wine is making you maudlin.'

'It's not the damn wine,' he said. 'We've been stuck in this room for twenty-three days, Karalyn. Twenty-three days of sitting here doing nothing. Edgar and the ironhides might have slaughtered everyone in the Holdings by now. And what about all of the other gods he freed? Where are they? There was one who drowned seventeen million mortals; do you remember? What's she doing? – that's what I'd like to know.'

'Bailey will come for us.'

'Maybe. If he can be bothered. He seems a wee bit cowardly to me. Hey, maybe they'll ask Sable to look for us.'

'Kelsey will be doing whatever it takes to get us out of here.'

'I've been thinking,' he said, as he swigged from the bottle. 'Should I kill you?'

Karalyn narrowed her eyes at him.

'If you were dead, right,' he went on, 'your spirit could roam free again. You could find a new body, and then come and let me out of here.'

'I happen to like this body.'

'But, you know, if it came to it? If it was the only way to escape?'

'It wouldn't work,' she said. 'I've already tried to find my way out of here with vision, and couldn't. If my vision is trapped in there, then my spirit would also be trapped.' She eyed him. 'If you killed me, I would haunt you for the rest of your days.'

'What about all of the ventilation shafts you were talking about?' He pointed into a corner of the chamber, next to where a tall pile of crates was stacked. 'There's one there.'

'I've tried it,' she said. 'That particular shaft is too narrow to crawl along, and it ends in a series of wire gauze barriers too dense for my vision to pass through. I've been trapped in the Palace of the Almighty before, Corthie, and I can tell you that Edgar knew what he was doing when he lured us into this chamber. We have air, we have food, we have water, but there is no way to get out.'

Corthie nodded, then he swigged from the bottle again.

'What's the best thing about your new body?' he said.

'The powers that came with it,' she said.

'And the worst?'

'Being much shorter. I miss being tall. Some of the shelves in the kitchens of Colsbury are too high for me to reach, and I have to crane my neck to look up at Cael and Kyra.'

'You're still taller than Aila,' he said.

'Barely. Still, I'm not complaining. Having a body is infinitely better than not having one. Even Lyla's body was better than nothing, despite the fact that it hindered the use of my powers.'

'Why did it do that?'

'I don't know the exact reason, but I suspect it was because Lyla had no powers of her own.'

'Would you take a man's body, if you had to?'

Karalyn grimaced. 'No, thanks. I'd wait until a suitable woman appeared.'

'But then you'd have to kill them.'

'I was lucky with Albany, I suppose. She was torturing Bailey, and she had just murdered Lyla, so I had no moral concerns about killing her in return. I would never take the body of an innocent woman.'

Corthie stretched out his legs and reclined. 'Will you live forever, do you think?'

Karalyn said nothing.

Corthie glanced at her. 'Does that idea worry you?'

'It fills me with dread,' she said. 'Think about how long the Ascendants were alive for – thirty thousand years. Can you imagine existing that long? But thirty thousand years is nothing when set against, say, a million years. What about ten million? But even ten million is nothing compared to *forever*. I don't want to live forever, Corthie. My mind can't even begin to fathom what it would be like. I know every god and demigod must go through the same feelings, but they understand that they aren't really immortal. The Holdfasts have certainly proved that over the past few decades. My experience differs from theirs, because even if I am decapitated, I will linger on until I can find a replacement body to occupy.'

'Do you have any of Albany's memories?'

'None. I made sure of that when I wiped her mind clean. I still have a few of Lyla's though, because Lord Malum made such a mess of forcing me into her body. I can remember Lyla walking to school with her brother when they were children, for example.'

'It occurs to me,' said Corthie, 'that you might know my children for thousands of years, while I only get to spend a few decades with them.'

'Aye.'

Corthie shook his head, feeling drunk and melancholic.

'Are you still planning on having twelve,' said Karalyn, 'assuming we get out of here?'

'Aye.'

'Why twelve?'

'Aila wants to emulate her father,' he said. 'He had twelve children. Aila is the only one left alive.'

'Then there will be fifteen immortal Holdfasts,' she said.

Corthie frowned. 'Fifteen? My twelve, and your two – who else?'

'Are you forgetting that Sable's daughter is also a demigod? Alindi'osso, or Lindi, as Sable calls her.'

'What about her son?'

'He's half-Kellach, so he's mortal.'

'Do you remember what Belinda used to say?'

'What did she say?' said Karalyn.

'That it was dangerous to be having immortal children. That, eventually, they will feel entitled to take power for themselves.'

'And do you believe that?'

'I don't know.'

'I wouldn't worry,' she said. 'Aila and I will be around to make sure that doesn't happen.'

Corthie sat up. 'I'm hungry.'

'Then eat something.'

'I don't know if I can stand any more tubbed meat.'

He got to his feet, and staggered over the smooth granite floor, passing the place where they had piled their armour. He reached the crates and began to rummage around in them.

'More gold,' he said, as he shoved a crate to the side. 'Jewels in this one; and more gold. Why did Edmond hoard so much gold?' He opened another crate. 'Look; broken Quadrants. How useful.'

Karalyn walked over to take a look inside the crate.

'If I had a forge, then I might be able to repair some of these. Not that they would allow us to escape, but it would pass the time.'

She picked up a Quadrant that had a sword blow cutting through its curved edge.

'I recognise this one,' she said. 'Mother broke it in Colsbury, while Agatha was attacking. I then gave it to Kelsey to take to Lostwell. Do you remember?'

'Aye. Vaguely,' he said.

'I wonder how it ended up here,' said Karalyn. 'Elbannon would be overjoyed if he got his hands on this crate.'

'Don't we already have plenty of Quadrants?' said Corthie. 'We have all the ones the Ascendants brought with them.'

'More wouldn't do any harm.'

'You say that, but Edgar has one now.'

Karalyn poked around in the crate, then she pointed at a tiny ingot of black metal.

'Tempest,' she said. 'Not the alloy that's in our armour, but raw Tempest ore.'

'What's it doing here?' said Corthie. 'How did Edmond get his hands on some, when it can only be found on Athumia?'

'It must be all that remains of the original stock that Theodora brought over to Implacatus after she had built the Sextant,' she said. 'Nathaniel used most of it to create the Quadrants, and this small amount might be all that was left over. I guess Edmond probably wanted to use it to repair the broken Quadrants, but he didn't have anyone who knew how to do it.' She smiled.

'What are you grinning at?' he said.

'I have just realised something,' she said. 'I now know how we are going to be found; it's just a matter of time.'

Four hours later, Corthie's hangover was developing into a mighty headache. Karalyn had been refusing to heal his hangovers for several days, telling him that it was the price he had to pay for consuming so much of Edmond's wine. He lay back on the granite floor, using a fur-lined satin robe for a pillow, and tried to get some rest.

Another oil lamp sputtered out, and the shadows inside the large chamber grew. Over in one corner, Karalyn was trying to read some tattered old documents she had found, and she muttered a curse under her breath as the light faded. She got up, and sat closer to one of the remaining lamps.

'I could do with a healing, sis,' Corthie said. 'My head is pounding.'

'Then don't drink so much.'

'You're cruel to me.'

'I'm just trying to teach you a lesson in taking responsibility for your actions.'

A blinding light appeared in the side of the wall as bright sunlight shone through into the chamber. Corthie narrowed his eyes and squinted, and Karalyn got to her feet.

Two people moved into the light, their figures silhouetted against the sunshine.

'Mother? Uncle Corthie?'

Karalyn stepped forward and one of the figures jumped down into the chamber. Karalyn embraced her.

'I knew you'd find us, Kyra; well done.'

'It's taken me fourteen days,' Kyra said. 'Fourteen days of Bailey opening up walls and ventilation shafts, until I finally found a small trace of Tempest.' She glanced over at Corthie. 'Is he all right?'

'He's hungover,' said Karalyn. 'Too much wine.'

She walked over to where Corthie was lying, and pressed her hand to his forehead. He felt a wave of healing powers ripple through his body, and all of his aches and pains vanished in an instant. He got to his feet, rubbed the side of his head, and gazed at Kyra.

'You found the Tempest sitting in that crate?' he said. 'How?'

'The same way I found the Sextant when Cael took it last summer,' Kyra said. She produced a small object from a pocket. 'The Compass. Your armour was also giving off a small signal; that's why I brought the Compass along with me, but I could sense the raw Tempest ore through the small ventilation shaft in the corner of the room.'

The other figure stepped down into the chamber and glanced around at the crates.

'Did Edgar trap you in here?' Bailey said.

'Aye,' said Karalyn.

'He left you with enough supplies to last you months,' Bailey said. 'Did he say much to you?'

'He seemed unsure about what to do.'

'Where is he?' said Corthie. 'Is he still on the Star Continent?'

'We have no idea where he is,' said Bailey. 'In fact, I was hoping he might have given you an indication of his plans.'

Corthie walked up to the new opening in the wall. A series of similar entrances were lined up in a row, leading directly to the outside of the Palace of the Almighty. Corthie climbed up, and walked to the edge of the building. Down on the ground below, dozens of soldiers were gazing up at him. Kelsey was among them, along with Frostback and Halfclaw.

'It's Corthie!' cried a soldier. 'He's alive.'

'Is Karalyn in there, too?' Kelsey shouted up.

'Aye. We're both fine,' said Corthie.

The silver dragon raised her head and peered past Corthie into the large chamber. 'Was this your prison for the last twenty-three days?'

'Aye,' said Corthie. 'We had food; we had wine. It could have been worse.'

'I see crates of gold.'

'There's plenty of gold,' said Corthie, 'and jewels, and broken Quadrants – all kinds of stuff.'

Kelsey gestured to a squad of soldiers. 'Get in there and bring it all out.'

'Is that safe?' said Corthie. 'There might be other gods or beasts lurking in the palace.'

Kyra climbed up next to him. 'The palace is empty, Uncle. The prisoners, the ironhides, the undead dragons – they're all gone.'

'We should still be careful,' said Bailey. 'There might be some secret chambers still undiscovered.'

'There might be,' said Karalyn, 'but if there are, they remain sealed up.'

Karalyn, Corthie, Kyra and Bailey used a ladder to climb down to the ground. The soldiers then ascended, to begin the process of removing everything of value from the chamber. Corthie embraced Kelsey, who laughed and pushed him away.

'You stink,' she said.

He smiled. 'No bath for nearly a third.'

'I assume your Tempest armour is still in there?'

'Aye. We took it off after a couple of days. Has Edgar really gone?'

'They have all gone,' said Bailey. 'The first place we looked were the dungeons. All that remain there are skeletons and corpses. Every living prisoner has been released. A pile of restrainer masks was sitting by a doorway, along with a few empty vials of salve.'

'I want to go back to Colsbury,' said Karalyn.

'We'll leave the soldiers here and go there now,' said Kelsey.

'Frostback and I should stay close to the palace,' said Halfclaw, 'in case the greenflies return.'

'The greenflies?' said Corthie.

'We think Edgar took the gods, undead dragons and ironhides with him,' said Kelsey, 'but he released sixty or so greenflies into the Holdings. They're ravaging the neighbouring Holds, and fanning out to the east and west.'

'I have a theory about that,' said Bailey.

'It can wait,' said Kelsey. She turned to the dragons. 'Keep watch over the soldiers, please. If the greenflies come, hurry to Colsbury and let us know, and we'll be back in no time.'

Frostback and Halfclaw tilted their heads, then Kelsey nodded to Karalyn. The air shimmered, and the group found themselves standing on the middle balcony of the Summer Palace on Colsbury. Cardova was there, with the four children. Karalyn hurried over to them. She embraced Carden, then she took Caitlyn from Cardova's arms and held her close.

'Happy birthday,' she whispered to the girl.

Cardova kissed his wife. 'It's good to see you, Karalyn,' he said. 'I missed you; the children missed you. What did Edgar want with you?'

'He needed me and Corthie out of his way for a while, so that he could leave the palace.'

'Sit down, everyone,' said Kelsey. She gestured to a servant. 'Order up lunch from the kitchens, enough for all of us.'

'Yes, ma'am,' said the servant.

Kelsey led the others over to a large round table and they sat.

'Right,' said Kelsey; 'here's what we know.'

'Who put you in charge, sis?' said Corthie.

'I did,' said Kelsey. 'Twenty-three days ago, Karalyn and Corthie walked into the Palace of the Almighty and disappeared. One day later, the sixty greenflies escaped from the palace, or were released by Edgar. Bailey – you said you had a theory about that?'

'I do,' said the god. 'The... greenflies are inherently uncontrollable. Edgar would not have been able to give them any orders, and so I think it's likely that they escaped by accident, when Edgar was releasing the prisoners. If that was the case, there was nothing he would have been able to do to recall them.'

'Why are you defending him?' said Kelsey. 'He imprisoned my brother and sister.'

'Yes, but he made sure they had plenty of food and water. More importantly, he didn't kill them.'

'He couldn't have killed me,' said Karalyn.

'Fair point, but he could have killed Corthie. He didn't. Why not?'

'Have you remembered why he was imprisoned in the first place?' said Karalyn.

'That's not quite how it happened,' said Bailey. 'Edmond announced that his brother had been slain. I had no idea that he was still alive until I saw him for myself in the palace dungeons. I have been through my memories, and I do recall the circumstances that led to Edmond's announcement. Karalyn, do you remember me telling you the tale of Theodora's murder?'

'Aye,' she said.

'Well, for the benefit of the others, I will quickly recap it. Theodora was busy creating Athumia, and when she came out of a Sextant trance, she discovered that Edmond had been conducting an affair with Belinda. This led her to move back into her own palace, in a different region of Implacatus. Edmond gathered the gods loyal to him, and they attacked Theodora's palace. Theodora herself was in the midst of another Sextant trance at the time, and Edmond's forces were successful. All Edmond had to do was wait for her to come out of her trance to kill her – and that is precisely what he did. When he returned from the battle, Edmond then announced that his brother Edgar had been slain in the fighting; but here is the vital point – Edmond claimed that Edgar had been fighting on the side of Theodora, not against her. Edmond pronounced Edgar to have been a traitor, and said that he had deserved his violent death.'

Bailey lowered his gaze. 'I remember hearing about it at the time. I was upon the world my sister had made for me when the news of Theodora's death arrived. To be honest, next to the murder of my sister, the death of Edgar did not seem quite so important. After all, Theodora was the first Ascendant to die since we had arrived on Implacatus. Even so, I recall myself questioning Edmond's words. There were rumours that Edgar and my sister had become close – too close for Edmond's liking, and some even suggested that they were having an affair.'

Corthie shook his head. 'It sounds as though all of the Ascendants were unfaithful to their spouses.'

'That might be true, Corthie,' said Bailey. 'Edmond and Theodora were married for millennia, and both might have strayed from time to time. Nathaniel was also known for having relationships with several of the Ascendants, before he and Belinda came together.'

'Weren't you and Edgar close friends?' said Karalyn. 'Wouldn't you have known if he was involved with Theodora?'

'We had drifted apart a little by that time. When Edgar's death was announced, I don't think I had seen him in over a century. That, too, is quite common when you live for thousands of years. Friendships wax and wane over great spans of time. Regardless, I now believe the rumours to have been false, for, if Edgar had truly been having an affair with Theodora, I doubt that Edmond would have allowed him to live.'

'Where do you think he has gone?' said Cardova.

Bailey raised his palms. 'Who can say? He is in possession of my recent memories, so he must know all about the fall of the Ascendants, as well as the Holdfast Empire, the Allied Worlds, and the Doomed Worlds.'

'What about the other gods he freed?' said Corthie. 'You told us that one of them had drowned millions of mortals.'

Bailey nodded. 'Her name is Allura, and she is a daughter of Edmond and Theodora. She was imprisoned around two thousand years ago, long after Edgar's capture, so it is possible that Edgar was unaware of her crimes when he released her.'

'There you go again,' said Kelsey, 'defending Edgar.'

Bailey shrugged. 'I would divide the six gods set free by Edgar into two groups – those who rebelled against Edmond's rule, and the dangerously criminal. Allura falls into the second category, along with Lord Ward, Allura's brother. Ward was a killer so deranged and vicious that his acts appalled even Edmond. Those two are the ones we should fear. The other four might not be altogether hostile, as they were all rebels fighting against Edmond's tyranny. Ballatar, for example, led a revolt long before Nathaniel and Belinda started their rebellion. He loathed Edmond and all he stood for, and he particularly hated Bastion, Edmond's favoured son. I assume Ballatar's life was spared because Edmond was his grandfather. So, you see, we should not make the mistake of imagining that all seven fugitives have the same motivations or attitudes. I would guess that this group will soon fracture, as I cannot believe that Edgar would want to be associated with either Ward or Allura.'

'What would you do if you were in his place?' said Corthie.

'A good question,' said Bailey. 'Let me think. I suppose I would want to get off the Star Continent as quickly as possible, without being followed; and it appears that Edgar has accomplished this. But where would I go? Dragon Eyre, Athumia and the City would be too unfamiliar to me. Two of those worlds were completely unknown at the time of Edgar's capture, and Dragon Eyre was an unimportant backwater in those days. So, what does that leave – the Doomed Worlds? Edgar would know all about them, although most of those worlds weren't *doomed* back then. Some of them used to be quite delightful. If Edgar has gone to one of those worlds, taking the others with him, then he would have met the remnants of the other gods by now. That would include Lord Elmhirst, who I imagine is leading the Doomed Worlds. Edgar's sudden arrival with six other gods would have unpredictable effects, as Edgar is as powerful as any Ascendant, and his pedigree is unquestionable. He still has the ironhides to somehow restrain, though…' He snapped his fingers. 'Elidus. The icefields on that world would force the ironhides into a deep stupor, like hibernation. It's far too cold for them there. That's where I would put them, in storage in case I needed them.'

'And the undead dragons?' said Kelsey.

'They would be simple to control,' said Bailey. 'Child's play for a god like Edgar.'

A group of servants arrived. One was wheeling a trolley, and the servants unloaded the plates and dishes of food, along with a few large flagons.

'Is that ale?' said Corthie, sitting up.

'It is, sir,' said a servant. 'Would you prefer wine?'

'Please, no,' said Corthie. 'I'm never touching that stuff again.' He filled a mug with ale, and drained it. He smiled. 'Thank Pyre for that.'

Karalyn glanced at Kyra. 'You have been very quiet.'

'I want to go back to Plateau City,' she said. 'I'm just waiting for a polite opportunity to leave. I've missed days of lessons looking for you and Uncle Corthie.' She looked at the others round the table. 'While you all sit here and talk about some crazy gods, the Empire is teetering on the brink of disaster. Wars in Rahain, Rakana, Na Sun Ka; huge tax rises, and now there are sixty greenflies terrorising the inhabitants of the Holdings. Thorn's ambition is destroying everything. We should overthrow her government before it's too late; and we Holdfasts are the only ones powerful enough to be able to do it.'

The others sitting at the table glanced at each other.

Kelsey started to laugh. 'It's nice to see you haven't changed, Kyra.'

'She has changed,' said Karalyn. 'Can you imagine her saying something like that this time last year?'

Corthie turned to his niece. 'Are you openly advocating treason against the Empress?'

'Aye,' said Kyra. 'Someone has to state the obvious, as you are all too cowardly to speak the truth. Thorn has to go; and Naxor, and Brogan, and Claudian. Bedig is harmless enough – all he does is police Plateau City; and Caelius is fine, if a bit of a yes-man. Apart from them, the Imperial Court is riddled with warmongers and imperialists who won't stop until they either rule over the Allied Worlds, or have driven the Empire into the ground.' She looked at Cardova. 'Are you going to have me arrested for speaking the plain truth?'

'Of course I'm not going to have you arrested,' said Cardova.

'I notice you didn't include him or Shella in your list of wicked criminals,' said Corthie. 'Aren't they members of the Imperial Court?'

'The Holdings has democracy,' Kyra went on, ignoring Corthie's comment. 'Why can't the Empire have the same?'

'Because we would have to impose it upon the nations that make up the Empire,' said Cardova. 'One of the founding principles of the Empire is that the nations are free to choose their own governments, and the Empress doesn't interfere in that. Are you saying we should force our beliefs onto everyone else?'

'But democracy would allow the people of every nation to choose their own government. What's democratic about the Matriarch of Sanang? And what about the governance of the Plateau? The Empress can do whatever she likes there.'

'The Clan Council of Kellach Brigdomin is democratic,' said Corthie. 'We vote for councillors every few years now.'

'And that rule was imposed by Empress Bridget,' said Kyra. 'Before that, the councillors were elected for life.' She turned to Kelsey. 'Why didn't you change things when you were Herald?'

'Was that rhetorical,' said Kelsey, 'or are you looking for a proper answer to that question?'

'A proper answer would be nice.'

'All right. I decided to focus what I thought would be my first ten years as Herald on two main objectives – stability and prosperity. Democracy does not thrive in chaotic, impoverished countries. Tyrants are more likely to be elected in places like that, rather than sensible, moderate leaders. I wanted to build solid foundations before experimenting with changes to the constitution. I wanted to improve the quality of life for all citizens of the Empire. If everything had gone according to plan, I would have started gradually changing more laws in my second decade as Herald.'

'I notice you didn't mention peace as one of your objectives,' said Kyra.

'Peace was implied. One cannot have stability and prosperity if one is constantly waging war.'

'But you invaded Rahain and Rakana!'

'I agreed with the invasion of Rahain,' Kelsey said, 'as a limited operation to restore order to the cities of that land, and to alleviate the terrible living conditions endured by the people there.'

'And Rakana?'

'The Rakanese campaign was never meant to happen,' said Kelsey. 'What was intended to be a humanitarian operation to allow starving refugees to cross into the Empire developed in ways we hadn't foreseen. The Empire made a mistake, and now we have to own the consequences, by ensuring that Rakana is allowed to choose its own government.'

'But that isn't happening.'

'I am no longer Herald, Kyra. For better or worse, I have no say in the direction of the Empire.'

Kyra turned to Cardova. 'But you do. You are the Constable. You are the commander of all armed forces.'

'That's right,' said Cardova, 'and my duty is to carry out the wishes of the Imperial Court, not to order the army to overthrow its legally-appointed sovereign. Right now, the armed forces of the Empire are more thinly stretched than at any time since the war against the Ascendants. Thanks to Queen Blackrose, we are having to govern Na Sun Ka, where Cael is based. Do you think we wanted to annex a part of Dragon Eyre?'

'Maybe you didn't,' said Kyra, 'but the Empress did. She is casting her greedy eyes over the rest of the Allied Worlds, wondering which part to attack next.'

Corthie groaned. 'I'd rather be fighting greenflies than listening to this. Is that the plan? Do you want me to hunt them down?'

Kelsey nodded. 'With the assistance of me, Frostback and Halfclaw.'

'I will also help,' said Karalyn.

'Will you take me back to Kell first,' Corthie said, 'so I can visit Aila and the bairns?'

Karalyn nodded. 'Aye, as long as we keep the visit short.'

'All I need is a quick bath, and then I'll be ready,' he said. He glanced at Bailey. 'Did you take Theodora's body back to Athumia?'

'I laid her to rest beneath the rose gardens of Zamata Gataza,' said Bailey. 'I think she would like it there.'

Kyra glared at the others. 'None of you care, do you? Thorn is transforming into a tyrant, and none of you give a shit.'

'I'm grateful that you came to our rescue, Kyra,' said Corthie, 'but, to be honest, you're right – I couldn't give a shit about the rest. I'm a father and a farmer. I just want to do my job and go home.'

# CHAPTER 21
# FROM BAD TO WORSE

**Colsbury Castle, the Holdings – 22nd Day, Second Third Spring 545**

Kyra got dressed in her bedroom in the Summer Palace in silence. Despite her desire to get back to the university in Plateau City, she had been persuaded to spend one last night in Colsbury. It hadn't gone well. She had bickered with Kelsey, Cardova and Karalyn all evening; and, when Corthie had returned from visiting Kell, he had made it clear that he wasn't interested in engaging in a political discussion with his niece. Even Shella had grown tired of her diatribes, and had wandered off with Olo'osso to smoke dreamweed by the island's small harbour.

Kyra packed her clothes into a bag, and laced up her boots.

No one understood her point of view. Not even her mother, who shared many of her opinions on violence, had given her much support. Instead, she had continually told her daughter that it was wiser to stand aloof from politics altogether. Cardova was too loyal to the Empress, Kelsey had overseen the invasion of Rahain, Shella supported the occupation of Rakana, and Corthie didn't care about any of it. Bailey had watched the Holdfasts squabble all evening with an attitude of faint amusement; but he was too in awe of Karalyn to ever stand against her family.

Kyra tapped her pocket to make sure the Quadrant was there, then she picked up her bag and walked out of the bedroom. She went along a palace corridor, then descended a flight of stairs to the ground floor. Corthie and her mother were there, strapping on their black armour.

'I'm going back to Plateau City now,' Kyra said.

Her mother and uncle turned.

'Already?' said Karalyn. 'Aren't you going to have any breakfast?'

'I can get some in the university canteen.'

'Well, thank you again for helping us.'

'Aye,' said Corthie. 'Thanks.'

Kyra frowned at the gleaming black metal encasing them both. 'Are you going out into the Holdings to hunt down greenflies?'

'Aye,' said Karalyn. 'Today will likely be the first trip of many. The dragons and Kelsey are waiting out in the forecourt for us. We're going to sweep over Hold Stringer first, and we won't stop until we kill them all.'

'Mother,' Kyra said. 'Thorn is a danger; you must listen to me.'

'Please don't start all this again,' said Karalyn. 'Say hello to Cole and Arrosa for me when you arrive at the university.'

'Is the wedding not meant to be happening soon?' said Corthie.

'Arrosa's eighteenth birthday is under a third from now,' said Karalyn, 'but I suppose it depends if Cael has managed to arrange some leave from the marines.'

'He might be dead by then,' said Kyra. 'Have you heard about the crazy risks he's been taking? Will you listen to me, Mother, if your son dies in a pointless war on Dragon Eyre?'

Karalyn narrowed her eyes. 'Cael is free to choose his own path; as are you, daughter. Good luck with your studies.'

Kyra said nothing as Karalyn and Corthie walked towards the main entrance of the Summer Palace. She placed a hand in her pocket.

*My room, the university. Go.*

The air shimmered, and she appeared in her bedroom in the accommodation wing of the university. She glanced at the mess, then she set her bag down onto a chair, and left the room. A few minutes later, she entered the canteen, and scanned the faces, hoping to see either Larron or Dazi. To her disappointment, Arrosa caught her gaze, and waved at her from where she was sitting with Cole. Kyra walked over to their table.

'I haven't seen you in ages,' said Arrosa. 'What have you been doing?'

'I was in Colsbury Castle, helping Mother with something,' Kyra said. 'She passes on her best wishes.'

'Have you heard the latest about Cael?' said Cole. 'Apparently, he single-handedly rescued an entire squad of marines from the middle of an underground Unk Tannic base; then he blew the whole mountain up, killing hundreds of terrorists.'

Kyra glanced down at the newssheet lying on the table and picked it up.

*More Daring Exploits of Cael Holdfast on Dragon Eyre*, ran one of the headlines.

'I wish he'd be more careful,' said Arrosa, 'though I can't help but be proud of him.'

Kyra repressed a desire to call her brother an idiot in front of the entire canteen. She put the newssheet back onto the table.

'When you were in Colsbury,' Arrosa went on, 'did you hear anyone mention if Cael has been granted leave for the wedding? I still haven't received any news about it.'

'My mother doesn't know,' Kyra said. 'She was talking about it just before I left.'

Arrosa shook her head. 'How am I supposed to arrange a wedding if I don't have a date?'

'There are bigger things to worry about, Arrosa.'

'Maybe for you. Oh, by the way, that guy called Larron was looking for you a few days ago. He came up to us to ask if we'd seen you.'

Kyra smiled. 'Thanks for letting me know. I'll look for him now.'

Arrosa narrowed her eyes. 'You like him, don't you?'

Kyra shrugged. 'Maybe.'

Arrosa burst into laughter. 'That is the funniest thing I've heard in ages. Poor Kyra.'

Kyra frowned. 'What are you talking about? What's so funny about that?'

'You mean you don't know?' said Arrosa, as laughter creased her face.

'Eh, Kyra,' said Cole. 'Sorry to be the one to tell you this, but Larron isn't interested in girls.'

'What?'

'He likes boys,' said Arrosa.

Anger rose within Kyra. 'And how would you know?'

'There was a big party in the quad while you were away,' said Cole. 'Arrosa and I went, along with a few hundred others, and the members of the Student Council were there. I think they'd organised it. Anyway, we saw Larron there with another guy. Half the university saw him.' He glared at Arrosa, and she stopped laughing. 'As I said,' Cole went on, 'I'm sorry you had to hear it from us.'

Kyra turned and walked away. As she was leaving the canteen, she heard her name being shouted out, and then she saw Dazi running towards her.

'Kyra, where have you been?' Dazi said. 'You've been gone for days. I need to tell you something.'

'If it's about Larron, then I already know,' she said.

Dazi frowned. 'You do? How? When did you get back?'

'Arrosa took great delight in telling me a few minutes ago.'

'Oh.'

'I am so stupid,' said Kyra. 'How did I not realise?'

'Well, I didn't know, either,' said Dazi. 'But, you know, it seems a little obvious now, if you think about it. You've been friends for a while, and he hasn't once tried anything. You practically threw yourself at him after going to his parents' tavern, and...'

'I did not throw myself at him.'

Dazi gave her a look.

'I kissed him. Once,' Kyra said.

'And he got up and left your bedroom,' said Dazi.

'I thought he was being decent and honourable, because I was so drunk. What was the other guy like, at the party?'

Dazi shrugged. 'He's a student, I think. From the Holdings. Why do you care?'

'I don't. I'd better tell Professor Achan that I'm back.'

'Are you going to be all right?'

'Of course. Why wouldn't I be? I will speak to you later.'

Kyra walked away. She took a set of stairs and ascended to the first floor, then she followed a corridor until she reached Achan's office. She knocked.

'Come in,' said a voice.

Kyra opened the door and walked in.

'Ah, you're back at last,' said Achan. 'I had started to wonder if you would return this term, Kyra.'

'My family needed me in Colsbury, sir.'

Achan glanced at a small calendar on his desk. 'Let's see; you were absent for sixteen days. That's a lot of missed lessons but, if you work hard, then you still have a chance to catch up with everything before the end-of-year examinations. I will inform your teachers that you have returned, but before I do that, there is something else I must tell you.'

'Is it about Larron, sir?'

Achan gave her a quizzical glance. 'Why would it be about Larron?' He went into a drawer and took out a letter. 'This arrived for you yesterday, and, as your tutor, I was told to pass it on to you if and when you returned to the university. It's from the Ministry of the Plateau, so I assume it's official.'

He gave her the letter. She cracked open the wax seal and unfolded it, her expression dropping as she read.

'It's a summons,' she said. 'I'm being summoned into the presence of the Empress.'

'I had suspected it might be something along those lines,' said Achan. 'Do you know why the Empress wishes to see you?'

Kyra shook her head.

'I will also inform the Student Council that you are back,' Achan said. 'Some of the members are a little aggrieved that you left Plateau City without any explanation. Is that what you meant when you asked about Larron?'

'Aye,' said Kyra. 'That's what I meant.'

'I think Larron was more concerned that you were all right,' said Achan. 'He seemed to be quite worried by your absence.'

Kyra decided to change the subject. 'Has there been any news about a possible strike?'

Achan smiled. 'There has been significant progress made in that area, and the terms of the strike have been agreed by the workers of the major industries across the entire capital. From the Rakanese dock workers to the Kellach wagon drivers, everyone will be taking part. Of course, they are protesting the tax rises rather than the illegal wars being waged by the Empire, but I will make sure the two issues are conflated. Slogans like *No taxes to pay for wars*, and others like it will be prominent on the banners we are making. Ten days from now, at noon, the walk out will begin, and the city will be paralysed.' He narrowed his eyes. 'I wonder if this is what the Empress wishes to discuss with you. I have no doubt that the Imperial Court is aware of our plans.'

Kyra nodded. 'I had better go to the Ministry of the Plateau. Thank you for offering to tell my teachers and the council that I have returned.'

'No problem, Kyra. Come and see me when you get back from your audience with the Empress, and we will take a look at your study schedule.'

Kyra let herself out of Achan's office, and went upstairs to her room. As soon as she had closed her door, she placed a hand into her pocket.

*The plaza outside the Ministry of the Plateau. Go.*

The air shimmered, and she appeared a few yards away from the Calendar Pole. Dragon Eyre accents were coming from a group of people by the edge of the plaza, and Kyra wondered if the portal to Ulna had recently been activated. She walked over to the side of the large Ministry of the Plateau building, and passed her letter to the soldiers standing guard by the door.

They gave it a glance, then they passed it back and allowed Kyra to enter. A courtier nodded to her in the cool, marble-lined hallway.

'I have been summoned to appear before the Empress,' Kyra said.

The courtier examined her letter. 'Come this way,' she said.

Kyra followed the courtier up a flight of stairs to the smaller of the two audience chambers. The courtier knocked, then opened the door.

'Your Majesty,' said the courtier, 'Miss Kyra Holdfast is here as requested.'

'Allow her to enter,' came the Empress's voice.

The courtier gestured towards the door, and Kyra walked in. Seated around the table were most of the Imperial Court, with the Empress on her throne at one end.

'Good morning, Kyra,' said the Empress.

Kyra curtsied. 'Good morning, Your Majesty.'

'We have summoned you here today,' the Empress went on, 'to offer our profound gratitude for your help in locating Karalyn and Corthie within the Palace of the Almighty. We received word from Karalyn yesterday that she and her brother were safe, and she also mentioned that your contribution was invaluable. Thank you also for sacrificing so many days of your university studies to lend a hand. We are very grateful.'

'You are most welcome, Your Majesty,' said Kyra.

'I want to make a little deal with you,' the Empress went on. 'In return for your discretion regarding the events surrounding the Palace of the Almighty, would you like to sit down and join today's meeting of the Imperial Court?'

Kyra frowned. 'I have already been discreet about what happened. I don't need to be bribed. And why do you think I would want to join a meeting of the Imperial Court?'

The Empress smiled. 'We are aware that you have been using your vision powers to covertly observe our meetings, Kyra. Wouldn't you prefer to find out what goes on here in a more straightforward and honest manner?'

Kyra's cheeks flushed. 'I... uh...'

'Sit,' said the Empress. 'Adjutant Claudian is currently overseeing operations on Na Sun Ka, so you may take his seat.'

Kyra saw a light smirk on Naxor's face as she sat down at the table.

'The first item of business concerns Na Sun Ka, Your Majesty,' said the demigod.

Kyra glanced at the others round the table. Across from her, Naxor was sitting next to Treasurer Slaeon and Jurist Holdsmith. To Kyra's left sat Brogan, while Caelius and Bedig were on her right.

'The *Horned God* has departed the city of Sun Ta,' Naxor went on, 'along with a few frigates. They should reach the *Wondrous Light* within the next six or seven days.' He glanced at Kyra. 'Second Lieutenant Holdfast is on board the dragon carrier, along with Commander Laimos and his dragon team.'

'It could be a trap,' said Caelius. 'The Unk Tannic are more devious than many might imagine. Back when I was on Dragon Eyre, we learned that lesson the hard way. They might be trying to lure Cael, Lahnos and the dragons away from Na Sun Ka, so that they and the Wystians can launch a counter attack.'

'Claudian has recognised this possibility,' said Naxor, 'as he also has vast experience of serving upon Dragon Eyre. However, we estimate that up to ten Wystians are travelling from Rigga to Gyle with every day that passes. If we allow this to continue, then the Wystians will be able to build up an army of dragons so large that even Lahnos would struggle to hold them back. Claudian feels, and I concur, that the best response is to recapture the *Wondrous Light* with speed and overwhelming force.'

Kyra wanted to start asking questions, but decided it would be better if she kept her mouth closed and listened for a while, rather than remind the others of her presence.

'What is the situation in Sun Ta at present?' said the Empress.

'The city is at peace, for now,' said Naxor. 'The main challenge to public order is the fierce animosity that exists between those who are native to Dragon Eyre, and those of Implacatus extraction – the Banner soldiers who were left behind when the others were brought to the Star Continent a decade ago, and the colonists they protected. Both sides have been guilty of enslaving and abusing the other; and so Claudian has taken the rather drastic decision to move the population into separate districts: the settlers in the eastern half of Sun Ta, and the natives in the west. Our soldiers are now employed in keeping the two sides apart, and separate civil administrations are being formed.'

Caelius shook his head. 'Do we really want to get bogged down in the politics and strife of Dragon Eyre? I understand that Queen Blackrose has placed us into a very difficult position, but perhaps it might be better if we ordered a full withdrawal. It is not the Empire's responsibility to protect the southern border of the Eastern Rim, and, frankly, those soldiers could be put to far better use elsewhere. Rakana, for example.'

'We did not wish to have to annex Na Sun Ka,' said the Empress, 'but now that we have, we cannot simply shrug off our duty towards the people there. If we withdraw, there will be a bloodbath, and the Unk Tannic and Wystians will return to the island in force. The former settlers and everyone who aided us would be massacred, and Queen Blackrose would be able to rightfully claim that we have broken our word.'

Brogan glanced at the Rahain Treasurer. 'How are we able to afford the occupation of Na Sun Ka? You told us that we were running out of money.'

'We *are* running out of money, Herald,' said Slaeon. 'At present, we have enough to fund the operations in Na Sun Ka for a further four thirds. After that, we shall have to severely curtail the subsidies being sent there. Na Sun Ka needs to be able to feed its own people by then, or the civilian population will starve.'

'There are serious difficulties with the food supply,' said Naxor, 'as both the settlers and the natives are each insisting that the arable land to the south of Sun Ta belongs to them. Historically, the land was all owned by the natives, but it was the settlers from Implacatus who greatly improved the yields, and who brought the farms up to modern standards. The settlers also drained the marshes, thereby increasing the amount of land available to farm.'

'I have seen a case study of the legal disputes,' said Jurist Holdsmith. 'It is a tangled mess of differing rights and ownership that will take years to unravel through the courts.'

'We cannot wait years,' said the Empress, 'not if the population will starve. The farms must be brought back into operation as soon as possible.'

'Then we give the land to the settlers, Your Majesty,' said Naxor. 'They have the skills and recent experience of tending the farms, while the natives, whose claim may be stronger, have lacked those skills for several decades. The natives are also unfamiliar with the new techniques the settlers brought with them, and would struggle to match the required yields.'

'The natives would revolt if we handed the farms to the settlers,' said Caelius. 'They have been fighting to get their land back for generations.'

The Empress frowned. 'We have two choices – we give the land to the natives, and retain the moral high ground at the risk of allowing the population to starve; or we give the land to the settlers, which will ensure enough food is grown, but would also be certain to antagonise the natives.'

'Or we allow the courts to do their job, Your Majesty,' said Holdsmith. 'If we diverted resources to the legal system, we could speed up the process of determining who owns what.'

'We have no money for that,' said Slaeon.

'That's your answer to everything,' snapped Holdsmith.

'Do not blame me for telling the truth,' said the Rahain Treasurer. 'If the legal system requires more funding, tell me which area of spending to cut.'

'We need more time to ponder our decision on this,' said the Empress. 'Please move on, Chamberlain.'

'Yes, Your Majesty,' said Naxor. 'The next item was brought to my attention by Marshal Bedig, and concerns the rumours of impending trouble here in Plateau City.'

'Thank you, Chamberlain,' said Bedig. 'I have it on good authority that entire swathes of the labour force in this city are planning to stop work, as a protest against the recent tax rises. A *strike*, they are calling it. The docks, the goods vehicles, the street lamps, the postal service, construction on the Blue Palace, the sewage works, the tanneries and factories – all work will come to a halt.'

'We used to have this exact problem in the City,' said Naxor, 'and it pains me to see it repeated here. The Evaders and Reapers were particularly fond of walking out of their places of work whenever they wished to protest about something. A secondary issue is that thousands of idle workers will be lingering on the streets. In the City, that usually meant riots.'

'How did the City deal with it?' said Brogan.

'That would depend upon who was running the City at the time. Princess Khora would allow the strikes to go ahead without interference, and merely wait them out until the workers ran out of food and money, and had to return to their places of work. Under Duke Marcus, troops were used to break the strikes. Under the Aurelians, there would be negotiations between the government and the striking workers, which often resulted in the workers getting whatever they wanted. Tell me – has the Star Continent never experienced a strike before?'

'Once, during the war with Agatha,' said Brogan, 'the Rakanese dockworkers threatened to strike over conscription.'

'Was that under your mother's regime?' said Naxor. 'How did Empress Bridget deal with the situation?'

'My mother used soldiers to prevent the strike from taking place,' said Brogan.

'This is a disease shared by the Rakanese and the City of Salve,' said Slaeon. 'I prefer Duke Marcus and Empress Bridget's approach. Marshal Bedig should put soldiers on the streets, and we should pass a law to make such strikes illegal.'

'Or we reduce taxes, and the problem goes away,' said Caelius.

'If we submit to their demands without a fight,' said Slaeon, 'then that will only encourage them to do it again. What will they demand next time, Quartermaster? Pay rises? The Empire literally cannot afford to be seen as weak on this issue.'

'Remember who is sitting among us,' said Naxor. 'I would imagine that Miss Holdfast is in close contact with Professor Achan, one of the chief organisers of the strike; and, of course, he is a man from the City, a Hammer dissident with much experience of these matters. If we announce our intentions, we will be giving Achan advance notice, and he will adjust his plans accordingly.'

The Empress caught Kyra's gaze. 'Not if she promises to remain discreet about what she hears.'

Naxor laughed. 'I do not believe that Miss Holdfast would be able to remain silent, Your Majesty. She will go running to Achan the moment she leaves this chamber.'

'Then tell Achan this, Miss Holdfast,' said Bedig; 'tell him that if the strike goes ahead, he will be held responsible for any violence that occurs.'

Kyra said nothing, her face a mask of calm reserve.

The door to the audience room burst open, and three officers from the army entered.

'Apologies for interrupting, Your Majesty,' said a major; 'but we have just received news from the Tempest mine on Athumia.'

'What news?' said the Empress.

'It has been re-taken by Dominion forces, Your Majesty,' said the major. 'The entire garrison has been slaughtered, along with every miner and civilian based there. Over thirty Dominion dragons were involved in the assault, and the report states that the dragons had help from at least one human with mage or god powers.'

The chamber fell into silence, and the Empress's features fell.

'How do we know this,' said Naxor, 'if everyone there was killed?'

The major turned. 'Bring the lieutenant in.'

Two soldiers escorted another officer into the chamber.

'This is Lieutenant Garrot of the seventh division of the Imperial Army,' said the major. 'He is the sole survivor.'

'Did you flee by using the Quadrant issued to the garrison?' said Naxor.

'The Quadrant was used, my lord,' said the lieutenant, his gaze lowered, 'but not by me.'

'Tell us your story,' said the Empress.

'Yes, Your Majesty,' he said. 'The attack began at dawn this morning. A wave of dragons appeared from the north-east, from the direction of Nom Karta. While we were preparing the Forty-Eighters to repel them, two gods appeared in the middle of our defences. They killed everyone up on the walls, and all of the artillery crews. When the dragons arrived, there was no one left to defend the civilian miners and workers, and the dragons slaughtered them all. I was kept alive, so that I could be brought here with the news. One of the gods took the Quadrant from the garrison commander, and he used it to bring me here.'

'A god was in Plateau City?' said Brogan.

'Yes, ma'am, but only for a few moments. He left me standing outside the Ministry of the Plateau, then he vanished.'

'Have the Doomed Worlds made common cause with the Dragon Dominion?' said Naxor. 'Did the god who brought you here have a name, Lieutenant?'

'He was called Ward, sir,' said the junior officer.

Kyra groaned aloud before she could stop herself.

All eyes turned to her.

'Have you heard of this god, Kyra?' said the Empress.

'Aye,' she said. She glanced at the officers.

'You can speak freely,' said the Empress.

'Bailey mentioned him, Your Majesty,' said Kyra. 'He was one of the gods released by Edgar from the Palace of the Almighty. Bailey said he was extremely dangerous – a callous murderer.'

'Have the lieutenant write up a full statement for us, Major,' said Brogan, 'with every detail he can remember.'

'Yes, ma'am,' said the major.

'Thank you, Lieutenant Garrot,' said the Empress. 'That will be all for now.'

The officers bowed and left the chamber. The members of the Imperial Court sat in a despondent silence for a few long moments, and Kyra watched the crushed and anxious expressions on their faces.

'This day goes from bad to worse,' said the Empress. 'What are our options?'

No one spoke, then, after a while, Slaeon glanced up.

'How important is the Tempest mine to the Empire, Your Majesty?' she said. 'That would seem to be the crux of the matter. If the mine is not essential to us, then I say we simply abandon our claim to it, and leave it to the Dragon Dominion.'

'But those bastards slaughtered our people!' cried Bedig.

'We must presume that this is but a first step in Edgar's scheme,' said Naxor; 'to deny us Tempest, and to ensure he has access to the mine. Edgar will be able to fashion Tempest armour and weapons for his gods, and for the dragons and armies of the Dominion, with whom we must now consider ourselves to be at war. It is a strategic necessity that we re-capture the mine as soon as possible. I recommend a full scale invasion force be rapidly assembled and sent to Inopei. We'll need dragons, powerful mages and elite soldiers.'

'And where are you going to find them, Lord Chamberlain?' said Slaeon. 'If it is truly the desire of the Empire to fight on Athumia, then we could perhaps follow the Quartermaster's advice, and withdraw from Na Sun Ka? That way, the Sanang, the marines, and Commander Laimos could be diverted to Inopei. Otherwise, I fail to see how we could gather the required forces.'

'There are plenty of unused army units scattered all over the Empire,' said Bedig. 'We could use them.'

'Ah, but the Lord Chamberlain specifically said he wanted *elite* forces. Do you think army garrison troops would stand a chance against the Dragon Dominion if Edgar's gods are assisting them?'

'Well then,' said Bedig, 'we send the regular army soldiers to take over the occupation of Na Sun Ka, and transfer the Sanang and the marines to Athumia.'

'That would be very expensive, indeed,' said Slaeon. 'Prohibitively so.'

'This meeting is at an end,' said the Empress. 'I would like to examine every possible way we could regain control of the Tempest mine. I want you all to formulate some detailed proposals, and I want to see those proposals before sunset this evening. Chamberlain, please inform the Constable and Chancellor in Colsbury of this development. We will require their presence here before any final decisions are reached. Dismissed. Kyra, would you please remain here for a moment?'

Kyra tilted her head as the members of the Imperial Court got to their feet, bowed, and left the room.

The Empress turned to her as soon as the door closed. 'Do you see the endless troubles we face?' she said. 'Do you think this is easy? We are trying to do our best, but there are no simple answers.'

'You have over-extended yourself,' said Kyra.

'We have, though each step we took seemed the best one at the time. I would ask you, no, plead with you – use any influence you have over Achan to postpone the planned strike. Crippling the economy of Plateau City will only hurt those we are trying to protect. If you do this, and the strikes are put off for the present, then I will establish a commission to look at the tax code. You have my word.'

Kyra's eyes narrowed. 'Are you begging me to help you, Your Majesty?'

'I am. For all the past that we have shared, Kyra, please do this for me.'

Kyra got to her feet. She looked into the Empress's eyes, and could see her desperation.

'Will you do it?' said Thorn.

Kyra placed a hand into her pocket.

'No,' she said, then she triggered the Quadrant and vanished.

## CHAPTER 22
## SPRINGING THE TRAP

**South-East of Rigga – 17th Duninch 5266 (18th Gylean Year 17)**

Sable had once told Cael that trying to locate a single ship in the midst of the ocean was an almost impossible task, and he had learned the truth of that statement over the previous few days on board the *Horned God*. Even knowing the approximate position of the captured dragon carrier had hardly helped, and he had spent hour after hour scanning the endless waters between Rigga and Gyle. Earlier that morning, he had caught his first glimpse of the anchored *Wondrous Light*. It had looked abandoned, with no signs of life anywhere, and its four masts had been broken. Jubilant with his discovery, he had told Lahnos and the captain of the *Horned God*, only to be unable to find the missing carrier again when he tried to plot its exact location on the sea charts. Three more hours had elapsed before he had seen it again, and was able to give the carrier's coordinates to the captain.

For all that time, the *Horned God* had sailed onwards with its escort of four frigates. A small course adjustment had been made when Cael had supplied the location of the *Wondrous Light*, and they were travelling directly towards it.

'Did you see any signs of life the second time you saw it?' said Lahnos.

'No, Commander,' said Cael, as they stood on the flight deck of the *Horned God*, surrounded by Bullan, dragons and officers. 'No crew; no dragons.'

'Perhaps the Wystians on Rigga have been having the same trouble locating the ship as you've experienced.'

'I would have to disagree with you there, Commander,' said Gallantmorn, who was standing close by. 'The eyes of a dragon, combined with their innate sense of direction, should allow the Wystians to easily find the *Wondrous Light*. We can accurately scan miles of ocean at a time. There must be another explanation for the ship being abandoned.'

Lahnos glanced down at the chart. Pencil marks showed both their current location, and the position of the *Wondrous Light*.

'We're only forty or so miles away,' he said. 'We'll launch when the distance is reduced to ten miles, and scout out the carrier for ourselves. I'll go with Lord Sigum, and we'll take Gallantmorn and Cloudeye with us.'

'What about me, sir?' said Cael. 'Should I come with you, or should I stay on the *Horned God*?'

'I'll decide that at the time,' said Lahnos. 'Be ready to go, but I want you to take one last look at the *Wondrous Light* before we take off. It'll take a few hours for the *Horned God* to cover thirty miles, so get some rest for now.'

Captain Doune frowned. 'Are you planning to purloin my young lieutenant, Commander? What if I need him?'

'Resources are allocated according to need, Captain,' said Lahnos. 'If I need Lieutenant Holdfast, then I'll be taking him.'

Cael saluted, then he walked to the forward hatch and descended into the humid interior of the carrier. He was sharing a cramped space with seven other marines from the Seaborne Company, and they glanced at him as he entered their section of the hold. Hammocks were strung up from a few posts and bulkheads, and Cael sat down by his own.

'Did you find the ship we're hunting?' said one of the marines.

'Aye. It's just sitting there, bobbing up and down on the swell. How can a ship possibly anchor out here in the middle of the ocean?'

'They call it an ocean, but it ain't,' said a marine. 'It's about as deep as the Inner Sea on the Star Continent. You can anchor just about anywhere.'

'All four of its masts have been hacked down,' Cael went on. 'Why did they bother doing that if there's no crew on board?'

'Because the fuckers know we're coming,' said a huge Kellach marine. 'They knew we'd have to respond, so they've gone out of their way to cripple the *Wondrous Shite*.'

'The Gift of Pain will fry the bastards if they try to ambush us,' said another marine. 'We can take a few days to allow the fish head carpenters time to repair the other carrier.'

'I was hoping for a fight,' said the Kellach. 'We'll have fuck all to do if there's nobody on board the *Wonderful Shite*.'

'I might be flying on Sigum's back to take a look when we're closer,' said Cael.

'Aren't you the lucky bastard?' said the Kellach.

Cael climbed into his hammock. 'I'm getting some rest,' he said. 'Even lucky bastards need to sleep.'

A few hours later, an Irlanian sailor shook Cael's shoulder, and he opened his eyes.

'Commander Laimos wants you, sir,' said the sailor; 'up on the flight deck.'

Cael stretched his stiff joints and clambered out of the hammock. He rubbed his face, then he followed the sailor up into the dazzling sunshine. The dragons, their riders and the Bullan had assembled on the flight deck, and Lahnos was speaking to them. Cael walked up to his side and saluted.

'Lieutenant,' Lahnos said; 'can you perform another scan of the *Wondrous Light* for us?'

'Aye, sir. It will take a few minutes.'

The others watched as Cael turned to face the direction in which the carrier was sailing. He sat on the deck, and sent his vision out over the waves. He kept his course steady, not wanting to be embarrassed if it took him too long to find the captured carrier again. He saw it when he was ten miles from the *Horned God*, and felt relief ripple through him. He pushed his vision on to take a better look, but nothing appeared to have changed, and the long, wide flight deck was empty. He searched the cabins and compartments in the only part of the ship's structure that rose above the level of the flight deck, then he pushed down into the lower decks, but saw no one.

He severed the connection and got to his feet.

'Nothing has changed, sir. The ship still appears to be abandoned.'

Lahnos nodded. 'All right; this is what we are going to do. Lord Sigum, Gallantmorn and Cloudeye will fly to the location of the *Wondrous Light*. Once there, we shall investigate the carrier, and Cloudeye will land if it is safe to do so, while Cael sends a message to the captain of the *Horned God.* Gallantmorn and Sigum shall patrol from the skies, and keep watch for any possible ambush by the Wystians.'

'What shall Mayscale and I do while the other dragons are away?' said Quicklime.

'You two will protect the *Horned God*,' said Lahnos. 'If this is a trap of any kind, the Wystians might attack the fleet in our absence. One of you should be aloft at all times until the fleet reaches the *Wondrous Light*.'

'As you will it,' said Quicklime, though Cael noted a gleam of hostility in the dragon's eyes whenever she glanced at Lahnos.

Captain Doune approached. 'Well, Commander?' he said. 'Are you taking my lieutenant?'

'I am,' said Lahnos.

'Make sure you bring him back, sir,' Doune said, then he turned to Cael. 'Don't disgrace the service, Holdfast.'

'I'll try not to, sir,' said Cael.

The riders of Gallantmorn and Cloudeye climbed up the harnesses of their dragons, then Lahnos and Cael did the same with Sigum. Lahnos signalled down to the watching officers, and Sigum ascended into the air. He circled over the carrier until Gallantmorn and Cloudeye had both risen up next to him, then the dragons sped off to the north-west.

'We will be there in ten minutes, my rider,' said Sigum.

'Thank you,' said Lahnos.

They flew over the empty ocean for a while, then Cael nudged Lahnos.

'Commander,' he said, 'either you're back with Ora'lya, or Quicklime likes to hold a grudge. Which is it?'

Lahnos said nothing.

'Did you do something else to upset her?' said Cael.

'Not that I'm aware of.'

'Tell him the truth, my rider,' said Sigum. 'I have seen the little looks that pass between you and Ora'lya; and, if I have noticed them, you can be sure that Quicklime has done the same.'

'Then you're back together?' said Cael. 'Wait; never mind, I can see the *Wondrous Light*.'

'I see it, too, Holdfast,' said Sigum. 'The flight deck is deserted.'

The three dragons approached the anchored carrier at high altitude, then, after observing it for a few moments, they began to descend.

'Cloudeye!' Lahnos shouted over to the blue and white dragon. 'Go lower, and if no one appears, land on the flight deck. We'll cover you from up here.'

Cloudeye tilted his head, then he soared down. He swept along the flight deck, flying just a few feet over the wooden beams, then he circled back and alighted on the deck, his rear claws gouging out marks in the wood. He sniffed one of the broken masts, then he peered down an open hatch.

'I can smell human blood,' he called out, 'but it is several days old. There might be crew in the lowest decks but, other than that, there is no one on board.'

'Perhaps the Wystians feared our arrival,' said Sigum. 'Perhaps they have given up trying to reach Gyle.'

'This is too easy,' said Lahnos.

'The *Horned God* will be here in less than an hour,' said Cael. 'Do you want me to send the captain a message?'

'Not yet,' said Lahnos. 'Could you use your vision to search the entire vessel? Every cabin, every hold, every deck?'

'That will take a while, and it would be easier if I was down on the flight deck.'

Cael and Lahnos leaned over, their gazes on the figure of Cloudeye, as the blue and white dragon was investigating the lift at the rear of the ship. It had been raised, and was level with the rest of the deck. The dragon moved away from it, and peered down another open hatch. The air shimmered next to him, and another figure appeared – a woman. Before anyone could react, the air shimmered again, and the woman vanished, along with Cloudeye and his rider.

'Pyre's arse, did you see that?' Cael cried. 'Who was it? Who was down there?'

'Cloudeye has been taken!' Gallantmorn roared. 'What should we do?'

'She had a Quadrant,' Lahnos said. 'For a moment, I thought it might have been Sable.'

'It wasn't Sable,' said Cael. 'I sensed self-healing powers, just for a fraction of a second. It was a god.'

'Are you certain?'

'I think so. It happened so fast. I don't know; I might be wrong. If she comes back, I'll be ready, and I'll know for sure.'

'I have an idea,' said Lahnos. 'When I give the order, make us invisible – me, you, and Sigum.'

'Aye, sir,' said Cael.

'Gallantmorn!' Lahnos shouted. 'We are going to be invisible for a few minutes. If that woman comes back, stay clear; we're going to ambush her.'

Gallantmorn tilted his head, then Lahnos nodded to Cael.

*You cannot see us.*

'It's done,' said Cael.

'Take us down, Sigum,' said Lahnos. 'Hover by the lift at the rear of the ship.'

Sigum soared down. He banked over the flight deck, and began to hover a few yards from the lift. On the deck, the air shimmered again, and the woman appeared. Next to her were the severed heads of Cloudeye and his rider. The woman gazed up at Gallantmorn, and her eyes began to narrow.

Lahnos extended his right hand, and Cael sensed the Gift of Pain leave his fingers. The woman on the flight deck screamed. She fell to her knees, and vanished.

'Shit,' cried Lahnos.

'She's definitely a god,' said Cael.

'I know,' said Lahnos. 'That blast of Pain would have knocked out any mortal.'

'She must be able to see us. She could be on Rigga right now, watching us.'

'Rigga is four hundred and fifty miles from here.'

Cael nodded. 'Then she's an extremely powerful god.'

'With a Quadrant.'

'Aye.'

'Make us visible.'

*You can see us.*

'Done, sir.'

'Sigum, get back up to Gallantmorn's altitude.'

'Should we not attempt to recover the remains of Cloudeye and his rider, Lahnos?' said the dragon.

'That's what she wants us to do. If we land on the flight deck the same thing will happen to us.'

'But we shall be prepared.'

'Let me go down,' said Gallantmorn, as Sigum flew up to meet him. 'I will bathe that witch in flames.'

'She's a god,' said Sigum; 'a mighty god.'

Gallantmorn's eyes burned with fear and rage. 'The gods have returned to Dragon Eyre? We need Sable Holdfast!'

'We have her nephew instead,' said Lahnos, 'but I'm not risking him. We're going back to the *Horned God* for now, to plan our next step.'

'This sits ill with me,' said Sigum. 'We have lost another dragon and his rider. I thirst for vengeance.'

'As do I,' said Gallantmorn.

'We'll get our revenge,' said Lahnos, 'but we'll do it properly. Let's go.'

A few minutes later, Sigum and Gallantmorn landed on the flight deck of the *Horned God*. Lahnos and Cael unbuckled themselves from Sigum's harness and climbed down to the deck, where a group of officers were waiting, along with Quicklime and the Bullan.

'Where is Cloudeye?' said Quicklime.

'He has fallen,' said Gallantmorn.

'We are facing a god with a Quadrant,' said Lahnos; 'a god who knew exactly where we were.'

'Why did Lieutenant Holdfast not see this god, sir?' said Efizel.

'Because she's not on board the *Wondrous Light*,' said Lahnos. 'She appeared from somewhere, killed Cloudeye and his rider, and vanished again, even after I hit her with the Gift of Pain.'

'We have sailed into a trap,' said Captain Doune.

'We will be alongside the *Wondrous Light* in forty minutes,' said the ship's captain. 'What powers does the god possess?'

Lahnos glanced at Cael.

'I don't know, sir,' said Cael. 'She was there and gone in a few seconds. I had no time to get into her mind, and she didn't use any powers. But, if she isn't on board, then she must be on Gyle or Rigga; and if she can see us from either of those islands, her powers are strong.'

'She could be on another ship,' said an officer.

'How do we know she's definitely a god, if she didn't use any powers?' said another.

'I could sense her self-healing,' said Cael. 'She is a god.'

'It appears that we are in need of a new plan,' said Doune.

'I am immune to god powers,' said Cael. 'I will go on board, and try to lure her out of hiding. Or, I could make myself invisible, wait for her to appear, and get inside her mind. If I can access her thoughts, I will be able to subdue her.'

'That might work,' said Doune. 'We would need a volunteer to act as bait, once the Holdfast lad is on board the *Wondrous Shi...*, the *Wondrous Light*.'

'I'll do it,' said Lahnos. 'If Sigum and I fly back to the other carrier, I could drop Cael off on the flight deck, then we can land and wait for the god to appear.'

'You saw how fast she was, Commander,' said Gallantmorn. 'Would Cael be able to do anything in the few moments it would take for her to appear and disappear? I think not. We need Sable.'

'Sable is two thousand miles away,' said Lahnos. 'It would take over a month to get to Ulna and back. We're on our own.' He turned and stared out to sea in the direction of the other carrier. 'We need a distraction,' he said; 'something to divert the god's attention while the marines board the *Wondrous Light*. Captain Doune, get your company ready. When the *Horned God* is alongside the *Light*, transfer to the other ship, and take up positions by the masts. Loose as soon as the god appears. Cael, you will be with them, but you will be invisible. Use your vision to get inside the god's head. Dragons, you will be circling above. Burn the god as soon as you see her. I will also use my Gift of Pain. We will have four different chances to kill or capture her, and we only need one of them to work, but we mustn't get in each other's way.'

'If this god possesses death powers,' said an old Banner officer, 'there will be carnage.'

'What's the alternative?' said Lahnos. 'Should we turn round and sail back to Na Sun Ka? Remember Adjutant Claudian's orders. If we cannot capture the carrier, we must send it to the bottom of the ocean.

That is exactly what we will do if our attack on the god fails. Dragon fire or explosives, it doesn't matter. We cannot leave the *Wondrous Light* here to be used by the Wystians.'

'Then I recommend that we instruct the frigates to use their Forty-Eighters, Commander,' said the captain of the *Horned God*. 'If this god has death powers, then we have no chance of bringing the *Wondrous Light* home with us. We should sink it.'

'But if we don't eliminate the god first,' said Lahnos, 'she could sink us long before we sink the *Light*. We will go with my plan, then, if it fails, we shall use yours, Captain.'

Lahnos strode away, and the officers began to disperse.

'It strikes me, young Holdfast,' said Doune, 'that all it takes is one rogue god to induce panic among the leadership. Isn't your family renowned for killing gods?'

'I have never killed a god, sir,' said Cael.

Doune smiled. 'Then isn't it time you started?'

The anchored dragon carrier came into view half an hour later, and the small fleet began to slow as it approached the stricken vessel. The *Horned God* manoeuvred its way to come alongside the other carrier, as the frigates took up position around it, ready to launch their Forty-Eighters at a signal from the carrier's captain. Cael was standing on the flight deck with the other marines from the Seaborne Company, as they prepared to board the other vessel. Above them, Sigum, Gallantmorn and Mayscale were circling over the fleet, while Quicklime remained in reserve, and was watching from the flight deck of the *Horned God*. Standing a few yards from Quicklime were the Bullan, who were strapping on their armour and loading their crossbows.

Cael scanned the deck of the *Wondrous Light*. The severed heads of Cloudeye and his rider were still there, untouched since the god had disappeared.

'Remember your orders, lads and lassies,' said Doune. 'Holdfast, how many other marines can you make invisible at the same time?'

'At least four, sir; maybe more.'

Doune gestured to a corporal. 'Assign four marines to the Holdfast lad.'

'Are they to watch his back, sir?' said the corporal.

'Certainly not. They are to attempt to kill the god while they can't be seen. Holdfast can look after himself.'

Four marines with maces and crossbows peeled off from the others and stood by Cael.

'Stay close to me,' Cael said, 'or you will become visible to everyone.'

Doune stared at the nearing carrier's flight deck. 'Where is that damn god? Show yourself! Come on, ya shitebag!'

Sailors rushed forward with long gangways as the distance between the two carriers shortened. The moment the first gangways were in place, Doune raised an arm.

'Board and disperse!' he cried.

A hundred marines began to race over the gap between the vessels before the ropes had been secured. Cael and the four marines next to him bounded over the nearest gangway. They jumped onto the flight deck of the stricken carrier and veered off to the right, their boots pounding over the wooden beams.

*You cannot see us.*

'We're invisible to everyone,' he said to the four marines. 'We'll take cover by the aft hatch, so we don't get hit by any stray bolts or bursts of flame.'

The other marines of the company scattered over the deck, many running towards the broken masts. There were two on each flank of the wide flight deck, and the marines positioned themselves next to the snapped beams, crouching with their loaded crossbows ready to loose. Cael led his detachment to the aft hatch, which was lying open, and they took cover behind it. Overhead, Sigum broke away from Gallantmorn and Mayscale, and began to descend.

'What kind of commander volunteers to be the bait?' muttered one of the marines kneeling to Cael's left.

'He's immortal,' said another.

'Aye, but his dragon isnae.'

Sigum landed in the middle of the flight deck, then the silvery-green dragon gazed around, his blue eyes narrow as he waited for the god to appear. Up on his shoulders, Lahnos was also staring at the deck, his right hand raised.

Screams broke out from the crowded flight deck of the *Horned God*, and Cael turned in time to see Quicklime's head explode in a crescendo of blood and skull fragments. As her headless body fell, swathes of sailors toppled over, screaming in agony. Two figures were walking down the middle of the *Horned God's* flight deck, pointing at any survivors, who immediately fell down dead.

To the left of Quicklime's body, the Bullan began loosing their crossbows at the two gods. One of the bolts struck the woman, who gazed over to see who had dared to loose at her. She raised a hand, and the Bullan fell, blood erupting from their eyes and ears as they collapsed to the deck.

The other god, a man, reached a hatch, and climbed down into it, disappearing from sight, then the woman vanished, leaving heaps of dead sailors and Bullan lying on the blood-slicked flight deck next to the decapitated dragon.

As the marines stared at the bodies, three naval officers emerged from the *Horned God's* forward hatch at a run. Three flags were raised. Two were directed at the four frigates, ordering them to sink the *Wondrous Light*, while the third was for the marines – summoning them back to the *Horned God*.

'What the fuck is going on?' shouted a marine. 'Are we giving up?'

'We cannae fight two gods,' said another, as the marines began to withdraw from their positions on the flight deck of the *Wondrous Light*.

'The Forty-Eighters are being prepared,' Captain Doune cried. 'Get yer arses off the flight deck!'

Cael relaxed his powers, and he and the four marines around him became visible again. They joined the others as they raced back towards the *Horned God*. More screams rose up, and the marines standing next to Cael fell, their eyes bursting from their heads. Cael felt death powers swirl around his defences as he dived to the deck, then he turned, and saw that the woman had reappeared behind the withdrawing marines. Her right hand was raised, and the marines were falling in numbers. Sigum rose into the air, and the god flicked her hand in the dragon's direction just as Lahnos unleashed his Gift of Pain. Both the dragon and the god screamed in agony, then the god vanished as Sigum plummeted back down to the flight deck. The dragon struck the wooden beams, gouging out furrows as he skidded, then he rolled over, crushing Lahnos, and his eyes closed.

Mayscale and Gallantmorn soared low over the two dragon carriers, as the four frigates prepared to loose their Forty-Eighters. Gallantmorn lowered himself next to Sigum, while Mayscale inspected the body of Quicklime. At that moment, the male god climbed up from the forward hatch, his eyes wild with delight. He raised a hand, and the three naval officers disintegrated in a cloud of red blood, Mayscale blasted fire in his direction, enveloping the god in flames, then the dragon cried out in terror and pain. His eyes rolled up inside his head, and he fell from the edge of the flight deck, crashing into the ocean swell and disappearing from sight. The male god emerged from the flames, his robes in tatters but his flesh healed, and Gallantmorn ascended, retreating from the deck of the *Wondrous Light* before the god could bring him down.

Cael glanced at the surviving marines, most of whom were taking cover by the starboard railings of the *Wondrous Light*, just a few yards from the deck of the *Horned God*, where the male god was looking for more enemies to kill. Cael raced over to the other marines, and brought them under his veil of invisibility. The god glanced over in their direction, but his gaze passed over them.

'He can't see us,' Cael cried. 'Loose at the bastard!'

Five marines knelt and pointed their crossbows at the figure stalking the flight deck. Bolts flew out, and three struck the god. He swayed and staggered, and Cael shot his powers in through his eyes. He barged through the god's thoughts, and was about to scour his mind when a ferocious blast of the Gift of Pain swept over him and the surviving marines from behind. Cael collapsed to the deck, hugging his chest as agony scorched his nerves. The god also fell, writhing in torment, as Lahnos leapt over the gap between the two ships.

Searing agony pulsed through Cael's body, but he managed to open his eyes. Lahnos was walking towards the fallen god with his right hand outstretched. The god was screaming and writhing, but he had no Quadrant, and Lahnos grew closer with every second that passed.

Over to their left, one of the frigates exploded, its masts and deck lifting from the hull in a roar and a cloud of white light and dust. Seconds later, another frigate exploded, and the wave of energy almost knocked Lahnos off his feet; and Cael felt the Gift of Pain flicker out for a moment. That moment was all the god needed. He raised a hand, and sent a huge blast of death powers at Lahnos. Lahnos fell onto the deck, convulsing, and his flesh started to rot and fall from his body.

The god got to his feet, his hand outstretched, as Lahnos's self-healing struggled to fight off the death powers.

'The *Horned God*?' he said. 'Now at last I understand.'

The last two frigates burst into flames, then their upper decks exploded as the fires reached the Forty-Eighters' munitions. Smoke and flames rose up into the blue sky, while pieces of the four destroyed frigates bobbed up and down on the waves, along with hundreds of bodies. Some of the sailors were dead, while others were clinging on to whatever was floating.

The female god appeared next to her colleague in a shimmer of air.

'I have taken care of the frigates,' she said, then she narrowed her eyes at the sight of Lahnos.

'This horned creature is immortal, Allura,' said the male god. 'Look at the way his skin is trying to heal.'

'Stop wasting time, Ward,' she said. 'Kill him.'

'I am trying, dear sister,' said Ward.

The marines next to Cael had begun to recover as soon as Lahnos had fallen, and some were reloading their crossbows. Despite the agony and exhaustion rippling through his body, Cael sent his vision back out. He entered the mind of the god named Ward and tried to scour his mind, but he was too weak, and the god fought back. Ward screamed as he struggled to resist Cael's powers, raising his hands to the sides of his head, before falling to his knees on the flight deck. Allura stared at the two decks, looking for whoever was harming her companion. Seeing no one, she swept her fingers over her Quadrant, then she and Ward vanished.

The two flight decks fell into silence, as the flames from the four frigates surrounded them. Smoke was billowing up, along with screams and cries for help from the sailors in the water. Three of the frigates slipped beneath the waves, while the carcass of the fourth continued to burn. Cael struggled to his feet, still invisible. Behind him, Sigum was sprawled out on the flight deck of the *Wondrous Light*, along with the bodies of the fallen marines, while the body of Quicklime lay in the centre of the *Horned God's* deck, also surrounded by bodies, including those of the Bullan.

A sailor staggered up from the forward hatch of the *Horned God*, and Cael dropped his invisibility.

'Over here,' Cael cried.

The sailor saw him.

'We need to summon the captain,' Cael shouted. 'We need to leave.'

'The captain's dead,' the sailor shouted back. 'They're all dead. Below decks looks like the inside of a butcher's shop.'

'What the fuck do we do now?' cried a marine, as he gazed at the carnage all around.

'Prepare one of the *Horned God's* launches,' said Cael. 'We need to get out of here before the gods come back.'

He jumped over the gap between the two ships, and staggered towards Lahnos.

'Was that an order?' said one of the other marines. 'Has anyone seen Captain Doune?'

Gallantmorn descended as Cael reached the side of Lahnos. Cael crouched, and watched as Lahnos's body continued to piece itself back together, his rotten flesh slowly reforming.

Gallantmorn landed next to them.

'I fled,' said the dark orange dragon, his head lowered.

'You survived,' said Cael.

'I have shamed myself.'

The last of the marines approached, along with a handful of sailors, but none of them were officers.

'As lieutenant,' said Cael, 'I am taking command of this operation. We might only have a few minutes before the gods return. We will take a launch, pack it with food and water, and get out of here.'

'I cannot survive at sea, Holdfast,' said Gallantmorn, 'and the launch is too small to bear my weight.'

'You might have to fly to Gyle, and then back to Na Sun Ka,' said Cael. 'For now, look for survivors from the four frigates, Gallantmorn, and start collecting them from the sea.' He turned to the marines and sailors. 'Ready the launch.'

Gallantmorn took to the skies, but the marines and sailors stared at him in silence.

Cael powered his skills of persuasion. 'Get the fucking launch ready,' he shouted, and the group ran off.

Gallantmorn swooped down to hunt for any survivors from the four frigates. He lined up those he found next to the rear lift of the *Horned God*, close to where the marines and sailors were preparing the ship's launch.

Cael watched Lahnos heal himself a little more, then he pulled himself back to his feet and gazed around at the devastation. Two gods – that was all it had taken to destroy an imperial fleet. Even with dragons, Lahnos, and a Holdfast on board, two gods with a Quadrant had been more than enough.

A marine ran over to him. 'Lieutenant Holdfast,' he said, 'the launch will be ready to sail in fifteen minutes, and, sir, we've found Captain Doune.'

'Is he alive?'

'Aye, sir. Badly injured, but alive. The marine standing next to him took the brunt of the god's powers.'

'Gather up a few others,' said Cael, 'and get them to transfer as much fresh water and food to the launch as it will take; but I need you to go below, to search the officers' wardroom for salve. Be as quick as you can.'

'Aye, sir,' said the marine, then he ran back to the rear of the ship.

Cael stared out to sea, his eyes on the dead sailors floating by the debris from the four frigates.

So much for his fabled good luck, he thought. The first real test, and he had failed.

# CHAPTER 23
# FAILURE OF COMMAND

**South-East of Rigga – 17th Duninch 5266 (18th Gylean Year 17)**

Lahnos opened his eyes, then he closed them again, the light from the sun overhead dazzling him. He groaned and rolled onto his side. His eyes flickered open, and he gazed at his hands. The flesh on them was tinged a greyish-green, and his fingernails were re-growing. Beneath him, patches of rotten flesh and pools of blood were staining the wooden beams of the flight deck. His flesh and blood, he realised, as his memories returned.

He tried to sit up, as agony continued to work its way through his body.

'They've gone,' said Cael, who was standing a few yards away.

Lahnos swayed, as though in a daze. 'Sigum? Ora'lya?' he gasped.

Cael said nothing.

Lahnos heard voices, and he turned to see a group of marines and sailors lowering the *Horned God's* launch over the stern of the flight deck, the pulley ropes straining. Bodies lay everywhere, including that of Quicklime. Lahnos got to his feet and stared at the corpse of the green dragon, but there was no sign of her rider on her back. He walked closer to the huge body, looking for Ora'lya, then his gaze fell on the remains of the Bullan.

Lahnos sank to his knees, his mind struggling to comprehend what he was seeing. Disfigured by the god's death powers, the faces of the fallen Bullan appeared indistinguishable, and Lahnos had to look at the insignia on their uniforms to know which one was Efizel, and which one had been Corporal Gaddiz. That was it – of all the Bullan, he had only learned the names of two; and now, because of him, they were all dead. Ten years of friendship and faithful service, and a god had ended it with one blast of death powers.

Gallantmorn landed close by, with two unconscious figures clutched in his forelimbs. He laid them down on the flight deck next to a row of wounded sailors and marines, then he took to the air again.

'Gallantmorn is gathering the injured survivors,' Lahnos heard Cael say. 'There are many more still in the water to collect.'

Lahnos tried to speak, but the flesh in his throat was still healing itself, and nothing came from his lips. He turned away from the Bullan, dreading what else he was about to see, but knowing he had to do it. On the flight deck of the *Wondrous Light*, the body of Sigum was lying outstretched. Lahnos had crawled out from under the dragon's back as soon as he had crashed into the wooden deck, in order to fight the gods who had struck him down. He got back to his feet and staggered towards the silvery-green dragon, almost slipping on the blood pooling by a gangway as he crossed over to the stricken carrier.

Gallantmorn circled overhead, then he alighted next to Sigum as Lahnos approached.

'Without salve or a healer,' Gallantmorn said, 'Lord Sigum will not last the hour.'

'He's alive?' said Lahnos.

'Barely. It should have been I who played the role of bait. I have failed the noble Sigum, and I have failed my kin from the Eastern Rim.'

'I have also failed, Gallantmorn,' said Lahnos. 'My decisions led us into this catastrophe.'

There was a creaking sound, and Lahnos turned to see the last frigate break up as it sank beneath the waves. All that remained of the fleet were the two dragon carriers, bound together by ropes, and held secure by anchors.

Lahnos turned back to gaze at Sigum. 'There is salve in the wardroom on board the *Horned God*,' he said, as his thoughts began to clear a little.

'The Holdfast boy has already sent someone to look for it,' said Gallantmorn.

'Did Cael take charge?'

'He did.'

Lahnos glanced up, and saw Annu'tila securely fastened to the harness on Gallantmorn's broad shoulders. 'Did any other riders survive?'

'Two,' said the dragon.

Lahnos stared at Gallantmorn. 'Who?'

'I plucked Mayscale's rider from the waters,' said the dragon. 'He is uninjured, and is helping the others with the launch. I will not be able to rest on the launch, however, as it will not bear my weight. The Holdfast boy told me I would have to fly to Gyle, and then...'

'And the other rider?'

'I found Quicklime's rider half-crushed beneath her dragon,' said Gallantmorn. 'She is grievously wounded, but she still lives.'

Lahnos ran back over to the deck of the *Horned God*, and raced to the stern, where Gallantmorn had placed the injured. He searched among the bodies, and found Ora'lya, her legs bloody and mangled. Lahnos crouched by her and took her hand, but her eyes were closed. He checked for signs of life, and felt her soft and failing breath against his cheek.

He looked up. 'Cael!' he shouted.

Cael hurried over.

'The salve, Cael,' Lahnos cried. 'Where is it?'

'A marine is looking for it below,' Cael said. 'There might be enough to heal all of the injured.' He glanced down at Ora'lya. 'Is she...?'

'She's alive,' Lahnos said, 'but I can sense her fading. Sigum, too. What have I done, Cael?'

'It wasn't your fault,' said Cael. 'How could we have known that two gods would be here?' He looked to his right. 'The marine's back. Over here!'

The marine ran towards Cael and Lahnos. 'The wardroom was full of bodies, sir,' he said, 'and the safe... it had been broken into. The salve has gone.'

'Shit,' said Cael.

Lahnos lowered his gaze, as tears welled in his eyes.

Another marine approached. 'The launch is in the water, sir,' he said, 'but there are too many survivors; they won't all fit on board. Should we prepare another one?'

Cael turned to Lahnos. 'You are in command, sir,' he said.

'No,' said Lahnos, as he clutched Ora'lya's hand. 'It was my plan that caused this disaster.'

The marines glanced at each other.

'How is Captain Doune?' said Cael.

'See for yourself, sir,' said a marine, gesturing at the line of wounded.

Cael walked over to look at Doune, as Lahnos closed his eyes and wept. The Bullan were dead, and Sigum was dying; Ora'lya too, and it was his fault. He had tried to strike down a god with the Gift of Pain, and the god's death powers had overwhelmed him. The full extent of his failure began to sink in, and he abandoned himself to grief.

'We need to make a decision, sir,' said a marine corporal. 'It is unlikely that Captain Doune will survive his injuries.'

Lahnos glanced up, but the marines were all looking to Cael to give the orders.

'How many will fit in the launch?' Cael said.

'Sixty, sir,' said the corporal. 'Seventy at a push. There are fifty able-bodied survivors on the flight deck, along with over thirty seriously wounded. And there are at least a hundred still down in the water, clinging on to whatever floats.'

'There are more survivors than we originally thought,' said Cael, 'and we're going to need a minimum of three launches to get us all out of here. The *Horned God* has two, and the *Wondrous Light's* launches might still be intact. Send a few sailors over to check them.'

'Aye, sir,' said the corporal.

Lahnos got to his feet, his heart torn. If both Sigum and Ora'lya were about to die, then no matter how fond he was of the rider, he knew his place was next to his beloved dragon. He left the others, and trudged back over to the flight deck of the *Wondrous Light*. The heads of Cloudeye and his rider were still lying in the centre of the deck, along with several dozen dead marines from the Seaborne Company, and Lahnos picked his way towards the body of Sigum. His self-healing had almost finished repairing his body from the damage inflicted by the god's death powers, and he could feel his strength returning. He reached Sigum, and placed a hand on the silvery-green scales.

'I'm sorry,' he whispered. 'We should never have left the Star Continent. I thought we were invincible.'

He sat down on the deck next to the dying dragon, as the scale of the catastrophe swept over his thoughts. The air shimmered a few yards away, and Lahnos flinched, then raised his hand.

'What a fucking mess,' said Sable, a drawn sword in her right hand.

Lahnos stared at her.

'Let's get you out of here first,' Sable went on. She dipped her left hand into a pocket. The air shimmered, and Lahnos found himself sitting on a large, open platform, surrounded by vine trellises. A few men and women were waiting, and they rushed forward.

'I'll be back soon with more wounded,' said Sable. 'The dragon needs salve.'

Sable vanished.

A man ran forward, a small vial clutched in his hand. He poured its contents into Sigum's mouth, and stood back. A blanket was placed over Lahnos's shoulders as he stared at Sigum. The silvery-green dragon's body convulsed for a moment, then he opened his blue eyes.

'My rider,' he said. 'Where are we?'

Lahnos ran to him, and embraced the dragon's face. 'I don't know,' he said, as tears ran down his cheeks.

'You are on Ulna,' said the man who had administered the salve. 'My name is Millen, and we are above the bridge palace of Udall.'

Lahnos glanced up, and saw several dragons circling overhead.

'How did Sable know where we were?' he said.

'I don't know,' said Millen. 'She's been gone for a few days, then she turned up here and told us to get ready to receive casualties.'

The air shimmered on another section of the large platform and Sable appeared, along with a few dozen sailors and all of the wounded. She nodded to Millen, then vanished again. Millen took out another vial of salve and hurried off towards the wounded. Others followed him, bearing blankets and water.

'Am I the only dragon left?' said Sigum.

'Gallantmorn also survived,' said Lahnos, 'but the others are dead.'

'I saw the Bullan fall,' Sigum went on. 'I saw what the gods did to them.'

Lahnos turned away, unable to bear the look of anguish on the dragon's face. He glanced over the edge of the platform. They were atop a high tower of a colossal building built into a long bridge that sat over a wide, brown river. Below, a town spread out on both banks of the river, with a harbour full of ships. Lahnos turned, and watched as Millen gave doses of salve to the wounded.

'Go to Ora'lya,' said Sigum. 'I am recovered.'

Lahnos walked across the platform, and came to where Ora'lya was lying. Millen had visited her, and her legs had healed. She glanced up at him with tears in her eyes, and he crouched next to her. He put his arms round her shoulders and held her close.

'Quicklime,' she whispered.

The air shimmered above them, and Gallantmorn appeared, with Sable and his rider Annu'tila on his shoulders. Sable vanished again, and Gallantmorn descended onto the platform.

The dark orange dragon tilted his head towards Sigum. 'My lord,' he said, 'the shame of this day will never leave me. Like a coward, I fled from the power of the gods.'

'Your death would have been for nothing, Gallantmorn,' said Sigum.

The air shimmered again, and a few dozen sailors appeared on the platform, along with gallons of seawater. The water flooded the platform, then it surged through the gaps in the railings, sending cascades down into the river below.

A dragon almost as large as Sigum began to descend. Lahnos looked up.

'Two dragons?' said Queen Blackrose. 'Is that all who remains? Lord Sigum, what have you done with those I gave you?'

Lord Sigum tilted his head as the queen landed in front of him.

'Two gods were waiting for us, Your Majesty,' he said. 'We were ambushed.'

Blackrose's red eyes burned. 'Two gods? Impossible.'

'Lord Sigum speaks the truth, Your Majesty,' said Gallantmorn. 'The gods – a man and a woman – had a Quadrant.'

The air shimmered, and more sailors appeared, along with Sable and Cael Holdfast.

'That's all of them,' said Sable, sheathing her sword.

'Did you see any gods, Sable?' said Blackrose.

'Not in the flesh, Your Majesty,' said Sable, walking forwards, 'but I saw them with my vision powers. I was hiding in a little cave on Rigga, keeping an eye on the captured dragon carrier.'

'Then why didn't you help us?' said Lahnos. 'We were slaughtered.'

Sable eyed him. 'I wasn't watching you continuously,' she said. 'I was checking in every few hours. I had to be careful that the dragons on Rigga didn't detect me while I was hiding. As far as I could see, the *Wondrous Light* was abandoned, and I had no idea that two gods were waiting to attack you. I came as soon as I saw what had happened.'

'Are the two gods on Rigga?' said Cael.

'I would have sensed them,' said Sable. 'They must be operating out of Gyle.'

'How did they get here?' said Blackrose. 'Every god on Dragon Eyre was killed years ago.'

'I don't know,' said Sable.

'I heard their names,' said Cael. 'The woman was called Allura, and the man Ward.'

'I've never heard of them,' said Sable.

'Why didn't you scour their minds?' said Lahnos.

'I tried to,' Cael said, 'but I was invisible, and you hit me with the Gift of Pain. It wasn't your fault, but it prevented me from being able to stop them.'

Lahnos rubbed his face. 'I take full responsibility. The dragons, sailors, Bullan and marines were under my authority, and it was my plan we were following. The Wystians on Rigga will now be able to use both carriers to escape to Gyle.'

'Not if I can help it,' said Sable. 'Were any explosives stored upon the *Horned God*?'

'No,' said Cael. 'They were all on the frigates.'

'Then I might have to steal some from Sun Ta. I'll destroy the carriers, and then I need to report what's happened to the Empress.'

'I know where we can get explosives on Sun Ta,' said Cael.

'Picture where they are being stored,' said Sable.

Cael nodded, and Sable looked into his eyes.

'Got it,' she said. 'I shouldn't be too long. Everyone else; stay here.'

'Are you going to face two gods to sink the carriers?' said Lahnos. 'On your own?'

Sable put a hand on her hip. 'Do you know who you're talking to, Lahnos? If there are enemy gods on Dragon Eyre, then someone needs to deal with them; and that someone is me.'

'I'm coming with you,' said Lahnos.

'No,' said Ora'lya, taking his hand. 'It's a miracle you're still alive, Lahnos. I heard what the gods did to you; you're not immortal.'

Lahnos gazed at her. 'I have to go. All those deaths were my fault. If I can help Sable sink the carriers, then some of the shame I feel may lessen.'

'I work better alone,' said Sable.

'I don't give a shit,' he said.

'Companions of mine have a habit of getting themselves killed,' Sable went on. 'You should stay here.'

Blackrose and the survivors had clustered around them, and all were listening to the exchange. Lahnos glanced at them. Irlanian sailors, marines from the Seaborne Company, and the three dragons all had their eyes upon him.

'Let him go,' said Blackrose. 'Take the horned one with you, Sable; I can smell his guilt and shame from here.'

Sable raised her palms. 'Fine. No one can say you weren't warned, Lahnos.'

'I'll come, too,' said Cael.

'No chance,' said Sable. 'You're staying here, nephew.'

'I'm not afraid,' said Cael.

Sable nodded. 'I can see that. Perhaps you should be, Cael. You're brave; no one here is doubting that, but you need a little more experience before you take on two gods who clearly know what they're doing. Their attack upon the fleet was exactly how I would have done it, and I can't give them any higher praise than that.' She turned to Lahnos. 'Are you ready?'

'I could do with a weapon,' he said.

Cael handed him his Tempest short sword.

'Thanks,' said Lahnos.

Sable turned to Blackrose. 'I will kill these gods if I see them,' she said.

'Must you sink the two carriers?' said the black dragon. 'They are of great use.'

'Right now,' said Sable, 'they are of more use to the Wystians.'

'But why would any god assist the Wystians?' said Blackrose. 'And why would any Wystian trust a god?'

'The Wystians have been trapped on Rigga for ten years,' said Sable. 'Imagine how desperate they must feel. Over the last few days, I have seen dozens make the journey to Gyle, using the *Wondrous Light* to rest overnight. They might not trust the gods, but if those gods are offering them freedom, then they have taken the deal. With two carriers now available, over twenty could flee every day.'

'That does not explain the actions of the gods,' said Blackrose.

'They are trying to harm the Empire,' said Cael. 'They must be from the Doomed Worlds. They are hurting us for what we did to the Ascendants.'

'But why now, after so long?' said Blackrose.

'I don't know,' said Cael.

'I will request a dozen volunteers to travel to Na Sun Ka,' the queen said, 'as it seems the promises of the Empire to defend that island are worthless. Without the carriers, and without Sigum's team, Na Sun Ka is vulnerable again. If the two gods are on Gyle, they may be coordinating a counter attack from there. You do not need to speak to the Empress Sable. When the portal to the Star Continent opens this afternoon, I will send emissaries to Her Majesty to inform her of this day's disaster.'

'Tell her that Lahnos and I will take care of the carriers,' said Sable. 'Do I have your leave to go?'

'Since when did you ask for leave, Sable? Go, if that is what is required.'

Ora'lya embraced Lahnos, and he kissed her; then Sable pushed the dragon rider to the side. She reached into her pocket, the air shimmered, and Lahnos found himself standing in a dark warehouse in the harbour of Sun Ta, with Sable next to him. They glanced at the racks of explosives arranged on rows of shelving.

Sable picked up a long cylinder.

'Not those,' said Lahnos. 'They're unreliable. They need fuse wire, and they have no detonators.'

She gestured to another shelf. 'What about these?'

'I don't know,' said Lahnos.

Sable eyed him. 'If you're going to come along, Lahnos, then you need to be of assistance.'

'My mind... All I can think about is the carnage on the two flight decks. What have I done, Sable?'

'You're no good to me like this,' she said. 'Get your head together, or I'm taking you back to Ulna.'

Lahnos nodded, then he glanced at the munitions on the shelf. 'They're for a new device called a mortar,' he said, 'but I've never seen them in action. You drop them into a metal tube, and the detonator at the bottom ignites.'

'They will do,' she said. 'We can drop them down the hatches on the flight decks. A couple of racks should be enough. Get ready.'

The air shimmered, and Lahnos found himself back on the flight deck of the *Horned God*, surrounded by Wystian dragons.

'Shit!' Sable cried, as the dragons turned to them.

'Insects!' shouted a dragon. 'Kill them!'

Sable triggered the Quadrant again, as flames burst out towards them from three different dragons. She and Lahnos appeared on the rear lift of the *Wondrous Light's* flight deck. The entire deck was crammed with Wystians, none of whom looked as tired as they should have been after flying from Rigga. Sable raised a hand, and four collapsed to the deck, their eyes closing, then Lahnos unleashed the Gift of Pain at the rest, flooding the flight deck with his powers.

The two gods appeared behind them, both armed with long swords.

'Stay back!' Ward shouted at the Wystian dragons. 'I want their Quadrant.'

Ward swung his sword at Lahnos's neck, and Sable parried the blow with her own blade. She leapt forward, her black sword slicing a wound across the god's waist. Allura joined the fight, her movements as quick as Sable's had been, and the Holdfast woman fended them both off.

'It's a Holdfast!' cried Ward. 'She has joined with the horned god.'

The two gods backed away a few steps, and Lahnos raised his hand to unleash the Gift of Pain, but Ward was quicker. He lifted a finger, and Lahnos felt his body flayed by a blast of death powers. He fell to the deck, writhing, as his self-healing got to work.

'The horned god is not immune to our powers,' said Ward, as he parried another attack by Sable.

'But the Holdfast is,' said Allura.

'Send them to sleep,' Lahnos cried, as he tried to get back to his feet.

'They are wearing eye-shields,' said Sable, as the tip of her blade ripped a long wound in Allura's side.

A dragon swiped a forelimb at Sable, and she rolled on the deck to avoid it, then she sprang back to her feet with her sword held out.

'What do you want?' Sable said to the gods.

'Power,' said Ward. 'We are going to bring the Holdfast Empire to its knees, and build a new world upon the ashes of the old.'

Sable ducked under a lightning-fast blow, then she lashed out, slicing through Ward's chest.

'This is only going to end one way,' said Sable, as Ward screamed in pain. 'I killed four Ascendants; you two are nothing special.'

Allura gazed at Ward, and fear passed over her eyes for the first time.

A dragon lunged forward, but not at Sable or Lahnos. Instead, his giant forelimb struck the rack containing the explosives, intending to push it into the depths of the ocean, but one of the mortars exploded with the contact, and the blast ripped through the stern of the *Wondrous Light*. Lahnos was sent flying through the air, blinded and deafened by the explosion. He landed on the wooden flight deck, but when he opened his eyes, he found himself lying on the high platform in Udall. Next to him, Sable was sprawled out, her clothes in tatters, and blood streaming from her body. Millen ran over to them, and held Sable's head as he poured a small dose of salve down her throat. The others on the platform crowded round as Sable's body jerked and healed.

A woman crouched by Sable, as the Holdfast woman's eyes opened.

'Hi, Lara,' Sable groaned.

'You stupid cow!' Lara cried. 'Are you trying to destroy me? We have two children; you can't do this any more.'

Lahnos rolled onto his front and got to his knees, as, for the second time that day, his body repaired the damage inflicted by death powers.

'Did you succeed?' said Blackrose. 'Are the gods dead, and the carriers sunk?'

'There was an explosion,' said Sable. 'The *Wondrous Light* might sink, but I don't know what happened to the gods. The Wystians were already there when we arrived.'

'The carriers are irrelevant,' said Lahnos.

'How so?' said Blackrose.

'There were twenty dragons on board the two carriers,' he said, 'and every one of them looked fresh. They didn't fly there; the gods used their Quadrant to bring them to the ships, to occupy them, not to use them as a stepping stone. They don't need a stepping stone any more. The gods will be transporting them directly from Rigga to Gyle.'

'He's right,' said Sable. 'The carrier was merely the bait, to provoke the Empire into trying to recapture it. Every stranded Wystian on Rigga will be in Gyle by this evening, if they're not there already.'

Blackrose's eyes burned with fury. 'It seems that we have been comprehensively out-manoeuvred.'

Sable got to her feet, then she glanced down at her torn and ragged clothing. 'The Empress needs to know about the Wystians now, not when the portal opens. As soon as I get changed into something that isn't falling apart, I'm going to Plateau City.'

'And then you will come right back here?' said Lara.

Sable nodded.

'What about me?' said Lahnos.

'I will take you and the other survivors to Na Sun Ka when I get back,' she said.

'We shall provide all the hospitality you need,' said Blackrose to the clustered groups of sailors and marines. 'Food, drink, and a place where you can rest until Sable returns. Millen, show our visitors to the guest quarters of the palace.'

Millen bowed his head, then he began to lead the survivors off the platform via a ramp that descended into the interior of the building.

'Sigum and Gallantmorn,' said Blackrose, 'you may rest here.'

The two dragons tilted their heads.

Lahnos walked up to Ora'lya, took her hand, and they followed the others down the ramp. Millen took them to a large suite of connected rooms, where palace courtiers were waiting with trays of food and drink for them. As they got settled onto long couches, Lahnos and Ora'lya walked out onto a wide balcony, which overlooked the town of Ulna.

'This is the worst day of my life,' said Ora'lya, as she sobbed. 'What will I do without Quicklime? I loved her with all my heart.'

Lahnos put an arm over her shoulder.

'This is my fault,' he said.

Ora'lya shook her head. 'Even Sable was unable to kill the two gods. Do you hear me? Even Sable. If she couldn't do it, then there is nothing you could have done, Lahnos. The Wystians are on Gyle; all seven thousand. They will be coming for Na Sun Ka, and then the Eastern Rim.'

Lahnos glanced back into the large chamber. Captain Doune, who had recovered from his wounds after a dose of salve, was organising the remnants of his Seaborne Company, but his eyes were grim as he stared at the two dozen survivors. Cael was among them, and he looked as though he was carrying the weight of the Allied Worlds upon his shoulders. Next to the marines, the Irlanian sailors looked exhausted and bewildered, and several were staring into space, or weeping in silence.

'There's only one thing I can do,' said Lahnos. 'I'm going to resign my command.'

Ora'lya looked at him, but said nothing.

'Because of me,' he went on, 'the Empire has suffered a terrible blow. Sailors, marines, dragons, riders... I lost the Bullan, and I almost lost you and Sigum. My failure allowed the gods to transport the Wystians to Gyle, and I need to take responsibility for that. I am going to kneel before the Empress and tell her that I am stepping down, and then I'm going back to Colsbury. Will you come with me, Ora'lya?'

'What about Sigum?' she said. 'What will he want to do?'

'I saw the look on his face after the salve had revived him. The Empress trusted us, and we led her fleet into disaster. We don't belong here. We've never belonged here. Sigum and I... this is not our war; this is not our fight. He will come with me if I ask him. Will you?'

'Without Quicklime, Dragon Eyre doesn't feel like my home any more. Do you really want me to come with you?'

He gazed down at her. 'Yes. I love you, Ora'lya.'

'I love you, too, Lahnos,' she said, 'but my heart is aching.'

'We have both lost those we loved. We can help each other.'

Ora'lya took his hand, and they stared out at the town of Ulna.

'Will you come with me?' he said.

'Yes, Lahnos,' she said. 'I will come with you.'

# CHAPTER 24
# INTRANSIGENT

**Hold Cane, Republic of the Holdings – 29th Day, Second Third Spring 545**

Corthie gripped the Clawhammer, and advanced between the tall lines of sugar cane. The four greenflies had been gorging themselves on the thick, syrupy sugar contained within the ripening canes, leaving a trail of devastation behind them. Corthie crept forward, then he charged the last few yards and burst into their midst. The Clawhammer ripped through the first greenfly, as the other three started to flee, then Karalyn appeared to their rear, and her Tempest sword sliced one of the beasts in half. Another one went for her, and Corthie launched himself at it, raising the Clawhammer and ramming the butt spike down into its brain. The shaft of the Clawhammer passed through the beast's eyeless head, before driving into the soil, pinning the greenfly to the ground. The last beast took to the air, but Halfclaw had been waiting. The green and blue dragon reached out with his forelimbs, grasped hold of the greenfly, and ripped it in half.

Karalyn glanced at the dead beasts. 'How many does that make today? Thirteen?'

Corthie nodded. 'Aye, I think so.'

He took hold of the Clawhammer with both hands, and ripped it from the head of the greenfly, as Halfclaw descended next to them.

'We have killed every beast that was ravaging Hold Cane,' the dragon said.

'Sixty-three in seven days,' said Karalyn.

Corthie sat down on one of the slain beasts. 'Are we done? I want to go home. I've only seen the family once since we got out of the Palace of the Almighty, and it's Cairney's birthday two days from now.'

Karalyn nodded. 'All right. We'll report to the Empress first, then I'll take you back to Clackenbaird.'

'And you'll leave me there?'

'I guess so. We still need Bailey to seal up the breaches in the palace wall, but we don't need you here for that.'

Corthie glanced at the dismembered bodies. 'I feel as though I've failed. The Empress asked me to destroy the monsters coming out of the palace, and I let more than half of them escape. Edgar could be anywhere. I want to go home, but not like this, not when the job isn't finished.'

'You defended the Star Continent,' said Karalyn. 'You kept Colsbury safe.'

'You could have done that on your own, sis.'

'Both of us were required to kill the three ironhides we came across.'

'And how many are still out there?'

'Let's go back to Colsbury for now,' she said. 'We'll get cleaned up, and then you can pack.' She glanced up at Halfclaw. 'Do you want to fly back to Colsbury, or do you want me to take you there?'

'I shall fly, Karalyn,' said the dragon. 'The days are getting warmer, and I love flying in the sunshine.'

Karalyn nodded to her brother. 'Up you get.'

Corthie stood, then the air shimmered, and he found himself standing next to Karalyn on the middle balcony of the Summer Palace. Kelsey was there, along with Cardova, and they glanced over.

'Did you get them all?' said Kelsey.

'We think so,' said Karalyn, as she and Corthie walked over. 'The sugar on Hold Cane was luring them, and we killed all thirteen that were there. Halfclaw will be along soon; he wanted to fly back.'

Kelsey eyed Corthie. 'So, is that it for you, brother? Is it time to go back to the farm and the kids?'

Corthie nodded. 'Aye.'

'You don't seem too happy about it.'

'I'll be happy to see everyone, but... I don't know.'

'He thinks he's failed,' said Karalyn.

'Edgar got the better of me,' said Corthie. 'It rankles.'

Cardova looked up from the pile of documents he was reading. 'If you want another go at Edgar, I'd be happy to send you to Athumia to help re-take the Tempest mine.'

Corthie half-laughed. 'No, thanks. Aila would kill me long before I got my hands on Edgar.'

'Who are you going to send, Lucius?' said Kelsey.

'That's what we'll be deciding in Plateau City later today. The entire Imperial Court will be sitting; even Shella will be coming.'

'I'll take you all together,' said Karalyn. 'Get ready, Corthie; we leave in an hour.'

'Where will I put the Tempest armour?'

'Keep it,' said Cardova. 'A gift from the Empire.'

'I hardly deserve it.'

'We managed to build up a large stockpile of Tempest before the Dominion launched their attack on the mine. We can spare one suit of armour.'

Corthie nodded, then he walked off the balcony and headed to his room within the palace. When he got there, he flung open the shutters, then he stripped the black armour from his body, laying it out on the bed. He pulled the coat of mail from over his shoulders, and hung it off the back of a chair. His underclothes went into a laundry basket, then he walked into his small bathroom, and turned on the shower taps. He stood under the flow of water, which started off cold, but quickly warmed up to a near scalding temperature.

A mixture of emotions tore at him. He longed to settle back into his life in Clackenbaird, with Aila and their seven children. The Clawhammer could return to its crate in the attic, and the Tempest armour could join it there, never to be worn again. At the same time, he felt regret that Edgar was still on the loose. The god had easily tricked both Corthie and Karalyn, two of the most powerful Holdfasts in existence; he had made them look like fools, and they had needed to be rescued by another god and a teenage girl. It was humiliating. Worse, following seven days of roaming through the Holdings to hunt down the greenflies, he felt as though he was just getting back into his natural fighting rhythm. After a decade of peace, it had taken him a while to regain the peaks of his youth, and now that he was there, it was time to go home again.

When his hair had been washed and his skin scrubbed, he turned off the taps, dried himself amid the steam, and walked back into his room. He dressed in his usual civilian clothing, then packed away his other belongings. He placed the plates of Tempest armour into a large crate, padding them with straw, and did the same with his Clawhammer. A dragon flitted by his window, and he glanced out, expecting to see the familiar blues and greens of Halfclaw. Instead, he saw a much larger dragon, its scales shimmering a silvery-green in the sunlight.

Lord Sigum alighted in the castle forecourt, his wingspan almost crossing the distance between the Summer Palace and the Great Keep. Three people were on the dragon's shoulders. One was Sable, and another Lahnos, while the third was a woman Corthie didn't recognise. The dragon raised its head up to the middle balcony of the palace, and Corthie left his room. He walked to the balcony, where the dragon was talking to Karalyn, Kelsey and Cardova.

The air shimmered, then Sable, Lahnos and the unfamiliar woman appeared on the balcony.

'Hey, Sable,' said Corthie.

She turned, and nodded at Corthie. 'Nephew,' she said. 'Do you know Lahnos?'

'We've met a few times,' said Corthie. 'How's it going on Dragon Eyre, Lahnos?'

The man with the horns glanced at him. 'Badly.'

Karalyn walked over. 'Is Cael all right?'

'Cael's fine,' said Lahnos. 'He's got the makings of a good officer, if he can keep his more reckless impulses under control.'

Karalyn glanced at the other woman. 'Who is this?'

'Her name is Ora'lya,' said Lahnos.

The woman sobbed, and Lahnos put an arm round her shoulder.

'What are you doing back on Colsbury?' said Cardova.

The silvery-green dragon leaned his head closer to the balcony. 'The fleet sent to recapture the stolen dragon carrier has been annihilated, Commander,' he said.

Cardova's eyes widened.

'We got our asses kicked by two gods,' said Lahnos. 'It was a slaughter. We lost the Bullan, along with three dragons, thousands of sailors, and most of Doune's Seaborne Company. That's why I'm here, Commander, to tender my resignation.'

Cardova kept his gaze on Lahnos, but said nothing.

'I took the other survivors back to Na Sun Ka,' said Sable, 'and I've already been to Plateau City to tell the Empress. Queen Blackrose is going to reinforce Na Sun Ka with a dozen dragons, but it's likely that every Wystian that was trapped in Rigga is now on Gyle.'

Cardova rose to his feet. 'What?'

'The gods have a Quadrant,' said Lahnos.

Sable eyed Karalyn. 'Where is the Sextant?'

'Why?' said Karalyn.

'I used it to send the Wystians to Rigga in the first place. This time, I'll send the bastards to Elidus; let their arses freeze in the cold.'

Karalyn said nothing for a moment, then she shook her head. 'The seven thousand Wystians represent the largest number of dragons on any world,' she said. 'Without them, the dragons are doomed to die out. I cannot allow you to kill them, Sable.'

'Then they will burn their way through the entire Eastern Rim,' said Sable. 'Blackrose's hundreds cannot withstand seven thousand.'

'Wait,' said Lahnos. 'What do you mean the dragons will die out? There are thousands of dragons on Athumia.'

'There are fewer than two thousand dragons on Athumia,' said Karalyn; 'and barely a thousand non-Wystian dragons on Dragon Eyre. Taken together, it's not enough to prevent the dragons from becoming extinct.'

'But this would happen centuries from now,' said Kelsey, 'if it happens at all.'

'And your point is?' said Karalyn. 'Lahnos and I will still be around centuries from now, and I don't want to live through the extinction of the dragons, not if I can prevent it.'

Sable sighed and shook her head. 'What if I put them somewhere else; somewhere they would survive?'

'Where?'

'I don't know. Give me the location of the Sextant and I'll find a suitable place for them.'

'I hid the Sextant for a good reason,' said Karalyn.

'Yes, to keep it away from Cael, in case he gets tempted to use it again.'

Karalyn eyed her aunt. 'It was also to keep it away from you.'

'Then *you* send them somewhere, Karalyn,' Sable snapped. 'If you don't, then the fall of the Eastern Rim will be your responsibility. While you speculate about events hundreds of years into the future, seven thousand Wystians are preparing to roll right over Na Sun Ka, Yearning and Haurn. They won't stop until they get back to Wyst, and guess who they will find living in their old homes? The fifty thousand Riggans I put there, that's who.'

'Can we get back to the gods for a moment?' said Cardova. 'Which gods are on Dragon Eyre? Did you recognise them, Sable?'

'No,' she said. 'Lahnos saw a lot more of them than I did.'

'It was a man and a woman,' said Lahnos. 'Ward and Allura.'

Corthie gasped, and the others on the balcony fell silent.

Sable narrowed her eyes. 'Who are they?'

'They were prisoners inside the Palace of the Almighty,' said Karalyn. 'Edgar released them, along with a few others.'

Corthie fell into a chair and put his head in his hands.

'Ward was also present at the capture of the Tempest mine,' said Cardova.

'The Tempest mine has been captured?' said Lahnos. 'When did this happen?'

'Seven days ago,' said Cardova, 'while you were sailing with the fleet. The Dominion dragons slaughtered the garrison, and the sole survivor was brought back to the Star Continent by Ward, who took the Quadrant that had been kept at the mine.' He glanced at Karalyn. 'Will you take us to Plateau City?'

Karalyn nodded.

'I'll fetch Shella,' said Kelsey, getting to her feet.

'Are you coming, too?' said Corthie.

'Why would I come?' said Kelsey. 'I have no job in the government, and I have no news to deliver to the Empress.'

'We will assemble in the forecourt in fifteen minutes,' said Karalyn. 'I will take everyone who is there to the Ministry of the Plateau.'

She walked from the balcony, and Sable cast an irritated glance in her direction. She turned to Cardova.

'I have no idea where the Sextant is,' he said, 'so there's no point in reading my mind to look for it.'

'She had no right to hide it,' said Sable. 'My home is on Ulna, and if the Wystians destroy it because of Karalyn's intransigence, then...'

'Then what?' said Cardova.

'I don't know,' she said. 'What can I do against Karalyn?'

'Very little,' said Kelsey. 'I'd better find Shella.'

'I'll come with you,' said Cardova, and they both left the balcony.

Corthie glanced up at Sable, Lahnos and Ora'lya. 'Are you all going to see the Empress?'

'I am,' said Lahnos. 'I intend to resign my position to Her Majesty in person.'

'Why are you resigning?'

'The slaughter at the dragon carriers was my fault,' he said.

'If anything,' said Corthie, 'it was my fault. I was supposed to defeat whoever was lurking inside the Palace of the Almighty, and Edgar tricked us and got away. If we had stopped him, then those two gods wouldn't have been on Dragon Eyre.'

'How did they trick you?' said Sable.

'Edgar lured Karalyn and me into the palace, then he used his stone powers to seal us inside, so that he could escape with the other gods.'

'Are you going to help us fight them?'

Corthie hesitated for a moment, as the others gazed at him. 'No,' he said. 'I'm going back to Kell. I'm going home.'

Sable glanced from Lahnos to Corthie. 'You two boys are the best the Empire has, and you're both about to give up?'

'I've had enough,' said Lahnos. 'I've given the Empire eight years.'

'And then you quit when things get rough? As for you, nephew, I'm disappointed, but not surprised. Kell is a good place to hide and pretend that everything will be fine, while Dragon Eyre is ravaged.' Sable shook her head. 'It's going to have to be me, isn't it? Again. Enjoy your holiday, boys; I have a home to defend.'

She put a hand into her pocket and vanished.

'Her words shame me,' said Sigum. 'They shame us all.'

Corthie got up and left the balcony without a word. He went to his rooms, and carried the crates and his luggage down the stairs of the palace to the large forecourt, where Lord Sigum was standing. The dragon's head was close to the middle balcony, and Corthie watched as he spoke to Lahnos and Ora'lya. Corthie sat on the crate of armour. He had promised Aila that he would only take up arms if the Star Continent was attacked by enemy gods, and he had attempted to do his duty when the Empress had asked him to destroy the beasts inside the Palace of the Almighty. Dragon Eyre and Athumia had experienced wars and chaos before, and he had never done anything about it, so why had Sable's words torn at him?

Karalyn appeared by his side. She glanced at her brother, a frown on her face.

'Are we shirking our responsibilities?' he said.

Karalyn said nothing.

'I want to go home, but...'

'Don't get involved, Corthie,' she said. 'Go back to your family and live in peace.'

'Will the dragons really die out if Sable kills the Wystians?'

'Aye. Even if, somehow, the dragons of Athumia were to join with the non-Wystians on Dragon Eyre, their extinction is only a matter of time. Even with the Wystians, the long-term future of the dragons is uncertain, but destroying them would make sure of it.'

'You're starting to think like a god,' he said.

'What is that supposed to mean?'

'You're looking at events in terms of centuries and millennia. To Sable, it must seem as though you're prepared to sacrifice the Eastern Rim because of something that might not happen for a thousand years.'

Cardova, Shella and Kelsey approached from the direction of the Great Keep, then Sigum glanced down. He reached out into the middle balcony, then he lowered Lahnos down to the forecourt.

'I will stay here with Ora'lya,' the dragon said.

'And I'll get out of everyone's way,' said Kelsey. She glanced around, frowning. 'Where's Sable?'

'She went back to Dragon Eyre,' said Corthie.

Kelsey nodded. 'Good luck.'

Karalyn glanced at those she was about to take to Plateau City, then the air shimmered, and they found themselves standing in the central courtyard of the Ministry of the Plateau.

'Are you coming inside?' said Cardova.

'No,' said Karalyn. 'I'm not getting drawn into a discussion about the future of the Empire. I'm staying out of it.'

Cardova looked unhappy, but said nothing; then Karalyn disappeared. Adjutant Claudian emerged from a doorway, and saluted.

'Constable Cardova,' he said, 'Commander Laimos, Chancellor Shella, and Corthie, welcome back to Plateau City. Her Imperial Majesty is awaiting you in the greater audience chamber.'

They followed the former Banner officer into the building, and Claudian gestured to a few soldiers to bring Corthie's luggage inside.

'It will be safe here until you are ready to leave,' Claudian said.

'Who will be taking me to Kell?' said Corthie.

'Lord Naxor has volunteered to take you,' said Claudian. 'He wishes to see his cousin, your noble wife. First, however, Her Imperial Majesty requests your presence at a meeting of the full Imperial Court.' He glanced at Lahnos. 'You are also invited, Commander.'

Lahnos said nothing, then Claudian led them up a flight of stairs, passing groups of courtiers and officials. The atmosphere within the building was tense, and most of those Corthie saw were wearing grim expressions on their faces. Claudian took them into a well-guarded room, where the Empress was seated upon a low throne. By a table in front of her, the rest of the Imperial Court was sitting. Corthie and Lahnos remained standing at the far end of the table, while Cardova, Claudian and Shella bowed and took their seats.

'Thank you all for coming,' said the Empress. 'This is the first time that the full court has gathered in over two years, and I wish it was under more favourable circumstances. My thanks also extend to Commander Laimos and Corthie for attending. Please be seated.'

Lahnos bowed. 'Thank you, Your Majesty,' he said, 'but I do not intend to take up much of your valuable time. I am here to tender my resignation in the aftermath of the catastrophe upon Dragon Eyre. As commanding officer of the operation, I take full responsibility for its failure.'

The Empress narrowed her eyes. 'It was, indeed, a catastrophe, as you say, Commander; however, we do not hold you to blame for the events that destroyed our fleet. You were ambushed by two of Edgar's gods, were you not?'

'So I have since learned, Your Majesty,' said Lahnos. 'Regardless, I pressed on with my plan to seize the captured carrier even after one of our dragons was slain by a god. If I had withdrawn at that moment, rather than attack, the fleet would have been preserved. We lost two thousand sailors, a hundred marines, and three dragons, along with four frigates and both carriers. If you do not relieve me of my command, then I have no alternative but to resign my commission.'

The chamber fell into silence.

'May I speak, Your Majesty?' said Naxor.

'Of course,' said Thorn.

The demigod turned to Lahnos. 'It seems to me, Commander,' he said, 'that you are taking all this rather personally. You were defeated, yes – no one is arguing that point – but wouldn't you prefer to make amends, rather than slink off into the shadows? Our plans involved sending you and Lord Sigum to Athumia, to lead the recapture of the Tempest mine. If you do this for the Empire, then you can resign in honour, rather than in disgrace.'

'My mind is made up, Lord Naxor,' said Lahnos. 'It was the Bullan who persuaded me to serve the Empire, and the Bullan are dead. They were my friends, they were loyal, and their deaths were my fault. I have served the Empire for eight years...'

'And the Empire thanks you for that service,' said the Empress. 'I will not accept your resignation, not yet; not until you have sat through this meeting. Sit.'

Lahnos lowered his gaze, then he and Corthie took seats at the other end of the table from the Empress. Thorn turned to Cardova.

'Please outline our current difficulties for the benefit of the Imperial Court, Lucius.'

Cardova stood. 'Yes, Your Majesty. Edgar and his gods are moving against us; that seems clear. Ward was seen on Inopei, and on Dragon Eyre, where he was accompanied by Allura. They have hit us hard, weakening our position on Na Sun Ka, and threatening the entire Eastern Rim; while also depriving us of our supply of Tempest. By now, it is likely that they will be equipping themselves with Tempest armour and weapons, while the Wystians will be preparing an overwhelming assault upon Na Sun Ka. Our first item of business, in my opinion, is to ascertain our priorities, for the imperial armed forces are stretched, and we cannot deal with both emergencies simultaneously. If we send a large force to re-take the Tempest mine, then we will not be able to withstand a massive invasion from Gyle. If, however, we reinforce Na Sun Ka, we will not be able to take back control of the Tempest mine.' He glanced at the Empress. 'This is a decision that only you can take, Your Majesty.'

'And what is your considered opinion, Constable?' said the Empress.

'Our treaty promises to Queen Blackrose would be broken if we allowed Na Sun Ka to fall without a determined fight,' Cardova said; 'therefore, I advise leaving the Dominion in control of the Tempest mine for now, until the situation on Dragon Eyre has been stabilised.'

'Stabilised?' said Caelius. 'With seven thousand dragons coming their way, the defences of Na Sun Ka will be obliterated, no matter how many reinforcements we send; and with gods and Dominion dragons defending the Tempest mine, any attack upon it would be disastrous.'

'I disagree, Quartermaster,' said the Empress. 'I believe that we can do both. We can defend Na Sun Ka, while sending an elite force to Inopei to strike at the Dominion, and at Edgar.' She glanced at Corthie. 'A small, elite force, armed with a Quadrant, could eliminate Edgar and his band of gods.'

'If I may, Your Majesty?' said Claudian. 'It appears that Edgar is employing the same tactics against us that Sable Holdfast used to defeat the Banner forces on Dragon Eyre ten years ago. Rapid movement, pinpoint strikes, use of powers, planned massacres – all aimed at sowing confusion and despair. Perhaps we should be considering where these gods will strike next.'

The door to the chamber opened, and Bailey walked in. He bowed low.

'Sorry I'm a little late, Your Majesty.'

'What have you learned, Bailey?' said the Empress.

Bailey glanced at the faces sitting round the long table, then he slipped a Quadrant into a pocket.

'Lord Edgar is not on Inopei, Your Majesty,' he said; 'though he has been there. He has departed Athumia, and is currently on Elidus, if, that is, he was telling the truth to the Dominion leadership. He has left

Lord Ballatar in charge of operations at the Tempest mine, along with several dragons, both alive and undead.'

'Were you on Inopei?' said Lahnos.

'I was, yes,' said Bailey.

'And do you have a new Quadrant?' said Corthie.

'The two things are related,' said Bailey. 'Lord Naxor was kind enough to lend me a Quadrant from the spares stored in the Ministry of the Plateau, and his condition was that I conduct a scouting mission on behalf of the Empire. I was on Inopei for two days, sneaking around the dragon palaces of Nom Karta, and investigating the defences of the Tempest mine. I had to be extremely discreet in the use of my powers, to avoid detection by the escaped gods.'

'Were you successful in that regard?' said the Empress.

'I was, Your Majesty,' said Bailey.

'Who is now running the Dominion?' said Naxor.

'Famula Min Gahad is now the undisputed Queen of the Dominion,' Bailey said. 'She has made her peace with the other members of the Royal Family, and rules from Nom Karta. She has met with Lord Edgar, and they have agreed to a treaty of mutual defence against the Empire. Soldiers have been summoned in large numbers from Aucteran, as they fully expect the Empire to launch an invasion to retake the Tempest mine. Indeed, I would go as far as to say that they want the Empire to attack, just as they wanted Commander Laimos to attempt to recapture the stolen carrier on Dragon Eyre.'

'It's a trap, in other words?' said Cardova.

'That is my belief,' said Bailey. 'I also discovered that Edgar has been compiling a list of other vulnerable targets within the Empire. Would you like to hear it?'

'We would,' said Thorn.

'The oil fields of Alef,' said Bailey, 'the salve mine east of the City, the coal and iron mines of Northern Kell, the Great Tunnel through the Grey Mountains, the mercantile houses of Amatskouri, the harbour facilities of Plateau City, and the university.'

'He means to cripple the entire Empire!' cried Caelius.

'Or,' said Bailey, 'Edgar guessed that we would send someone to Inopei to read the mind of Queen Famula, and told her all this to keep us unbalanced.'

'That seems a bit of a stretch,' said Naxor.

'I know Edgar well, Lord Naxor,' said Bailey. 'He will be planning schemes within schemes, all designed to drive the Empire to distraction. We still have no clear idea of his aims. However, that logic does not apply to Ward or Allura, who were given the task of transporting the Wystian dragons from Rigga to Gyle. That is what Edgar ordered them to do on Dragon Eyre. The destruction of the fleet was carried out on their own initiative. If you want my advice, it is this – eliminate Ward and Allura as quickly as possible.'

'Are they still on Dragon Eyre?' said Claudian.

'As far as I know,' said Bailey.

'What other orders has Edgar given them?' said Shella.

'That information was not in the mind of Queen Famula, nor any of the other dragons or humans whose memories I read while on Inopei.'

'Now I must ask you something, Lord Bailey,' said the Empress. 'Would you be willing to lead a small, elite group to assassinate Ward, Allura and Ballatar? This small group would include Commander Laimos and Corthie Holdfast.'

Bailey glanced down. 'I... uh, well, Your Majesty, I am not a fighter. My nerves were shredded by simply going to Inopei, even though I was not recognised. I do not react well when my life is in danger. I panic, or freeze. I would be useless to you.'

'I will not be a part of this group,' said Lahnos. 'I will not be leading any more imperial forces.'

'Nor I,' said Corthie.

The members of the Imperial Court stared at him.

'But, Corthie,' said the Empress, 'the gods escaped from the Palace of the Almighty, and it was your job to apprehend them.'

'I agreed to defend the Star Continent,' he said. 'I will not be chasing gods over the Allied Worlds.'

Anger rippled across the features of the Empress. 'Lord Naxor,' she said, 'it might be better if you were to escort Lahnos and Corthie out of my presence before I say something I will regret. Take Lahnos to Colsbury, and Corthie to Kell; then return here, so that those who care about the Empire and its people can decide its future.'

Naxor stood, and bowed.

Lahnos and Corthie also got to their feet.

'Does this mean you have accepted my resignation, Your Majesty?' said Lahnos.

'No,' said the Empress. 'I am placing you on indefinite leave Remain on the island of Colsbury, if you do not wish to incur my wrath.'

Lahnos bowed his head.

Naxor gestured to the door. 'This way, gentlemen.'

The demigod led Corthie and Lahnos downstairs, to where Corthie's luggage was sitting. When they reached it, Naxor withdrew a Quadrant, and swept his fingers over its surface. The air shimmered, and they appeared on the middle balcony of the Summer Palace on Colsbury. Ora'lya was there, talking to Sigum, whose head was level with the balcony.

Lahnos walked over to Ora'lya and the dragon, then Naxor triggered the Quadrant again, without saying a word. The air shimmered, and Corthie appeared by Naxor's side in the courtyard in front of the farmhouse of Clackenbaird, the crates on the ground next to them.

Corthie breathed in the fresh spring air of Kell, as Naxor regarded him.

'In all the years I have known you, Corthie,' the demigod said 'I have never taken you for a coward. You have been a champion of the Bulwark, a drunken oaf, destroyer of Banners, killer of gods, hero of the Kell Pass, and the slayer of Edmond. In my humble opinion, your words in front of Her Majesty have destroyed your reputation in an instant.'

'Then it's lucky I couldn't give two shits about your opinion, Naxor,' said Corthie. 'This is my home; this is where I belong. I have never made a secret of that.'

'Well, well,' said Naxor; 'the day has finally come when I am perceived to possess more courage, honour and integrity than the famed Corthie Holdfast. I do hope you enjoy your little farm, while others fight and die to preserve your way of life. Goodbye.'

The air shimmered, and Naxor disappeared.

The front door of the farmhouse opened, and Aila came outside, three children running out after her.

Corthie tried to smile. 'Good morning, Aila,' he said. 'I'm home.'

# CHAPTER 25
# THE NOON BELL

**Plateau City, The Plateau – 3$^{rd}$ Day, Last Third Spring 545**

Elbannon beamed in delight as the students walked into his classroom. He was sitting at his desk, a walking stick held in one hand, while a large wooden crate lay by his feet.

'Hurry up and sit down,' he called out to the class.

Kyra sat next to Dazi, her mind on other things as Elbannon continued to smile. Noon was only a short time away, and her nerves were jangling.

'Do you all see this crate?' Elbannon said, once everyone was seated. 'I got this delivered to my office this morning. You are my third-year class – the most advanced Tempest students in the university, and the contents of this crate are going to be your focus for the rest of the academic year. *But what is in this crate?* – I hear you ask. That is the question.' He grinned, then he stooped down and removed the lid from the crate, revealing a layer of straw. He reached in, and took out a Quadrant.

'This one has scorch marks and three jewels missing,' he said, placing it onto the surface of his desk. He took out another one. 'This has a crack right down the middle; something heavy was dropped on it, I think.' He took out a third. 'And some fool bashed this one with an axe or sword blade. Altogether, there are seventeen broken Quadrants in this case. Seventeen! I haven't been this excited in years. Seventeen broken Quadrants, all retrieved from a storeroom within the Palace of Almighty, Lord Edmond's old home. The Ascendants may have been powerful, but without Theodora and Nathaniel, it appears that none of them had the knowledge or skills to repair a Quadrant. Or perhaps they did, but they had no Serpent Eye jewels or spare Tempest to effect any repairs. Regardless, any Quadrants that were broken were simply put aside. Dazi – get up here, girl, and lay out every Quadrant on my desk; my back is getting sore.'

Dazi got to her feet and walked up to the front of the class. She crouched by the crate, and Elbannon watched as she placed every one of the Quadrants onto the professor's desk.

'Our job, if it wasn't obvious to you, is to repair as many of these Quadrants as possible,' Elbannon said. 'Three of them in particular look to be beyond repair; we can use those ones for spare parts. That leaves fourteen. Some of them require new Zamatan Coils, some need jewels, and some will have to be re-wired.' He glanced at Kyra. 'I have heard that your family were responsible for breaking a few Quadrants over the years – is that true, girl?'

'Aye,' said Kyra. 'My Aunty Sable broke two, or maybe three; and my grandmother broke one in Colsbury.'

Elbannon scanned the desk and picked up one of the broken Quadrants. 'This is the one that was struck by a sword held by Daphne Holdfast, eighteen years ago. I know that because Kelsey Holdfast, who sent these Quadrants here to the university, was kind enough to write me a few notes.' He held up the copper device, and Kyra saw the large score mark that had split its curved edge in two. 'This Quadrant,' he said, 'used to belong to Lady Agatha, who fled to this world from Lostwell. Assassins used it to murder Lady Isobel, a high vision mage, and then they used it to maim Empress Bridget, by plucking out one of her eyes. It was stolen by Kyra's mother, and then, when the gods tried to steal it back, Daphne Holdfast whacked it with a sword. A few years later, Kelsey took it to Lostwell with her, in the hope that she would find someone able to repair it. Instead, she was arrested by two Ascendants, and the Quadrant was confiscated. Somehow, it then made its way back to Implacatus; most likely in the possession of Lord Bastion, when he and Lord Edmond withdrew from Lostwell just moments before that world was destroyed. And then it was placed with the other useless Quadrants, and forgotten about.' He smiled again, his joy seemingly unbounded. 'We don't know much about the other Quadrants assembled here, but we can be sure that each one has had a long history of being used by the gods and Ascendants of Implacatus.' He glanced at Dazi, who was still standing by the table. 'Select one, Dazi, and it will become your project for the rest of the term.'

'Thank you, sir,' said Dazi.

Her eyes went to the table, and she picked up a Quadrant that had a large dent in one corner, where a jewel was missing.

'Kyra, you next,' said Elbannon. 'I want you to take the device your illustrious grandmother so carelessly whacked. After that, everyone else can form a queue. There is enough for the whole class.'

Kyra got to her feet, and passed Dazi as she returned to her seat. Elbannon handed Kyra the broken Quadrant. She touched its surface, but heard no voice, then she sat down again, the Quadrant on the desk in front of her. She gazed at it as the others in the class lined up to pick their own device.

'You must be very careful when you handle them,' said Elbannon, 'as they may react unpredictably. Treat them as if they were working, and do not try to activate any of the coils. The first thing I require from you all is a short piece of written work. Record your observations regarding the Quadrant you have selected, and outline a simple plan to investigate the cause of the damage, along with the appropriate remedial steps you intend to take in order to repair it. It may be that you have picked one of the devices that I deem irreparable; even so, I wish you to carry out this first exercise. You may begin now.'

The students took out sheets of blank paper and pencils, and began to write. Kyra noted the date and her name at the top of the page, then she jotted down a few observations. All five jewels were still in place, and the damage consisted of a cut around two inches long, between the second and third jewels arranged along the curved edge. She suspected that at least two of the internal coils had been sliced through by the blade her grandmother had been wielding. To repair it, the cover would need to be carefully prised off, then the damaged coils could be removed, and the two sheets of copper welded back together. After that, she imagined that she would have to fit two new coils of Tempest, and the Quadrant would once again be operable. A thought occurred to her, and she raised a hand.

'Yes?' said Elbannon.

'What will happen to these Quadrants once they have been repaired, sir?'

'I haven't the faintest idea, girl,' said Elbannon. 'That will be up to the imperial authorities – they own the Quadrants. The university is merely borrowing them in order to fix them.'

'So, they could be used to transfer soldiers to other worlds?'

'I suppose so.'

'Then we should refuse to repair them, unless we get a solemn guarantee from the Ministry of the Plateau that they will only be used for peaceful purposes; otherwise, we shall be supporting imperialist aggression.'

Elbannon groaned.

At that moment, the noon bell sounded. The students glanced at each other, then most of them got to their feet, including Dazi and Kyra.

'What are you all doing?' said Elbannon. 'That wasn't the lunch bell; the class hasn't finished.'

'The strike has begun,' said Kyra. 'The noon bell will be ringing all over Plateau City, sir, and today is the day. Did you not see the posters nailed up in the quad? This has been planned for days.'

Elbannon raised an eyebrow. 'I have no idea what you're talking about, girl. What is a strike? Who are you striking?'

'Every worker is walking out of their jobs as we speak, sir. The dockworkers, the postal staff, the bakers, the wagon drivers. That is a strike.'

'Why would they do that?' said Elbannon. 'They won't get paid if they leave their jobs.'

'The city will be utterly paralysed until our demands are met. It would be wonderful if you walked out in support of the ordinary workers of this city, sir. Will you join us?'

Elbannon snorted. 'Let me get this straight in my mind – you would rather wander around the city like aimless fools than repair broken Quadrants? Do none of you wish to stay in this class?'

Three students who had remained seated raised their hands.

'We are not joining the strike, sir,' said one.

'Why not?' said Elbannon.

'We think it's pointless, sir,' said the student.

'You agree with the wars, you mean,' said Kyra. 'You don't care how many civilians are slaughtered by our soldiers.'

'My sister's in the army,' said one of them. 'She hasn't *slaughtered* anyone.'

'And my brother is Cael Holdfast,' said Kyra, 'and I'm sure you've all read the propaganda the newspapers have been printing about him. Even so, I have to act according to my principles. I do not blame the individual soldiers and marines in our armed forces. No, I blame the warmongering politicians and generals who have sent them to kill and die in Rahain, Rakana, and on Dragon Eyre.'

Elbannon clutched his walking stick and got to his feet.

Kyra smiled. 'Are you coming with us, sir?'

'Certainly not,' he said. 'I intend to make myself a nice cup of tea. When I return in a few minutes, every student who is still here will have automatically passed this course for the year; and we shall begin work on repairing the Quadrants. All those not here, on the other hand, will be required to complete their assignments right up to the last day of term. No exceptions.' He walked to the door, then he stopped and glanced at Kyra. 'I hope it rains.'

Kyra's smile faded as Elbannon left the classroom.

'I could really do with passing this class,' said Dazi.

'Me too,' said another Rakanese student. 'It would boost my average.'

'He is trying to bribe you,' said Kyra. 'It's outrageous.'

'Maybe,' said the student, 'but my parents are using up all their savings to send me here. They aren't rich like your family, Kyra.'

'Do they work in Plateau City?'

The student nodded. 'In the harbour district.'

'Then they're joining the strike,' said Kyra. 'I want to support them, and every worker who is being impoverished by the new taxes – taxes that are being used to massacre people on Dragon Eyre. I know it's a risk, but we have to take a stand. We have to show the Empress and her government that we are not frightened of them, that they can't push us around and treat us like this.' She raised her chin. 'I'm going, and I hope you all join me.'

She walked out of the class and began to descend the stairs. The corridors and hallways of the university were bustling with students, all heading towards the quad. A few teachers and professors were with them, along with some of the staff from the kitchens and the laundry services. Kyra glanced over her shoulder as she walked down the steps. Dazi was right behind her, followed by the majority of the class.

Kyra turned back to face the front, and smiled. She led them out into the crowded quad, and made for a wooden platform that had been erected the previous day. Achan was up on the platform, talking to Larron and a few others she knew from Achan's circle of dissidents. Larron caught Kyra's glance, and gestured to her to approach.

'This is a wonderful response,' he said, as she reached the side of the platform. 'Look at all these students. How many from your class walked out?'

'Most of them,' she said. 'Professor Elbannon wasn't too happy about it. He told us that anyone who didn't walk out would automatically pass the Tempest course for this year.'

'I will lodge a complaint with the Student Council,' said Larron. 'Elbannon is breaking all kinds of administrative rules by making rash promises like that. Leave it with me; I'll sort it out.'

'Thanks.'

She gazed up at him and smiled. They had yet to have any kind of conversation about what she had learned about him, and he had never once mentioned the occasion when she had tried to kiss him. Instead, they had both acted as though nothing had occurred to disrupt their friendship, and she was glad that she hadn't chased him away.

'Come up and join us, Kyra,' said Achan. 'I am about to make a speech, though it will be a short one, I promise.'

Larron held out a hand, and then he pulled Kyra up on to the platform. Achan raised his arms in the air, and the gathered crowd began to hush.

'The noon bell has pealed!' Achan cried, and the crowd cheered. 'All over this city,' he went on, 'workers are beginning their great protest against the tax rises and naked aggression of the Empire. For too long we have been patient, waiting for the Empress to see sense, but, as it is clear that Her Majesty needs a little encouragement for this to take place, we shall demonstrate our collective power. As of today, this city will be brought to a complete standstill. As long as we remain united, we shall prevail, and the strike will go on for as long as it takes for the government to bow to our demands. These demands are simple. First, we want all recent tax increases to be repealed; and second, we want all imperial forces to be removed from Dragon Eyre, and the Empire's claim to Na Sun Ka revoked forever!'

The crowd of students and staff cheered.

'In a few moments, we will be marching to Duncan Gardens, where the workers out on strike will be gathering,' Achan went on. 'Do I need to remind you all that violence will not be tolerated? The imperial garrison will be watching us. Do not give them any excuse to intervene. This is a peaceful march, and a peaceful strike. Our aims are noble and just; do not tarnish them by petty acts of violence, vandalism, or intimidation. Banners and placards are piled up by the entrance of the quad – take one on your way out; first come, first served.'

He lowered his arms, and the crowd began to file out of the quad, spilling into the streets by the front of the university.

'Kyra,' said Achan, 'could you please check that the route to Duncan Gardens is clear? I don't want any nasty surprises.'

Kyra nodded, then she sent out her vision powers, lifting them clear of the tall university spires and towers. She glanced down at the roads they would be taking. Their route went through the Old Town, then it crossed part of the Kellach Quarter to reach the largest open space in the city, where the huge statue of Chief Duncan stood next to the preserved section of earthen rampart. Soldiers had been posted along the route, but all were standing back from the street, and none were blocking the way. In the gardens, large crowds were already assembling, streaming south from the Kellach Quarter, and north from the bridges over the river, from the Rakanese and Rahain Quarters. Crowds of Holdings folk were also coming through the gap in the Emergency Wall, leaving the New Town behind as they marched towards Duncan Gardens.

Kyra came out of her vision trance. 'The route is clear, sir, and strikers are gathering from every corner of the city.'

'Excellent. Any sign of violence?'

'None that I could see, sir. The soldiers are out in numbers, but they aren't blocking any of the roads, and they haven't entered Duncan Gardens.'

Achan nodded and rubbed his hands together. He glanced at the quad, which was starting to empty, as most students had already departed.

'Ideally,' he said, 'we need to be leading the student march. Shall we go? We will have to hurry to get to the front.'

'Or,' said Kyra, 'I could take us there in an instant.'

Achan smiled. 'Then please do so, Kyra, with my gratitude.'

Kyra glanced at the others on the platform. 'All of us?'

'Yes,' said Achan. 'But please, try not to startle anyone.'

Kyra scanned for a suitable location, then she touched her Quadrant through the hole in her pocket.

*The alley behind the bakery I just saw. Go.*

The air shimmered, and the leadership of the student protestors appeared in a narrow alleyway, just out of sight of the main road.

'We are in the Old Town,' Kyra said, as she saw the surprise on the faces of the others. 'Follow me.'

Kyra led them to the main road. On their right was a set of gates leading to the New Town and the university.

'The front of the march will be here in a moment,' she said.

'I enjoyed that,' whispered Larron, as he stood by her side. 'It was worth it for the look on their faces.'

The first marchers appeared, holding up their banners and signs as they approached the gates. Achan stepped out on to the street, along with the others, and they greeted the first ranks of the march. A few of the students appeared a little bewildered by how Achan and the others had got in front of them, but Achan merely smiled, then he turned, and began to lead the others through the Old Town.

They joined a large stream of Rakanese workers coming from the harbour, and then hundreds of Holdings and Kellach merged into the march from their left, where they had walked out from the building site where the enormous Blue Palace was being constructed. Kyra glanced up at the half-built structure, its two tall towers piercing the cloudy sky. By the time the marchers had left the Old Town, their part of the demonstration was thousands strong, with more joining the closer they got to Duncan Gardens. A festive atmosphere pervaded the air, and many were grinning and joking as they passed the soldiers on duty by each junction. The soldiers remained where they were, their faces giving nothing away as they watched the huge mass of people enter the gardens from the west, joining the thousands already gathered there. There were Kellach and Holdings, and Rakanese and Rahain – the only people from the Star Continent that Kyra didn't see were the Sanang, and she wondered if their loyalty to their Sanang Empress had influenced their decision.

The march ground to a halt as they passed further into the vast park. Many had assembled near the statue of Duncan, but Achan and Kyra were still several hundred yards from it when they were forced to stop by the weight of the crowds.

'Can you get us closer to the old rampart, Kyra?' Achan whispered to her. 'I need to let the other organisers know that we have arrived.'

'Who should I bring?' she whispered back to him.

'Just me, Larron and you,' said Achan. 'A larger number appearing out of nowhere might cause panic.'

Kyra nodded, then her vision powers scanned the long earthen rampart that ran behind the statue. She saw a quiet spot on the far side, under the branches of a cedar tree, and touched her Quadrant.

*Next to the cedar. Go.*

The air shimmered, and then she, Achan and Larron appeared in the shade of the tree's branches, just a few yards from the base of the rampart. They climbed up the turfed slope, and gazed out at the enormous crowds from its summit. The entire park was a heaving mass of humanity – men, women, young, old. The majority of the banners being held aloft were clear about the main reason for the protest – they wanted the new taxes repealed; but there were also a few banners demanding an end to the various wars being conducted by the Empire dotted here and there. Achan led them along the ridge of the rampart, until they came to a large group. Achan's back was slapped several times, and hands were shaken, as Kyra and Larron stood back a little.

'Good to see you, Achan,' said a tall Kellach man wearing a blacksmith's apron. 'Is that Larron?'

'It is,' said Achan.

The blacksmith gestured to Larron. 'Your folks have sent over baskets of food and jugs of ale for the strikers, lad. Tell them it's much appreciated.'

'I will,' said Larron.

'Are the taverns still open?' said Kyra.

'That they are, lass,' said the blacksmith, 'but many of them have pledged to offer free meals for the striking workers, for as long as the protest lasts.'

'This is Kyra Holdfast,' said Achan.

'I thought it might be,' said the blacksmith. 'I'm glad to see you here, lass. If yer looking for something useful to do, there's a pile of tents needing to be set up.'

'Tents?' said Kyra.

'Aye, lass. This strike won't be done in a day. We'll have to stay here until the Empress starts to feel the squeeze.'

'Have we sent our demands to the Ministry of the Plateau?' said Achan.

'Aye,' said the blacksmith.

'And did they include our demand about pulling out of Dragon Eyre?'

The blacksmith nodded. 'Just as you insisted, Achan; though it's the taxes that are occupying the minds of most folk here.'

'It is essential that we keep the two issues connected.'

'If you say so, Achan. But, if the taxes are paying for these wars, then lowering them should result in a withdrawal anyway.'

'Perhaps, but it's a chance to educate the strikers about the war crimes being committed in their name. It is important that they know what the Empire has become.'

Larron nudged Kyra. 'The tents? Shall we?'

She nodded, and they walked down the slope of the old rampart, and joined a group of people who were erecting tents over a flat, grassy area of the gardens.

'We're here to help,' said Larron.

An old Rahain woman smiled at them, and gestured towards a heap of canvas and poles.

'The ground has been marked out with string,' she said. 'Keep the tents within the lines.'

'Aye, ma'am,' said Larron.

He picked up a bundle, and Kyra followed him to the edge of where the others were setting up the lines of tents. They found the string, which had been attached to a long line of pegs, and began to pitch the tent.

'I will have to go back and forward between here and the university a lot,' Kyra said, as she picked up a wooden pole.

'We will be relying on you for that, I think,' said Larron. 'You will be able to get food and supplies quicker than anyone else. We could be here for days.'

The air shimmered, and Lord Naxor appeared next to them.

He smiled. 'Enjoying yourself, Miss Holdfast?' he said. 'It's a lovely day for camping out in the gardens, though I hear a heavy downpour is forecast for this evening. Such a pity.'

'What do you want, Naxor?'

'I am here to reply to the list of demands that was received by the Ministry of the Plateau, and you were the first person I recognised. Might I assume that you know where the leadership of this... gathering is based?'

She nodded, then she turned to Larron. 'I'll take him to Achan and the others.'

'All right,' said Larron, as he eyed Naxor warily.

Kyra led Naxor away from the tents, but, as the demigod's face was little known outside of the upper circles of government, no one commented or stared in his direction. They climbed the rampart, and Kyra walked over to where Achan and the other leaders were talking in a large cluster.

'Sir?' she said. 'Professor?'

Achan and a few others turned. Naxor walked forward, then he bowed with a flourish.

'For those who do not recognise me,' he said, 'I am the Imperial Chamberlain – Lord Naxor of Port Sanders and Plateau City, and I have been empowered by Her Imperial Majesty to give you an official response to your list of demands.'

The others on the rampart stared, and a few even edged away a little.

Naxor smiled. 'Now,' he went on, 'as none of you will be getting paid by your employers for as long as this little strike lasts, I felt it would be in your best interests that I come here as quickly as possible to deliver the government's response.'

'Let's hear it then,' said the Kellach blacksmith.

'There were two demands,' Naxor said, 'and I have two responses. No and no.'

Achan chuckled. 'Let us see if the government maintains that position as Plateau City grinds to a halt. No ships are being loaded or unloaded, no rubbish is being collected, no wagons are available to haul cargo or passengers around the city, no letters are being delivered, no…'

Naxor yawned, loud and sustained. 'You ridiculous little Hammer,' he said. 'Do you think I have never dealt with a strike before? You rabble used to paralyse Reaper, Evader and Hammer territory for years, to very little effect. Stay here as long as you like. Consider this, though – I have experience of several differing regimes that ruled the City. I have served under Prince Michael, Princess Khora, Duke Marcus, Lord Simon, and the Aurelians. Whose approach to dealing with strikers should I take, Mister Achan? Should we crush you, ignore you, or bow to your pathetic demands?'

Achan blinked, and his face paled a little.

'If you are here to negotiate,' said the blacksmith, 'then I suggest that we…'

'I am not here to negotiate,' said Naxor. 'I am here to tell you that this strike is futile. You will achieve nothing, except your own impoverishment. Go back to work, and support this Empire, and your Empress. That is all. Good day.'

The air shimmered, and Naxor vanished from the rampart.

'Who were those princes and princesses he mentioned, Achan?' said the blacksmith.

'Former rulers of the City,' said Achan. 'Many were cruel and ruthless.'

'Was he threatening us?' said another.

'Not overtly,' said Achan. 'He was just trying to frighten us. Michael, Marcus and Simon would have already sent in troops by now, or they would have come in person, to begin a dreadful massacre.'

'The Empress won't do that though, will she?' said the blacksmith. 'None of us are armed, and we have pledged to remain peaceful.'

'As I said, it was an attempt to intimidate us. We have to stay united, and strong. They cannot beat us if we stick together. All the same, we should be careful.' He gestured for Kyra to approach. 'Keep a watch out for any odd troop movements in the city,' he said to her. 'If the Empress has appointed Lord Naxor to deal with the strike, then things could get messy.'

Kyra nodded, then the first drops of rain landed around her.

'Get those tents up,' cried the blacksmith, 'and the pavilions, before we're wading through a sea of mud.'

Kyra turned and hurried down the slope of the old rampart, as the rain got heavier. Despite the weather, she knew they were going to win, as she gazed out over the tens of thousands gathered in the gardens.

They had to.

# CHAPTER 26
# IMPRINTED

**Sun Ta, Na Sun Ka, Western Rim – 24th Duninch 5266 (18th Gylean Year 17)**

Cael and a few other marines of the Seaborne Company sat on the pier, their legs dangling over the waters of Sun Ta harbour. Captain Doune had been keeping the survivors of his company busy since Sable had transported them from Ulna, but he had departed that afternoon, after a summons had arrived for him from the marine headquarters based on the waterfront. The remaining marines had carried out every job on the list Doune had left them, and, following that, they had taken a rare chance to relax in the sunshine.

The entire city knew what had happened to the fleet. The Sanang soldiers occupying the streets had mocked the marines for their defeat, but most inhabitants of Sun Ta were anxiously awaiting news regarding a possible invasion from Gyle by over seven thousand Wystian dragons.

'What do you think will happen to us?' said a corporal.

'There are two options,' said a tall Kellach. 'They disband us, and send us back to our old battalions, or Doune is given permission to recruit new members of the Seaborne. The Holdfast lad can read minds; maybe he could find out.'

'I'll get hauled before a court martial if I get caught reading the thoughts of a senior officer,' Cael said.

'Then don't get caught.'

'Aye, but I've already been reprimanded for going into an officer's head, back when we were taking this city from the Unk Tannic.'

The Kellach marine laughed. 'I heard about that, sir. It was a navy officer, aye? And you shouted at him, in his head.'

Cael nodded. 'Aye. I was lucky to keep my rank.'

'They won't be putting you back into an ordinary battalion, Lieutenant,' said another marine. 'I reckon the high command have big plans for you.'

'Even after what happened with the carriers?'

The marine shrugged. 'None of that was your fault. You emerged from that shitstorm pretty unscathed, in my opinion, sir. Who was it who organised the survivors, eh? And if Commander Laimos hadn't hit you with his Gift of Pain, then you might even have taken out one of those damn gods. Nah; they'll just be glad you're still alive.'

'I heard Laimos has done a bunk,' said the tall Kellach. 'He's fucked off out of the armed forces, because his precious Bullan were killed. We wouldn't have taken Sun Ta without him and his big dragon, and we've no chance if seven thousand Wystians turn up.' He glanced at Cael. 'You know him, sir. Is he coming back?'

'I don't know,' said Cael. 'Gallantmorn's still here, and I was told that he'll be the only dragon on Na Sun Ka until Queen Blackrose's reinforcements arrive in a few days. But I don't know if that means Commander Laimos is never coming back. Maybe he needed a break.'

'We all need a break, sir. When are you meant to be getting married?'

'By the end of Tradinch.'

'And what's that in real calendar-speak?'

'Before Summer's Day,' said Cael. 'Today is the Fourth Day of the Last Third of Spring back on the Star Continent.'

'Is it? I'd lost all fucking track, to be honest, sir. Every day is like summer on Dragon Eyre.'

'Aye,' said another; 'it's just a pity about the folk who live here. Ignorant natives and arrogant colonists; I don't know which side I dislike more.'

'The Sanang will always be top of my list,' said the tall Kellach. 'I cannae stand those uncivilised bastards.'

'Someone's coming,' said another marine. Cael got to his feet and glanced along the pier. A young marine was hurrying towards them.

'Lieutenant Holdfast?' he said.

'Aye, that's me.'

'Captain Doune wants you in the marine headquarters, sir.'

'Did Captain Doune say what he wants the rest of us to be doing?' said the tall Kellach.

'Aye,' said the young marine. 'He wants all equipment on the cutters stowed away into the boatshed; all of it. He said you won't be needing it.'

The marines on the pier frowned and glanced at each other. Cael followed the young marine to the stone quayside, and they walked into the large building where the senior officers of the marines had their offices. Cael's escort led him to a large chamber on the ground floor, where several senior officers were standing, along with Captain Doune of the Seaborne Company. Adjutant Claudian and Herald Brogan from the Imperial Court were also there.

Cael saluted as they turned to look at him.

'Come in, Lieutenant,' said Claudian.

'They're reassigning us, lad,' said Doune.

Claudian smiled. 'I would prefer to deliver the news myself, Captain.' He glanced at Cael as he approached. 'The Empire has another small crisis to deal with, Lieutenant, and we are of the opinion that your particular skills might make all the difference.'

Cael stood to attention, and said nothing.

'Twelve days ago,' Claudian went on, 'the Dragon Dominion launched a surprise assault upon the Tempest mine on Inopei. Are you aware of the presence of this mine?'

'I am, sir. I was there once, many years ago.'

Claudian narrowed his eyes. 'You have been to the Tempest mine?'

'Aye, sir; with my mother and sister. I was there when my mother killed King Gahad, sir.'

'Ah, of course; I have heard of this event. You will most likely remember the barren terrain where the mine lies – a wilderness of volcanoes, hundreds of miles from any town or village. The mine itself is quite small. A settlement lies next to it, as well as a fortress, and the entire area is surrounded by a defensive wall. When the Dominion launched their assault, the soldiers on duty fought bravely, but they were too few to contain the attack, and the garrison was slaughtered. There was but one survivor – a junior officer, who was deliberately left alive so that he could inform the government of what had taken place. We have recently sent a spy to scout out the current situation, and it seems that the Dominion is expecting us to counter attack in great force. We will not be so obliging as to fall into their trap. Instead, we will first hit them where it hurts, in the city of Nom Karta. This attack upon the dragon city will distract them, and only then will we send in forces to re-take the mine. I assume you know how to use a Quadrant?'

Cael suppressed a groan. 'No, sir. I have never used a Quadrant.'

Claudian and the others looked a little shocked, while Doune chuckled quietly.

'Never?' said Brogan.

'That was always my sister's area of expertise, ma'am,' said Cael. 'The Sextant speaks to me but not her; and Quadrants speak to her, not me. Whenever I needed to go anywhere, Kyra or my mother was always able to take me.'

Claudian leaned in close to Brogan. 'Perhaps we could ask Bailey to imprint the information he needs into his mind?'

'Would that work?' said Brogan. 'Isn't Cael's mind protected? Cael, would it work?'

'It would work if I allowed it to work, ma'am,' said Cael. 'If Lord Bailey were to link his thoughts with mine, I could allow him to imprint the necessary knowledge into my mind.'

'Then we shall do that,' said Claudian. 'Lord Bailey is still in Plateau

City, so I will take you there after I have briefed you on your operation. Lieutenant, you will be second in command to Captain Doune. You will travel surreptitiously to Nom Karta in Inopei and, once there, you will sow devastation and chaos. You will be taking a very large amount of explosives with you. Use them. The greater the panic you cause, the better. Remain in Nom Karta for as long as practicable, then flee when your situation becomes untenable.'

'Aye, sir,' said Cael. 'Who shall be coming with us?'

'We're taking the survivors of the Seaborne, lad,' said Doune. 'I know them, trust them, and they can all handle explosives.'

'When will we be leaving, sir?'

'This evening,' said Claudian. 'I will take you to Plateau City now, while Captain Doune summons the Seaborne Company and prepares them for action. Captain, I shall bring Lieutenant Holdfast to you when we return. The marine commanders have been instructed to supply you with everything you need. Take enough food for several days, and enough explosives to level a mountain range.'

'Aye, sir,' said Doune, saluting.

The Adjutant of the Empire withdrew a Quadrant from a deep pocket, then he glanced at Cael.

'Prepare yourself, Lieutenant,' he said.

He brushed his fingers over the surface of the device. The air shimmered, and Cael found himself standing in a courtyard, surrounded on all four sides by a large building.

'We are at the centre of the Ministry of the Plateau,' said Claudian. 'This way.'

They entered the building, and went up a flight of stairs. They stopped by a door.

'The Empress would never forgive me if I brought you to Plateau City without giving her a chance to greet you,' said Claudian.

He opened the door, and they walked into a small reception room. The Empress was speaking to a few people Cael didn't recognise, and her eyes widened when she glanced over and saw him. She got to her feet, smiling.

'Cael,' she said. 'What a lovely surprise. What are you doing here?'

'I need Bailey to show me how to use a Quadrant, Your Majesty,' he said.

Thorn walked over and embraced him tightly.

'Have you any idea how proud I am of you?' she said. 'What you have achieved in such a short time in the marines has been nothing short of marvellous.'

He smiled back at her. 'Thank you, Your Majesty.'

'No, Cael, thank you. And thank you for agreeing to go on this new operation. Remember, though, you must flee if your life is in danger. Do what you can, but return to us alive. I have plans for you, Cael.'

Claudian coughed gently. 'Do you happen to know the whereabouts of Lord Bailey, Your Majesty?'

'He will be in the library, Adjutant,' said Thorn. She smiled again at Cael, as though she was reluctant to let go of him. 'You coming here has made my day,' she said.

'It was an honour to see you, Your Majesty.'

Thorn released her grip on him. 'Good luck.'

Cael bowed. 'Thank you, Your Majesty.'

Claudian escorted Cael out of the room, then he glanced at him.

'The Empress mothers you, Lieutenant.'

'She was legally my mother for several years,' said Cael, 'and my earliest memories are of her. I wonder where my sister is. I guess she is studying at the university?'

Claudian said nothing.

'And Arrosa?' Cael went on. 'Do you know of Arrosa, sir? She is my betrothed. We are due to be married less than a third from now. Do you think I might be able to see her for a few minutes?'

'Unfortunately not, Lieutenant,' said Claudian. 'I need to get you back to Sun Ta as soon as Bailey has taught you how to use a Quadrant. Do you have leave organised for this wedding?'

'I put in the request some time ago, sir, but I haven't received any confirmation.'

'I will see to it personally, Lieutenant. You will need some leave when you return from Incpei, of that I am sure.'

They ascended a flight of stairs and entered a small library. The books were all dry academic records and chronicles of the Empire, detailing its legal system, decrees and constitution, and Bailey was sitting at a desk, his eyes on the text of a large volume.

'My lord,' said Claudian.

Bailey looked up. 'Adjutant,' he said, 'and Cael Holdfast. How curious.'

'I would like you to imprint instructions on how to use a Quadrant into Lieutenant Holdfast's mind, my lord.'

Bailey frowned. 'One of Karalyn's twins doesn't already know how to use a Quadrant?'

'I have never used one,' said Cael.

'But you are one of the very few mortals who can use the Sextant.'

'Quadrants do not speak to me, and I have never learned how to use one manually.'

'I will need you to grant me permission to enter your mind.'

'I understand. Should I be seated for this?'

'I will leave you both to it,' said Claudian. 'How long will it take, my lord?'

Bailey shrugged. 'A few minutes.'

'Then I shall return soon. This unexpected trip back to Plateau City has given me an opportunity to catch up with some other business.'

Claudian left the library, and closed the door behind him.

Bailey turned to Cael. 'Do you know why you are being sent to North Karta?'

'To blow up a few dragon palaces and sow some chaos,' said Cael.

'Yes, but why you? You weren't the first choice, did you know that? They asked Lahnos and Corthie, and both refused. They also asked me, and my reply was the same.'

'I can understand why you don't want to go,' said Cael. 'Uncle Corthie, too. He's never wanted to get involved in the Empire. But Lahnos also refused?'

'He did.'

'So, the rumours are true? He has resigned his post?'

'He tried to. The Empress wouldn't allow it. She has sent him to Colsbury on indefinite leave.'

'I saw him after the battle for the two carriers,' said Cael. 'It hit him hard.'

'Weren't you also there, Cael? You seem fine.'

'It was rough. The Seaborne Company sustained heavy losses, and the sailors were slaughtered.'

'And yet I heard that you remained calm enough to assume command of the survivors.'

'I did my job. It was nothing special.'

Bailey smiled. 'I wonder what else they haven't told you. You met Ward and Allura, didn't you?'

Cael nodded.

'One or both of those gods might be on Inopei now. They helped the Dominion capture the Tempest mine.'

Cael lowered his gaze and shook his head.

'Did Adjutant Claudian neglect to tell you that part?' said Bailey.

'It doesn't matter,' said Cael. 'Show me how to use a Quadrant. I'm ready.'

Cael felt Bailey's powers trying to enter his mind. He was a powerful god, but Cael's defences were more than a match for him. Cael relaxed his control, and allowed Bailey into his consciousness.

*Hello,* said Bailey.

*Is this going to hurt?*

*It might. Apologies in advance. Here goes.*

A tremendous wave of power swept over Cael's mind, as Bailey imprinted everything there was to know about Quadrants into his brain. It was over in a few seconds, and Cael rubbed his head. He entered Bailey's mind.

*Thank you. Wait – do you know Gunstian? I can see it in your mind. Can you teach me that, too?*

*Why would you want to learn Gunstian? Oh, Arrosa – of course.*

Cael's mind began to throb in pain as Bailey imprinted the entire Gunstian vocabulary into his head, along with its grammatical structures.

'Ow,' said Cael.

Bailey shrugged. 'You asked. Be warned – the version of Gunstian I have given you is actually a Zamatan dialect of the language, rather than the original, purer variety spoken in Gunst. They are very similar though, and as Arrosa is a Zamatan Gunstian, you should be fine. I learned it from Karalyn, you see; and she learned it from Lahnos.' He pulled a Quadrant out from his robes and handed it to Cael.

'Is this mine now?' said Cael.

'No. It's mine. I just want to check that you know how to use it without having to think too much. You might not have a lot of time on Inopei to stop and stare at the surface of the device. I will give you a little task to carry out for me, and you will operate the Quadrant through instinct alone. Draw upon what I have imprinted into your mind. All right. Stand.'

Cael got to his feet.

'Pick me a flower from the rose bushes in the gardens of Colsbury, then return here.'

Cael swiped his fingers over the Quadrant, as though he had used the device a thousand times before. The air shimmered, and he appeared in the garden behind the two keeps on Colsbury. He laughed to himself, then he plucked a rose from its stem, and hovered his hand over the *Go back* command. He hesitated, then he changed his mind. He swiped the Quadrant, and appeared in the quad of the university in Plateau City. It was deserted, and Cael frowned. Where were all the students? He reached out with his vision, and located a small group of students and staff sitting in the canteen. Among them was Arrosa, and he smiled again. He triggered the Quadrant, and arrived a few feet to her right.

'Good morning, my beloved,' he said, bowing, and handing her the rose.

She stared at him. 'Cael?'

She got up, and Cael wrapped his arms around her. They kissed, and several of the students laughed or cheered.

'I'd better go,' he said, then he switched to Gunstian. 'I wasn't supposed to come here, but I couldn't resist.'

'You speak Gunstian now?' she said.

'Aye, and I can use a Quadrant. Adjutant Claudian has said that he will personally make sure I get the leave I requested. We'll be married within the month.'

She kissed him. 'I can't wait.'

He triggered the Quadrant, and appeared in the library. Bailey frowned.

'That took too long,' the god said, 'and you have no rose.'

'I know,' Cael said. 'I gave it to Arrosa.'

Bailey raised an eyebrow, and started to laugh.

Claudian opened the door and entered. 'Are we all set?' he said.

'Indeed we are, Adjutant,' said Bailey. 'Lieutenant Holdfast is now proficient in the use of a Quadrant.' He held out his hand, and Cael passed him the copper device.

'I have the one you shall be using, Lieutenant,' said Claudian. He reached into his uniform and handed another device to Cael. 'Thank you, Lord Bailey. Now, Cael, do you think you could take us both back to the marine headquarters in Sun Ta?'

'Aye, sir.'

'Then do so.'

Cael used three fingers to swipe the device. The air crackled, and then he and Claudian appeared in the same chamber from where they had left.

Cael laughed, and the Adjutant narrowed his eyes.

'Sorry, sir,' Cael said, 'but this is incredible. Ten minutes ago, I had no idea how to use a Quadrant, and now... now it seems easy.'

'I am glad you are feeling confident with the device,' said Claudian. 'It goes without saying that you must take good care of it while you are on Athumia. Without it, it may prove very difficult to get you and the other marines home again.'

Herald Brogan walked over. 'The survivors of the Seaborne Company are being briefed by Captain Doune by the pier,' she said. 'Before you leave to join them, Cael, we have something else to tell you.' She glanced at Claudian.

'I'm afraid it isn't good news, Lieutenant,' said the Adjutant. 'Those two gods you encountered on Dragon Eyre – there is a chance that they are on Athumia at the moment. We also know that another god, by the name of Lord Ballatar, is based at the Tempest mine. I doubt that he will travel to Nom Karta to oppose you, but keep your eyes open for Lord Ward and Lady Allura. If in doubt, you have the authority to cut short the operation and return here, to Sun Ta, if you feel it necessary, and even if Captain Doune disagrees with the decision. The Quadrant is yours, not anyone else's, and I am granting you sole authority over it Is that understood?'

'Aye, sir.'

'There are two things the Empress wishes to prevent,' Claudian went on; 'the loss of another Quadrant to the enemy, and your death. Her Majesty was quite clear on this. Do your duty, but refrain from making any more reckless decisions. I know we are asking a lot of a young officer with relatively little experience, but you have proved that you are good in a crisis, and the Empire is depending on you to cause a distraction large enough for the Dominion to take their eye off the Tempest mine.'

'I love this job, sir,' said Cael. 'I won't let you down.'

Brogan gave him a strange look, then Claudian nodded.

'Rejoin your company, Lieutenant,' the Adjutant said; 'then assemble back here at sunset.'

Captain Doune led Cael and the others remaining from the Seaborne Company back to the quayside as soon as the sun neared the horizon to the west. Adjutant Claudian and a few senior officers from the marines were waiting for them by the front of their headquarters, along with stacked-up crates of explosives and supplies.

'Good evening,' said Claudian, as the marines lined up on the quayside. 'Do you have the map of Nom Karta, Captain?'

'Aye, sir,' said Doune.

'Be warned that the information held within it might be a few years out of date,' said Claudian, 'but I have been assured by recent intelligence that the palace of Lady Natali Min Gahad remains abandoned and empty. It is one of the smaller palaces of Nom Karta, and it lies close to the northern perimeter of the city. It has its own wells, and its cellars are more than adequate to house you all during the operation.' He gazed at the marines. 'Your orders are simple – use whatever means necessary to cause a major distraction to the Dominion authorities. The Dominion and its immortal allies are waiting for the Empire to assault the Tempest mine; they will not be expecting a bold attack in the heart of their capital. I now invite Lieutenant Holdfast to enter my mind, to glean the precise location of Lady Natali's palace, as noted by Professors Elbannon and Gallea of Plateau City University.'

'Aye, sir,' said Cael. He pushed his vision powers into the mind of the Adjutant. Claudian was concentrating on an image of the city of Nom Karta. In particular, his thoughts were focussed on a large palace of purple and black marble near the tall curtain wall of the vast settlement.

'I have the location, sir; thank you,' said Cael, as he withdrew from Claudian's mind.

'Very good,' said Claudian. 'You may now depart, Captain Doune. Good luck.'

Doune nodded to Cael, who took out the Quadrant from behind his Tempest breastplate. He gazed at the symbols on the copper surface, and the knowledge of what he had to do to travel to Nom Karta appeared in his mind. The information was coming from the memories Bailey had stamped into his brain, but the god hadn't merely imparted a few destinations – he had given Cael a full understanding of how Quadrants worked. Cael would need three fingers – altitude, direction and distance, and the location of the world of Athumia. One tiny mistake, and he would transport the marines of the Seaborne Company into the flank of a mountain, or deep underground, or high above an ocean. Kyra had no such concerns; she simply told the Quadrant where to take her, and it obeyed; while Sable was so proficient at using the device manually that she could operate it with a hand in her pocket.

'Do you know what to do, lad?' said Doune.

'Aye, sir,' said Cael.

'Then proceed.'

Cael brushed his fingers over the surface of the device, and the air crackled over the quayside of Sun Ta. A moment later, Cael found himself standing in darkness, a faint smell of damp coming from the cellars around him. One of the marines lit a match, and ignited the wick of an oil lamp. He shone it around, revealing the inside of a large basement storage room. Cael had brought the crates with them, and they were lying a few yards to their right.

Doune gestured to a set of stairs leading upwards to their left.

'Take a marine and get up there, corporal,' he said. 'Check the surrounding area is clear before we start to make a racket down here.'

'Aye, sir,' said the corporal. He lit another lamp, then he nodded to a marine and they stole up the stairs.

Doune spread his map out on the stone floor.

'Gather round,' he said. He pointed at the outline of a palace on the map. 'We are here.' He glanced at Cael. 'Aye?'

'That's right, sir,' said Cael. 'Lady Natali's palace.'

'We are going to take an hour or two to settle in before we start blowing things up,' said Doune. 'We need to find somewhere free of damp to sleep and to store the explosives, and somewhere we can light a small fire without the smoke being detected. I am going to split the company in two – the first team will be responsible for guarding and maintaining our new home, while the second will take charge of offensive operations. Lieutenant Holdfast, as you possess both mage powers and the Quadrant, you will lead the second team. Whatever else happens, lad, do not lose that Quadrant, eh? I have no intention of living out the rest of my days upon Athumia.'

'Aye, sir,' said Cael.

The corporal returned with the other marine.

'We are two floors below ground level, sir,' the corporal said. 'Above us is another layer of cellars, all empty, and then the upper part of the palace rises above that. We didn't see any signs of human or dragon occupation.'

'Did you venture outside?' said the captain.

'No, sir.'

'Did you see anywhere without damp?'

'Aye, sir. The floor above us is dry, and we found a well.'

Doune stood. 'We shall get everything moved upstairs,' he said, 'and set up our camp in a drier part of the basement. Get to it, lads and lasses; the corporal will lead the way.'

Cael watched from the low balcony of the palace as three dragons flew past in the night sky. In front of the balcony, four other massive palaces were spread out in an arc, each one larger than Lady Natali's. Of them, three had lights glinting out from various windows, while the other was shrouded in darkness. Cael had ensured that he and the four marines crouching by him were all invisible, and they had been scouting out the immediate vicinity.

'This is like no city I've ever seen before,' said one of the marines. 'There are no houses, no shops; just palaces.'

'And did you see the soldiers up on the curtain wall?' said another. 'They're Bullan, just like the ones Commander Laimos has around him... well, like he used to have around him.'

'These ones are still loyal to the Dominion,' said Cael. 'Treat them as hostile. Also, invisibility might not work on them, as they have their own language, so we'll stay well clear of the outer walls.'

They fell into silence as another five dragons soared overhead. In their midst was a huge dragon, her body enveloped in plates of black Tempest armour.

'That's the new queen of the Dominion,' Cael whispered. 'Lady Famula.'

'Is she a target, sir?' said a marine.

Cael smiled. 'That depends how successful we are. We'll start off by blowing up a few of the smaller palaces, and see what kind of reaction we get. Are the explosives ready?'

Two marines were carrying packs full of the devices Claudian had given them, and they nodded.

'Aye, sir,' said one.

Cael nodded. 'Let's cause some havoc.'

# CHAPTER 27
# REGRETS

**Colsbury Castle, the Holdings – 5th Day, Last Third Spring 545**

'Friel, Reyn, Leona, and now the Bullan,' said Lahnos. 'I am used to loss. Piece by piece, my old life is disintegrating, and all that remains of those I loved from Athumia are Sigum and Arrosa.' He glanced at Karalyn. 'It will only get worse for the two of us. A hundred years from now, everyone we know will be dead, but we won't.'

Karalyn said nothing as she knelt by the grave. She removed some withered old flowers from a vase, and replaced them with freshly-cut ones. Lahnos and Kelsey remained silent as they watched Karalyn arrange the flowers by Lennox's last resting place. She stood, and brushed some soil from her hands.

'I could take you back to Zamata,' said Kelsey.

'I don't want to go back there,' Lahnos said. 'My memories of the island are not good ones. Besides, the Empress ordered me to stay here.'

They walked away from the row of graves, and Lahnos felt a warm mountain breeze against his face. Colsbury was milder than Dragon Eyre, but the garden behind the two keeps was blossoming in the spring light.

'If you are still here at the beginning of summer,' Karalyn said, 'you will have to prepare yourself for the arrival of the Imperial Court. The

Empress usually gets here on her birthday – Summer's Day, and then the entire court stays until Autumn's Day.'

'At least I will get to see Arrosa,' he said.

'Arrosa might be back before that,' said Karalyn. 'The wedding? Did you forget?'

'I confess that I did,' he said. 'When is it?'

'The exact date is still uncertain. Arrosa will be eighteen in fourteen days from now, and then it depends if Cael has managed to get any leave. I'm ready to spring into action; a wedding can be arranged at short notice, though I still have to find a Gunstian priest for the ceremony.'

Lahnos frowned. 'Why would you… Never mind; it's obvious. Arrosa asked for a Gunstian priest, didn't she? Even though they think I'm a soulless demon. I'll wear a bag over my head for the ceremony.'

'Do you know much about Gunstian weddings?' said Kelsey. 'Do they have any strange rituals we should know about?'

'I've never been invited to one,' said Lahnos.

They reached the apple orchard, and stopped in a small clearing, where the nanny and a servant were sitting on a large rug on the grass. Three of Karalyn and Kelsey's small children were also there. Caelius and Carden were chasing each other over the soft turf, while two-year-old Caitlyn was crawling on the rug. Lahnos, Karalyn and Kelsey sat down on the rug next to them, and Karalyn picked up Caitlyn and set the girl down on her knee.

Lahnos glanced at the children for a few moments. At some point in the future, if he and Ora'lya remained together, then she might bring up the subject of children again.

'I should check on Ora'lya,' he said.

'You haven't left her side in five days,' said Kelsey. 'Give yourself, and her, an hour apart. It won't hurt, and you need some fresh air.'

Lahnos glanced in the direction of the Summer Palace, then he nodded. 'I wish I'd never signed up to serve the Empire,' he said, 'but then I wouldn't have met Ora'lya.'

'It was the Bullan who persuaded you to assist the Empire,' said

Karalyn. 'I remember it well. You were quite reluctant, and they wore you down over the space of about a year.'

'And, as Herald, I was very grateful for your help, Lahnos,' said Kelsey. 'You and Sigum secured the Great Tunnel, and drove away the bandits who had been terrorising the farmsteads down there. You did a good job. You still have brothers and sisters on Zamata, don't you?'

'One brother, three sisters,' he said.

'Wouldn't you like to visit them?'

'Not really. Does that sound terrible? My sisters loathe me, and my brother barely tolerated me. We parted on decent terms, but there was still a lot of anger between us. Much of that is my fault; I had no time for my family after they rejected me for growing horns. I cut them out of my life, and by the time I tried to make amends, it was too late.'

'There must be others on the island that you know,' Kelsey went on. 'What about Bauchlie?'

Lahnos shook his head. 'Bauchlie is my cousin, but he would have a heart attack if I suddenly appeared on Zamata. He'd assume that I intended to take over the island.' He eyed the former Herald. 'You seem to be keen to get rid of me.'

'I'm not,' she said. 'I'm thinking of what might be the best for you and Sigum. As Holder Fast, I own Colsbury, and you will always be welcome here.'

'You *own* Colsbury?'

'Aye,' said Kelsey; 'in its entirety. The Empire pays me to have the Imperial Court based here for the summer. Officially, I rent the Summer Palace to Her Majesty.' She smiled. 'Karalyn is also my tenant.'

Karalyn glanced at her younger sister. 'Are you thinking of evicting me?'

Kelsey laughed. 'And what would you do if I tried that?'

'Well, I'd first take you to court,' said Karalyn, 'and win back the right to be called Holder Fast; then I would transfer Colsbury into my name; and then I would let you be Holder Fast again.'

'That was a more peaceful response than I was expecting.'

'Peaceful, and legal,' said Karalyn. 'I was thinking of visiting Corthie soon. Do you want to come?'

'Aye,' said Kelsey.

'Are you going to try to persuade him to work for the Empire again?' said Lahnos.

'Of course not,' said Karalyn. 'Corthie is back where he belongs – at home with his family. We shouldn't have asked him to fight the... things that were inside the Palace of the Almighty. It's taken my brother years to get used to a peaceful life, and Thorn and I risked all that.'

'Why?' said Lahnos. 'I mean, what was the harm in asking him to help?'

The two sisters glanced at each other.

'Corthie is... well, he has his own monster living inside him.' said Kelsey. 'Once he starts fighting, he doesn't know how or when to stop.'

'I was worried that he might get a taste for it again,' said Karalyn, 'and I suspect Thorn was hoping that would be the case. Fortunately, he saw sense, and returned to Clackenbaird.'

'I have heard the stories,' said Lahnos, 'but I have never seen him fight. He can't be better than Sable.'

Kelsey smiled. 'So Sable would like to believe, but even she would admit that Corthie is better. Out of everyone I've seen, only Belinda came close to Corthie. Besides, Sable's forty-one. She's past her prime.'

Karalyn shook her head. 'Don't ever say that to her face. Sable has kept herself in shape, and her battle-vision remains more than enough to defeat most people.'

'She told me that she will fight the Wystian dragons on her own if she has to,' said Lahnos.

'She's going to get herself killed,' said Kelsey. She glanced at Karalyn. 'Unless...'

'Unless what?' said her older sister. 'I'm not going to Dragon Eyre.'

'I was talking about the Sextant. Use it. Move the Wystians somewhere out of harm's way.'

'I can't,' she said. 'If I put them onto an isolated world, then that would guarantee the extinction of the dragons on the Allied Worlds.

And I can't place them onto one of the Doomed Worlds – they would either fight the gods there, or ally themselves to them. Where else is there? The City of Salve? Can you imagine?'

'Drop them off in the middle of the Gunstian Empire,' said Lahnos. 'You know, just for a laugh.' He gazed out over the gardens. 'Have I made a mistake? Should I have volunteered to lead the operation to retake the Tempest mine? Failing that, should I be in Na Sun Ka, defending the island from the imminent invasion of seven thousand Wystians from Gyle?'

'You have suffered a great loss,' said Karalyn. 'The Bullan were your friends.'

'I led them to their deaths.'

'They wanted to fight,' said Kelsey.

'Then shouldn't I be fighting for vengeance?'

'No,' said Karalyn. 'Vengeance is always wrong. Fight to defend your loved ones, or to protect the weak, but not for revenge.' She narrowed her eyes, and fell silent.

'What is it?' said Kelsey.

'Lucius is back,' Karalyn said, as she got to her feet, Caitlyn still held in her arms.

'He was away for a long time,' said Kelsey.

'Seven days. I'll bring him to the garden. Wait here.'

Karalyn and Caitlyn vanished.

'Do you miss being Herald?' Lahnos said to Kelsey.

'Aye. I don't miss the hard work, but I know I could do a better job than Brogan. But, what can I do? The Empress demanded that I give her every moment of every day, and I can't do that, not with two children to look after. And I enjoy writing. I've nearly finished the first draft of my book on the history of the Star Continent. I'm up to the Allied invasion of Rahain in five-oh-five. All I have to do now is work out how the book should end.'

The air shimmered, and Karalyn re-appeared with Cardova and Caitlyn. Lahnos started to get to his feet to salute his commanding officer, but Cardova gestured for him to remain where he was.

'You are on leave, Lahnos,' he said, as he sat down on the rug next to them.

'What news do you have for us, Lucius?' said Kelsey.

'The Empire can wait,' said Karalyn, as she sat and placed Caitlyn onto the rug; 'I want to hear about Cael first.'

'I have news about both of the twins,' said Cardova.

'Why would you have news about Kyra?' said Karalyn. 'Did you visit her at the university?'

'She isn't in the university. Have you heard about the strike currently paralysing Plateau City? Kyra is at its heart, helping the leaders organise the protests. They have been in Duncan Gardens for two days now – tens of thousands of workers who walked out of their jobs. Cole and Arrosa are among the few students still attending classes at university; neither was interested in joining Kyra.'

Kelsey shook her head. 'And I wonder where they got the idea of a strike from? It was Achan, wasn't it?'

'Achan is heavily involved, yes,' said Cardova. 'It's like the Reapers and Evaders all over again. Naxor has been put in charge of overseeing a settlement.'

'What do the strikers want?' said Karalyn.

'They have demanded two things – that the recent tax increases are overturned, and that the Empire withdraws all military forces from Dragon Eyre. Naturally, the Empress is opposed to both demands. Lord Naxor is rushing through a new law which will criminalise striking during an emergency. He is also drawing up papers to have Kyra and the other student leaders expelled from the university, if they remain on strike once this new law has been approved by the Empress.'

'Expelled?' said Kelsey. 'I'm the patron of the damn university; don't I have a say?'

'Naxor's new law will allow authority over individual students to be placed into the hands of the Imperial Court.'

'Kyra will be throwing away her entire future if she carries on like this,' said Karalyn. 'I should go down to Plateau City to speak to her.'

'Will she listen to you?' said Cardova.

'Probably not.'

Cardova glanced at Lahnos. 'How have you been? I am very sorry about the loss of the Bullan during the battle for the two carriers.'

'Am I being allowed to resign my commission?'

'The Empress has not changed her mind, Lahnos. You are to remain on indefinite leave. She asked me to pass on a message – Her Majesty says that you should take some time to rest and grieve, and then she wants you to report back for work.'

'Does she still want me to lead an attack on Inopei?'

'No,' said Cardova. 'Another leader has been found for that. Her Majesty wishes you to defend Na Sun Ka from the Wystians.'

'Which other leader has been chosen?' said Kelsey. 'Is Adjutant Claudian going to lead from the front?'

Cardova gazed into the distance. 'That brings me to the other twin. Cael has gone to Inopei, along with the surviving marines from the Seaborne Company. Adjutant Claudian has loaned him a Quadrant.'

Karalyn stared at him.

'I didn't think Cael knew how to use a Quadrant,' said Kelsey.

'Bailey imprinted the knowledge into his mind,' said Cardova.

'Aye, all right,' Kelsey went on, 'but Cael is an eighteen-year-old second lieutenant; he can't be leading this operation.'

'Technically, Captain Doune will be in command, but Cael has been told that he is to make the decision on when to return home.'

'You can't be serious,' said Karalyn. 'The Empress asked Cael to lead the attack on the Tempest mine?'

'I thought it was a trap,' said Lahnos.

'It is a trap,' said Cardova, 'which is why we decided to send Cael and his marines to Nom Karta. They are to cause a massive distraction, to draw the attention of the Dominion away from the mine. The Imperial Court felt that we should try to match our enemies' tactics – they hit our weak points, so we shall hit theirs. Cael has enough explosives with him to turn every dragon palace in Nom Karta to rubble.'

'What did you say to the Empress?' said Karalyn. 'Surely you objected? Cael is too young for this.'

'Is he?' said Cardova. 'I love the boy, but I had already been in the Banner of the Black Crown for two years by the time I was eighteen. And Lennox was a similar age; so was Corthie. I swore I wouldn't show any favouritism towards him; how could I object?'

Karalyn's eyes flashed anger at her husband. 'So you said nothing?'

'No. I suggested a few alternatives, but none were accepted by the Imperial Court. The orders were issued, and I fell into line. That is what I do, Karalyn – I obey the commands I am given. The Empress was anxious about Cael going; she cares very much that he comes back in one piece.'

Karalyn got to her feet. 'I'm going to Inopei. Cael is my son, and I will not allow this to happen.'

'Then go,' said Cardova. 'I cannot stop you. But, before you leave, should I tell you what Cael said when Claudian gave him his orders?'

'What did he say?' said Karalyn.

'He said, *I love this job*. That's what he told Claudian. Cael wants to be a marine, and he wants to take part in the risky operations. You'll be doing him no favours if you swoop into Inopei to rescue him from what he wants to be doing.'

'And what if I went there to help him?'

'Then the Empress would be overjoyed. You could destroy Norn Karta, topple the Dominion government, and retake the Tempest mine. In fact, you could probably do all that in one day. After that, you could accompany Cael back to Na Sun Ka, and defeat the Wystians. Should I inform the Empress that you have decided to help us?'

'You go too far, Lucius,' she said.

'I have commanded the armed forces of the Empire for almost a decade,' he said, 'and you have been my wife during that time. You have never objected to my decisions before, not until one of the twins decided to join the marines. Cael is an adult, Karalyn. He is capable of forging his own path in life; as is Kyra.'

A tear rolled down Karalyn's cheek. 'He is just a boy.'

'He is an officer in the Imperial Marines – an officer who has already carried out dangerous operations in Sun Ta, and in the western region of Na Sun Ka. He also took charge after the disaster caused by the battle for the two carriers, when...' Cardova fell silent, then he glanced at Lahnos.

'When I was too numb to give orders,' said Lahnos. 'You can say it, Lucius; I know I let everyone down that day.'

'You were overcome with grief,' said Cardova. 'No one blames you for that.'

'But you all blame me for trying to resign.'

'Some in the Imperial Court were... disappointed by your words, yes. However, you remain a formidable ally, and it is hoped that you will return to your post once you have had time to recover.' He turned his gaze back to Karalyn. 'Until then, Cael is the Empire's best option. His powers should keep him safe.'

'I feel sick,' Karalyn said. 'If only I could give Cael my self-healing powers; I would gladly go without them to keep him alive. What if Ward and Allura are on Athumia? What if Edgar is there? Cael cannot fight gods of that calibre.'

'He has been told to evacuate as soon as things get too dangerous,' said Cardova. 'Trust him; trust that he will know what to do.'

Karalyn cast a glance of contempt at Cardova, then she walked away.

Kelsey raised an eyebrow. 'I sometimes wonder how you two have managed to stay together all these years, Lucius.'

'We argue,' he said, 'and then we put it behind us.'

'That might have worked before Cael joined the marines. Back then, Karalyn didn't have a personal stake in the decisions you were taking – it was all a bit theoretical. Now, her children are involved. If something happens to Cael...'

'You don't have to say it,' said Cardova. 'I know.'

'Did Cael really say that he loved being a marine?' said Lahnos.

'Yes. Brogan was quite taken aback when he said it. She had been expecting him to look a little anxious by what was being asked of him.'

Lahnos got to his feet. 'I think I'll check on Ora'lya.'

He set off through the gardens, then took the tunnel under the two keeps. He emerged into the castle forecourt, but there was no sign of Karalyn, so he carried on into the Summer Palace. He passed a few guards and courtiers, and ascended to the floor where he was staying with Ora'lya. He pushed the door open, and saw her gazing out of the window.

'How are you feeling?' he said.

'I've not long woken up,' she said, 'and now I'm waiting for the dragons to get back. Where have they gone?'

'Frostback and Halfclaw took Sigum for a long flight over the mountains; they might be gone all day.'

'Do you want to go for a walk? I still haven't been to the mainland.'

'Sure,' he said, as he sat down on a chair close to her. 'First, though, I need to speak to you.'

'What about?'

'The Empire has sent Cael to lead the operation in Inopei.'

'Have they? He seems a little young for the responsibility.'

Lahnos nodded, then he glanced out of the window at the blue sky. 'It should have been me.'

Ora'lya narrowed her eyes.

'An eighteen-year-old is doing the job I was supposed to do,' Lahnos went on.

'And now you are feeling guilty about it?' she said.

'Yes.'

'Are you seeking my permission to go back to Athumia, Lahnos? I can't stop you.'

'I don't know what to do. I dread going back to Inopei. What if Ward and Allura are there? They were too strong for me on the carriers. If I did go, then I would leave Sigum here with you. I can't put him at risk again; he almost died on that ship.'

'I think Sigum would refuse to be left behind,' she said.

'What do you think I should do?'

'You are too mired in sorrow to think straight. If you returned to Plateau City, then I think the Empress would be happy to send you back to war, but wouldn't she send you to Na Sun Ka? Why would she send you to Inopei if Cael is already there? You and Sigum would be deployed against the thousands of Wystians about to invade. That's your real choice – stay here, or return to Na Sun Ka.'

'You're right,' he said. 'If I wanted to help Cael, then I would have to ask Karalyn or Kelsey to flout the Empress's commands and take me to Nom Karta. I doubt Kelsey would do it, but Karalyn might.'

'And then what? What would Cael think if you just turned up? There's something about Cael; something that tells me that he wouldn't understand why you had arrived. And then, if you tried to explain that you were there to help him, he might even feel insulted. On top of that, you would have disobeyed a direct order that came from the mouth of the Empress herself. It's Na Sun Ka or nothing, Lahnos. You can't just decide where to deploy yourself in the midst of a war spanning several worlds.'

Lahnos frowned. Ora'lya was right, but her words had done nothing to assuage the guilt festering within his guts.

Someone knocked at their door, and Lahnos stood. He went to the entrance and opened it, to see a servant standing outside.

'Commander Laimos,' he said, 'a young woman has arrived on Colsbury, and she has requested a few moments of your time.'

'What young woman?' he said. 'Is it Arrosa?'

'No, sir,' said the servant. 'She gave her name as Lieutenant Dolwyn.'

Lahnos narrowed his eyes.

'Who?' said Ora'lya, as she walked to the door. 'Who is she, Lahnos?'

'She's a... soldier,' Lahnos said. 'I knew her when I was stationed in the Great Tunnel. We... uh, she and I were involved for a couple of months last year.'

'What does she want?'

Lahnos shrugged. 'I have no idea.'

Ora'lya turned to the servant. 'What does she want?'

'She informed me that she wished to have a few moments to talk to Commander Laimos, ma'am. She did not reveal her reasons.'

'How did she get to Colsbury?'

'By wagon, ma'am. She arrived around twenty minutes ago. I guided her to the lower balcony. Shall I take you both there now?'

Ora'lya nodded. 'Yes. I think I will come along. Do you mind, Lahnos?'

'No,' he said.

They followed the servant along a hallway, and then they descended a flight of stairs. The lower balcony was long and wide, but it was almost empty when they stepped out on to it. The servant gestured to a tall woman who was standing by the balcony railings with her back to them.

'Thank you,' said Lahnos.

The servant bowed. 'I shall remain close by, sir, in case I am needed.'

Lahnos and Ora'lya walked towards the woman.

'Is she Kellach Brigdomin, Lahnos?' said Ora'lya, her eyes tight.

Lahnos nodded.

'Good morning, Dolwyn,' Lahnos said, as they reached the railings.

The woman turned, and smiled. 'Lahnos.' She glanced at Ora'lya. 'Is this yer new woman?'

'We've been together since autumn,' said Lahnos. 'Her name is Ora'lya, and she's from Dragon Eyre.'

'Then I obviously didnae mean that much to you,' she said.

'That's a bit unfair,' he said. 'I was upset when we broke up but, in the end, I moved on with my life.'

'It was you who ended it, after you told me about... Does Ora'lya know?'

'She knows.'

Dolwyn took a breath. 'I've been thinking long and hard about coming here. I was down in Plateau City when I heard the news about the Bullan, and that ye were on Colsbury.'

'It takes a wagon ten days to get from Plateau City to Colsbury,' said Ora'lya, 'and we have only been here for seven days.'

Dolwyn narrowed her eyes. 'I didnae come here by wagon. I only told the servant that, because if I had told him the truth it might have looked a bit weird. As I said, I was in Plateau City when I heard about the Bullan, so I went to the Ministry of the Plateau, to ask about Lahnos's whereabouts, and to check that he was still alive. I spoke to a few folk there, and then, eventually, I got a few minutes with Herald Brogan. She used a Quadrant to drop me off in the village, on the mainland.'

'Why would Brogan bring you here?' said Lahnos.

'I guess she sympathised with my situation. It only took her a couple of minutes, so it was hardly a major sacrifice for her. I told her what I wanted to tell ye, and she helped me out.'

'Out with it,' said Lahnos. 'Say what you have to say.'

Dolwyn turned to face the balcony doors, and an older woman emerged from the shadows of the palace.

'This is my ma,' Dolwyn said, as the woman approached, 'and the baby she's carrying is yours, Lahnos.'

Lahnos stared. The older woman was holding a bundle in her arms, and she gave Lahnos a nervous smile.

'You have a son,' Dolwyn went on. 'I thought you ought to know. He was born two thirds ago, in the army hospital in Rainsby.'

Dolwyn's mother glanced up at Lahnos's horns. Lahnos ignored her, and gazed down at the baby she was holding.

'Did you know you were pregnant when we broke up?' Lahnos said.

'No,' said Dolwyn. 'Do ye remember you tried to talk to me in Tahrana City, a wee while afterwards? I knew then, but I had decided to keep it a secret from you. It was only later, after the birth, that I realised that ye should know the truth. I'm not looking for money or anything, and I'm not expecting ye to drop everything and reorganise yer entire life because you have a bairn. But, I have to report back to work in a few thirds. I'll be leaving Dermot with my ma and da in Plateau City while I go back to the regiment. If you like, you can play a part in his life.'

'Dermot?' he said.

'Aye. Dermot ae Lahnos ae Domm; or Dermot Laimos; take yer pick.'

'Is he healthy?'

'Aye.'

'No, I mean… has he had any injuries or illnesses?'

Dolwyn frowned at him. 'He's half-Kellach, so he doesnae get affected by many illnesses.'

'I think,' said Ora'lya, 'that Lahnos is trying to ask if the child is a demigod; immortal, like him.'

'Ah,' said Dolwyn. 'The answer to that is no. He got a small cut a while ago, and it didnae heal on its own. He's a mortal wee lad.'

Lahnos felt dizzy. 'I need to sit down.'

He collapsed into a chair, and put a hand to his face.

'Are ye sure this was a good idea?' said Dolwyn's mother.

'It had to be done, Ma. I couldnae not tell him.' She glanced at Ora'lya. 'Sorry, hen. Did Lahnos give ye the whole *I don't want children* speech?'

'He did, yes.'

'I didnae plan on getting pregnant. And then, I didnae plan on ever telling him; but it felt wrong. Lahnos, do ye want us to leave ye alone? I can get a carriage back to Plateau City.'

'That doesn't seem fair,' said Ora'lya. 'Are you hungry? We could speak to the Holdfasts, and arrange food, and a place for you to stay overnight. Ten days in a carriage is a long time for a baby. Kelsey Holdfast has a Quadrant.'

Dolwyn smiled. 'Thank you for being so reasonable about all this, Ora'lya, but I think maybe Lahnos doesnae want us here.'

Lahnos looked up. 'No. Wait. May I hold him, please? May I hold my son?'

The three women looked at each other, then Dolwyn's mother passed him the bundle. Lahnos cradled the child in his arms, and gazed down into his face. The boy appeared to be sleeping, and Lahnos stared at him.

'I'm not going back to Na Sun Ka,' he said. 'Not now.'

'Does that mean ye want to play a part in Dermot's life?' said Dolwyn.

Lahnos nodded. 'But how? Sigum... and Ora'lya. How could it work? Can I speak to Ora'lya alone for a moment?'

Dolwyn nodded, then she and her mother retreated to the other side of the balcony.

'I had no idea,' Lahnos said.

'I know,' said Ora'lya.

'I thought you might be angry.'

'I'm not angry; these things happen. I'm... sad. I'm sad that it's not me presenting you with a baby. He looks like you.'

Lahnos held the child in his left arm, and took Ora'lya's hand. 'I can't ignore this.'

'I don't want you to be the kind of man who ignored it.'

'But what will we do? Sigum can't live in Plateau City, and I'm under orders not to leave Colsbury.'

Ora'lya bit her lip. 'Do you still have feelings for Dolwyn?'

'No. They had faded away before I met you. It's you I want to be with, Ora'lya.'

Ora'lya crouched down next to him, and he put his free arm over her shoulder.

'You are the boy's father,' she said. 'If you want to be part of his life, then I will support you.'

'But where will we live? What do I do about the Empress's orders? Should we move to Plateau City; or should we ask Kelsey if Dolwyn's parents can live on Colsbury?'

'One thing at a time, Lahnos,' said Ora'lya. 'We'll figure it out.'

# CHAPTER 28
# WEAK POINT

**Marchside, Kell – $7^{th}$ Day, Last Third Spring 545**

Corthie walked down the paved farm track, holding Carron's hand as the boy jumped in the puddles caused by the morning rain. The sky had cleared up by the afternoon, and the sun was shining down on Clackenbaird. Corthie smiled. It wasn't as warm as Colsbury and the Holdings had been, but it was a beautiful day in Kell. The track led down the slope of Marchbrae, and below ran the road that led from Marchside to the Brig Pass. Beyond, the hills and glens of Southern Kell were lit up by the sunshine into a dozen shades of green. The trees were out in blossom, and the track was covered in tiny pink petals.

At the bottom of the hill, five children were beginning the ascent up towards Clackenbaird Farm, and Corthie paused on the track to wait for them. He released Carron, who crouched on the track, and started to poke at a snail with a stick. A farm cat paused by the side of the track to lick its paws, as the children grew nearer. Carron got up to chase it, and the cat bolted into the thick undergrowth by the edge of the field.

Corthie kept his eyes on the approaching children. Killop was in the lead, looking impatient at the slow progress of his siblings, while Carter and Clova came next. They were in the youngest class of the school in Marchside, and Clova had started her lessons in the New Year, while

Corthie had been in Colsbury. Lagging at the rear were Konna and Cairney. Cairney had turned nine a few days before, and it was his voice Corthie could hear rising up to him.

'How was school, son?' Corthie said, as Killop reached him.

The boy shrugged. 'All right, Da, though I'm fed up having to walk the others home. It used to take me half the time to get back before Carter and Clova started school.'

'You're their big brother,' said Corthie; 'they're too little to walk here on their own.'

Clova and Carter arrived, and Clova hugged her father. She produced a crushed-looking daisy chain from a pocket.

'I made this for you, Daddy,' she said.

Corthie held out his hand, and the girl placed the bracelet of flowers over his wrist.

'It's beautiful,' Corthie said.

'It's rubbish,' said Cairney, as he and Konna approached.

Corthie opened his mouth to say something, then he noticed blood on the boy's fists.

'Have you been fighting again, Cairney?' he said.

'He hit a boy two years older than him, Da,' said Konna.

'And why did you do that, son?'

Cairney glanced away. 'He was annoying me.'

'Am I going to receive a visit from his parents?'

'Nah,' said Cairney. 'He's too scared to tell them it was me.'

The boy walked past Corthie and carried on towards the farmhouse. Corthie lifted Carron out of the undergrowth, and then he and the others followed Cairney up the track.

'Did you see what happened, Konna?' Corthie said.

'No, Da. I saw the other boy crying after, but. Cairney split his lip.'

'He's always getting into fights,' said Killop.

'I know,' said Corthie, 'and I have a letter from Chief Kallie to prove it. If he keeps this up, they're going to throw him out of the school.'

'The school would be nicer without him,' said Clova.

'Aye, but then I'd have to teach him from home,' said Corthie. He glanced up the track at Cairney, knowing that he would have to sit the boy down and speak to him later, once none of his siblings were around to hear what was said.

They reached the brow of the hill, and the farmhouse came into view, along with several large buildings that had been constructed by the Banner of the Sapphire Throne, but which now belonged to Aila's Marchbrae whisky business. A few workers were assembling oak barrels by the cooperage, and they waved at Corthie and the children.

'Boots off at the front door,' Corthie said, as they reached the farmhouse. 'Hang up your coats.'

The children halted by the open front door of the large house as they unlaced their boots. Corthie supervised, making sure that each child stacked their boots in the correct place, then he noticed a woman walking down the hallway towards him.

'The chaos returns,' she said.

'Hi, Kelsey,' he said. 'Visit, or business?'

'Just a visit,' she said. 'I wanted to see how you've been doing since you got back. Karalyn was going to come down as well, but she has her own dramas to deal with.'

'What kind of dramas?' said Corthie, as he shepherded the last of the children into the house.

'The twins,' said Kelsey. 'I'll tell you all about it later.'

'Is Aila in?'

'Aye. She's in the kitchen with Kilholm and Ceres. I was having a cup of tea with her when we heard you all coming back.'

They walked to the kitchen, which was crowded with the children saying hello to their mother, who was sitting with baby Ceres on her knee. Kilholm had prepared a large tray of food and drinks for the children who had come home from school, and he set it down on the table.

Kelsey raised an eyebrow as the children devoured the food in seconds. 'Like little wolves,' she said.

'Get changed out of your school clothes,' said Aila, and the room quietened, as five of the children ran off.

Corthie set Carron down onto the floor, and he hurried off after the others, who could be heard shouting and laughing from the neighbouring rooms. Corthie and Kelsey sat, and Kilholm placed a fresh teapot onto the table.

'Thanks,' said Corthie.

'Did you know that Lahnos has a son?' said Aila.

Corthie frowned. 'What?'

'Kelsey was telling me about it,' Aila went on.

'The Kellach woman he was seeing a while ago turned up on Colsbury with a baby,' said Kelsey, 'and Lahnos is the father. We're letting them stay on the island for now, until we work out what to do. Lahnos is in shock.'

'What about that Ora'lya girl?' he said.

'Aye, she's in shock, too,' said Kelsey.

'The baby is mortal,' said Aila. 'Poor Lahnos. It made me remember how lucky I am.'

'Now that I'm back,' he said, 'should we be thinking about number eight?'

'That sounds like a good idea,' Aila said. 'I'm ready for another one.'

Kelsey shook her head. 'Are you really going for twelve? The house is already overrun with kids.'

'It might be more ideal to space them out a bit more,' said Aila, 'but Corthie isn't getting any younger. Twenty-four years to have a dozen children, then another ten years to move out of the little children stage. Corthie will be in his fifties by then.'

'Thanks for reminding me,' he said.

Kelsey smiled. 'So, are you happy to be back?'

'Aye,' he said.

'Good. Lahnos is tearing himself inside out with guilt.'

'Are you saying that I should feel guilty?'

'No. Karalyn and I think that the Empress should never have asked you to go to Athumia.'

'I agree,' said Aila.

'Why?' said Corthie. 'Do you both think that I'm past it?'

'Don't be a numpty,' said Kelsey. 'I had the opposite fear – that you'd enjoy yourself a little too much, and decide to get back into fighting full time.'

Corthie rolled his eyes. 'Do you think I enjoyed getting tricked by Edgar? And my reward for being rescued by Kyra was being forced to listen to her lecture me about the evils of the Empire – aye, that was enjoyable, right enough.'

'Kyra's views have got her into a bit of trouble,' said Kelsey. 'Right after she left Colsbury, she went back to the university, and helped organise a huge strike that's crippling Plateau City. I guess nobody in Kell will have heard about it yet, but it's pretty serious.'

'A strike?' said Aila. 'I didn't think they happened on the Star Continent.'

'Aye, well, they didn't, not until the idea made its way over from the City. Tens of thousands of workers and students are occupying Duncan Gardens. They're upset about taxes, and the war on Dragon Eyre.' She eyed Aila. 'Naxor has been put in charge of reaching a settlement.'

Aila shook her head. 'Naxor? What does he intend to do?'

'He's preparing a new law that will come into force tomorrow at midnight, outlawing strikes during an emergency. He's also going to declare an emergency, naturally, and then, if the strikers don't disperse and go back to work, then... well, I'm not exactly sure what he's going to do. I'm just glad it's not my responsibility.'

'I could tell you a few of the tactics Naxor has deployed over the centuries,' said Aila. 'You see, it all depends on who is in charge; Naxor takes his cue from them. Under Prince Michael, Naxor would send in the troops; but under Princess Khora, he would ignore the strikes, as if they weren't happening, and wait for them to run out of food and money.'

'I remember how he behaved under Simon,' said Kelsey, 'but the Empress is no Simon.'

'Praise Malik for that.'

'Whatever Naxor does, we'll have to assume that the Empress has given her approval.'

'What about Cael?' said Corthie. 'Has he recovered from the battle on Dragon Eyre?'

'He's more than recovered, brother,' said Kelsey. 'The Empress has sent him to Athumia, to take the fight directly to the Dominion.'

Corthie lowered his gaze. 'They sent Cael? That was the job the Empress asked me and Lahnos to do.'

Kelsey nodded. 'Do you now see why Lahnos is wracked with guilt?'

'There is absolutely no reason for you to feel guilty,' said Aila. 'You have made it clear a hundred times that you would only fight if the Star Continent was invaded. They twisted the rules a little when they summoned you to kill the monsters in that palace, but going to Athumia or Dragon Eyre? I can hardly believe the Empress had the gall to ask you that.'

'Aye,' said Corthie, his mood souring.

Aila and Kelsey eyed each other.

'How long can you stay for?' said Aila.

'Well, I was planning on only being here for an hour,' said Kelsey, 'but... I could stay longer.'

'How about dinner,' said Aila, 'then you and Corthie could share a couple of whiskies? Unless you have the children just now?'

'Calpurnia and Caelius are with their father today and tomorrow,' said Kelsey, 'but I'd have to return to Colsbury to deal with a couple of things first, and then I could come back?'

'Thanks,' said Corthie. 'That'd be good.'

Aila glanced at Kilholm, who was at the kitchen counter washing vegetables in the sink.

'One more place for dinner, please,' she said.

'No problem, ma'am,' said Kilholm. 'Should I also prepare the spare room?'

'Aye, just in case,' said Kelsey. 'I don't plan on getting drunk, but you never know.' She finished her cup of tea. 'I think I'll go to Colsbury now, so I can be back here in time for dinner.'

She got to her feet.

'See you soon,' said Aila.

Kelsey smiled, then she activated her Quadrant and vanished.

'I think you need an evening to relax,' said Aila.

'I'm not feeling guilty,' he said.

She eyed him. 'Are you sure? Part of me thinks you'd be quite happy to wade into battle again.'

'I have responsibilities here. That part of my life is over.' He tried to smile. 'How was your day?'

'It was fine, Corthie. You know, I think I'll raise the wages of everyone who works at Marchbrae; just by a little. They're bound to hear about the strikes in Plateau City eventually, and I want to keep them loyal.'

He nodded.

Aila smiled. 'Did you hear anything I just said? Go and play with the children for an hour, and I'll call you when dinner is ready.'

Corthie stood, then he walked out of the kitchen. He knew he shouldn't feel bad about declining the Empress's offer, but his thoughts went to Cael. He seemed too young to be off fighting on Athumia, and Corthie tried to remember that he had been the same age when he had arrived in the City to battle greenhides. That was different, he told himself; he had battle-vision, while his nephew didn't. He walked into the large sitting room. Korna and Clova were on a couch, while Carter and Carron were playing on the rug. Corthie wondered how he would feel if it was his own children joining the armed forces and going off to war, then he recalled that they were immortal. They would be living their lives long after their father was dead and gone.

He sat on the rug, and watched Carter playing with a wooden greenhide. The boy seemed a little obsessed with the green-skinned beasts, and was forever drawing pictures of them or pretending he was one to terrorise his younger siblings. Corthie picked up one of the other greenhide toys, and they began to play.

An hour later, Corthie was watching Clova as she made another daisy chain, this time for her Aunty Kelsey, whom Corthie had told her would be coming back for dinner. He had only had to leave the sitting room once, when he had heard Killop and Cairney shouting at each other in a nearby bedroom.

'Do you think Aunty Kelsey will like it, Daddy?' said Clova.

'I'm sure she will, sweetheart,' he said.

A clatter came from the hallway, then Kilholm staggered inside, his apron smeared in blood. Konna let out a cry at the sight, then Kilholm collapsed to the floor, a long kitchen knife embedded into his back. Corthie jumped to his feet, as the children began to wail in terror, then Killop ran through from his own room. He stared down at the body of the cook, then Corthie pulled him aside as another figure entered the sitting room.

'A lair of little Holdfasts,' the man said, his eyes scanning the five children in the room.

Corthie grabbed a poker from the hearth and stepped in front of the children.

'I don't care who you are,' Corthie said, 'but you made a mistake coming here.'

'Edgar told me about you, Corthie,' said the man. 'He told me that you were immune to the power of the gods. Are your children the same?'

He raised a hand, and Corthie leapt forward, powering his battle-vision as he swung the poker. The iron bar connected with the side of the man's head, and he was flung backwards by the blow. He collided with the doorframe, then he reached to his belt and threw a knife at Corthie's head. Corthie ducked, and the blade struck his left shoulder. The man raised his hand again. Clova screamed, but nothing happened.

'I see,' said the man. 'How is it done? How can your children not be affected?'

'I am going to kill you for that, god,' said Corthie, as he tried to suppress the pain coming from his shoulder. He advanced with the poker, and the man drew a sword.

Corthie lunged forward but, this time, the man was prepared. He parried Corthie's blow, his body moving with a speed given only by battle-vision.

'You say you do not care who I am,' the god said; 'but I care very much about you, Corthie. This is your last day alive. Once you are dead, I will cut off the heads of your children in front of their mother, and then I will kill her, too.'

Corthie got in another blow, driving the poker into the stomach of the god. He gasped in pain and staggered back a few steps, then he regained his composure.

'Your family of immortal Holdfasts are too dangerous to be allowed to live,' said the god, 'but I am not here for any noble reason. The Second Ascendant was my grandfather, Corthie, and you murdered him. I am here for your blood.'

The god lashed out with his sword. Corthie blocked it with the poker, and the god rammed his fist into Corthie's face, breaking his nose. Corthie reached out with his left hand, and gripped the god's throat, squeezing, then the blade of another sword was punched through the god's chest from behind.

'Stand clear,' said Aila, the sword in her right hand, 'so I can take the bastard's head.'

Corthie released the god, who slumped to the floor, his wounds healing. Aila raised her sword, then she was flung off her feet by a massive wave of death powers. Corthie felt them swirl around him, but only Aila was affected. She was thrown against a wall by the force of the blast, her skin falling in strips from her face and arms, and her sword clattering to the floor.

Another god appeared at the end of the hallway, his right hand raised. He regarded Corthie's bloody face, then he looked down at the god on the floor.

'Get up, Crennic,' he said. 'You are embarrassing yourself.'

'He has battle-vision,' Crennic gasped, as he got to his feet, 'and his young are as immune to our powers as he is.'

'Do you know who we are, Corthie Holdfast?' said the other god.

'No, and I couldn't give a shit,' said Corthie. 'You're just more gods to kill.'

'Do you think you can defend your children from two of us? Didn't Leksandr and Arete once get the better of you?'

Corthie frowned.

'You fight him, Ward,' said Crennic, 'and I'll deal with the children.'

'No,' said Ward. 'We kill Corthie together, and only then shall we turn this house into an abattoir.'

Ward drew his own sword, and Corthie saw it had a black blade. The two gods advanced, stepping into the sitting room, but Corthie held his ground as the children clustered behind him. Killop had a hunting knife in his right hand, but Corthie kept a hand raised to stop his son from charging.

'Edgar should never have allowed you to live,' said Ward. 'It was a mistake that we are here to put right.'

'Konna,' said Corthie, 'open the window and get the little ones out. Run with them down to Marchside and go to Chief Kallie's house.'

There was a loud shout behind Ward and Crennic, then the blade of a war axe struck the side of Crennic's head, shearing off his left ear. Corthie didn't hesitate. He charged forward, and rammed the poker into Crennic's face, the tip entering just under his nose, and then smashing through the back of the god's skull. Corthie let go of the poker as Ward slashed out with his sword, slicing through Corthie's waist. Corthie rolled to the floor, blood streaming from him, then he glanced up to see Cairney standing in the hallway with the war axe. Had it been Cairney who had struck Crennic? Ward raised his sword, and Cairney swung again, aiming at Ward's legs. Ward skipped back out of the way.

Corthie extended his hand. 'The axe, Cairney.'

His son passed him the axe. Corthie took it, then he summoned all the strength he had, and hurled it at Ward. It struck the god in the chest, and Ward screamed in pain; then Killop ran forward, and stabbed the god in the stomach with his knife. With one last effort, Corthie staggered to his feet. He barged into Ward, and they fell to the floor together. Corthie rammed his fist into Ward's face, breaking several bones. Killop stabbed the god again, then Cairney picked up Crennic's knife, and rammed it into Ward's left eye.

The god screamed as the three Holdfasts were upon him, then his left hand broke free, and he vanished. Corthie fell into the space where Ward had been, and his blood seeped onto the rug.

'Da!' Killop cried, dropping the knife and kneeling by his father. Cairney was still clutching Crennic's blade, a wild look in his eyes. He went to the prostrate body of Crennic, the poker still driven through the god's skull, then he began to saw away at the god's neck. A hand pushed him away.

'Let me do it, son,' said Aila.

She brought down her sword, and cleaved Crennic's head from his shoulders.

'Ma,' said Konna. 'Da's dying.'

Corthie's eyes were still open, as blood pooled under him. The pain from the wound in his shoulder, and from his broken nose, were nothing compared to the agony coming from the injury inflicted by Ward's black sword. The blade had cut deep into his waist and abdomen, and he could feel his life ebbing away. His children crowded round him, crying and sobbing, and Aila took his hand.

'Stay with us, Corthie,' Aila said.

Corthie nodded, then his eyes closed.

When Corthie next awoke, all pain had ceased. He was lying in an unfamiliar bed, next to which several chairs had been placed. Aila was sitting on one, her hands clutching Corthie's right arm, then Konna was in the next chair, then Kelsey and Shella, while Cardova, Karalyn and Killop were standing.

'How are you feeling?' said Karalyn.

'Better,' he said. 'Tired, but all right. Where are we? Colsbury?'

'I brought your entire family here,' said Kelsey. 'I don't think Clackenbaird is safe at the moment.'

Corthie nodded. 'And the children?'

'They're all fine,' said Aila. 'Kilholm was the only one to die, apart from that god we killed.'

'His name was Crennic.'

'He was one of Edmond's grandsons,' said Karalyn, 'released by Edgar from the Palace of the Almighty.'

'Did you heal me, sis?'

'Aye,' said Karalyn.

'You were unconscious when I returned to Kell,' said Kelsey. 'You killed another god, brother.'

'I didn't do it alone,' he said. His eyes fell on Killop. 'Thank you, son. And Cairney... Where's Cairney?'

'He's swimming in the lake with a few of the other children,' said Shella. 'Lahnos and Olo'osso are keeping an eye on them.'

'Is he all right? He's only nine, and he...'

Aila nodded. 'We know. I saw it. I couldn't do much until my self-healing had repaired the damage Ward inflicted on me, but I could see what was happening. How did they know where we lived?'

'They know everything Bailey knows,' said Karalyn, 'and there isn't much Bailey doesn't know.'

'Will they attack Clackenbaird again?' said Corthie.

'It's possible,' said Kelsey, 'but we doubt it. The Holdfasts were the only reason they went there, and the farm should be safe if you're all here. Colsbury is a far more likely target.'

'But we have three dragons here,' said Cardova, 'and we have Karalyn and Lahnos, as well as the greatest mortal warrior of all time.'

Corthie lowered his gaze. 'Don't say that. I was unable to defend my own home from attack.'

'Unable?' said Kelsey. 'Are you joking, Corthie? Who else could have fought off a son and a grandson of Edmond and Theodora? They're as powerful as the Ascendants; and now one of them is dead. Ward must have thought it would be easy, but now he's gone crying back to Edgar.'

'We don't know that Edgar sent them,' said Karalyn.

'It doesn't matter, sis,' said Kelsey. 'They failed. The bastards tried to attack the Holdfasts, and they got their arses handed to them.'

Corthie sat up, then he pulled back the covers and put his feet on the floor.

'Where are you going?' said Aila.

'I'm healed,' said Corthie. He glanced down at his ripped clothes. 'We need to go back to Clackenbaird.'

'It's not safe,' said Karalyn.

'Just for two minutes,' he said.

'Why?' said Aila.

'Why do you think?' he said. 'So I can get my Clawhammer.'

The others said nothing.

'Do you think I'm going to cower here while Edgar plans his next attack on us?' Corthie cried, as rage started to fill him. 'I'm going after those bastards. I'm going to hunt them down. They tried to kill my children...' He almost broke down, then he steadied himself. 'All I wanted was to live in peace. That's all I wanted. Who's going to take me to Kell?'

Kelsey and Karalyn glanced at each other.

'I'll do it,' said Kelsey.

'No,' said Karalyn. 'Let me go. The gods might return to collect Crennic's body, and my powers match theirs. I'll throw clothes into a bag while Corthie gets his Tempest armour and the Clawhammer.' She glanced at the others. We shall be as quick as we can.'

The air shimmered, and Corthie found himself standing in the sitting room of the farmhouse. Blood was smearing the rug, and the body of Kilholm was still lying by the doorway. Crennic, however, had gone.

'The god was there,' Corthie said, pointing at the floor.

'Was he definitely dead?' said Karalyn.

Corthie nodded.

Karalyn placed a hand on his arm. 'I want you to think very carefully about what you said in Colsbury, brother. Shouldn't your place be with your children, protecting them? If you go off to hunt the gods, who will defend your family?'

'You,' said Corthie. 'You, Lahnos, Frostback, Halfclaw, and everybody else on Colsbury.'

'But you are their father.'

'Then you go!' he cried. 'You go and hunt down the bastards who tried to slaughter my family.'

'I… I'm not getting involved…'

'Then shut up,' he said. 'By going after the gods, I will be defending my family in the only way I know how. I am going to wade in those bastards' blood. They fucked with the wrong Holdfast.'

Karalyn said nothing.

'I'm going to bring the Clawhammer and my armour down from the attic,' he said. 'Grab a few bottles of whisky from the kitchen.'

He walked away, leaving his sister staring at his back.

Forty minutes later, Kelsey was helping Corthie fit his Tempest armour, as Aila watched with Ceres cradled in her arms. Corthie's fury had not abated since the attack, and he could feel his battle-vision longing to be unleashed. He thirsted for death; he could feel it in his fingers. He yearned to kill, and his thoughts were turning dark with images of what he would like to do to Ward when he found him.

'You're all done,' said Kelsey, stepping back a pace.

Corthie nodded.

Kelsey eyed Aila. 'I think I will leave the two of you alone for a moment; but Lucius wants a word, Corthie. Should I send him in?'

'Give us a minute first,' said Aila.

Kelsey nodded, then she left the room.

'I can feel your anger from here, Corthie,' Aila said.

'And do you think I should be more relaxed about what happened?'

'No. You are reacting as I had imagined you would if something like this ever occurred. But please, be careful. Kill those bastards, but do it right. Don't leave your children fatherless.'

He glanced down at her. 'You want me to hunt them down?'

'Yes, I do. Find them, and kill them all.'

'Karalyn tried to tell me that I should stay here.'

'Of course she did; what else did you expect her to say? But I am your wife, Corthie, and I am asking you to show no mercy to the gods who tried to take our children from us. Do you hear me? No mercy.'

She leaned up and kissed him, then the door opened and Cardova walked in.

'Sorry for interrupting,' he said.

'What is it, Lucius?' said Corthie.

'Do you want to fight the gods who attacked your home?' he said.

'Aye.'

'Then let me help you. I can put the entire armed forces of the Empire behind you, but only if you agree to serve the Empress.'

'I want to kill the gods who attacked Clackenbaird,' Corthie said.

'And that is exactly what the Empire is doing. Edgar's gods are basing themselves on Dragon Eyre and Athumia, in order to bring the Empire to its knees. The Empire's fight is your fight, Corthie; should we not coordinate our efforts? If you go off on your own, we might inadvertently get in each other's way. Wouldn't it be better if we worked together? You can't be on Dragon Eyre and Athumia at the same time; and who would transport you from world to world? Listen; I can have a team of elite soldiers assigned to you within a matter of hours, and I can secure a Quadrant for your personal use. The team could take you straight into the heart of the fight, and they would watch your back.'

'If I agree,' said Corthie, 'then would the Empire expect me to obey orders? I've never been very good at that. And any team assigned to me usually ends up dead.'

'I understand the risks, but having you on our side changes everything. We would allow you freedom to carry out operations on your own initiative, but as a part of a greater effort; as part of a grand strategy to defeat our enemies. What do you say?'

Corthie glanced at Aila.

'It makes sense,' she said. 'The Empress is bound to send you directly against the gods, Corthie, while her armies deal with the other threats.'

'I'll do it,' said Corthie. 'Give me an hour with my family, and then take me to Plateau City.'

Cardova gave him a grim smile. 'Thank you, Corthie. We will keep your children safe; I swear it.'

An hour later, Corthie gave Aila and their children a last hug, then he stood next to Cardova and Kelsey, who was holding her Quadrant in her hands. Karalyn had refused to take Corthie to see the Empress, and had declined his invitation to say goodbye.

'Kill them all, Da!' Cairney shouted.

Corthie nodded to his son, then Kelsey triggered the Quadrant, taking her, Corthie and Cardova to the inner courtyard of the Ministry of the Plateau.

'I'm not going inside,' Kelsey said. 'Should I come back for you in a little while, Lucius?'

'I will ask Brogan to take me back to Colsbury later,' he said. 'Thanks.'

Kelsey shrugged. 'It was the least I could do, Lucius. I don't think Karalyn will be speaking to you for a while after this, but.'

'I know,' he said.

Kelsey vanished, and Cardova led Corthie into the building. Courtiers, soldiers and officials were crowding the hallways, and many stopped to stare at the sight of Corthie in his Tempest armour, with the Clawhammer over one shoulder, and they cleared a path for him and Cardova.

They ascended a flight of stairs, and Cardova led him to a guarded door.

He glanced at Corthie. 'Are you sure?'

'Aye. I'm sure; it's time.'

Cardova knocked on the door, then he pushed it open. Inside, the Empress was seated with a few other members of her Imperial Court. She glanced up, and her eyes widened.

'There has been an attack on Clackenbaird, Your Majesty,' said Cardova.

The Empress got to her feet. 'Oh no,' she said; 'are the children all right? Aila?'

'The resident cook was killed, Your Majesty, but Corthie and his family were able to fight off the attackers. One of them was Lord Ward, and the other, whom Corthie killed, was called Lord Crennic. It appears as though they might have been sent by Lord Edgar, in order to slaughter Corthie's family.'

The Empress stared, as anger burned in her eyes.

Naxor got to his feet. 'One of Edgar's gods was killed, you say? A Lord Crennic?'

'Yes,' said Cardova. 'Ward fled before Corthie could kill him, too.'

'What do you need, Corthie?' said the Empress. 'Do you want me to send a battalion of marines to Clackenbaird?'

'My family is in Colsbury Castle, Your Majesty,' said Corthie. 'Kelsey took them, and they will be safe there.'

'I am glad they are safe,' she said. 'Then what can I do for you?'

Corthie got down to one knee before her.

'Your Majesty,' he said, 'I want to kill the gods for what they tried to do to my family. I will not rest until every one of them is dead. Take me into your service, and unleash me against our enemies.'

A faint smile flitted over Thorn's face. 'If you work for me, Corthie, then I can promise you nothing but blood and death.'

'That suits me fine, Your Majesty,' he said, 'because that's all I want.'

# CHAPTER 29
# TWO MOTHERS

**Plateau City, The Plateau – 8th Day, Last Third Spring 545**

Kyra used her vision to watch the approaching mass of soldiers and officials walk all the way from the Ministry of the Plateau to Duncan Gardens. In the midst of the soldiers was the red-headed son of Empress Bridget – Bedig, the Lord Marshal of the Empire. As commander of the local garrison of Plateau City, Bedig was dressed in military attire, with a polished steel breastplate, and with a sword hanging from his belt.

Kyra snapped her vision back to her body.

'They will be entering the gardens in a couple of minutes,' she said to Achan and the other leaders of the strike. 'They came via the Emergency Wall, and are approaching the gardens by the river gate.'

'Who has the Empress sent?' said a Kellach leader of the strike. 'Lord Naxor?'

'No,' said Kyra. 'Lord Bedig.'

Several of the leadership smiled and relaxed a little, especially the ones of Kellach extraction.

'I don't trust that demigod Naxor,' said one, 'but what harm would one of Bridget's sons do to us? He's probably on our side.'

Achan frowned. 'I wouldn't be so sure about that. Power changes people. Even those with the noblest principles will find themselves making compromises to retain authority.'

'Do you think we should bar the entrance to the gardens to keep him out?'

'No. I think we should listen to what he has to say, but we should be prepared for disappointment. In my opinion, it is far too early for the imperial government to meekly surrender to our demands.'

'Too early? But we've been here for five days.'

Achan smiled. 'I have said this before, but I will repeat myself so that there is no doubt – in order to secure the acquiescence of the Empress, we may have to continue the strike for months. It comes down to economics. By striking, we are hurting the finances of the Empire, but we are also hurting ourselves. If both sides hold their nerve, then the winner will be the ones that can hold out the longest.'

The other leaders looked away, their features grim.

'May I speak?' said Kyra.

'Of course,' said Achan. 'You do not need to ask permission, Kyra; your help has been invaluable.'

Kyra nodded. 'I don't like to disagree with you, sir,' she said, 'but I believe that the imperial finances are in a worse state than you might imagine. Plateau City is one of the largest sources of tax income in the entire Empire, and the strike is placing a great strain on their ability to pay for all of their commitments. I do not believe we will be here for months.' She smiled. 'Although, might we call them *thirds*, sir? This is the Star Continent.'

Achan nodded. 'I hope you are right, Kyra. Perhaps I am being overly pessimistic. I have endured many long strikes in the City of Salve, you see, and the various governments there were well used to them. Plateau City is not.'

A Holdings man gestured to a group of nearby volunteers. 'Clear a path all the way from the river gates to the statue of Duncan, and allow Lord Bedig safe passage. Remind everyone you see that this is a peaceful protest.'

'Aye, sir,' said one of the volunteers. They turned and walked down the slope of the long rampart.

Kyra watched as the masses of strikers were cajoled into moving aside, so that a way was opened up through them. Tents were littered all over the gardens, and dozens of thin tendrils of smoke were rising from the little camp fires. The odour of so many people crammed together had been increasing over the days, and strict rules about toilet ditches had been brought in to keep it under control. The river ran along the southern flank of the gardens, and that had helped with washing, collecting fresh water, and the disposal of waste, but most of the strikers were too far from its banks.

To Kyra's left, the large statue of Chief Duncan rose into the darkening sky. The sun was setting over the roofs of the Old Peasant District to the west and, beyond that, the two towers of the abandoned Blue Palace construction site were silhouetted in the red sky.

'So, Kyra,' said Achan, 'who was this Duncan fellow?'

'The Sanang once tried to attack Plateau City before its walls had been finished,' she said. 'Duncan was the leader of the Kellach Brigdomin refugees who had gathered here. They built the rampart to keep the Sanang out.'

'He is a hero to the Kellach?'

'Maybe up here. Down in Kellach Brigdomin, most people have never heard of him.'

Achan pointed. 'Here they come.'

In the distance, the soldiers and officials that Kyra had seen were making their way through the vast crowd. A few of the strikers were shouting out insults at the group, but the majority seemed relieved that something was happening after five days of hearing nothing but silence from the authorities. Lord Bedig approached the statue of Duncan, flanked by well-armed soldiers, then he came to a halt.

'Join us on the Auld Rampart, Lord Bedig,' one of the leaders of the strike called out. 'Talk to us.'

Bedig ignored the shout. He gestured to an official, who stepped forward, a document in his hands.

'On behalf of the Imperial Court and Her Majesty the Empress, Holder of the Worlds,' the official said, 'I hereby declare that a new law regarding strike action has been passed, and shall come into force when the dawn bell rings tomorrow. From that moment onwards, it shall be a criminal offence to withdraw labour during times of emergency; and such an emergency has been declared. Therefore, anyone remaining in Duncan Gardens beyond that time will be treated as though they are in breach of the law, and will be dealt with accordingly. Those who do not report for work tomorrow shall be dismissed from their places of employment with immediate effect. Those who do not return to their lessons at the university shall be expelled from that establishment forthwith. The penalty for breaking this new law shall be two years imprisonment or four years of service in Her Majesty's armed forces; however, for the organisers and leaders of any illegal strike, the penalty shall be twenty years imprisonment.'

The official lowered the document and bowed his head towards the Lord Marshal.

'You have all heard what the new law has decreed,' Bedig called out in a loud voice. 'You have until dawn to peacefully disperse and return to your homes. I pray you make the right decision.'

The group turned to leave, and the crowd erupted in anger. Fights broke out as the soldiers were jostled, and an official was hit on the head by a thrown stone.

'No!' cried Achan. 'Remain peaceful. Do not resort to violence!'

The soldiers around Bedig closed ranks, and barged their way through the crowd, their tall shields raised. The boss of one shield battered into the face of a Holdings striker, and the man went down. The volunteers who were supposed to keep order among the crowd were trying to push the protesters back, but they were heavily outnumbered, and screams rose up into the evening sky as the soldiers shoved and pushed their way free of the gardens. More soldiers positioned by the edge of the gardens went to the assistance of their colleagues, and Lord Bedig made it back to the streets unscathed, as the crowd roared out its fury at the new law.

Achan sat down on the grass of the old rampart, his head in his hands.

'What now?' said a Kellach leader. 'Have you seen this tactic used before, Achan?'

'I have,' he said. 'Either the government is bluffing, or they mean to use force to break the strike.'

'Then we should arm ourselves,' said one. 'If they want a fight, let's give them one.'

'Are you insane?' cried another. 'Hundreds will be killed if we resist. It's over, but we've made our point. The Empress can't pretend that we agree with her; she knows how we feel about the taxes.'

'We can't give up,' said a Rahain striker. 'If we go home, the Empress will have beaten us. She'll know that we are too scared to do anything to stand up to her government.'

'But twenty years in a prison? That's what we're all facing. Every one of us standing on this rampart will be included as the leaders of the strike, and I have no desire to become a fucking martyr.'

Kyra sat down next to Achan as the others continued to argue.

'What do you think we should do, sir?' she said.

'I admit,' said Achan, 'that I wasn't expecting such a ruthless response from the government, not this early in the strike. We may have underestimated the resolve of the Empress.'

'Aye, but what should we do?'

Achan gazed out over the crowd. 'You should go back to the university, Kyra,' he said.

Kyra gestured towards the masses of people in the gardens. 'But no one else is leaving.'

'They will. As soon as their anger begins to fade, they will start to drift away. No one will want to be the first to go, but a trickle will quickly turn into a flood.'

'And you?'

'Me?' He shook his head. 'I imagine that the government will send me back to the City, if I'm lucky. I will stay here, and take whatever punishment they mete out.'

'You might get twenty years.'

'I might. I have been in prison before, Kyra; jailed for refusing to surrender my principles. If it happens again, I will continue the struggle from within my prison cell.'

Several hours later, as far as Kyra could see, Achan's prediction was wrong. She watched the crowd throughout the evening, but saw no one leave the gardens. Then, not long before midnight, she noticed a few Rahain protesters slipping over the bridges that led to their quarter of the city, and the effect was like a dam bursting. Large groups of Rakanese flooded out of the river gates, then hundreds of Holdings and Kellach started to leave by the northern entrances to the gardens. By the time the midnight bells pealed over the city, fewer than half of the strikers had remained. The grass was littered with abandoned tents and piles of rubbish, while those who had decided to stay tried to get some sleep before dawn.

Kyra retired to her tent next to the old rampart. Larron was sitting outside its entrance, tending a small fire as he heated some water.

'Are you not going to bed?' she said to him as she sat on the grass.

'I don't think I'd be able to sleep,' he said.

'I half wondered if you would have gone back to the university,' she said, 'or perhaps to your parents' tavern.'

'I was tempted, but I didn't want to leave you here on your own, Kyra.'

He poured some of the hot water into two mugs, and passed her one. 'Tea?'

'Thanks.'

She took the mug, and sat closer to the fire.

'When the sun rises,' Larron said, 'we will still have a choice. The soldiers won't be able to block every entrance to the gardens – there are over a dozen of them, and much of the rest is unfenced. We could even climb over a low wall and flee into the Kellach Quarter.'

'If we're going to run away,' she said, 'we should do it now. At least then we'll get a decent night's sleep.'

Larron poked the fire with a stick. 'What do you want to do?'

'I want to stay. Achan is prepared to spend twenty years in prison. Running away would feel like abandoning him.'

'We would be expelled from university.'

'I know.'

'We might even face two years in prison.'

'Or four years in the army.'

'I honestly believed the Empress would be more reasonable,' he said. He exhaled. 'All right; I will stay if you stay, and then we can decide what to do when the sun rises.'

They finished their tea in silence, then they crawled into their tent, wrapped themselves in blankets, and tried to sleep.

Kyra awoke with Larron's hand on her shoulder.

'What is it?' she whispered.

'Something's happening,' he said in a low voice. 'I heard shouting.'

Kyra sat up and rubbed her head. She opened the tent and gazed outside. It was still dark, and there was no sign of the coming dawn. A loud cry rang out in the distance, followed by more in quick succession, then a group of terrified-looking Holdings strikers ran past the line of tents.

'Run!' cried one. 'They're coming!'

The group reached the rampart, then they sprinted up and over it, disappearing from sight.

More cries rose up from all over the gardens, then screams. Kyra pulled her boots on and laced them up as quickly as she was able, as Larron crawled out of the tent. He ran up the slope of the old rampart, gazed around in all directions, then he hurried back to Kyra. He took her hand and pulled her to her feet.

'What's going on?' she cried.

A large group of over a hundred Sanang men burst into view from their left, some with lit torches, and others wielding long wooden staves. They were pulling people out of their tents and clubbing them, then they were ripping the tents down and stamping on the camp fires, as the strikers fled in terror. Any who resisted were thrashed without mercy, the long wooden staves battering them to the ground.

'The Sanang are everywhere,' Larron said, as he tried to pull Kyra away.

'Where should we go?' said Kyra. 'The bridges?

'Soldiers are blocking every bridge over the river,' said Larron, 'and they've sealed off the streets leading from the gardens. They're standing back, and allowing thousands of Sanang to do whatever they like.' He gripped her hand and gazed into her eyes. 'It's too late to run.'

Larron pushed Kyra to the ground as another armed mob of Sanang approached, then he lay on top of her, covering her with his body as the first Sanang men ran towards them. Three Holdings were dragged from a neighbouring tent and beaten with the staves, then another group ran up to Larron and Kyra.

'We are not resisting!' Larron cried.

The staves battered down onto Larron's back, shoulders and legs.

'Striking scum,' shouted one of the Sanang as he beat Larron. 'Fucking traitors!'

Kyra was crushed under Larron's weight, but his body was shielding her from the staves, and the Sanang moved on, eager to attack the leaders of the strike, who were now surrounded on the rampart. The Sanang ran up the slope from both sides, lashing out at anyone within range, then passing over them like a storm.

Larron groaned and rolled off Kyra. Blood was coming from the side of his head, and he was gasping in pain.

'I have a Quadrant, you idiot,' Kyra said, as tears came to her eyes.

Another group of Sanang ran by the tents. They glanced around at the cowering and beaten strikers, and one smiled at the sight of Kyra crying by Larron's side.

'Enjoy your prison cell when they come for you at dawn,' he shouted.

Drums and horns sounded in the distance.

'Do you hear that?' cried another Sanang man. 'There will be no more sleep for any of you bastards tonight if you stay in the gardens. Go home! And be glad we have sticks instead of swords!'

The other Sanang laughed as they pressed on, spreading out into the other parts of the encampment. The area of the tents began to stir back into life as the wave of Sanang passed the rampart. A few fortunate individuals who had been missed in the attacks crawled out of their tents and peered around, while others were weeping and bleeding where they sat on the grass. A steady stream of strikers began heading off in the direction of the gates, some limping, some furious, and others in tears.

'They lied to us,' Larron groaned, as he lay on the ground. 'Lord Bedig... they lied to us, Kyra.'

'Is anything broken?' she said. She put a hand to the side of his head, and it came away covered in blood. 'I'm taking you to my mother,' she went on.

'Your mother?'

'Aye, and then I might pay the Empress a little visit.'

She raised her head, and listened to the pounding drums and the horn blasts echoing over the darkness of the gardens. More and more people were trudging towards the bridges, or the gates along the northern flank of the park, while screams were still coming from the areas the Sanang mobs were passing through.

Kyra put a hand into her pocket.

*Middle balcony, Colsbury. Go.*

The air shimmered, and she found herself kneeling by Larron on the balcony of the Summer Palace. The balcony was deserted, apart from two people huddled together round a table in the corner. One of them, a man with horns, got to his feet.

'Kyra?' he said. 'Is that you?'

'Lahnos?'

He hurried over, and a woman followed him. Lahnos crouched down, and took a glance at Larron's injuries.

'Who are these people?' said the woman.

'This is Kyra Holdfast,' Lahnos said, 'Karalyn's daughter; but I don't know who the man is. I'll fetch Karalyn.'

Lahnos ran into the building, leaving the woman, who was looking down at Kyra and Larron.

'Was he in a fight?' said the woman. 'He looks badly beaten.'

'He was protecting me,' Kyra said. 'Listen; ask my mother to heal him when she gets here. There's something I have to do.'

She got to her feet.

'Will you be coming back?' said the woman.

'Maybe. We'll see how it goes.'

'No, Kyra,' groaned Larron. 'Stay here; don't go.'

'I have to go,' said Kyra. 'My mother will look after you.'

She placed her hand into her pocket again.

*The Ministry of the Plateau, Plateau City. Go.*

The dark air shimmered, and Kyra appeared in the inner courtyard of the ministry building. A couple of soldiers stared at her and she entered their minds.

*Sleep.*

The soldiers fell to the ground, their crossbows clattering off the cobbles. More soldiers started to emerge from the doors of the building, and Kyra kept her hand in her pocket.

*The Empress's private rooms. Go.*

Kyra found herself in a small study, where a few candles were burning. Standing alone by a tall window was the Empress. She was staring out in the direction of Duncan Gardens, her hands clasped tightly together in front of her.

'You bitch,' said Kyra.

Thorn started, then she turned her head, and her eyes widened.

'You sent in thousands of Sanang to beat up peaceful protesters,' Kyra went on. 'You told us we had until dawn.'

The Empress said nothing.

'My friend was nearly killed,' Kyra said. 'You threatened us with prison sentences, or losing our jobs; or being expelled from university, and for what? Because we disagree with you?'

'The strike was bringing us to the edge of the abyss, Kyra,' said the Empress. 'I did not want to use force, but...'

'You liar!' Kyra cried. 'You are unfit to rule. You have done nothing but send our soldiers to slaughter people all over the Star Continent and Dragon Eyre; and you have bankrupted the Empire. Why? Was it all for your own glory? When I was younger, you used to say that you wanted to be remembered as a great Empress, as an Empress who cared for those you ruled over. And now? I'm ashamed of you. I'm ashamed I ever loved you.'

Thorn lowered her gaze.

'Nothing to say?' said Kyra.

'I have plenty I could say, Kyra,' said the Empress, 'but I don't think you would listen to me.'

'Tell me why you sent armed Sanang thugs into the gardens.'

'To break the strike.'

'But you said the law didn't come into force until dawn.'

'We gave you sufficient time to leave Duncan Gardens,' said the Empress. 'Those who were still there after midnight had made up their minds.' She raised her chin. 'We needed to show that we could be ruthless, without actually killing a single citizen. Do you think anyone will dare to organise another strike, after this? For the sake of the Empire, I had no choice. Your demands were childish, Kyra. We are in a defensive alliance with Queen Blackrose; did you truly expect me to abandon her? Thousands of Wystians are amassing on Blackrose's borders, and you wanted me to withdraw our forces? The Wystians and Unk Tannic will slaughter and enslave hundreds of thousands of people in the Eastern Rim if they get past Na Sun Ka. But that doesn't mean anything to you, does it? You think I am to blame for all the ills of the Allied Worlds.'

'Don't tell me this is about alliances. You annexed Na Sun Ka.'

'I had to. Blackrose refused to send any of her own forces to the island. She lured us into Dragon Eyre, without any intention of committing her own resources to defend Na Sun Ka. If there is anyone to blame for this, it is the Queen of the Eastern Rim. And yet, I do not blame her. She was acting in the best interests of her realm. She knew that I would be obliged to use imperial forces to defend her southern flank. And then Edgar and his gods appeared. How could I have planned for that? According to you and your band of dissidents, I should withdraw our forces. We shall then watch as Dragon Eyre is consumed by slaughter and fire. And then what? Do you think Edgar will be content to rest there? We are fighting on Dragon Eyre to stop the war reaching the Star Continent.'

'Your ambition has led us to this disaster.'

'My ambition? You are right – I am ambitious. I do want to be remembered as a great Empress. I want my reign to be a time of peace, prosperity and stability, an age that people will look back on with fondness. I want all people, on every world, to be free to live their own lives without poverty and oppression. I want to ring the Empire with steel, to protect the lives of all who dwell here. That is my ambition, Kyra.'

'You will be remembered for what you did this night,' said Kyra. 'You will be remembered for ordering Sanang mobs to crush a peaceful protest.'

A flicker of a smile touched Thorn's lips. 'I doubt that, Kyra. Plateau City may well be the capital of the Empire, but no one else will care. Most of those living in Plateau City won't care. Those who do, will be relieved that everything will go back to normal. A few bruises and broken limbs are not going to bring about the collapse of civilisation. For some, though, it is too late. Achan will be arrested, along with the other leaders of the strike. Anyone who does not turn up for work this morning will find themselves unemployed. Any student who does not return to their classes will be expelled. An example must be made, to show everyone the price of trying to foment rebellion.'

'You make me sick.'

'What happened to you, Kyra? This time last year, you were my chosen successor. If you had only held your tongue and kept your opinions to yourself, then you would have been best placed to become Empress after me; and then you could have ruled as you wished. You could have overturned every one of my laws, and rewritten the constitution in any way that pleased you. No more. Now that I understand how dangerous you are, I will never allow you to get close to the throne. It breaks my heart, but I want nothing more to do with you. Your brother, on the other hand – now there is someone upon whom I can rely. Cael will do great things, I think. He may even be the next Emperor.'

Kyra's temper snapped. She clenched her fists and lunged towards the Empress. Thorn moved back a few steps, her eyes calm; then a door burst open, and Naxor led over a dozen heavily-armed soldiers into the study.

'Are you all right, Your Majesty?' Naxor cried.

'I am quite well, Naxor,' said Thorn.

The demigod pointed at Kyra. 'She attempted to assault the Empress. Arrest her.'

The soldiers aimed their crossbows at Kyra, and edged forward. The air crackled, and Karalyn appeared between them and her daughter.

'Do nothing rash,' said Karalyn, her palms raised.

'Kyra tried to attack the Empress,' said Naxor. 'We cannot allow her to go unpunished.'

'I will see that she is punished,' said Karalyn. 'Your Majesty, allow me to take my daughter back to Colsbury. I am removing her from this city, and from the university. There is no need to make this public.'

'No, Mother,' said Kyra. 'I refuse to be expelled for doing nothing illegal. You agree with me, don't you? You think the wars are wrong. Tell her! Tell the Empress.'

Karalyn glanced at Thorn. 'Do I have your agreement to take her?'

'You do,' said the Empress. 'Please confine her to Colsbury for now, Karalyn. Naxor, pull back your soldiers; there will be no arrest.'

Karalyn tilted her head slightly at the Empress, then the air shimmered, and Kyra found herself back on the middle balcony of the Summer Palace on Colsbury. Before Kyra could react, her mother whipped out a hand, and tore the Quadrant from Kyra's clothes, leaving a ripped hole in the side of her dress.

'What are you doing?' Kyra cried. 'That's mine!'

'Not any more,' said Karalyn. 'I no longer trust you with a Quadrant.'

Kyra clenched her fists again, her eyes smouldering with fury. 'Give it back.'

'No.'

'Give me my Quadrant!' Kyra shouted.

'Or what?' said Karalyn. 'My powers are far stronger than any you possess. It pains me to discipline you, daughter, but I am doing this for your own good. I forbid you from crossing over to the mainland.'

A short surge of agony rippled through Kyra's mind, and she fell to her knees.

'Aye,' said her mother; 'that was a block I have just placed in your head, rendering you unable to walk, sail or swim off this island. In time, I will remove it, once you have calmed down and are acting reasonably. Until then, you will remain on Colsbury.'

'Why, Mother?' Kyra sobbed. 'Why are you doing this to me?'

'You raised your fists to the Empress,' Karalyn said. 'I will not tolerate it. What would you have done if Naxor and I hadn't intervened?'

'I would have punched her in the face. I would have kicked the shit out of her.'

A wry smile appeared on her mother's lips. 'Well, at least you are honest. However, you have broken the rules. We are dream mages, the most powerful mortals in existence; but I will not allow any of us to abuse our powers. Thorn was elected to be our Empress; and though we are not obliged to serve her, neither are we permitted to act against her.'

She extended a hand, but Kyra pushed it away and stood on her own.

Kyra turned, and saw a small crowd standing by the balcony doors –

Cardova, Kelsey, Shella, Lahnos, and a few others, and in their midst was Larron, who was staring out on to the balcony with wide eyes.

'Give her some space,' said Karalyn.

The others cleared a path, and Kyra walked from the balcony. She paused by Larron.

'Will you come with me?' she said.

'Aye. Of course.'

Larron followed her as she went to a well-lit flight of stairs.

'Where are we going?' Larron said.

'I have rooms,' she said.

'Rooms in the Summer Palace?'

'Aye. They are kept available for me, so that I can stay here whenever I wish.'

'Your mother healed my injuries,' Larron said, as they climbed the stairs.

Kyra nodded. They reached a landing, and Kyra led Larron to a door. She opened it, and they went inside. Kyra sat on her bed as Larron closed the door.

'I have never been so humiliated,' she said. 'And now I am expelled from university, and unable to leave Colsbury.'

Larron sat down next to her.

'Everything I have ever strived for is in ruins,' she went on; 'and worse, nothing I did has made any difference. The wars are still going on, and no one in Plateau City will dare defy the Empress again. Where did I go wrong, Larron?'

'I don't know,' he said. 'We underestimated the Empress and Karalyn Holdfast.'

'My two mothers,' she said. 'For years, I have swung between one and the other. When my mother was missing, I clung on to Thorn, and when Thorn's ambition clouded her judgement, I swung back to my mother. I was wrong to trust either of them. Thorn wants nothing but power, and my mother wants nothing to do with power. One will burn down the worlds, and the other will stand by and watch.' She glanced at him. 'You should leave. Ask Aunty Kelsey if she will take you back to the university. If you attend classes tomorrow, you won't be expelled.'

'How can I leave you here?' he said. 'If you need a friend, then I would rather stay.'

Kyra started to cry. 'I don't deserve you.' she said.

'Don't be silly,' he said. 'I will stay here for as long as you like, but I do have one small condition.'

'Aye?'

He smiled at her. 'Don't try to kiss me again.'

# CHAPTER 30
# DISAGREEABLE

**Nom Karta, Inopei – 9th Tradinch 1597**

The dragon soared overhead, his eyes scanning the empty boulevards that connected the huge palaces of Nom Karta. As soon as the dragon's shadow had passed over them, the five marines crept out from their hiding place in the rubble by the side of the road. They edged along the wide street, then ran up the stairs of an abandoned palace and entered through a human-sized door.

'It's working,' said Cael, his gaze on the street outside. 'They're coming.'

Cael gestured to a large hallway, and the marines raced through into it. They lingered for a few moments by the top of a flight of stairs, then they descended into the darkness of a basement. As they reached the bottom, they each avoided stepping onto a particular flagstone, then Cael led them to the side.

*You cannot see us.*

'Now we have to get back outside,' Cael whispered to the other four, 'without making any sound.'

They crouched down and pulled off their boots, then each marine tied them over their shoulders. They secured their crossbows, and anything that might rattle, then Cael led them back up the stairs, his feet padding softly on the worn stone steps. At the top of the stairs, they stuck to the left-hand wall, as over forty Aucterian soldiers entered the chamber, coming through the same doorway the marines had used. They fanned out, their crossbows loaded and ready. One of their sergeants crouched to examine a few marks in the dust by the top of the stairs, then he pointed down into the darkness. Their officer nodded, then he gestured to a couple of squads, and signalled that they should descend.

By the left wall, Cael and his four marines were edging round the circumference of the chamber with as much silence as they could muster. One of them scraped the butt of his crossbow against the stone wall, and a couple of Aucterians glanced over, their crossbows aimed into the shadows. They stared into the gloom, saw nothing, and their attention went back to the top of the stairs, where the two chosen squads were preparing to descend. Cael and the others kept moving. They reached a side passage, and took it, increasing their speed as they left the chamber and the Aucterians behind. They came to a ransacked storeroom, where they halted to put their boots back on, then they sprinted down a corridor. They had just reached another doorway leading to the outside, when the explosives they had planted under the loose flagstone in the basement were set off. The explosion rocked the huge palace, bringing down walls and ceilings, and sending a huge cloud of dust and debris flying out into the road in front of the building.

Cael ran across the boulevard, the four marines keeping pace with him. More Aucterian soldiers had been positioned on the road by the main entrance to the palace, but the explosion had driven them back; while other Aucterians were staggering out from the rubble at the collapsed doorway, covered in blood, their uniforms in tatters. Two dragons began to circle over the site of the explosion, their gazes passing over Cael and the marines as they ran down a side street.

Cael and the four marines took a circuitous route back to Natali's palace, remaining invisible for the entire journey. Aucterian soldiers had set up numerous roadblocks throughout Nom Karta, while there were always dragons patrolling from above, and Cael's nerves were jangling from exhaustion by the time they reached the safety of the cellars that had once belonged to Lady Natali. Cael relaxed his powers as they entered the underground refuge, and then he and the four marines slumped onto a long stone bench, as others from the Seaborne Company handed out food and water skins to them.

'Successful trip, lad?' said Captain Doune, as he walked over. 'I heard a rumble.'

Cael nodded. 'Aye, sir. We lured a few squads of Aucterian soldiers into Lord Irvan's palace, where we had rigged up some explosives under a loose flagstone. There was enough to bring down that wing of the building. I estimate maybe thirty to forty enemy casualties.'

Doune nodded. 'Good work. I wonder if we're having the desired effect. Have you managed to read the thoughts of any dragons in the last day or so?'

Cael shook his head. 'I'm pretty sure the dragons would be able to sense me if I went into their heads, sir, but I read the mind of a senior Aucterian officer who works in Queen Famula's palace.'

'And what did you learn?'

'I learned that we're upsetting the dragons of Nom Karta, but I don't think it's been enough to draw major resources away from the Tempest mine.'

'I don't suppose you know if the Empire has begun its operation to retake the mine?'

'If we have, then the officer knew nothing about it, sir.'

'And the gods?'

'Lord Ballatar is still guarding the Tempest mine, and Ward and Allura are believed to be on Dragon Eyre. No one seems to know the location of the other gods, including Edgar.'

'We have enough food for another three days,' said Doune. 'Get some sleep, lad, and we'll cook up another scheme for tonight.'

Cael nodded. He passed a water skin to another marine, then he got up and walked through to the darkness of a neighbouring chamber, where those off duty were able to rest. Cael unrolled a blanket, and lay down on the stone floor, using a folded uniform as a pillow. Six days and nights of using his powers almost continuously had tired him out, but he remained unsatisfied by what they had achieved. Despite their best efforts, they hadn't managed to kill any of the Dominion dragons. They had injured two, and they had killed and wounded over three hundred of the Bullan and Aucterian soldiers defending Nom Karta; and they had also damaged several palaces, but it wasn't enough.

Cael closed his eyes. If they returned to the Star Continent without killing at least one of the Royal Family of the Dominion, he would consider the operation a failure; but, as the captain had reminded him, they only had enough food left for three days. The beginnings of a plan began to form in his mind. Some might regard it as stupidly reckless; his mother would certainly think so, but Cael felt as though he had something to prove. The Empress had chosen him to attack the heart of the Dominion, and the last thing Cael wanted to do was disappoint Her Majesty.

He allowed his dream powers to gaze over the city as he slept. The Dominion soldiers were furious. Several groups of Bullan had come down from guarding the city walls, and they had watched as the Aucterians had carried over two dozen bodies out of the collapsed portion of Lord Irvan's palace. A few yards away, their senior officers were speaking to Lord Konran and another dragon about how to catch the saboteurs who were loose in the city. An entire regiment of Aucterian soldiers had recently arrived, partly to make up for the Bullan casualties, and partly to increase security in Nom Karta, and Cael had been pleased by this development. The Bullan spoke and thought in their own, impenetrable language, and Cael found it impossible to use his powers of persuasion or invisibility on them; while the minds of the Aucterians were far more malleable. With the Bullan, Cael had been obliged to sneak about in the shadows, but he was able to walk right in front of the Aucterians without them seeing him, and that had made it far easier for the marines to carry out their acts of sabotage and destruction. More was needed, though; much more, before Cael would be content to call the operation a success.

He moved his dream vision closer to the massive palace used by Queen Famula. It had once belonged to King Gahad, and was the largest building in Nom Karta. Cael swept through the enormous main entrance, and into a great, domed reception hall, where over a dozen dragons had congregated. As the only dragon who possessed Tempest armour, Famula was easy to recognise. Cael had tried to access her mind on more than one occasion, but had been forced to withdraw each time, as the dragon had seemed able to sense his presence. The queen was a daughter of the mighty Gahad, of whom Cael had a few memories. He recalled that his mother had entered the dragon king's mind in order to destroy him, and Cael wondered if he would be able to do the same to his daughter.

Would it work? Cael didn't know, but it was worth a try; and if the Empire needed a distraction, then what he was about to attempt would guarantee one. He would only have a few seconds in which to act; a few seconds before Famula would be able to sense, and then, perhaps, repel him.

He summoned his powers, and drove them into the queen's head. With no time to be discreet, he began to tear through her mind, ripping up connections and scouring memories. He managed to get into her eyes, and blinded her, flaying the nerves that conveyed vision to her brain.

Famula screamed, her roar of anguish causing the chamber to shake. The other dragons cowered back for a moment, then Konran and Abda hurried forward as Famula fell to the floor and convulsed. Cael could feel Famula's mind attempting to assert itself against his powers. The inner core of her identity became shielded from him, but he was able to imprint a frantic sense of panic and fear into the queen's mind, a terror beyond imagining.

*They all want to kill you, Famula; trust no one. They hate you. Kill them.*

Famula screamed again, then the strength of her mind began to prevail.

*Who are you?* cried the queen.

*I am the son of the Demon Witch, Famula,* he said. *There is no escape.*

*Get out of my head!* she screamed at him.

At once, the connection to her mind was broken, and Cael opened his eyes as sweat ran down his forehead. He rolled over, and gagged, as cramps and pains rippled through his body. A pounding headache hammered at his temples.

'Lieutenant, sir,' said a marine, 'are you all right?'

Cael steadied himself. 'Give me a minute.'

Captain Doune entered the dark chamber. 'What's going on? Who cried out?'

'It was Lieutenant Holdfast, sir,' said the marine.

Doune walked over, and crouched by Cael. 'What happened, lad? Was one of the gods inside your head?'

'No, sir,' said Cael. 'I was inside the mind of Queen Famula.'

'But you said she would be able to sense you, and you went in regardless? Why?'

'To cause a bigger distraction, sir.'

Doune narrowed his eyes. 'Will she be able to trace us to this building?'

'I don't know. Maybe.'

Doune got to his feet. 'Everyone, pack up your things and prepare to evacuate. The Holdfast boy has blown our cover. You have ten minutes.'

He walked into the other hall, and repeated the message. The marines hurried into action, placing explosives back into their crates and throwing their kit into bags. Doune returned to the dark chamber and shook his head at Cael.

'And things were going so well,' he said. 'You just couldn't resist, could you, Holdfast?'

Cael opened his mouth to respond, then he heard, or sensed, god powers being used somewhere in the city. His mother had always described the sensation as akin to hearing a sound, but to Cael the feeling was more nebulous than that, as though a buried and undefined sense within him was being activated. It was vision powers, he realised. A god was in the city, and was using vision powers to search for the being that had invaded Famula's mind. The god using the powers seemed to know where to look, and Cael felt them enter the basement of Natali's palace where the marines were hiding.

Cael tried to stand, but his legs buckled under him. Doune and a nearby marine took hold of his shoulders and hauled him to his feet.

'They've found us,' Cael gasped.

Two marines came running in from the direction of the stairs.

'Every dragon in Nom Karta is taking to the air, sir,' said one.

Doune eyed Cael. 'Get your Quadrant ready, lad. It's time to get the fuck out of here.'

The captain and the marine helped Cael through to the other room, where all of the marines had gathered. Cael felt the vision powers swirl around the chamber. They passed over him, but latched on to several of the other marines and, one by one, they fell to the floor, unconscious.

Doune stared at the falling bodies, then his eyes rolled up into his head, and he collapsed, bringing Cael down with him. Cael raised his head from the stone floor. Every marine in the basement was lying helpless and unconscious. A burst of dragon fire lit up the stairs that led to the ground floor, but the marines were too deep underground to be harmed by any dragon attack from the exterior of the building. They would send in the Aucterians and the Bullan instead; or perhaps the god that Cael had sensed would come in person.

Cael pulled the Quadrant from his clothes. Angry with himself, he swiped his fingers over the copper surface.

The air shimmered, and the unconscious marines appeared on the quayside of Sun Ta harbour, outside the front door of the marine headquarters. Around them lay untidy piles of half-packed crates, along with bags of clothes, kit and food, and a few loose explosives.

The dock workers ran away at first, then a few returned to stare at the scene. Cael staggered to his feet in time to see a group of marines and officers spill out of the front of the headquarters building.

'Lieutenant Holdfast?' said a major.

Cael swayed, then he stood to attention and saluted. 'All marines accounted for, sir.'

A crowd was forming on the quayside, surrounding the two dozen unconscious marines.

The major crouched by Captain Doune, and checked that he was breathing.

'A god sent them all to sleep, sir,' said Cael. 'They will be fine in a few minutes.'

'Were you on Athumia, Lieutenant?' he said.

'Aye, sir.'

'Then I must assume that your operation in Nom Karta is at an end.'

Cael frowned. 'Could I have permission to return there, sir? The operation was only a partial success.'

'I don't have the authority to allow that,' said the major. 'Wait until Adjutant Claudian returns from Plateau City the day after tomorrow. Until then, you had best give that Quadrant to me.'

'What was that, sir?' said Cael. 'I'm afraid I've gone a bit deaf. Did you say that I was to return to Nom Karta?'

The major frowned at him, then Cael swiped his fingers over the Quadrant.

The air shimmered, and Cael appeared on the roof of the palace of Lady Tirna in Nom Karta. He crouched by the battlements that ran along the edge of the flat roof, and gazed out in the direction of Natali's palace as his body started to recover from the ordeal Famula had put it through. Dozens of dragons were circling over the palace of Natali, while companies of Aucterian and Bullan soldiers were funnelling in through several entrances. Cael scanned the dragons, but saw no sign of Famula among them. He made a decision. If Famula had been permanently incapacitated by what he had done, then he would return to Sun Ta to announce the success of the operation; if not, he would stay until he had a tangible achievement that he could give to Adjutant Claudian.

Cael tried to summon his dream vision powers, but felt exhaustion ripple over him as he watched the soldiers entering Natali's palace. His eyes started to close, and he slipped into a deep sleep.

When Cael next awoke, the sun was shining down on the city of Nom Karta. Over to the left, beyond the river, the city of Sat Orma sprawled out in a chaotic fashion. Half of the buildings had been destroyed in the civil war among the children of Gahad, and many of the humans dwelling there were living in squalor. Compared to that, Nom Karta seemed like a beacon of cleanliness and order. Cael gazed out at Natali's palace. A solitary dragon was on its roof, keeping watch, while soldiers had been posted by every entrance.

Cael was feeling much better, despite the uncomfortable position in which he had slept through the night. He stretched his arms, and tried to ignore the thirst and hunger. He hadn't eaten or drunk anything since the previous evening, but knew he would have to wait. He remained lying on the flat roof, sheltering in the shadows of the battlements, and sent out his vision towards Famula's palace.

He reached the huge reception chamber. Several dragons were there, but many of the senior ones, including Famula, were not present, so Cael went deeper into the interior of the vast palace. He came to another enormous hall, and saw Famula lying on the floor, surrounded by half a dozen dragons. Standing next to them, looking tiny, was a tall young man. Ward. Cael went straight for the god's head, but he was wearing eye-shields. He scanned the dragons in the chamber – Abda, Tirna, Saphben, Konran, Marda and Shana were there, but they were all children of Gahad, and Cael knew that they would detect his presence if he entered their minds. Cael turned, and saw a small number of Aucterian soldiers by the entrance. He drove his powers into one of their minds, and hid there, in silence.

'The internal politics of the Dominion are of absolutely no concern to me,' Ward was saying. 'If Queen Famula has gone insane, then you must choose another ruler.'

Abda's eyes glowed with fury. 'That is what we are trying to decide, god,' she said.

'I should be prince-regent while the queen recovers,' said Saphben. 'Apart from Her Majesty, I am the last remaining child of Snowdrift, the mighty King Gahad's first mate.'

'You do not deserve the title,' said Abda. 'You supported the coward Tegru during his rebellion. I am the senior of those who remained loyal.'

'Will Her Majesty recover?' said Tirna. 'God, do you know this?'

Ward shrugged. 'That depends upon what exactly the Holdfast boy did to her brains.'

'The who?' said Tirna. 'Before she lost consciousness, Her Majesty claimed that she had been attacked by the son of the Demon Witch.'

'Indeed,' said Ward. 'The Demon Witch is Karalyn Holdfast, and she has only one son old enough to harm Queen Famula – Cael. It seems the boy was too stupid to realise that I would be able to unravel his little riddle. Too stupid by far. So stupid, in fact, that he has decided to return to Nom Karta alone.'

'He is here?' cried Abda.

'He is probably watching us right now,' said Ward. 'I would know for certain had I not been obliged to wear these awful eye-guards. I sensed him use his powers last night, and again when he returned. He was observing the assault upon the palace of Lady Natali from the roof of your palace, Lady Tirna. That was when I put my eye-guards on, to protect myself.' Ward gazed around the room. 'If you are watching us, Cael Holdfast, it might be a good idea to take a little look around you. The Bullan are immune to your tricks, are they not? Regardless, I look forward to seeing you soon in person.'

Cael severed the connection and opened his eyes to see over a dozen heavily-armed Bullan pointing their crossbows at him. He reached for his Quadrant, and a Bullan soldier kicked it out of his hand. The Quadrant skittered along the roof of the palace, and another Bullan soldier picked it up.

'Hands in the air!' shouted a Bullan sergeant.

Without a weapon, without a Quadrant, and without any way to penetrate the minds of the Bullan, Cael lifted his arms. They were grasped by two Bullan soldiers, and forced behind his back.

'I surrender,' said Cael. 'I will not resist.'

His hands were bound, and he was pulled to his feet. A bag was placed over his head, and Cael smiled, knowing that his enemies were unaware that he didn't need his eyes to use his dream powers. That wouldn't matter if Ward continued to wear eye-shields, but it was an advantage, no matter how slim.

The Bullan led him off the roof and down several flights of stairs. Cael declined to use any of his powers to see where they were going, as something Ward had said had stuck with him – the god had claimed that he had sensed him use vision to watch the attack on Natali's palace. Had he been bluffing? Was it possible that any god could sense a dream mage? Or were Cael's powers so much weaker than his mother's that he didn't qualify as a full dream mage? He had lost the ability to place blocks in the minds of others to shield them from vision attacks, and he was unable to hear the voice of a Quadrant; still, he had retained persuasion and invisibility, which seemed far more useful.

It was a twenty-minute walk to Famula's palace, and the Bullan led him inside. They went down long hallways, their boots clacking off the smooth marble floor, then they entered a chamber. Cael could make out a few oil lamps burning through the fabric of the bag over his head. If they were hanging from the walls, then the room he had been brought into was small.

'Thank you, Bullan sergeant,' said Ward's voice. 'Did you know that the best way to inhibit someone from using their powers is pain? When one is in agony, one cannot concentrate properly.'

'Is that right, sir?' said a Bullan.

'It is,' said Ward.

Cael cried out as a blade was punched into his stomach. The Bullan soldiers were gripping on to his arms and shoulders, and he remained on his feet, as his guts burned in agony.

'Secure him to the rack,' said Ward.

Cael was dragged across the room, then his legs were lifted and he was placed onto an uncomfortable grid of metal. The cords binding his hands were cut, and his arms were pulled out to the side. Shackles were attached to his wrists, and then to his ankles, the Bullan hammering in iron pins to lock them into position.

The bag was pulled from Cael's head.

'Does that hurt, Holdfast?' said Ward, as he looked down at the wound by Cael's waist. 'Try to use your powers.'

'Fuck you,' Cael groaned.

'How disagreeable,' said Ward. He glanced at the Bullan. 'You may leave us alone while I interrogate the prisoner.'

The Bullan saluted, then they walked from the room and closed the door.

'I do like the Bullan,' said Ward. 'They clearly detest all humans, including gods, and yet they are unfailingly loyal. Well, I like these Bullan. I didn't care for the ones who followed the horned god around, which is why we had to kill them. The best thing about the Bullan is that the Holdfasts are unable to read their minds; don't you agree? No matter. I have other, more relevant questions to ask you. Firstly, you will tell me all you know about the Empire's plans to attack the Tempest mine.'

Cael said nothing, as the pain in his abdomen grew.

'Come now,' said Ward; 'I only stabbed you a little bit. That wound isn't going to kill you, not when you have the constitution of the Kellach Brigdomin. A normal human might die of infection, but you will be fine. Tell me about the Empire's invasion plans, or I will do something worse to you.'

'You will get nothing from me,' gasped Cael.

'That isn't quite correct. I have already taken your Quadrant. That makes three, so far, that your side has foolishly lost to us. I think I will give this new one to my sister Allura, in advance of the imminent reconquest of Na Sun Ka; I am sure she will find it very useful.'

'How can you sense my powers?'

Ward smiled. 'You overheard that, did you? Do you recall the fight for the dragon carriers? Edgar had warned me about the powers of the Holdfasts, but I had been sceptical, to say the least. And then you were able to penetrate my mind, twice – before and then after the horned god swept me off my feet with his Gift of Pain. Both times, I could feel you try to rip through my consciousness. It was painful, and, I must confess, a little terrifying, but I learned from the ordeal. Your powers are faint, almost too faint to be detected but, having experienced them at first hand, I was in no doubt that it was you we were facing in Nom Karta.' The god gazed into the middle distance. 'The dragons of the Dominion are most impressed with my abilities, as they should be. I am a son of Edmond, the greatest being who has ever lived. I remember the days before Implacatus; I was there when Theodora created the Sextant. I walked upon the green fields of Implacatus while it was still a paradise, long before Nathaniel sent Gahad to this world.' He placed a knife blade against Cael's face. 'Invasion plans. I am waiting.'

'You're wasting your time,' said Cael. 'Why would I know anything about a plan to attack the Tempest mine? I'm a fucking second lieutenant.'

'Yet you were sent here with explosives and a Quadrant. Why?'

'For a holiday.'

'If I were to hand you over to the dragons, they would tear your body to pieces for what you did to Queen Famula.'

'Then do it. Throw me to the dragons, and I'll see how many of them I can bring down before they kill me.'

Ward slid the razor-sharp point of the knife down Cael's cheek. Cael grimaced, the pain flaring, but he said nothing.

'Tell me about the planned invasion,' said Ward.

'You don't care about what I know,' said Cael. 'You're doing this because you enjoy it, not because you think I'll give you any information. Admit it, you sick bastard.'

Ward laughed quietly. 'I have met very few mortals as fearless as you, Cael.'

'Aye? I'm a Holdfast. I thought you knew things about us.'

'I think I will flay the skin from your body,' said Ward. 'That used to be my speciality. I could drag it out for days, cutting off a mortal's skin piece by piece while keeping them alive. I would sprinkle maggots onto the open wounds, for two reasons. They would eat any flesh that started to rot, prolonging the victim's suffering, and they would also wriggle and squirm, which sometimes drove the victims mad.'

'Is that why your father locked you up? Were you too insane for even Edmond to cope with?'

Ward laughed again, but louder. 'Do you think my blessed father cared about what I did to mortals? No, Cael. I upset him by torturing other gods to death, which is a far trickier and yet more fulfilling pastime. Let us begin. This blade is as keen as any razor.'

Ward stretched his knife out towards Cael's left arm, then he began to gently slice through the skin. Cael clamped his mouth shut, determined not to betray any fear or panic. He tried to think of his formidable grandmother, and how she had always told him never to give comfort to an enemy, and that he was a Holdfast, and therefore he had to behave like one.

The door opened, and Ward looked up. His eyes widened, then something flung him backwards, and his body slammed off the wall. Cael glanced at the doorway, as a young man in gleaming white stone armour walked into the room.

'What have I told you, Ward?' said the man. 'First you try to kill Corthie, and now this?'

Ward groaned, and staggered upright.

'We agreed not to kill any Holdfast,' the man went on.

'I didn't agree to that,' said Ward. 'You ordered us not to kill any, but I didn't agree.'

'If we start killing Holdfasts,' said the god in white armour, 'it becomes personal. We will enrage the entire family, and they will come for us. Has the slaughter of the Ascendants taught you nothing?'

'But I have this one at my mercy,' said Ward. 'It was easy to ensnare him.'

'This one is still young and inexperienced,' said the other man. 'Tell me; was it so easy to kill Corthie? No. Instead, he killed Lord Crennic, and he almost killed you.' He gestured to the door. 'Out.'

Ward narrowed his eyes, then he brushed the dust from the front of his clothes and strode from the room.

'Thank you,' said Cael.

The man in white armour came up to the rack, and began to release the shackles by Cael's ankles.

'Don't thank me,' he said. 'I am not going to release you, Cael Holdfast, but neither will I torture or kill you. You are now my hostage. Do you know who I am?'

'No.'

'My name is Edgar.'

'Edmond's brother?'

'The same. I could have killed Corthie in the Palace of the Almighty, but I spared him. Did he tell you that?'

'I haven't seen my uncle for a while.'

'Then you will have to take my word for it.' He placed a hand onto Cael's forehead. 'Your immunity to our powers does not seem to apply to touch. Interesting. I could kill you, or heal you.'

'I would rather you healed me, if I'm being honest.'

'And if I do so, will you promise not to try to escape?'

'No.'

'You would rather be in pain than utter a few words that might mean nothing to you?'

'They wouldn't mean nothing to me. I am going to escape.'

A faint flicker of a smile passed over Edgar's face, then Cael felt a wave of powers flood his body. The wounds on his arm and face closed up, then the injury in his stomach healed. Edgar disconnected Cael's wrist shackles from the rack, and dragged him onto the floor. Cael fell, then, before he could react, Edgar took out a Quadrant and glided his fingers over it.

The air shimmered, and they appeared inside another building, with a barred door between Edgar and Cael.

'This cell will be your new home for now,' said Edgar.

Cael got to his feet. He eyed the walls of the small, windowless cell, then he gripped the bars of the door. He tried to drive his powers into the god's mind but, like Ward, he was wearing eye-shields.

Edgar smiled and shook his head. 'A little predictable, don't you think? Did you imagine that I wouldn't take steps to protect myself?'

'Where are we?' said Cael.

'You have been here before,' said Edgar. 'We are close to the Tempest mine. Lord Ballatar is one of my most trusted friends, and he has requested my help to repel the imminent invasion by the Holdfast Empire.'

'I'm not going to reveal anything I know about that to you.'

'I don't care,' said Edgar. 'What information could you possibly have that would interest me? The invasion will come, and we shall annihilate it. The waste of life will be tragic, but how else will the Empire learn?'

'What do you want?'

'Peace.'

Cael snorted. 'You want peace, and yet you also want to slaughter the soldiers of the Empire?'

'The two things are not mutually exclusive, Cael. In order to bring the Empire to the negotiating table, I will have to show the Empress that I have the will to defeat her armies; otherwise, she will not respect me. And how can I negotiate with an enemy who doesn't respect me?'

'And where do I fit in?'

'You are my hostage, and my prize. You are the golden boy, beloved by Karalyn, and by the Empress. They would do anything to keep you safe, would they not?'

'I think you might be underestimating how ruthless my family can be.'

'Those days passed with the death of Daphne Holdfast, Cael. The younger Holdfasts lack the resolve that she possessed. You see, as well as reading Bailey's memories, I have since spoken to Lord Elmhirst, who was present on your world when the Ascendants were massacred. It was Daphne Holdfast who held your family together, through sheer will and determination, and now it is divided.'

Cael said nothing.

'You know that I speak the truth,' said Edgar. 'Is there a single member of your generation who has the same strength of will as your grandmother?'

'Aye, there is.'

'Come now; who?'

Cael held the god's gaze. 'Me.'

# AUTHOR'S NOTES

NOVEMBER 2024

Thank you for reading ***Palace of the Almighty***, the second book of the Twins Trilogy. After writing the first two books of the new Masters & Makers series, it took a shift of perspective to go back into the world of the Magelands. By ***Palace of the Almighty***, I felt truly at home with the Holdfasts again. Switching between the two worlds is essential, as I seem to be unable to keep both in my head at the same time. It has to be one or the other, with no middle ground. I store away the series I am not working on in a dark corner of my mind and try to forget all about it, so that I can give all of my focus to what I am doing.

I hope you enjoyed it.

## RECEIVE A FREE MAGELANDS DOMINION SHORT STORY

Building a relationship with my readers is very important to me.

Join my newsletter for information on new books and deals and you will also receive a Magelands Dominion short story that is currently EXCLUSIVE to my Readers' Group for FREE.

www.ChristopherMitchellBooks.com/dominion

# ABOUT THE AUTHOR

Christopher Mitchell is the author of the Magelands epic fantasy series.

*For more information:*
www.christophermitchellbooks.com
info@christophermitchellbooks.com

Printed in Great Britain
by Amazon

55711029R00274